THIRTEEN
O'CLOCK

By Thurston Clarke

FICTION
Thirteen O'Clock

NONFICTION
Lost Hero
By Blood and Fire
The Last Caravan
Dirty Money

THIRTEEN O'CLOCK

A NOVEL ABOUT GEORGE ORWELL AND 1984

Thurston Clarke

DOUBLEDAY & COMPANY, INC.
GARDEN CITY, NEW YORK
1984

All of the characters in this book are fictitious and any resemblance to actual persons, living or dead, is purely coincidental.

Library of Congress Cataloging in Publication Data
Clarke, Thurston.
    Thirteen o'clock.
    Includes bibliographical references.
    1. Orwell, George, 1903–1950, in fiction, drama, poetry, etc. I. Title.
PS3553.L339T4   1984   813'.54
        ISBN: 0-385-19211-8
    Library of Congress Catalog Card Number: 83–25306

For Judith Wederholt

In February, 1945, George Orwell gave up the literary editorship of *Tribune* because he had been invited by David Astor to go to liberated Paris, and thence into Germany, as a war correspondent for the *Observer*. Leaving Eileen to cope with the baby, he went to Paris in March, 1945, and stayed, like all allied war correspondents, at the Hotel Scribe, near the Opera. . . . Among the stupendously-salaried Americans . . . [in Paris] was Ernest Hemingway.[1]

To [Orwell's] delight he found Hemingway's name. He had never met him. He went up to his room and knocked. When told to come in, he opened the door, stood on the threshold and said, "I'm Eric Blair." Hemingway . . . saw another war correspondent and a British one at that, so he bellowed, "Well what the ying hell do you want?" Orwell shyly replied, "I'm George Orwell." Hemingway pushed the suitcase to the end of the bed, bent down and brought a bottle of Scotch from underneath it and still bellowing said, "Why the zing hell didn't you say so? Have a drink. Have a double. Straight or with water, there's no soda."[2]

Orwell looked nervous and worried. He said that he feared that the Communists were out to kill him and asked Hemingway for the loan of a pistol. Ernest lent him the .32 Colt . . . Orwell departed like a pale ghost.[3]

There is a curious lack of any letters to any of [Orwell's] friends while in France and Germany and none of them can remember him talking about the time. . . . It is puzzling.[4]

[1] Peter Lewis, *George Orwell: The Road to 1984* (New York: Harcourt Brace Jovanovich, 1981), p. 100.
[2] Paul Potts, *Dante Called You Beatrice* (London: Eyre & Spottiswoode, 1960), p. 82.
[3] Carlos Baker, *Ernest Hemingway: A Life Story* (New York: Charles Scribner's Sons, 1969), p. 442.
[4] Bernard Crick, *George Orwell: The First Complete Biography* (Boston: Atlantic–Little, Brown, 1980), p. 332.

It was a bright cold day in April, and
the clocks were striking thirteen.
                    Nineteen Eighty-four

PART I

Early October in a year soon after 1984

CHAPTER 1

A tuba blast of anger and lust shattered the silence and echoed through the hills. Gina Baldwin turned to see if the stag was behind her. Malcolm tugged on her sleeve and pointed to a grassy plateau overlooking the Atlantic. Two beasts—the intruder and defender—paced parallel to one another, bellowing and preparing for battle. The prize, three hinds, stood fifty yards away, awaiting the outcome.

Go on, run, Gina thought. What do you care? Let them kill each other.

The larger stag charged. Antlers slammed together and the two animals butted back and forth until the smaller one slipped backward down the slope. Finally he wrenched free and retreated. The hinds trotted after the victor and all four disappeared up a glen.

"Too much sex on the hill today," Malcolm said cheerfully.

Gina shuddered. Sex was one of the things she had come to Jura to avoid.

Malcolm picked up the binoculars. "Sex excites the beasts, keeps them on the move, hard to stalk. What we need is a loner."

A minute later he had one. "He's on that ridge." He gestured vaguely to the northeast. "Easy to spot."

She took the glasses and scanned a patchwork of purple heather, hill grass, bracken and boulders.

She could not pick out the stag, but admitting that would give the old man too much satisfaction. Already this morning what she thought were antlers had proved to be a bush, and a silhouette she dismissed as a bush had darted across a barren corrie and disappeared. She had pointed to a brown hump in the heather and asked,

"Stag or wild goat?" Without raising his binoculars Malcolm had said, "Rock."

"Yes, now I see him," she said. It was her second lie that day; she had also said she enjoyed hunting.

"Not there, lassie. Find the wee burn and follow it down the slope fifty yards. He's to the left."

Her legs ached from crouching, her thighs shook with fatigue. To conceal her exhaustion she lay down in the heather and, her elbows resting on a flat rock, panned across the ridge. It was part of a line of rocky hills reaching up to 1,500 feet which ran the length of the island from north to south. From her vantage point she could look east to where the Sound of Jura flooded into rocky bays and inlets. To her west, Atlantic surf pounded granite cliffs and white beaches comprised of thousands of stones, each the size of a baby's head and bleached skull-white by the sun.

Finally she saw him: graceful antlers, a finely proportioned head and a body the size of a horse. Rutting in the peat he had blackened his fur. He was moving, rubbing himself against the mossy bank of the burn. Slowly she realized he was masturbating.

Malcolm was watching her. She could feel her face flushing but she refused to admit the embarrassment. She swung the binoculars away, as if scanning the surrounding slopes.

"You're right, Malcolm," she said. "He is alone."

Then her lens caught the light: just a flash, but dazzlingly bright. She blinked and looked back. It flashed again.

She pointed to the ridge. "Look over there. The sun is reflecting off something."

The boy focused first on the old man. He saw a mean red Protestant face, a Catholic-hating face. Now he knew how the young Scottish soldiers in Belfast would look in fifty years. Killing the old man would be easy.

He moved the glasses to the left, stopping when he saw the second target. She had long brown hair, freckles like his sister's, a pretty face. She could be Irish. "What's her name, Jack?" he asked.

"Gina."

"Gina who?"

"Do you need to know a fox's name before you shoot it?"

"Never shot a fox. I'm from the city, you know that. Only thing I've ever killed is rats."

"Then think of them as rats. That's what they are, rodents on two legs. Don't trouble yourself; don't make your first kill so hard."

The boy had thought it would be easy. He had imagined lying behind the hedges of a misty Irish field, waiting in ambush for a Brit patrol. Then tossing a grenade, detonating a mine, firing at armed men. Instead he was on an island in the Inner Hebrides, just five miles off the west coast of Scotland, stalking a pretty woman and a toothless old fart.

"Is she British, Jack?" That would be something.

"No more questions, Charlie." No more questions because Jack had asked himself the same ones all morning. He supposed the American knew the answers, but he had stayed in Belfast. Thought it best, no doubt, to leave the dirty work to the Micks.

Malcolm glanced up as a line of clouds extinguished the sun. "There's nothing on this end of the island that would reflect light. Nothing here but wind, water and stone."

He crawled next to her so that their elbows touched. "Did you see the beast, then, lassie?" he whispered.

She turned and stared. Their faces were inches apart. His leer showed off ill-fitting dentures and inflamed gums. "You mean the one that's wanking off?" she said.

He blushed, ripped up a handful of grass and tossed it in the air. The wind blew it southeast. "Aye, poor lonely beast, left out of the rut. We'll soon put him out of his misery."

He tossed up more grass. "He's lying with his back to the wind. If we approach from downwind, he sees us; come from upwind and he smells us."

Gina turned her face to the wind and drew a deep breath. She was sensitive to smells, particularly bad ones. This wind carried the gamy stink of a large wet animal. The winds on Jura brought the fast-changing Atlantic weather: the fog, mist and drizzle, the violent squalls, dazzling sunlight and lines of fair-weather clouds racing across the sky like express trains. They stunted trees, slapped tiny fish against cliffs and carried lime from beaches to gardens, so that bushes bore raspberries the size of eggs. They carried for miles the bellowing of stags, the roar of the Corryvreckan whirlpool and the stench of goats, deer and humans.

Malcolm gestured east to a line of rounded hills. "We'll walk along the side of that ridge, then crawl up through the bracken— they're good camouflage." He pointed to where she had seen the light. "You can take a shot from up there. Watch out for hinds; they're the sentries. If they panic and run, he'll follow."

She boxed the binoculars and crept backward. Camouflage, sentries, she thought, the vocabulary of war romanticizing a duel between armed intellect and unarmed instinct. How would we fare if the stags stalked us? she wanted to ask Malcolm, but didn't. She needed him.

"Malcolm?" They were downwind of the stag now, walking east.

"Aye."

"Did Orwell ever stalk?"

"Who?" Most of the islanders knew him by his real name, Eric Blair.

"Mr. Blair, Malcolm. You know who I mean." She had learned that Eric had been fond of Malcolm. Yet he stubbornly refused to answer her questions. Luckily, the other elderly people on Jura were more cooperative. Flattered by her interest, they submitted to lengthy interviews. Only Malcolm and his wife, Mary, resisted. Usually they changed the subject.

Once Mary had said, "We don't gossip about Mr. Blair in this house."

Gina had abandoned hope until Malcolm had suggested they stalk together. He claimed it was her duty as the Barnhill tenant to help thin the herd. She agreed, hoping that away from Mary he might finally discuss Eric. For that she could endure his constant winking and pinching.

She repeated the question. "Did you take Mr. Blair stalking, Malcolm?" He glanced toward his cottage at Kinauchdrach, as if his wife could hear them. Finally he spoke.

"Mr. Blair didn't approve of stalking. Said it was sport for the lairds, and no help to the crofters. But he didn't object to eating venison, or to killing in general. He liked blasting away at the rabbits."

"So he had a shotgun?"

"Aye, and a revolver."

"A revolver on Jura? What did he hunt with that?"

"It was a war souvenir. He carried it for protection against the bulls. He was scared of them—or so he said." He stopped and pointed to the ocean. "While we waste time talking that fog is coming in. You'll miss your shot."

I hope I do, she thought.

"I've lost them, Jack." He was relieved. "They must have given up and gone home."

They had planned to shoot her earlier that morning, when she left the house to dig her garden or feed her hens. It should have been easy; the boat would have come back at noon and they'd have been home by evening. Instead the old fart had appeared at her front door and they had set off together.

"Even better," Jack had said. "It'll look like a hunting accident. If we hide the bodies well, they won't be found for weeks, months, perhaps never."

But the old fart knew the land and they did not. They had already lost and then found them again twice. All morning Charlie had watched her crawl, bend over and trot ahead. Christ, she was in good shape. And all morning he had had to study her face, see her toss back her hair like a frisky colt and watch her quick nervous smile. She even shared some of his sister's nervous habits: chewing on her nails and picking at her lips.

"Don't worry, lad," Jack said. "They've sighted the stag below us.

We'll sit tight. They'll have to come up here to have their shot. Another hour and it'll all be over."

The boy looked away. He was about to cry.

"You volunteered," Jack said quickly.

"I'm seventeen. You said it was time." Charlie remembered the story of his grandfather's first kill. He had planted a bomb under a manhole cover in Dublin, to divert attention from a bank robbery. He was to detonate the bomb when the others dashed out of the bank. Then a young Irish police cadet, about his own age, had walked into the intersection and stood over the manhole, directing traffic. He had prayed the cadet would feel the urge to eat, or piss, or chat up a pretty girl on the curb. When the time came, though, he told his grandson, "I prayed for his soul and pushed the plunger." Now Charlie swore he would do the same.

Gina saw the fogbank moving toward them. Malcolm was right. They would have to hurry. If the fog settled they might be forced to spend the night in one of the caves that lined the island's west coast. The caves had once served as hideouts for poachers, shipwreckers and thieves; as prisons, chapels, stills; and as funeral parlors where corpses awaited transportation to graveyards on the "Holy Islands" of Iona and Oronsay. Now they were like the rest of Jura's Atlantic coast, deserted. For four hundred years a skull had sat undisturbed on a stone ledge overlooking the Atlantic inlet of Glenngarrisdale. A Gaelic inscription carved in the stone identified it as a McLaine, but the writing was only visible when struck by the setting sun at certain times of the year. Glenngarrisdale was so remote that the skull survived until the early 1970s, when an expedition of Boy Scouts examined it and forgot to return it to its ledge. Finding it on the ground, the famished deer devoured it. The islanders were surprised it had disappeared; Gina was amazed it had survived four centuries in plain sight. For her, it illustrated why Eric kept returning to Jura to write *Nineteen Eighty-four*.

He had chosen to write his utopian nightmare in the most isolated corner of one of the wildest, most inaccessible and least visited of Britain's inhabited islands—a twenty-eight-mile-long island with two hundred inhabitants where the present was indistinguishable from the past or future, where four-hundred-year-old skulls sat on ledges and rings of Druid stones stood in fields unmarked and untouristed; an island dominated by the prehistoric constants of wind, water and stone, where one expected pterodactyls rather than eagles to sail between misty cliffs and brontosauri to emerge from marshy lochs. Gina believed Eric had come to Jura expecting rural isolation and then found something more vital, a place beyond time in which to create a nightmare of time.

She was finding Jura much the same. There was still no electricity or telephone service on the north end, and Malcolm and Mary were the only neighbors for miles. For Gina, as for Eric, the isolation was convenient. Piers could not telephone and the trip from London took a full day even if one flew via Glasgow—only sixty miles due west—to the neighboring island of Islay. Her brief letters exaggerated the discomforts, and Piers never made good his threat to visit. She had spent the summer alone, with Eric.

Malcolm dropped into a crouch and motioned her down. They had rounded the corner of a ridge and could see the stag.

"Crawl, lassie," Malcolm whispered. "Keep to the shade and keep down." As if for emphasis, he patted her rear.

She dragged herself forward with her elbows. The ground was like a sponge. Water seeped through her trousers and flowed over the tops of her Wellingtons. Clouds of midges stung her cheeks and disappeared into the tangle of her hair. Pellets of deer excrement smeared her jacket. But she had to persevere; if she proved herself, Malcolm might open up about Eric.

The Orwell thesis was more than Gina's work. It was her future. If, after she completed it, she received an offer from a good university, then she would be independent again, back where she had started when she arrived in Oxford ten years before, just after graduating from Wisconsin. It had been her first trip abroad and her first time away from the Midwest. She had been awarded a fellowship for two years of postgraduate work in literature. Immediately she had fallen in love with England, particularly Oxford. She wanted to stay so badly, to become a part of the university rather than always being the American outsider, that she became infatuated with the first young don who showed any interest. Unfortunately it was Piers.

Eric would have hated Piers, and the more she read about Eric, the more she did too. The two men had only one thing in common: both had changed their names. Piers Michael Baldwin had discarded his first name when he left the university to run for Parliament. He was now known to supporters as "Mike" Baldwin, a name with more proletarian appeal. Otherwise he and Eric were opposites. Eric was suspicious of pacifists; Piers was often photographed leading demonstrations denouncing war or praising "anti-fascist freedom fighters." Eric detested political lies; Piers told them hourly. Eric was a socialist but put truth before ideology; for Piers, ideology was truth.

Now Eric would provide her with the means to escape Piers with honor, without the humiliation of needing his money. If her thesis was a failure she would still leave him, but not on her own terms, and the last ten years—the seven with Piers and the three with Eric —would have to be judged a failure. Her thesis was a last chance to rescue something from a disastrous decade.

"There they are." Jack pointed to the burn. "I told you they'd come to us."

The boy trained his binoculars on the burn and saw two khaki shapes crawling through the bracken. He caught a glimpse of her face and then her ass wiggling back and forth as she slid over the ground. She slapped at midges and stopped to pour water out of her boots. Christ, he thought, she hates it here as much as I do.

"Time to move, lad. We're on their spot." The line of boulders ran for about a hundred yards along the crest of the ridge. "We'll hide and wait while they have their shot, then we'll crawl back and have ours."

"Is she a politician?" He needed something to go on. What had she done, or what might she do, to Ireland? Was she a future Thatcher? A cousin of the queen?

"And what difference does it make if she is, or isn't?"

"None, I suppose," he lied.

"Good. Better not to know," Jack said, although he was as curious as the boy. He had been told this killing was a "favor." It had nothing to do with the struggle. The woman was not their enemy but the enemy of an unnamed friend. The American who had briefed them might be representing anyone: the Soviets, Arabs, or their American "cousins." All he knew for sure was that the friend had supplied them with weapons and money and demanded in return the only thing they could offer: boys like Charlie to pull the trigger.

Malcolm pulled the rifle from its canvas case and slipped five cartridges into the chamber. They were wrapped in pretty blue paper. He handed it over and said, "Crawl up to that line of rock. From there you'll look down on him. Adjust for the angle and mind you don't slam the rifle against a rock and scare him."

She hesitated.

"Go on, then, or we'll lose him in the fog."

She crawled slowly up to the rocks. The animal was eighty yards below, grazing. Could she squeeze the trigger? She knew the island was overrun with deer. Every winter hundreds died of starvation. They devoured young birches and ravaged vegetable gardens. When they collapsed with hunger hooded crows swooped down with ratchety cries and plucked out their eyes while they were still alive. All morning she had walked past piles of bleached antlers and corpses rich with flies and maggots.

But still she wondered if she could fire. It was the usual problem: she convinced herself that an action was correct, yet when the time came to act she procrastinated. Two years after vowing to leave Piers she was still perfecting her escape.

She released the safety and, cradling the rifle in her arms, sighted just below the shoulder for a heart shot. She wrapped a finger around the trigger but didn't fire. She had shot small animals—rabbits and grouse—but it seemed sinful to kill something so large.

Malcolm crawled forward whispering, "Shoot! Shoot!" She sighted again and then, remembering that Piers was a vegetarian, squeezed the trigger.

The explosion echoed through the hills. The stag darted toward her and froze, unsure where the danger lay, unsure which way to run.

She fired again. He jerked his head back, started running and then, as if remembering something, abruptly stopped, sank to his knees and fell. His legs twitched convulsively, like those of a dog running through a nightmare.

Malcolm gave a shriek of victory and bounded off the ridge. She imagined Campbells swooping from ambush into the hated McLaines. By the time she reached the stag the old man had rolled up his sleeves, removed his watch and plunged a knife into the deer's jugular. As blood spurted onto the grass he patted its side and crooned, "What a lovely beast. What a handsome lad you were." When the bleeding subsided he reached his knife into the mouth and carved out the tusks. "The Huns are fond of these," he explained, wiping them clean on his shirt. "They turn them into cuff links."

The sky darkened and drizzle fell. Malcolm rolled the stag onto its back, cut the penis and testicles free and tossed them into the heather. To her surprise Gina found herself saying, "I killed it. I'll butcher it. Tell me what to do."

"Do you want me to do it?" Jack asked. They had crept back along the ridge until they were less than a hundred yards above Malcolm and Gina.

The boy shook his head. What was it his grandfather had said? "The tougher the job, the greater your love for Ireland." If he could do this he could do anything.

He sighted the woman. The cross hairs intersected just above her left ear. He could not miss on purpose, not at this range, and not with a telescopic sight. Then she bent over to take the knife from the old man and he lost her.

"Now, lad, do it now. First her, then him."

"She moved." He took his eyes off the sight. Jack was staring at the ground so he wouldn't see it happen. The fucker.

"Good lad. Wait for a killing shot. We can't afford to miss. They're armed too."

He's a fucking coward, Charlie thought.

Gina took the knife. It was slippery with blood. She hacked off the head and set it carefully on the grass, but Malcolm pronounced it "not fine enough for mounting." Then, under his direction, she cut the legs off at the knees, sliced open the chest and pulled out the stomach, heart, lungs and intestines. The stomach burst, filling the air with a warm musty odor and scattering clumps of partially digested grass. Flies and midges descended and she slapped her face with bloody hands.

Malcolm slit the thighs and threaded ropes through them so they could drag the carcass. Then he dipped his fingers in blood and, before she could protest, stroked her cheeks.

"First kill, first blood," he said. "Customary to be blooded after your first stag."

The boy sighted again, just above the ear. She had dressed the deer herself; that took guts and spirit. He liked her.

"Shoot, lad!"

He moved the cross hairs a millimeter to the left, away from the freckled face that reminded him of his sister. He squeezed the trigger and burst into tears.

"You little bastard." Jack tore the rifle from his hands and fired wildly at the woman. When he reached into his pocket for spare cartridges he saw the boy had fled, vanished into the mist. Good riddance, he thought. Leave him here, let him starve. His bones would lie there on the hill along with the deer's and that fucking woman's.

Gina felt as if she were at the center of an explosion. Pain shot up her arm like an electric shock and blood spurted from her wrist. For a second she thought Malcolm had fired by accident. Then more bullets slammed into the stag's carcass, splattering her with blood and fur. Instinctively she froze, listening as the shots echoed and re-echoed. Had they come from the ridge above or the glen below? There was a boulder nearby—would it shelter or expose them?

From the ridge she heard the click of a cartridge being ejected. "Behind the rock," she shouted. Malcolm grabbed the rifle. More shots rang out as they dived for the boulder.

Malcolm cursed. "Bloody poachers!" he shouted. "You've done more than scare us, you've drawn blood."

He lowered his voice. "I think they're Catholics over from Ireland, come here in boats to poach the stags. I ran off a gang last month; now they're back for revenge."

Gina shook her head. The shots were too close. She could have been killed. She remembered the reflecting light and suddenly realized that all morning someone had stalked them.

Malcolm peered around the rock. Fog and mist had descended, obscuring the ridge. Neither side could see the other, both were armed. The stalk was equal, a standoff.

Malcolm pointed into the glen. The fog was thickening. They might slip down the hill unnoticed. He would go first; if they didn't fire she could follow.

After he disappeared she counted silently to ten. There were no shots, but as she crept away from the boulder she heard someone call out. Malcolm was right about the stalker's nationality. The accent was Irish, and he sounded like a boy. But the old man was wrong about him being a poacher. This boy knew her. His soft Irish voice was calling her name.

CHAPTER 2

What made an overweight, middle-aged, twice-married former CIA agent decide to hang a gold band from his left earlobe?

As the fishing boat pitched and rolled in the Caribbean swells, the sun glittering off the earring had focused Adam's mind on the question. Earrings were popular with the trust-fund hippies who lived along the island's northern coast. But it was easier to imagine Stan Hacker ripping those earrings out than admiring them.

The boat mounted a swell and there was another flash of sun and gold. It plunged into a trough, and Adam saw the flat tropical coastline, a green snake on the horizon. The chimneys of TropicAmerican's sugar refinery puffed white smoke into a clear sky. It was one of the rare days when the wind blew east to west, carrying the sicksweet smell across TropicResort's designer golf courses, Olympic and Polynesian swimming pools, tennis villages, poolside bars, cabanas, bungalows, VIP villas and "native village." It was a fine day to be offshore, fishing.

Adam returned to contemplating the earring. Hacker had been a partner in a D.C. "consulting" firm of other former FBI, CIA, DEA, and NSA agents. Now he was head of security for TropicAmerican. Why would such a man put on an earring to go fishing? Was it a good-luck charm? An act of rebellion? After years of upholding convention did he enjoy flouting it? All of TropicAmerican's "Inner Circle" were along on this fishing expedition, but only Victor Gore himself had mentioned the earring. Were they all, except of course for Gore, intimidated by Hacker?

Through a haze of sun, Dramamine and beer Adam heard a voice, his own voice, say, "Stan?"

Hacker pushed up the brim of his khaki bush hat and grunted. Adam was pleased to see that his face was gray-green under its tan. He was as seasick as the rest of them.

"I was asleep," Hacker said, straightening up his beefy cop's body.

Don't say anything about the earring, Adam thought, don't stir up trouble. But the real trouble was that they both had the same title, "special adviser to the president," both reported only to Victor Gore and both were known as "Gore's fair-haired boys," even though Adam was thirty-five, Hacker at least forty, and both were dark. They were included in the Inner Circle only because of Gore's obsession with publicity and security. Adam guarded Gore against verbal assaults, Hacker against physical ones. Adam "handled" the media and wrote—the term was "crafted"—Gore's speeches and the sermons he placed in liberal newspapers. Hacker protected Gore from kidnapping, extortion and terrorism, worried about industrial espionage and "managed sensitive exchanges with foreign governments." He also supervised the background investigations of new executives. He had rummaged through Adam's past and frequently told him what he thought of his summer as a civil rights worker in Mississippi—"You guys were all Reds"; his three years in Peru with the Peace Corps—"Saved your ass from Vietnam" (which was true); his graduate degrees in journalism and Latin American studies— "professional student"; and the liberal East Coast newspaper in which he had invested three dreary years.

Adam thought that, like many cops, Hacker was better at collecting information than at analyzing it. To him it seemed obvious he had only been looking for excitement, for "experience." If he were a committed liberal, why on earth would he have joined up now with TropicAmerican? In Peru he had hunted seedy bars searching for Nazi fugitives and listening to the romantic fantasies of alcoholic expatriates. In Mississippi he joined the most dramatic sit-ins but avoided the voter-registration drives. He resigned from the newspaper when they posted him to the dreary state capital "for a few years of seasoning." TropicAmerican had promised responsibility and adventure without apprenticeship. But Gore had yet to give him an important assignment, and the exotic countries he visited for TropicAmerican were all alike: steamy airports, frigid hotels and awkward meetings with dark little men who spoke the brisk jargon of American business schools.

Hacker removed his sunglasses and squinted at Adam. "O.K. What is it? You woke me, you must want something."

Be polite. "Sorry to disturb you, Stan." Stop there, don't say more. "But there's something I've been dying to ask you."

The unaccustomed courtesy disarmed him. "Sure, sure old buddy, ask away."

"Are there any special counters in the boutiques?"

"I don't read you, old buddy." He was wary again.

"What I'm asking is, how does someone, a man, that is, go about choosing an earring? Do the jewelry boutiques have 'For Men Only' counters?"

Hacker raised a middle finger the size of a hot dog. "Fuck you, old buddy." He pulled the hat back over his eyes and slumped down in the fishing chair, swiveling around so the earring was out of sight.

In the adjoining fishing chair, Gore frowned. His fair-haired boys were squabbling again.

Adam cursed himself. "Stan, I wasn't trying to offend you." He spoke loud enough for Gore to hear. "I'm really interested. Was it something you always wanted or was it a sort of Road to Damascus situation?"

Hacker swiveled back. To him, the word "Damascus" meant PLO. "A what?"

"A sudden conversion. Did you see an earring on someone and think, 'Damn! I'd like one of those'?"

Hacker jumped from his chair. One of the two rods trolling from the upper deck was bent almost double. Its reel clicked like a stock ticker. A hundred yards astern a huge sailfish leaped into the air, arching its back as if preparing for its future as a wall decoration. It rose again, wriggling frantically, trying to tear itself away from the hook, and then fell with a splash and swam parallel to the boat, its sail cutting the water like a shark's fin.

The boat came to life. The captain, a weary old man wearing a "Virginia Is for Lovers" T-shirt, pulled a wooden club from a footlocker. His mate, a young boy in a stained and faded bathing suit, screamed at the fish in Spanish and leaped around the deck like a monkey as he reeled in the other lines to prevent their becoming tangled.

The passengers forgot their seasickness and imagined the elegant fish mounted over a wet bar or a fireplace. Tropic's senior vice-president for marketing, Bill Hochmeyer, shouted, "What a beauty! Must be seven feet!"

"No way," snapped Jim Fiore, senior vice-president for finance. "Nine feet or more; twice as big as that salmon you snagged in Nova Scotia."

"A steak dinner says you're wrong."

"Done." Both men stared intently at the water, waiting for the fish to leap again.

Victor Gore trained his binoculars on where it had last jumped and said, "I told you we'd nail one." As if he had commanded the fish to swallow the bait.

But Adam wondered if any of them could take credit for "nailing" this fish. After boarding they had sprawled out on deck chairs and cushions and opened beers. Except for Hacker, no one had sat in the uncomfortable fishing chairs or bothered deciding who was "fishing" with which rod.

Adam noticed Nat Beale edging toward the empty fishing chair that had hooked the fish. The rod was locked into a cup fastened to its seat. Beale had recognized their dilemma: Who would actually catch this magnificent animal?

Beale was a tall, genteelly impoverished Yankee aristocrat who had exploited his brief tenure as Director of the Central Intelligence Agency to land positions on the boards of several companies, including TropicAmerican. Gore included him in the Inner Circle because he added "class," and called him "my Kissinger." Beale usually suffered Gore's expeditions in silence, his clothes expressing his distaste for the proceedings. When they hunted bear in Canada and the others dressed in bush jackets with too many pockets, he appeared in a patched tweed jacket. Today, everyone except Gore and Beale had put on designer tennis outfits crisscrossed with racing stripes. Gore wore immaculate white trousers—he was never seen in shorts or swimsuits—while Beale was clothed in baggy khakis, a faded polo shirt and a tennis hat, ready for a day's sail off Martha's Vineyard.

Beale was too late. His Topsiders were still several feet away from the empty chair when the boy grabbed the rod. He let out more line and motioned frantically for someone to replace him. The captain shouted a string of Spanish obscenities.

"What's Juan so upset about?" Gore asked. No one knew the captain's real name. The entire trip, including a 20 percent gratuity, was prepaid. When Adam asked why they had chosen this surly captain and his shabby boat, Hacker, who had organized the trip, uttered his favorite word: "Security." Gore wanted to be out of range of microphones and eavesdropping waiters. This captain spoke no English.

Adam censored the obscenities and translated. "He wants someone to reel in the fish. The boy is too weak."

Everyone stared at the rod, then at Gore, wanting to land the fish themselves but only if he chose not to.

The sailfish leaped again, whipping the rod forward. The boy screamed for help. Finally Gore gave his verdict: "Adam. You're the youngest. See how fast you can bring him in."

As Adam slid into the chair Gore clicked the stopwatch feature on his complicated wristwatch. Adam had seen him use it to time Haitian migrants cutting sugarcane, Brazilians boxing parts for Tropic's chain of auto-supply centers, Taiwanese women nimbly assembling Tropic's video games and a TropicResort bartender assembling a piña colada.

Adam jerked up the rod and cranked the reel. What he knew about deep-sea fishing came from *Sports Illustrated,* beer commercials and Hemingway. The boy cried *"Lentamente! Lentamente!"* and pulled back gently on an imaginary rod. Adam copied the boy's motions, reeling in several feet and then pulling back gradually until the line became taut, then dipping forward and reeling again. During the next ten minutes the fish jumped twice, each time rising lower in the water and nearer the stern. Gore said it was putting up a splendid battle, but Adam thought it was twitching through its death throes. He had pictured long tests of endurance between man and fish, blistered hands, aching backs and sweaty, good-natured male camaraderie.

The fish flopped around next to the stern. Adam reached into the water and caught its tail. The old man grabbed its bill and whacked it over the head with the club. Its thin, graceful body lit up like a neon sign, becoming a rainbow of electric blues and deep purples. The shutter of Gore's camera clattered like a machine gun as it recorded the colors.

Once the fish had been hauled aboard it turned black. The boy kicked it and said, *"Muerte."* The old man asked Adam if he wanted it mounted. Otherwise he would sell it for fertilizer. The meat was oily, and so many were caught even the poor had tired of eating it. Adam paid a deposit. In celebration the boy poured more beer into plastic cups, tossing the cans overboard.

Gore raised his cup. "Well done, Adam. Eleven minutes, ten seconds, a company record. After you all hear what I have to say you'll want to raise these cups again. Adam, tell Juan to cut the engines. We'll start up again when the meeting is over."

The boat lurched and bobbed, but Gore kept his balance easily. Fiore and Hochmeyer stared determinedly at the horizon, a remedy for seasickness. Gore ignored their agony. He stood facing the Inner Circle, hands on hips like a football coach delivering a pep talk, his legs spread far apart on the swaying deck.

"I want your help," he said, "in convincing the board at next month's meeting to authorize a substantial new investment in the R-Tube."

"You'll need help convincing me first," Fiore spoke up. "That damned gadget is a financial disaster."

"But a technical success."

"Agreed. It's the most sophisticated interactive system in the world. It does everything Warner's Qube can do and more."

"So what's your objection?"

Fiore shrugged. "You know damn well—the cost. Even for a small test market, the cost of establishing a control-center computer and laying the cables is too high. And we can't enter large markets until we have greater consumer acceptance."

"And the result?" Gore asked. As long as someone followed the script he was happy to let them talk.

"The result is that we've tested in diddly-shit places: a hundred units in that godforsaken Arizona condominium and five hundred in that depressing Los Angeles suburb. We could generate more excitement testing in Alaska."

"Which is precisely why I want to wire Washington, D.C."

Fiore pulled himself upright and gripped the arms of the fishing chair. "Christ almighty, Victor, you can't be serious. Washington is seventy percent black. What kind of a test market is that?"

"I'm not talking test market. We've tried that, so has everyone else. Big deal. Warner has its middle-American households in Columbus. Some bank in Minneapolis has two hundred North Dakota farmers plugged into a Videotex system. They're all moving too slowly. Interactive cable is the first breakthrough in two-way communication since the telephone. The difference between watching television and using it. The marriage of the TV and the computer."

Gore paced back and forth across the deck as he spoke, snapping his fingers in the air as if, like a magician, he was reaching into thin air to produce these catchy phrases. His posture was perfect, his energy unlimited. He was at least seventy but looked ten years younger. When he became sixty-five he had persuaded the board to raise the retirement age for senior executives to seventy-five. Adam wondered if he would soon make them lift it to eighty.

"The television is king," he said. "The computer is queen. Now they've given birth to a prince, the R-Tube. And it's growing up faster than our competitors imagine. Kids are educated by television and computers—screens and buttons. This generation will demand interactive cable because it's computer television. If we take a few risks now the interactive they'll demand will be the R-Tube."

Adam recognized the phrases. They all came from speeches he had written for Gore. The R-Tube was Gore's obsession, and Adam had come to know it well. The "R" stood for "Relationship," signifying that the device permitted subscribers to "talk back" or have a "relationship" with their television. They could take college courses at home and then answer tests by pushing buttons on their consoles. They could vote in town meetings, order from department stores, execute bank transactions and respond to surveys. They could even vote between different endings for a favorite soap opera.

A subscriber could summon an ambulance by activating the medical-alert feature and know that simultaneously the R-Tube was delivering his medical history to the ambulance and hospital emergency room. The R-Tube's smoke detectors transmitted alarms and the floor plan of an endangered house to the local fire station, and its security sensors on doors and windows alerted the police to intruders.

Gore often visited the factories where R-Tube components were manufactured and assembled. He had installed a modified system in the two Caribbean TropicResorts and had rented houses in the two American test markets. He played with the R-Tube, invented new features and sometimes oversaw the computer sweeps that monitored and tabulated subscribers' test scores, merchandise orders, entertainment choices, bank transfers and survey responses.

Fiore interrupted Gore's monologue. "It'll take those ghetto blacks a lifetime just to learn how to operate the R-Tube."

Gore stopped pacing. "Fuck the blacks. We wire a few middle-class black neighborhoods—that keeps the liberals happy. Meantime we wire Georgetown." He snapped his fingers twice. "And Cleveland Park, and that renovated neighborhood where the congressmen and their staffs live." Another snap. "Chevy Chase." Snap! "Arlington, Bethesda and McLean." Snap! Snap! Snap!

A wave crashed over the stern, drenching everyone and cutting short the list. Gore shook himself like a wet dog and continued. "I want to showcase the R-Tube. Put it on display in the most influential market in America. Every evening legislators, journalists, lobbyists, diplomats and senior bureaucrats will come home to the R-Tube. During the day their wives and children will play with it. They'll be our ambassadors to the rest of the nation and the world. Foreign diplomats will want it for their countries. Congressmen will recommend it to their districts. The Washington press corps will love it. They can write about it without moving off their couches."

Adam saw Fiore shut his eyes and swallow hard. He had worked for a decade to become the company's next chief executive officer. Now Gore refused to retire and Fiore was too old to look elsewhere. Instead, he was waiting for Gore to become ill, die or disgrace himself. Adam wondered why, if he thought the R-Tube was such folly, he did not encourage Gore. Or was he worried it would be so successful that Gore's position would be ensured for another decade?

"Suppose we invest in a head-end computer and in laying cables," Fiore said, "and then only a handful of households subscribe, especially when they discover the R-Tube comes with a thousand-dollar installation fee. Some damned microwave company has already gone into Washington and sold about fifty thousand microwave antennas. They cost fifty bucks and you pay an additional twenty a month for a scrambler to pick up movies and sports from the entertainment satellites."

"Microwave is a one-way cable, dead television," Gore said. "It's irrelevant. I guarantee we'll sell the R-Tube to households that already have dishes on their roofs. We'll sell it by offering what everyone in these expensive Washington neighborhoods needs."

Everyone waited. When he was sure he had their attention, Gore pulled five manila envelopes from a sail bag and tossed one on each lap. "I had Stan Hacker prepare this report on the Washington firms that install and maintain burglar-alarm systems. In Washington the wealthy and powerful live in cute Georgetown houses or sprawling suburban mansions, a burglar's dream. Check out the appendix. It's got all the details, the addresses of most of our target households— congressmen, journalists, diplomats, law partners and members of the executive branch. Over ninety percent live in projected R-Tube neighborhoods."

Everyone leafed through the report. Hacker stroked the vinyl cover of his as if it were a favorite child. This was his moment. Adam saw Gore give him a nod.

"I've studied the security companies," Hacker began. "They install alarms, intrusion-detection sensors, and offer fire and medical services. Like our system, theirs also rely on a two-way wire between the residence and the monitoring point, whether it's the police station or the security office. The big difference is that we install the R-Tube for a thousand dollars and then charge fifteen dollars a month to monitor a subscriber's home; the security outfits charge an average of three thousand dollars for installation and then up to fifty a month."

"Why the difference?" Adam asked.

"Because we use our own cable television lines while they have to tap into the phone lines, and Ma Bell rapes them and the subscriber. Which means that by purchasing the R-Tube a subscriber gets an alarm system and the other R-Tube services for much less than the security companies charge. It's irresistible."

"Except for anyone who's already paid three thousand to install a conventional alarm system," Fiore said. "They won't want to invest again."

Gore waved his hand. "We cancel the installation fee for anyone already wired into a conventional system. Remember that our purpose is to showcase the R-Tube. We want everyone to have it."

"And remember too," Hacker said, "that we're bound to sign up people who want protection but resisted the conventional alarm companies because of the expense and because wiring their homes struck them as slightly unsavory or paranoid. Furthermore, the security firms have a bad image, like undertakers. Everyone thinks they're staffed with ex-mobsters and cashiered cops."

And people like you, Adam thought.

"Whereas we," Gore said, "are a jolly family entertainment company. People will welcome us into their homes as protectors rather than invaders of their privacy. And once we're inside we've got an electronic highway smack through the most influential households in the country." Gore flattened out his hand and swept it down an imaginary superhighway.

"We'll showcase every new R-Tube feature in D.C. Within a decade we'll be handling every essential household function: entertainment, shopping, security, banking, home computing, messaging and education. We'll have become a utility, like the phone or electric company."

"O.K.," Hochmeyer said. "I'll support you. It's good. Fear of crime gets us into these influential homes. We give them security and the R-Tube at a fair price. Then when old cable franchises expire or are abandoned and when new ones are awarded we'll have earned their support."

"Jim?" Gore asked. "Are you with me?"

"I'll go along," Fiore said weakly. "Provided the report supports your conclusions. I'd also like to submit it to the board."

Hacker jumped up. "No!" he shouted. "I don't want that bitch or the professor to see this. They might leak it to the press." The "bitch" was a vice-president of a liberal foundation and the "professor" was a distinguished black who taught economics at Yale. They were the tokens—black, female and liberal—on Tropic's board of directors.

"Nine feet seven inches," Beale announced, holding up a tape measure he had borrowed from the captain.

Hacker spun around. "What do you mean?"

"The length of Adam's fish. It's almost ten feet. Quite a catch."

"Don't you think you should pay attention to what Victor's saying?"

Beale squinted at Hacker as if just noticing him. "Mr. Hacker, I'm fully capable of listening and measuring a fish at the same time. Would it make you happier if I proved my interest by asking a question?" Beale not only resembled Henry Fonda, Adam thought, he was beginning to sound like him.

Beale addressed himself to Gore. "Let's assume the board buys this. Are you sure we can get the necessary franchises? I imagine Congress has to approve the award of the D.C. franchise. Then you've got to worry about the county authorities in Virginia and Maryland. Some have already granted cable franchises."

"You're right. We can't get all the suburbs we'd like but there'll be no problem with the D.C. franchise."

No one needed to ask why. Gore was a close personal friend of the President. He had rented a house in Washington after the election, and his wife—"the Duchess"—frequently shopped and lunched with the First Lady. For the President to facilitate the award of a franchise to TropicAmerican would be a small favor.

"There may be more opposition than you think," Beale said. "The Democrats won't like handing this to one of the President's buddies. That's how they'll see it."

"But, Nat, you're going to reassure them. Why do you think I'm taking you into my confidence before the other directors? I need your support. You've held important posts in two Democratic administrations. The liberals and moderates on our board will listen to you. Afterwards, I'm counting on you to reassure your friends that this is not some crazy Watergate plot to bug their houses."

Beale plunged his hands into a bucket of water and rinsed off the sailfish's blood. He said, "I can't make these kinds of promises until I know more about—"

"You know enough already," Gore interrupted. "First"—he snapped his fingers and pointed his index finger like a pistol straight between Beale's eyes—"you know the R-Tube is not some fucking spy. No one has to subscribe and if they do no one forces them to turn it on.

"Second, a half dozen companies are developing and testing interactive cables. Columbus, Ohio, has had Qube since 1977 and I'm not aware of it turning into a police state.

"And third"—his finger was now a few inches from Beale's forehead—"data from the computer sweeps will be stored under tight security. Hacker himself will be in charge of the facility."

"Is that so reassuring?"

"He was promoted while you headed the Agency."

"He's not with the Agency any longer."

"Neither are you. Instead we pay you handsomely to ornament our board of directors. For once, I'd like to see you prove you're worth it."

Adam slowly swiveled his chair so that he faced the sea. He felt embarrassment for Beale, but wondered why the older man subjected himself to this treatment. Did he need money that badly?

"Meeting adjourned," Gore said. "Adam, tell Juan to crank up those engines and head back."

At the dock, the captain and the boy dragged the fish across the dock to a scaffold, tied a rope to its tail and hoisted it into the air, all the while cursing its weight. Adam put his arm around it, and an old man snapped a picture with a battered Polaroid.

"Nice fish, old buddy." Hacker stared over Adam's shoulder at the picture. The fish was green, Adam's face yellow, but there was no sarcasm in Hacker's voice. Apparently Gore had ordered a truce.

"I'm having it mounted. But it wasn't what I expected. You'd think a fish that size would fight more."

"Maybe he didn't want to piss off Victor." Adam found himself laughing with Hacker. Now was the time to apologize.

"Stan, about what I said on the boat . . ."

"Enough said, old buddy. All forgotten." Hacker examined the picture again. "You pay that fucker anything yet?"

"A deposit."

"Turn around, old buddy."

Adam turned. The old man had unhooked the fish and was slicing it into thick steaks with a machete. Market women in flowery dresses were handing tattered bills to the boy.

"What the hell . . . ?"

"No sweat. You still get your fish."

"How, reincarnation? That old pirate is selling it."

"The mounted fish are plastic."

"Plastic!" He had imagined them stuffing it, like a moose head.

"Sure, but sometimes they do a nice job. They paint on all the pretty colors you saw when it died. The real fish would just be an old ugly mud-brown color. Who'd want that?"

"Who'd want a plastic fish?"

"Plenty do. Don't worry, the bill is genuine. They cut it off a real fish and paste it on your plastic one." Hacker chuckled. "Only problem is that it may not be the bill off your fish. They've got dozens lying around, and who's to know the difference? They all look the same. So do the fish. Not much difference between one plastic fish and another."

Gore grabbed Adam by the arm and led him toward one of the waiting limousines. "No more bickering between you two. You're going to have to work together on this R-Tube business."

"I've already apologized."

"Good. I knew you would." He gripped Adam's forearm so hard that Adam expected bruises.

"Exactly how will we be working together?" He did not relish spending time with Hacker.

"This whole thing was largely Stan's idea. He'll be working on our marketing strategy and will report directly to me. You'll have a similar liaison position with our public relations people. I also want you thinking about the type of PR campaign we want. I'm going to persuade the President to have an R-Tube installed in the family quarters of the White House. There could be a ceremony, similar to lighting the White House Christmas tree, with the First Lady turning on the first Washington R-Tube."

He squeezed Adam's arm so violently that Adam almost cried out. "I think you're going to have a lot of fun with this," he said.

The market women elbowed past. The fish's head peeked out from one of their baskets.

"There's one more thing," Gore said, putting his arm around Adam's shoulders, a gesture reserved for bad news. "I may want to change the location of the October board meeting."

Adam winced. Gore insisted on rotating the quarterly board meetings among countries where TropicAmerican had substantial holdings. The actual site had to meet Hacker's rigorous security standards, as well as offer good hunting or fishing. Gore had blasted moose in Maine and wild boar in Germany, hauled salmon from Scottish streams and stalked elk in Canada. Next month's meeting was scheduled for Mexico. Gore was going to shoot white-winged doves.

"Are you certain it's necessary?" Adam asked. Lining up the Mexican shooting estate had proven particularly expensive and difficult. "The meeting is less than a month away."

"I only said it *may* be necessary. Hacker is worried because we've had another threat from the Puerto Ricans; he'd rather bypass Latin

America. And I wouldn't mind switching to somewhere more isolated. It would encourage the board to concentrate."

In other words, Adam thought, you want to hold everyone hostage, just like this morning, in some miserable, uncomfortable place
until they agree to anything in order to escape.

"Hacker and I have settled on a possible alternate site with great
security and fabulous hunting. I'll decide by tomorrow evening.
Meantime you might call around there to see if there's a good hotel
or an estate we can rent."

"Where is it?"

"An island off the west coast of Scotland, very remote but only an
hour from Glasgow by helicopter. It's called Jura."

CHAPTER 3

The helicopter landed on the meadow as Gina walked up the driveway. Piers, Dorothy and a long-haired young man clutching a camera with a telephoto lens climbed out.

Gina wanted to turn and run but she hesitated too long and then Piers was on her. Catching her in his arms, he lifted her off the ground and she heard the rapid clicking of an automatic shutter. It would be a stirring, poignant picture: husband and wife locked in rapturous embrace, reunited on a windswept Scottish field after her ordeal. She glared at the photographer and squirmed out of Piers's embrace.

"No more pictures," she whispered. "I'm filthy, exhausted, and I've spent the night in a cave full of goat shit."

Piers ignored her. "Thank God you're safe!" he shouted. The young man scribbled in a notebook. A goddamned journalist, she thought, come to report my dramatic rescue, or tragic death. How had Piers organized it all so quickly? She had been missing less than twenty-four hours.

"You're too damned late!" she shouted back. But the journalist had pocketed the notebook and was pointing his camera at Barnhill.

"The police thought you might have fallen off a cliff or twisted an ankle. I came to help search for you."

"Half an hour earlier and you could have plucked me off the moor. I needed a ride home." She turned away and walked toward the house.

Piers followed. "You should be more grateful," he said. "Renting that thing is costing a packet."

She shrugged. "Political expense."

"And Dorothy insisted on coming even though she loathes flying. She became terribly airsick on the hop over. Good God, it's windy here!"

A gust of wind swept away his cap, the cheap cloth kind worn by "workers" in television comedies. Dorothy and the handsome young pilot chased it across the meadow.

"Don't complain, Piers. That picture should be worth something. They can headline it 'Mike Comforts Wife After Hebrides Ordeal.' How about 'Thank God You're Safe!' as a caption?"

Dorothy and the pilot pounced on the hat like rugby players on a loose ball and rolled in the grass, pretending to fight over it.

Gina said, "Your 'political adviser' has recovered from the flight."

"She's only twenty-five," he said proudly. "The young are very resilient."

"Was this stunt her idea?"

"No, all mine, but she suggested bringing the reporter. He's from one of those tabloids that excel at football scores, royal gossip and pictures of undressed girls. But its editorials support the workers."

"Good."

They were less than twenty yards from the house and she did not want him coming in. "Are you still banging her?"

"That's a vulgar expression. Is it American? You know, I heard an amusing joke at a diplomatic party recently. What's the definition of a happy diplomat? Give up? It's someone with an American salary, a French cook and an English wife."

She stared at the ground. He was wearing woolly black socks underneath his sandals. Would the reporter mention that? A good thing Eric could not see him trotting about his meadow. He had once written an essay vilifying "professional do-gooders and vegetarians in sandals."

"And then there's the unhappy diplomat."

She had thought the joke was finished.

"He has a French salary, an English cook and an American wife."

"In other words, you *are* still banging her."

For a moment he halted and actually looked at her. But his expression told her nothing. Though he was forty-five his face was virtually unlined, so smooth and featureless that it never betrayed his emotions. He claimed his vegetarian diet was responsible for his youthful looks. She thought he looked like a decayed boy.

"No, I've stopped," he said. "Pleased?"

"Yes. For her sake." That should be enough to send him packing, she thought.

But he was still there. "She loves me, but I've told her it's impossible."

"Why?"

"Haven't you read? There's going to be a general election. I can't afford any scandal."

"I thought they'd promised you a safe seat this time." He had lost his seat in the last election. "One of those places that would elect a murderer to Parliament as long as he wasn't a Tory."

As she opened the gate to the front garden she searched again for a reaction. Nothing.

"It's not the election worrying me, it's afterwards. I've a good chance for a cabinet post. Or, if we lose, a position as a shadow minister. But the party's right wing will be looking for excuses to veto me. Dorothy understands that."

"She should. Political advice is what you pay her for, isn't it?"

"She *wants* me to succeed. In fact, she's keen to have you back in England. It will be awkward explaining why you're sitting out the election up here, instead of coming home to pitch in."

"I am home." She pushed open the front door of the fortress-like gray stone house. Barnhill was one of Jura's few middle-class dwellings. It had three bedrooms upstairs and a parlor, kitchen and bedroom on the ground floor. Two parallel wings attached to the rear contained garages and barns and also created a small U-shaped courtyard. Altogether, it was about twice as large as the average farmer's cottage and a third the size of a manor house. Because of this, it suited Gina as much as it had Eric.

The moment she stepped into the hallway she smelled it: the rank odor of male exertion. It reminded her of undergraduates jogging through the quad in filthy rugby clothes and of Piers's thick woolen shirts after a demonstration.

Piers followed her into the hall.

"Were you poking around here earlier?" she asked.

Piers let himself look annoyed. "You saw us land. We flew from the mainland in convoy with the police helicopter. This man you were with—apparently his wife called the police by shortwave when you failed to return."

"My fellow survivor is an elderly man with dentures and wandering hands." Her mind was racing. If Piers hadn't been in Barnhill, who had? One of the islanders in search of Barnhill's tenant? Or just a burglar? She preferred almost any possibility to the thought of the owner of that soft Irish voice she had heard yesterday.

"The police said you'd gone stalking. I told them it was impossible. You detest blood sports."

"You detest them. I don't recall having an opinion."

"So you were stalking!"

"I liked it," she lied. "But I didn't go for fun. It was part of my job."

"Can't you get by on your allowance without working as a gamekeeper?"

"I meant my thesis. I went stalking to coax someone into an interview."

"Is that what you call it? Your 'job'?" He smiled.

She resisted pushing him out the door. For the first time in years she needed him. He had to stay until she was positive Barnhill was empty. A housebreaker, so soon after the shooting incident, seemed ominous. But she couldn't bring herself to tell Piers. Within moments he and Dorothy would be publicizing it as a right-wing plot to intimidate the candidate. No one would believe she was important enough to be shot on her own account.

"You've come this far," she said. "You might as well see the house."

He peered out the hallway window at the helicopter. Dorothy had put on the pilot's cap. The pilot wore Piers's hat. They were posing by the helicopter with their arms draped over each other's shoulders, laughing. The reporter was taking pictures. "Aren't you going to invite them in as well?" he asked.

She realized he was reluctant to leave Dorothy alone with the pilot. "Look, I've been out all night and I'm not up to running a guided tour. Besides, they seem to be amusing themselves."

As she hung up her jacket she tried to separate any strange sounds from the familiar ones. The house was never silent. It was situated high on an open meadow without trees or neighboring buildings to break the wind. From a distance it looked like a ship floating on a grass-green sea, and like a ship it creaked and shuddered in the wind. All the sounds she heard now were familiar: windows rattling and curtains flapping, a trapped fly buzzing against a windowpane and a faucet dripping in the larder. Every floorboard had a distinctive groan. If anyone was inside he was not moving.

She nudged open the door to the downstairs bedroom with one foot. It too reeked of the same odor as the front hall. Gina looked out the windows. To the west she could see the dirt track to the moor and to the east the Sound of Jura and the bleak purple hills of the mainland. There were no vehicles on the track, no boats on the sound. Her intruder was long gone, or still there.

She threw open the windows and a damp cross draft swept through the room, carrying away the odor.

"Is this where you sleep?" he asked, eyeing the narrow cot and thin mattress.

"It's the guest room. Care to stay?"

He looked out the window again. The reporter was sitting alone in the doorway of the helicopter, pouring tea from a thermos. Dorothy and the pilot had disappeared. "I wouldn't mind a cup of tea," he said.

He's giving them time, she thought. He doesn't want to flush his mistress out of the bushes in front of an audience.

"Perhaps the others would like some tea too?" she asked brightly.
"Why not ask them?"

"They've brought their own. Besides, this is our chance to be alone."

Traces of coal dust spotted the kitchen's linoleum floor. Someone had used the metal tongs to rummage through the coal bin and poke inside the Aga, her coal-burning stove. She filled the kettle and took cups and saucers from the kitchen cabinet. Her intruder had pulled it out from the wall and then pushed it back several inches to the left, scratching the floor. Was he searching for something, there or in the coal bin? Or was this just someone's way of frightening her?

She pried off the top of the tin labeled "Tea" and found scones inside. Someone had switched the tops of the tea, scone and sugar tins.

Piers sat at the scarred kitchen table drumming his fingers, his eyes locked on the helicopter. "You still haven't told me what happened," he said absentmindedly.

"We were trapped on the west coast by fog, so we slept in a cave. The fog lifted and we walked back. Malcolm went to Kinauchdrach, where he's now being scolded by his wife and the police. I returned to see you and your mistress land on my meadow. End of story."

And she hoped Malcolm remembered to tell the same story. Malcolm, who had the usual islander's distrust of outsiders, was as unwilling as she to report the shooting. He had even argued that it was not her name the Irishman had called out in the mist. And Gina had let herself be persuaded. After all, her wound was no more than a scratch; it would quickly heal. But if Piers learned something was up, he would use it to his own advantage—not just by calling in the tabloids but by forcing her to return home where she could be properly guarded. No, she could never ask his help.

"Sugar?" she asked, holding a heaping tablespoon over his mug. He jerked the mug away. "It's poison. You know I never take it."

She heaped twice her usual ration into her mug and lit a rare cigarette. When she sat down she saw that someone had shuffled the positions of the sugar bowl, egg cups, marmalade jar and toast rack that lived in the center of the kitchen table. She wiped them furiously with a damp dishcloth and returned them to their proper positions. Someone had violated her kitchen—Eric's kitchen, the heart of Barnhill.

She liked thinking that the table, kettles and cabinet were there when Eric had first come to Barnhill during the summer of 1946. At the age of forty-three and after years of neglecting his health for the sake of his writing, he planned to relax and regain his strength before beginning *Nineteen Eighty-four*. But the summer was unexpectedly hectic. He shared the house with his housekeeper and her boyfriend, his adopted son, his sister and friends he had invited up from London. The kitchen was the center of activity.

Gina had also spent most of her summer in the kitchen, with her notes and manuscript spread out on the table. At first she had played the wireless during meals, and even looked forward to visits from Malcolm and Mary. But after several weeks of reading and rereading Eric's books and essays, of transcribing interviews about him and of writing and revising her chapters, she had stopped being lonely. And sometimes during a still summer evening, with the kitchen warmed by the setting sun and the perpetual heat of the Aga, with the wind briefly stilled and the sea the color of polished silver, with insects buzzing in the overgrown garden and the cuckoos crying their hypnotic refrain—sometimes during these summer evenings she looked up and saw his graceful hands filling a cigarette paper with dark Turkish tobacco. He had a pencil-thin moustache and translucent skin. He smiled shyly, lit a cigarette, and a soft, purring tubercular cough rose from his lungs. He stood up, a thin figure in a patched tweed jacket and baggy corduroys, and moved around the kitchen filling kettles and buttering toast. Then he poured himself a cup of India tea and sat across from her. When he looked up from his mug she stared into pale blue eyes protected by sockets as deep as Jura's caves. They never spoke, at least out loud.

"Did you shoot him?" Piers asked.

She coughed up a swallow of tea. "Who?"

"The stag, of course."

"Straight through the heart. A clean kill. I gutted him myself: the heart, liver, stomach and intestines just spill out, and in five minutes flat it looks like something hanging in a butcher shop. Did you know that the Germans make cuff links from the teeth?"

"I think you should leave this place. There's room in the helicopter."

She looked outside. Still no sign of Dorothy and the pilot. "No, thanks. I plan to stay and finish." She paused. "You know, my job."

"There can't be many people still here who knew him. Surely by now you've completed your interviews. You've been on Jura all summer."

"And I plan to stay the winter."

"But why? It must be ghastly here: damp, dark and perpetually windy."

"I have a year's lease."

"Break it. I'll pay the owners."

"All right, then, I'm staying because it inspires me."

"You don't need inspiration. You're writing a thesis, not an epic poem."

She knew he would ridicule her if she told him that she would stay the winter because Eric had and she wanted to share his experience. He had returned to Barnhill for a second visit in the spring of 1947, exhausted after a long wintry struggle with tuberculosis in London. The guests that summer only saw him at meals if he was well enough to join them. Most of every day he spent writing. He was determined to complete a first draft before his health failed. He finished in October and promptly collapsed, unable to leave his bed. Two months later he entered a Glasgow sanitarium, afraid he would die before he could finish the revisions. Gina knew by heart the chilling letter he had written his publisher: "It's such a ghastly mess as it stands but the idea is so good that I could not possibly abandon it. If anything happens to me, I've instructed Richard Rees, my literary executor, to destroy the manuscript without showing it to anybody."

He left the sanitarium in July 1948 and returned to Jura. His friends thought he was mad. The island was damp and isolated, the nearest doctor a two-hour drive. But he had written most of *Nineteen Eighty-four* on Jura and was determined to finish it there. In some way, her own connection with Eric depended on Jura—if she left the island, it might be broken. She would have to finish there too.

"You're right, of course, Piers," she said, trying to sound calm.

"It's only a thesis, but it would give me pleasure to do it properly and I think I can accomplish more here than at home while you're campaigning."

She snatched the mug from his hands and tossed the remaining tea into the sink. Time to send him off, before he destroyed the confidence she had slowly erected over the summer. Better to face her intruder alone than share Barnhill with Piers.

"What about my tour?" he said quickly, as if sensing her mood. "Then I'll be on my way."

In the parlor the armchairs were grouped at a different angle around the fireplace. She straightened them out. Her intruder had shuffled the cushions on the leather couch so the one with the stain was on the left. The disturbances were so minor that a policeman investigating her death would have thought the house untouched. Only she, who knew the position of every pot of marmalade, could see the place had been thoroughly searched.

Piers sat in one of the chairs, toying with a box of matches. She hoped he would not light the fire.

"I fail to see the charm," he said. "Why did he keep coming back here? What kind of a socialist shuts himself away on an upper-class estate, miles from the workers, and then writes Red-baiting, anti-socialist fantasies?"

"He didn't write *Animal Farm* here, only *Nineteen Eighty-four*, and they were anti-totalitarian, not anti-socialist."

"What good did either do the workers?"

"Is that the test of literature?"

"No, the test of a sincere socialist. You know, the workers have no use for Orwell, but he's immensely popular with the Tories and those thugs in the White House. They're always quoting him to prove socialism means the end of liberty instead of the liberation of the exploited."

"I've heard this before. I think you should go. It gets dark early here, even in early October."

He ignored her, as if she were a heckler at a rally. "If he were still alive he'd be, how old? In his mid-eighties? He'd probably have accepted a peerage: Lord Jura." He laughed. "He'd be living on a vast estate, giving the odd speech at Tory conventions and writing reactionary columns in the newspapers about Poland and Afghanistan."

"Instead of progressive columns justifying them?"

"When you began this project you still had the vestiges of a political conscience. I hoped you might write a revisionist interpretation, explode some of the old myths. Instead you've just become another right-wing sycophant. You know, if your thesis was ever published, it would embarrass me. I'd be tarred by your brush."

"Don't worry, 'Mike,' " she said. "I promise to use my maiden name."

"Oh, I'm not really worried. This will probably be like your other hobbies, never properly finished."

Dorothy and the pilot walked across the garden. She was wearing his cap at a jaunty angle and he had put his uniform jacket around her shoulders. He was picking something—bits of hay?—from her blond hair. It was the first time Gina could remember being glad to see her.

She pointed out the window. "You can go now, Piers. They've come back."

He stared at his watch for a long time. "We do want to catch the last London plane. Glasgow is a dismal place to spend the night. Why not go upstairs and pack your bags?"

"No."

"I can drain the pipes and nail the windows."

"No. And if I *were* leaving I could manage that myself."

"You don't have to stay home for long, just a week or two. The gossip columns have already made snide comments about your absence."

"Goodbye, Mike."

"You know I could force you."

"I doubt it." Perhaps he had already tried—a fake assassination attempt that had come just close enough. And now the smell of an intruder.

"I could cut off your funds."

"I could sue for divorce and name Dorothy."

"I'd countersue for desertion."

"It's a stalemate, Piers. I need your money to finish my work and you need a wife until after the election."

"Not necessarily." He gave a blank stare.

"And if you're so concerned about a scandal you might think about hiring a more discreet political adviser. Dorothy is such an obvious slut."

"The next time you get into trouble up here," he said, walking to the door, "don't expect me to come rescue you."

As soon as he left she lit the fire and watched the helicopter become a black speck in the sky. Was someone—the Irish boy?— also watching it disappear, but from one of the upper-floor windows? She had to find out. She turned to face the stairs.

Charlie woke to the sound of the helicopter. He had fallen asleep under a rocky ledge within sight of Barnhill, clutching his pocketknife and dreaming of Belfast. He woke cold, hungry and exhausted but confident.

He was alone but not lonely. There were no older brothers or sisters to give orders, yet he had survived. He had found shelter, waited out the storm and fog and then walked east, keeping to the high ground and scanning the countryside with his binoculars for any sign of Jack. When he reached the coast he had checked the stone jetty in the neighborhood inlet where they had landed yesterday morning. It was deserted. Jack had left; by now he would be in Belfast, telling them Charlie was a traitor, or a coward. Fuck him.

Charlie knew the truth: he was no longer a boy who took orders.

In an hour it would be dark. Time to take stock, make a decision. He crawled from under the ledge, removed his possessions from the knapsack and arranged them on the ground. There was a map of Jura, half a packet of his favorite biscuits (chocolate-orange Jaffas), a pocketknife and the binoculars, worth thirty quid. He could sell them for fifteen. In the pocket of his windbreaker he found the box of spare cartridges he had grabbed at the last moment. Lucky he had taken these, or Jack might have hunted him down and then waited for the woman to return. He had saved her life twice, then; for that she owed him.

He spread out the map to orient himself. He was at Barnhill, at the extreme northern end of the island. The only ferry, he saw, was at Feolin, thirty miles south. From where he sat he could see the road to Feolin, a miserable, rutted dirt track that not a single vehicle had used all day. He leaned over the map and traced the road with his finger. Ten miles south of Barnhill, at Ardlussa, it became dotted red. He consulted the key. Dotted red was a paved road with passing lanes, which meant traffic. The road hugged the shoreline until it reached Craighouse. He remembered from the briefing that here were the island's only store, church, distillery and hotel. After Craighouse the road cut inland across the southern tip to Feolin, where a dotted line marked the ferry service across narrow straits to Islay. From there another dotted line, a larger ferry, ran to the mainland. Islay also had an airport.

He could begin walking and hope to hitch a ride after Ardlussa. In Craighouse he might sell the binoculars for enough money to reach the mainland. But by now word was out about the shooting. He had seen a police helicopter coming from the mainland. He would be arrested in Craighouse if not before. Even if he hiked overland they would catch him at the ferry dock. And suppose he did escape? He could not return to Belfast, or anywhere else in Ireland. Jack would kill him.

He looked up from the map and noticed smoke spiraling from one of Barnhill's chimneys. Perhaps Gina hadn't left in the helicopter after all. Good. She could feed him, give him money and smuggle him off the island. Who would believe she would help her assailant escape? He would tell her how he had missed her on purpose. He had saved her life; now she had to save his.

It was only as he strode down the hill toward the house that it occurred to him she might refuse. Then, surely, he would have to kill her. Charlie hesitated, trying to think it through. Then it came to him: if she resisted and he killed her, he would have accomplished his mission. Then he could go home.

Gina dashed through the upstairs bedrooms, opening and closing closets and peering under beds. The rooms were empty and undisturbed. They all looked identical: white walls, a single bed, a bureau with sticky drawers and framed pictures of wildflowers razored from magazines.

She checked her own bedroom last. Once she was certain it was empty, she collapsed on her bed in relief. This room was the largest and most comfortable, the one she imagined to have been Eric's, probably the one in which he had typed the final draft of *Nineteen Eighty-four*.

During that last summer in Jura, the summer of 1948, he had gone to great lengths to conserve his health, even sleeping outdoors in a tent on dry nights in the belief that fresh air was beneficial. Half of each day he puttered in the garden and answered mail. During the other half he revised his first draft. When he finished in October there remained only to submit a clean copy to his publisher. But the manuscript had become such a maze of additions and corrections that it could not simply be sent off to a typist. He tried to hire a stenographer, but none could be found who was willing to brave Jura in November, and Eric was too ill to travel himself. His lungs were painfully inflamed and any exertion raised his temperature. Determined to submit *Nineteen Eighty-four* by the end of 1948, he decided to type it himself.

For three weeks he lay propped up in bed, typing. He smoked heavily and warmed himself with a paraffin stove. Its fumes aggravated his lungs. When he finished he was too weak to leave Barnhill and pessimistic about what he had written. He told one friend that it was "a good idea ruined." To another he said, "I ballsed it up rather, partly owing to being so sick while I was writing it." Gina believed his suffering had enhanced the book, that the island's hardships had challenged his physical and intellectual courage, igniting the manuscript, creating a masterpiece.

By January 1949 he had recovered enough to travel to a sanitarium in England. "I ought to have done this two months ago," he wrote, "but I wanted to get that bloody book finished." He never regained his health, never was well enough to leave the sanitariums and hospitals. He died a year later, killed by the lethal combination of tuberculosis, *Nineteen Eighty-four* and Jura.

Thinking of Eric's manuscript made Gina think of her own. She jumped off the bed and ran back into the small upstairs bedroom she had converted into an office. It appeared untouched. Her desk was still covered with notes and articles, and on top was the fireproof box containing her manuscript. She had purchased the box in London after reading how T. E. Lawrence had lost the manuscript of *The Seven Pillars of Wisdom* at the Oxford train station. He had no copy, and it had taken him four years to write the book again from scratch. Doubting she could summon such courage and determination, she had bought the fireproof box. Whenever she left Barnhill she locked her manuscript and notes inside.

Her manuscript. It had never occurred to her that someone might want to steal *that.*

She grabbed the box by the handles. The lid came off in her hands and the bottom crashed to the floor. Her intruder had neglected to refasten the clasps after forcing the lock and stealing the contents.

At first she was relieved: she had solved the mystery. Then she doubted her eyes. It was an illusion. Perhaps if she closed the box and opened it again the manuscript would be there.

Had Piers taken it to force her into leaving? She had seen him land, but he could have paid someone else to do it. Or was it an unbalanced academic competitor? She knew about medical students ruining one another's experiments and law students ripping important cases from library books. Last week someone had read her manuscript and shuffled several pages out of order. She had assumed that Malcolm was the culprit; now she was not sure.

What was the first sentence of her first chapter? Her mind was blank. How many interviews had she lost? The people she had interviewed were elderly. How many would still be alive if she went looking for them again?

She heard hinges creak downstairs as someone opened the front door. There were footsteps in the hall and then a faucet running in the kitchen. She slipped off her shoes and tiptoed to the stairs. A floorboard groaned beneath her. She prayed the running water had muffled it. Once she escaped from Barnhill she would run to Kinauchdrach. The police might still be there.

She paused on each step. The intruder turned off the faucet and she heard a clanging as he set the kettle on the Aga. The son of a bitch was fixing himself a cup of tea.

On the last step but one she stumbled and grabbed for the banister. Her elbow crashed into the wall. She picked herself up and raced for the door.

A small man darted from the kitchen. He dropped his mug and it shattered, splattering her with tea.

"Mrs. Baldwin! What a fright you gave me," he said, bending down to collect the pieces. It was Euen, the postman.

She hugged herself. "Don't bother, Euen. I'll sweep it up. Nothing of value, just a mug commemorating the Queen's visit to, oh, I can't remember where."

"I knocked as usual but no one answered. Were you asleep?"

"I suppose." She was so stunned by her loss that she had not heard his van. "Go brew yourself another cup and bring it into the parlor. Scones are in the usual box."

When they sat across from one another with fresh tea he said, "Terrible time you must have had. I was up at Malcolm's. The police had left but he was having a row with his wife on account of her calling them."

He handed her a parcel of letters and newspapers wrapped in elastic bands. "Not as much as when your adverts were running. But the Islay airport was fogged in this morning, so we missed a day's delivery. There's this from Malcolm to make up for it." He held up a small package wrapped in brown paper. "I shouldn't be delivering it for free but I know you won't snitch."

She opened the envelope attached to it. The note said, "In case they return. Open it when he leaves."

Euen held up a dry scone. "Do you have a wee bit of butter?"

"I'm sorry, I'm out." Perhaps that would make him leave sooner and she could open the mysterious parcel.

"I'll get your provision box from the van then. The store's out of butter but they might have sent up some marge."

She slipped the rubber bands off her mail. Three days of newspapers uncurled. She scanned the front pages—nothing about "Mike" this week. One envelope was a bill from the London *Times* with a copy of the notice she had inserted in the personals column. She had sent a similar inquiry to *The New York Times Book Review*. It read: "ORWELL. Scholar writing thesis seeks information about George Orwell in Paris/Germany during 1945. All replies strictly confidential. Baldwin, Barnhill, Jura, Scotland." She had decided against paying extra for a box number. It seemed an unnecessary expense, and she worried that they might hold her replies for weeks.

The details of Eric's life were important to her thesis. He was a writer who always drew heavily on his own experiences. He had been a colonial policeman in Burma for five years, and his novel *Burmese Days* described the stultifying life of the British in that country. He lived and worked among the destitute and then wrote an account of his experiences in *Down and Out in Paris and London*. In one of his novels, the middle-class hero chooses to explore poverty and becomes a hop picker in Kent, as Eric himself had once done. Gina believed that the same held true for *Nineteen Eighty-four*, that it was based closely on his own real-life experiences. But because it was a fantasy these experiences were more subtly disguised. She hoped to ferret them out and reveal them.

A variety of people in England and America had responded to her ads. But now, she suddenly realized, the file containing those replies were also missing. The only one she could remember had come from London. It had said something like: "Dear Mr./Mrs. Baldwin. I will visit Jura during the third week of October and will make myself known to you. I believe I can assist in your research and that the reason for my caution will soon become obvious. I trust you will, as promised, treat this letter in strict confidence." The letter was signed "Dawney" and contained a postscript asking her to send him a note in care of some London pub—she could not remember its name—if she planned to be away in October. Dawney had included in the letter a copy of a brief note Orwell had written him in 1948, shortly before leaving Jura for the last time. In it Orwell had promised that once he regained his health, he would return to Barnhill to write the "Ekman" book. In the meantime, he was leaving his notes behind in a safe place. Now this and all her other carefully gathered contacts were gone, stolen. This had to be academic sabotage.

Euen returned to the kitchen and unpacked the provisions. She flipped through the other letters.

"Not much there," he said. "But could you check this before I leave for Craighouse?" He held up a letter addressed to "George Baldwin," at Barnhill, Jura.

She recognized the writing and the return address: "Brigadier Geoffrey Paget, 'Parade Rest,' 7 Bramble Walk, Bournemouth." There had been a Paget among those who answered her *Times* advertisement.

The letter was penned in the same cramped, spidery writing as his earlier response and she needed several readings to decipher it.

"Dear Mr. Baldwin. I so enjoyed our talk yesterday, although I fear I may not be much use to you since my acquaintance with Orwell, as you now know, was all too insubstantial and brief. I trust it was not too boring for you to listen to an old man go on about the war and his experiences in the Middle East. I find it encouraging that a fine young man such as yourself has such a knowledge and interest in History. Perhaps you Americans are keener on these things than we are, although I expect you are something of an exception. I wish you good luck in your research and if your thesis is ever published I shall put down for it at the library, if I'm still alive. At your request, I have dug out my 1945 diary. If you care to stop by again I shall be only too happy to read you the portions describing my meetings with Orwell in Paris. I have taken the liberty of sending this to the address in your advertisement since I seem to have mislaid the London telephone number you left with me. Thank you again for an interesting afternoon."

As Gina finished the letter she could feel her pulse accelerating. Chills stabbed the back of her neck and her mind raced. Suddenly she found herself encircled by anonymous enemies. Someone was impersonating her; someone had stolen her manuscript; and someone else, perhaps the same man, had tried to kill her. There had been nothing in her advertisement to indicate that she was a woman. If the stalker's shot had been more accurate, Brigadier Paget need never have known that he had been interviewed by an impostor. How many of her other respondents had this young American interviewed? To have reached the Brigadier so quickly he must have entered Barnhill sometime during the previous weeks and read her correspondence. But why hadn't he stolen her papers then? And why had he returned later to kill her?

She thrust the letter into the pocket of her jacket, keeping her hands concealed so Euen could not see them shaking. Finally she looked up. He was waiting for an explanation. She took a deep breath and said, "Actually it *was* for me, Euen." She paused and searched for something more convincing. "Sent by an old gent who must have muddled my name."

"I'll be off, then," he said. "Anything to post?"

"No, nothing." Now she had to act, make a decision without her usual procrastination and moral equivocations. She was afraid to stay in Barnhill alone. That made her furious. Her house, Eric's house, had suddenly become a place she feared.

She gulped the rest of her tea. She would visit Brigadier Paget, taking her passport and the bill from the *Times* as identification. She would explain what had happened—but what *had* happened?—and ask him for a description of her competitor. He had, after all, seen him.

She caught Euen at the front door. "Is there anyone staying at the hotel?"

"Empty at present."

"Good. I'll need a room there tonight. I want to catch the early ferry to Islay. Can you wait while I pack and close up? I'd like to ride down with you to Craighouse." She did not want to drive in her own Land-Rover, alone.

"Shall I hold your mail in the village or leave it here?"

"No, not here," she said quickly. "I'll be gone at least a week. I'd be grateful if you'd look in and feed my hens." She remembered the letter from Dawney. He would be arriving soon. "If anyone asks, say I'll be back next week."

Charlie had taken cover when the postal van pulled into Barnhill. At first he was dismayed when he saw Gina leave carrying a bag. But then he realized it was small; she would not be gone too long.

When the van was out of sight he headed toward the house. It would be easy breaking in and there was bound to be food. He was in no hurry. No one would search for him here. He could make himself comfortable and wait until she returned. Provided she did not meet Jack, or whoever else wanted her dead.

As Euen's van bounced along the dirt track Gina was still struggling to control her quivering hands. She sat on one and then shoved the other deep into her shoulder bag. It brushed against the barrel of Malcolm's revolver. She tensed but then willed herself to hold the handle and curve one finger around the trigger. She had unwrapped Malcolm's parcel while she was upstairs packing, and this old, well-oiled and loaded revolver had tumbled onto her bed. She had stared at it for several moments before picking it up between two fingers, examining it at arm's length and then dropping it into her shoulder bag.

The van nosed into another pothole and she let go of the gun and withdrew her hand to steady herself. Once she was alone she would release the safety and make herself fire it in practice. That would be easier than aiming it at someone, even in self-defense, and even if the target was her mysterious enemy.

CHAPTER 4

Brigadier Geoffrey Paget slid the magnifying glass down the page. When he found the first sentence he began reading in a booming voice: "So in the morning, which, though we meant it to be seven, became eleven, partly on account of difficulties in packing the camel so that things did not slide off, but mostly because starting at seven tends to become eleven—"

Bella Stevens interrupted. "What utter nonsense! I can assure you nothing ever slid off *my* camel. And when I said 'Wheels rolling' at seven, they jolly well rolled at seven."

"But, Bella, you always traveled alone."

"Of course I did. Who wants some thieving guide creeping about, or a lot of chattering fools complaining about the nosh and pointing out every mosque and minaret as if it were Agia Sophia?"

"Towers of Trebizond is only a novel, Bella. Rose Macaulay may not have behaved this way on her own explorations. It's simply her characters who do. Perhaps she was punctual and loaded her camels with great care. So what? She was never a real explorer, not like Gertrude, or Freya, or you." Last week he had read Freya Stark, Gertrude Bell the week before, and before that Bella's own book, *Dead Sea to Damascus.*

"Shall I continue?"

She nodded.

The magnifying glass had slipped down the page. Rather than admit to losing his place he picked up where it had stopped. There was no reason to feel guilty. He had already read *Trebizond* to her once this year. Even though the book had large, clear print, he still had to press his best eye against the glass to make out the words. Last year he had held the glass several inches from his eye.

He continued: "The camel paced briskly after the jeep with Aunt Dot sitting astride in blue linen slacks and a topee in front of the hump and holding the reins, which were scarlet, and Father Chantry-Pigg in khaki riding breeches and puttees riding on top of the hump, with luggage slung on each side, though most of it was in the jeep—"

"Jeep!" she shrieked. "What luxury! When did she write this rot?"

"Published in 1956, although I imagine Miss Macaulay visited Turkey several years earlier, perhaps just after the war." Bella's heyday had been between the wars. Her book jackets still bore the same picture: Bella in a white blouse and a billowing khaki skirt standing erect, her posture perfect, in front of a Crusader castle. One hand clutched the reins of her donkey, "Memsahib," the other held a pith helmet. She had removed it to show off the thick blond hair pinned to her head. She wanted her readers to know she was not a butchy public-school games-mistress type with a boxy haircut.

How he had admired her, and worried about her. She was more courageous than hardy; she sickened easily and ended up recovering in monasteries. She was also bloody-minded and ignored warnings and advice from the authorities. He was often the authority she ignored. Between the wars they had crossed paths in Palestine, the Transjordan, Iraq and Egypt. During the Arab Revolt, when he was a major in Palestine, she had made what she called her "D to D Walk," the Dead Sea to Damascus. He had begged her to reconsider and then forbade her to go. The fedayeen had already murdered British civilians and what if they took her for a Jew? She simply laughed at his fears and he was powerless to stop her; already she was too famous to be ordered about by a major.

Her book about that trip was her best—romantic, not romanticized. She wrote without exaggeration or embellishment, stressing the passions and frustrations that linked mountain Arabs and the average Englishman, diminishing the effect of the exotic clothes and customs that separated them.

And how he respected her! Unlike others who trekked through the Middle East between the wars, she never ridiculed the "bloody wogs" in private while glorifying their nobility and hospitality in her books. She saw them as he did, people who could be kind or evil, charming or boring.

He had always contrasted her with Elinor. His wife had come out twice to join him with the twins, and both times she had returned immediately to her mother in Wales. She had hated the noise, the heat and the hollow, ritual pleasantries; the way Arabs touched and came so close you smelled their last meal. He was proud of his Arabic, but to her it was "the key to an empty room." And the Middle East was "no place to raise the boys." Fat lot of good it had done them, growing up in Britain. Both were middle-aged salesmen, one in houses, the other in stocks. Every year they jumped on a plane and went to the Costa something, got sunburned and sent postcards which the Brigadier tossed away. It was not worth dragging out the magnifying glass to examine the brand-name skyscrapers where they stayed. Did they imagine he would be proud they were "seeing the world," following in their father's footsteps?

"Get on with it, Geoffrey," she insisted. "Or have you dozed off again? No wonder. These chairs are much too comfortable and your parlor is like a Turkish bath, although of course it's cleaner. At home I always sit in a hard-backed wooden chair. Keeps me alert."

"That reminds me never to accept your invitations." She was right about the chairs and the heat. The leather club chairs almost filled the small front sitting room and they *were* comfortable. That was why he had shipped them from post to post. And it was too hot. Whenever Bella visited, Perkins always cranked up the radiators. Why did the young think the elderly flourished in a tropical environment?

To prove he was alert, he began reading loudly. "The people of Trebizond ran after us and cheered," he shouted. "The children learned a little English at school and had also mixed up with some tough young Britons who had been employed on the harbour works, and had picked up from them uncultured remarks such as bye bye; cheerio; cheery bye, old trout; and so on. So they called these after us shouting 'Bye bye old trout,' as the camel went by with Aunt Dot and Father Chantry-Pigg on its back and its ostrich plumes tossing on its head."

"Ha!" Bella exclaimed. " 'Old trout' would have been a compliment some of the places I went." But she had never been an old trout, and even now she was handsome. She still had the graceful legs that had covered great distances, the pronounced cheekbones that saved her face from being horsy and the same dark green eyes, although they could no longer focus on the printed page. She had never married, although he had asked her when they had their fling in Paris near the end of the war. She had been there as a special correspondent for one of the Sunday papers. After decades of intriguing and fighting against the French in the Middle East, the army had sent him to Paris to coordinate Franco-British planning for the occupation of Nazi Germany. His wife had died the previous summer and for a month he and Bella were lovers. Then she left to cover the last of the war in Italy and he followed the forces into Germany. She refused to become an army wife and refused to let him resign for her sake.

He had lost track of her until two years ago when he read in the *Journal of the School of Oriental and African Studies* that, like him, she had retired to Bournemouth. It was not her kind of place, too many old pussies bundled up in deck chairs listening to military bands. As it turned out, they had both come there to live with relatives who had then died within months of their arrivals. He had invited her to lunch and after several meetings they admitted to one another that their sight was failing, but, as it turned out, in conveniently complementary ways. He had cataracts and could read with the aid of a magnifier but was almost blind to objects and people several feet distant. She, on the other hand, was farsighted; she had trouble reading but could see clearly across a room. Their meetings soon evolved into a routine: three mornings a week he read to her and afterward she walked him around to the shops. They finished off with a curry lunch at the Moti Mahal, an Indian restaurant.

The telephone on the hall table just outside the parlor rang when he was midway into the next paragraph. Perkins left the kitchen and answered it. Paget disliked the telephone, particularly now that his hearing was failing. He used it in extremis and relied on Perkins to relay most conversations. Usually he terminated these by ordering the caller to write him a letter.

Perkins poked her head into the parlor and, putting her hand over the mouthpiece, said, "It's that young American again. He wants to know about your diary."

"Tell him I'm too busy to come to the phone and besides I've already written him about it. I've no intention of repeating myself over the phone."

She relayed the message, frowning as she heard the reply. "He's very put out, Sir Geoffrey. Wants to know why you didn't contact him in London."

"Lost the damned number." He had thrown it away, like his sons' postcards. "So I decided to write to the address in his *Times* advert. Anything the matter with that?"

"What *is* this all about?" Bella asked. "Doesn't he know you never use the telephone?"

"I don't think Americans know how to communicate except over that damned instrument. He's a young chap at one of their state universities who's writing some sort of paper about George Orwell. Did I ever tell you that I had a few drinks with him at the Scribe during the war?"

"No, you didn't." She shook her head. "But I distinctly remember us all lunching together. Perhaps you have him confused with someone else."

"Nonsense. My memory is every bit as keen as yours, perhaps more so. Of course I recall that lunch, but I also recall the two of us meeting for drinks sometime afterward."

"Are you sure? How extraordinary! I didn't think you and Eric had hit it off. Whatever did you find to talk about?"

The Brigadier sighed. "All right, dammit, maybe I can't remember *that*. Why do you think I've had to dig out my diary."

"Well, *I* can certainly remember a great deal about that strange lunch we all had together. Eric took us to a very posh hotel where he claimed to have worked in the scullery. Ordered a lovely lunch and then told a lot of ghastly stories about how they prepared the food when he was there before the war. Chefs licking the steaks and spitting in the soups, chickens dropped down service lifts and then rubbed off and sent out—that sort of thing. I always thought he made those stories up, but we were never quite sure. He had such a peculiar sense of humor."

Paget strained to focus on her lovely face. "But you already knew him before Paris, didn't you?" She blushed; or did she? Damn his old blind eyes.

"Oh yes," she said after a pause. "I'd met him in London several times in the thirties, before he was so well known. I think he worked in a bookshop in Hampstead. I liked him tremendously because he was such a 'doer.' Not one of those academics sitting in a senior common room talking rot over decanters of port. He didn't just babble on about the fascists in Spain; he went there. And when he arrived he didn't just hang around a lot of bars and soak up atmosphere; he fought. You know, Geoffrey, he was a man of great physical courage."

And so was I, thought Paget.

"That lunch in Paris reminded me what a doer he was. He decided to write about poverty, so he lived it, even worked at that hotel. Reminded me of my own career. That's why I liked him. We were both doers." She sensed his jealousy. "Of course, you were too, but it was easier for you. You were a man and always so fit, but he and I had handicaps. I was a woman and he was always so ill."

"I really don't think that's terribly much to have in common."

" 'As the corpse went past,' " she said, " 'the flies left the restaurant in a cloud and rushed after it, but they came back a few minutes later.' "

"What?" said the Brigadier. Old girl has finally lost her marbles, he thought.

"That was the first sentence of his essay about Marrakesh. Wish I'd had the nerve to start books that way. But of course, he never knew half as much about the Arabs as you do."

He knew her well enough to know that compliments were usually strategic, a means of distracting him or changing the subject. He pushed himself forward to the edge of his chair and willed every muscle in his eyes to focus on her face. "Exactly how well did you know him?"

She stared right back. "We were *very* good friends."

"As good friends as we were?" He was enjoying this; he had thought he was too old for jealousy.

"Different. You loved me; he confided in me." There, I've finally gone and said it, she thought. That should shut him up.

"Sir Geoffrey!" Perkins shouted in an exasperated voice. She had relayed Paget's last message and was waiting, with her hand over the mouthpiece, to transmit the American's reply. "He wants to know if you'll read parts of your diary over the telephone."

"Certainly not! I refuse to strain my eyes poring over my old scribblings, but you can, provided you've nothing better to do. I haven't bothered to reread it myself yet, but you can go ahead and read any entries mentioning George Orwell. Be sure you shut the door first."

A few minutes later Perkins poked her head into the room. "He wants to come interview you again, Sir Geoffrey. Says your diary is most interesting."

"I suppose he can stop at noon Saturday week. No, make it this Saturday. Sooner the better when you're my age. Might be dead in two weeks."

"Anything else?"

"Yes. Since it's your day off, tell him to bring me a beef sandwich and a bottle of pale ale. Rare beef. I'm not giving him tea a second time. On second thought, double that order. You're invited too, Bella. I'm curious what you make of him, and after all, you knew Orwell too. Better than I did." He winked.

"If it's Paris he's interested in I could probably help," she said. "But first I'll have to see if I like him."

"Oh, I'm sure you will. Nice enough chap, for an American. I told him what I remembered, and he asked if I kept any kind of diary. A diary! I must have forty. I made the mistake of promising to dig out the Paris one, see if it would jog my memory, and now he's badgering me about it. But don't worry, Bella." He paused. Perkins was still safely on the telephone. "She'll only read out the parts about Orwell in Paris," he whispered, "not the passages about us."

Before she could react he closed the book and set down the magnifier. "Well, my appetite seems to be vast today. Shall we off to the Moti? I'm in the mood for a prawn vindaloo."

The phone rang again as they left the house. Perkins caught up with them at the gate. "Sir Geoffrey, now there's a Gina Baldwin on the phone wanting to see you in regard to her Orwell advertisement."

"Baldwin never spoke of being married, but of course she could be a sister."

"She does have traces of an American accent," Perkins said.

"Probably helping out with the research chores and the typing, Not very well organized, both of them calling for an appointment."

"What shall I tell her?"

"That her husband, or brother, or whatever, just made an appointment for Saturday noon. If she wants to come too she'll have to bring her own sandwich."

CHAPTER 5

The R-Tube said: "You are the plunderer of ancient pyramids in a dangerous land of decayed forests and scorpion-filled deserts."

Adam sat up on his bed at the TropicResort and pressed buttons on the hand-held keypad and a diagram of a maze within a pyramid flashed onto the television screen. Cobras and ancient curses blocked entry to a secret chamber. Too difficult. He erased it and called up Adventure Five: "You are the leader of a heroic underground group sent to rescue a beautiful Allied agent imprisoned by the Gestapo in a mist-shrouded fortress high in the Bavarian Alps." This was more like it. He grabbed the R-Tube joystick. A digital clock in a corner of the screen ticked off seconds beginning at 300. He had five minutes to rescue her.

The hero, Adam, appeared on the screen as a stylized green dollar sign with red, white and blue striped arms. Adam jerked the joystick, jabbed the action button and ducked through a hole in the electrified fence. Safely reaching the other side, he raced across a brilliant yellow meadow, dodging black Dobermans and leaping over cherry-red nipples that represented German land mines. He reached the moat unscathed. The R-Tube chirped a computer-harsh hurdy-gurdy "Star-Spangled Banner." Two hundred and eighty-seven seconds left on the clock.

The Gestapo had stocked the moat with sharks and electric-blue piranhas. Adam jumped in, and a line of piranhas shifted course and tracked him, their blue jaws snapping in unison. He leapt back onto the bank. Was he being cautious or cowardly? He lost fifteen seconds racing around the moat. He vaulted onto a rock in midstream, then to another and onto the opposite bank. He had reached the castle. Seconds remaining: 249. Enough to save the girl and shoot the moon—use every feature on the TropicResort's closed-circuit R-Tube. He could easily alternate back and forth between the game and the other R-Tube services.

He bounded off the bed and into the chair facing the R-Tube keyboard, laid the joystick on the rug and gripped it with his bare foot. Like a pianist before a concert, he paused for a moment to exercise his hands, and then wondered what Hacker would make of the bizarre "guest profile" he was about to create. Every six seconds the head-end computer in the control room swept the guest rooms, recording all R-Tube activity. The personnel manager found the sweep results helpful for evaluating employee performance, for determining how long it took a maid to make a bed or a waiter to deliver a drink. The marketing manager also checked the sweeps, to see which hotel services were purchased by which type of guest. Hacker used them to compile guest profiles. When someone failed to settle a bill or a gambling debt, entertained unauthorized overnight visitors or damaged hotel property, then Hacker would direct one of his men to "use the profiles aggressively." Hacker had four special assistants, all blond southern boys he had lured away from some government agency. They went by the names "Ash," "Birch," "Pine" and "Maple" and, like Secret Service agents, they wore colored pins in their lapels and spoke with polite menace. Adam referred to them as Hacker's "trees."

Adam leaned over the keyboard and played a fugue. The Gestapo castle disappeared, replaced by live video of a pretty young woman who flashed a mechanical smile and said, *"Buenas días . . ."* She looked up and checked the overhead monitor displaying the room number and name of the guest plugged into "TropicResort Elementary Spanish Conversation." She continued: *"Buenas días, Señor Frost."*

TYPE REPLY flashed across her chest in squat computer letters.

Adam's fingers flew across the keyboard. BUENAS DIAS, SENORITA. COMO ESTA USTED?

She glanced at the monitor. *"Muy bien, Señor Frost. Vamos a comenzar lección uno."*

Adam zapped her. She would shrug and charge for a full lesson. He punched more keys.

Superimposed over a mortar and pestle were the words TROPICRESORT PHARMACY . . . PLEASE ORDER.

Adam responded: VITAMIN C—1000 MG; DOLOMITE; VITAMIN E—200 IU; STRESSTABS—600 + ZINC.

When he ran out of screen he erased the pharmacy and punched another combination of letters and numbers.

ROOM SERVICE. A smiling cartoon waiter held a tray in one hand and in another a decision tree: A) BREAKFAST B) LUNCH C) DINNER D) BAR.

Adam pressed D and ordered twelve Prestige beers and three bowls of fried banana chips, no salt.

He tapped into the casino and an electronic roulette wheel spun across the screen: WELCOME TO THE TROPICASINO.

He chose BLACK: $15 and slapped the action button. No time to watch the spin. Seconds left: 221. Back to the adventure.

He twisted the joystick with his foot and was inside the Gestapo castle, racing through a maze of hallways, just ahead of dogs and guards. Three women sat in three rooms in the center of the maze. Adam chose one. The R-Tube boomed out "Deutschland, Deutschland über Alles." The woman was a Gestapo decoy. The maze dissolved and the room became a gigantic red swastika. It filled the screen and revolved like a pinwheel, accelerating until it spun him out of the castle. Two hundred and one seconds left in the game.

He checked his TropicResort account. There were already charges for a Spanish lesson and vitamins. He had lost at roulette. He shifted cash into his gambling account, returned to the casino and played a hand of blackjack. A three for the dealer. He had a twelve. He computed the odds and drew. A ten. Bust.

TROPICRESORT EXERCISE SALON. A girl in red leotards pretended she could see him. "Come on, Señor Frost, let's see if we can touch our toes, that's good, now arms bending and stretching. One-two-three-four . . ."

She could not see him yet he followed her instructions. He typed in a request for squat jumps. She checked the monitor and hopped across the floor like a frog.

A buzzer sounded. He dashed to the front door. A huge woman in an Aunt Jemima costume carried in a tray of beers. His order had taken less than a minute, no doubt because room service had a mini-bar in each wing. Seconds left: 170.

His waitress clocked out by inserting her computer identity card in the R-Tube slot. Adam ran back to the console. His exercise instructor was still hopping. "Time for a new exercise, Mr. Frost?" she asked hopefully.

NO. He felt his pulse. Very fast. Perhaps he could activate the medical alert. Hacker would have a fit.

SERVICE POLL replaced the exercises. This feature appeared automatically on the screen exactly twenty seconds after an employee clocked out of a room. Adam gave the waitress a perfect 10 and a 20 percent tip. He knew that employees scoring below the mean were terminated.

His fingers jabbed the keys. Too fast. The signals were scrambled. Three images convulsed onto the screen at once, flaring into a rainbow of neon colors, all fighting for precious moments of interactive time. Adam thought of a speech he had written that Gore particularly liked. It began: "Interactive time is power. Whoever controls it controls the future."

Adam punched TB 101.

TROPICBOUTIQUE

He ordered bottles of perfume, a dozen ladies' panties and bathing suits. What would Hacker think?

He struck another combination of keys. GOLF RESERVATION . . . ELEVEN P.M. . . . TENNIS LESSON . . . FOUR A.M.

Suddenly he was back in the Gestapo castle. His foot slipped off the joystick. He grabbed it in both hands and maneuvered himself into the center of the maze. The woman jumped into his arms. This time he'd picked the real heroine. They escaped and the castle exploded. Ninety-seven seconds. Still time to shoot the moon.

There was a thud. The vitamins from the pharmacy shot through the front-door delivery chute. How had they done it so quickly? Did they know from his profile what he would order? He swallowed a Stresstab and chugged two Prestiges.

A movie! He punched it up and saw that this decision tree was complicated. He chose FEATURE FILM, then ADULT, and then a title. Naked bodies coupled on the screen and he ran around the room waving his arms, jumping up and down, attempting to activate the security system. Each room was networked with pressure pads, heat- and motion-sensitive sensors, strobe and infrared detectors. They alerted the head-end computer to how many people occupied a room and where they were standing, sitting or lying. They informed on burglars, unauthorized service personnel and overnight guests. He jogged opposite the front door, directly over a pressure pad.

Ten seconds left. He twisted the joystick. He and the girl flew over the moat and raced across the yellow meadow hand in hand. Like Olympians, they hurdled the land mines and ducked under a fence. Once again the R-Tube played "The Star-Spangled Banner." Three seconds left. He had won and shot the moon! Fuck Hacker.

Two guards with pistols drawn burst through the front door. Two more came through the terrace door. Adam raised his hands.

The sergeant recognized him. "Oh, Mr. Frost. It's only you. We were told someone was being attacked. All the heat sensors and pressure pads were going bananas. It's the first time the alarm has ever sounded. There must be a fault in the system."

"That's all right. I'll change rooms so you can check it out." He wanted to get rid of them before he collapsed in hysterics.

"We'll have to report this to Mr. Hacker."

"Yes, yes, fine, you do that."

As soon as they left, he chugged two more beers and rolled onto the bed laughing. Would Hacker think there was a bug in the R-Tube or that Adam was a drug-crazed, hyperactive, alcoholic, sexually ambidextrous compulsive gambler?

Beale would enjoy hearing about this. He detested Hacker, and the R-Tube. Adam punched into the keyboard to summon directory assistance. One typed in the name of a guest and the R-Tube shot back the room number and phone extension. The listings were instantaneously amended whenever a guest or a Tropic employee checked in or departed.

TROPICRESORT INFORMATION SERVICE READY

Adam typed: BEALE, N.

NOT LISTED

He prefixed his request with the special ex-directory code. Some Tropic employees and celebrity guests demanded unlisted numbers.

NOT LISTED EX-DIRECTORY

Had Beale checked out ahead of schedule? He typed: DEPARTURE?

NO DEPARTURE

ARRIVAL?

NO ARRIVAL

It had to be a mistake. Beale had been on the fishing trip. Adam had seen him in the restaurant the following morning. He certainly had not slept on the beach.

A tiny red light on the lower left-hand corner of the console flickered, signaling that someone had logged in a message. Adam punched in his room number and the message appeared on the screen.

TO: ADAM FROST. FROM: NO NAME. MESSAGE: MEET AT HEMINGWAY BAR. ONE P.M.

"No Name" had to be Beale. He and Adam often went to a decrepit café in the neighboring town in order to escape the resort and the Inner Circle, and Beale had dubbed it the Hemingway Bar. Had Beale been afraid to sign his name to his message?

CHAPTER 6

The painting was dominated by the rear view of a man. He had short blond hair and wore a red beret. Then one saw his muscular arms and delicate white hands. They were gripping the handles of an antique machine gun. Its muzzle, wreathed in smoke, was trained out a second-story window, firing into the plaza below. Here men and women sprawled in grotesque positions, hands clutching wounds, mouths screaming. A decapitated horse gushed blood, palm trees smoldered and flames shot from the roof of an overturned tram. The surrounding buildings flew a rainbow of flags: the anarchists' black and red, a hammer and sickle, red for the Trotskyites, and the faded red-yellow-purple tricolor of the Spanish Republic. Puffs of smoke clung to the façades of buildings, identifying the positions of other guns joining in the murderous cross fire.

"What do you think, Mr. Baldwin?" Dawney asked. He slid two more pints of beer onto one of the pub's scarred tables.

"Well, sir . . . it's a bit depressing, but . . ."

"It's meant to be," he snapped. "Ever seen Goya's 'Disasters of War' at the Prado?"

The blond young American shook his head. It was bad enough being in London; he had never heard of Goya or the Prado.

"Then I've saved you a trip to Madrid." Dawney gestured at the four paintings lining the dark nook where they sat drinking. "Goya depicted the horrors of the Spanish rebellion against Napoleon: the methodical firing squads, women raped in front of their children, men impaled on trees and split in two by swords, soldiers becoming beasts of cruelty. It happened again during the Spanish Civil War and I painted these modern atrocities as Goya would have. Look at the title of the first masterpiece."

The light was so poor that Baldwin had difficulty deciphering the smudged words in the lower left-hand corner. Dawney became impatient. "It says, 'I saw this. And this.' The same title Goya used for one of his wartime etchings. He witnessed the horrors he portrayed; so did I. Did you know that afterwards he went mad?" He locked his eyes on Baldwin's. "I asked for your opinion."

As Baldwin swiveled around to re-examine the paintings, some of the adhesive tape anchoring the concealed microphone to his chest came loose, yanking out a patch of body hair. He winced in pain.

Dawney glared. "Come now, they're not that bad."

"No, no. It isn't that. I have a crick in my neck." He leaned forward and squinted at the paintings. Somehow he had failed to notice them during the week he had spent in the Tattered Flag waiting for Dawney to appear. Off in this dingy corner, they had been darkened by years of cigarette smoke and grease from the sausage and chips fried up in the next-door kitchen.

"They're fascinating . . . startling . . . very impressive." He searched for flattering words. "But why not hang them somewhere more public?"

"Because this is where I come to remember Spain; the only place where they know Dawney, hero and martyr." He dug out a small penlight and moved its beam across the first canvas. Like a miniature spotlight it illuminated the white hands gripping the machine gun, then the crumpled bodies in the plaza.

The light pinpointed one of the faceless corpses. "That's me," he said.

The light hovered over another body. "And that's Orwell."

"I'm sorry, sir." Baldwin smiled boyishly. "But Orwell didn't die in Spain, nor, quite obviously, did you."

"Of course not, dammit!" Dawney shook his head so violently Baldwin worried he was having a fit. "Of course we weren't physical victims. But, laddie, we were victims of a political cross fire as deadly to the spirit as bullets to the body."

"I thought we were going to discuss Paris. Isn't that why you answered my ad?"

Dawney's eyes became wary; they scanned the room for the first time since the two men had sat down. The young man cursed himself. An academic researcher would want to hear everything about Orwell. Until now everything had gone smoothly. Dawney had accepted his explanation that he had closed the house on Jura for the winter and come to London before returning to the States.

"We'll do this my way," Dawney said. "First Spain, then Paris. If you want to understand what happened to Orwell in Paris, you first must understand Spain. But even before that . . ." He drained his mug and banged it on the table. "Your round."

Baldwin returned quickly with the drinks. He smiled, said "Cheers!" and wondered how this pitiful old bag of shit could be important enough to justify the orders: "Tape him, find out where he lives, then kill him and search his house." During their fifteen minutes together Dawney had smoked four cigarettes and drunk two pints and a shot of gin, all the time coughing, wheezing and picking brown stubs of teeth with scarred nicotine-stained fingers. He was bald and shrunken, as gray and grimy as his fucking paintings, and his filthy jacket and paint-splattered red beret looked as if he never took them off. His breath smelled like low tide, and bits of a paper napkin, hastily removed, hung from his frayed collar. Imagining those stained fingers touching food made Baldwin queasy. He rubbed one leg against the other and felt the reassuring outline of the pistol strapped to his calf.

No one should live to be so old and filthy, Baldwin thought. He was already half dead; finishing the job would be an act of charity. The only thing about him not decayed were his damn eyes, the luminous sparkling blue eyes of a teenager, or a madman.

Dawney said, "When I met George Orwell at the Lenin Barracks in Barcelona it was December of 1936. He was thirty-four, and I was twenty-two, about your age . . ."

"Oh, I'm a bit older than that, sir." He grinned and his perfect white teeth sparkled.

"Despite our differences in age, Orwell and I were equally stupid and naïve. He thought all of us leftists—anarchists, Communists, socialists, liberals and Trots—really were 'comrades,' all united in a gallant crusade against fascism and Franco and Hitler and Mussolini and . . . et cetera, et cetera. On the other hand, all I thought about was this." He pointed to his crotch.

Baldwin tried to chuckle. The thought of Dawney screwing repelled him.

"We learned very quickly that what really mattered the most was which militia you joined." He clicked on the penlight again. Its beam darted across the first canvas like a firefly, picking out first one flag and then another. "You could enlist in the International Brigades, which were controlled by the Communists, or in the anarchists or, as Orwell and I did, you could fight in the militia allied to the smallest, weakest and most doctrinaire of the Marxist parties, the Partido Obrero de Unificación Marxista." He pronounced these words in perfect Spanish. "Of course, you probably recognize the party by its initials, POUM."

Baldwin nodded, although it was the first he had heard of it.

"I joined the POUM after spending a year walking, painting, working and begging my way through northern Spain. I ran out of money in Barcelona and fell for a girl who worked in the POUM headquarters. I enlisted to impress her. Orwell was even more of a fool. He actually came to Spain to fight. He brought a letter from some obscure British socialist party with ties to the POUM. But he didn't know anything about the party's politics; all that mattered was that its militia fought fascists.

"In fact, it didn't really fight much at all. We were sent to the front in January. Some front. There were no battles, only skirmishes. We were in constant danger of freezing, starving or being bored to death, but not of being shot. When we returned to Barcelona on leave we witnessed more bloodshed in one day than in three and a half months in the trenches."

Dawney leaned across the table and tapped on Baldwin's open notebook. His finger left a smudge on the empty page. "I'm risking my life by meeting you, and you're not even bothering to take notes. You may think you know everything because you've read Orwell and a few histories, but you don't. What's really important are my experiences, my perspective. Write!"

Baldwin swept up the notebook and, holding it close to his chest, wrote again and again, first in a precise schoolboy script and then in larger and larger block letters: "I CAN'T WAIT TO KILL THIS CRAZY OLD BASTARD!"

"Orwell and I hadn't realized that two civil wars were being fought simultaneously. There was the aboveground war between the Republic and the fascists; we all knew about that. But there was an equally vicious underground war, pitting the anti-Stalinists, such as the anarchists and the POUM, against the Stalinists. And the Stalinists were winning. Because the Soviet Union was the Republic's only source of arms, the Stalinists came to control the central government in Madrid.

"Barcelona, though, was an anti-Stalinist stronghold. The POUM had its headquarters there and the anarchists controlled municipal services such as the telephone. At the beginning of May, at Stalin's instigation, Republican police and soldiers in Barcelona attacked the anti-Stalinists. During the previous months our ranks had been infiltrated by Stalinist agents posing as POUM members. During the Barcelona disturbances they fired randomly into crowds, provoking reprisals and even greater bloodshed."

To emphasize this point, he held the beam of light on the white hands gripping the machine gun. "The violence was random, insane. Any moving cars, any pedestrians, became targets. There was a cease-fire and armistice after several days, but by then we had lost control of the city. Crack Republican troops from Valencia took over.

"As much as the fighting itself, Orwell was appalled by the lies that followed it. The Stalinists launched vicious attacks against their former POUM comrades. We were a 'fascist spying organization' in contact with Franco's forces through secret radio transmitters. We had started the Barcelona fighting to destroy the Republic. We had vast secret stores of arms. In fact, as Orwell and I knew from our experiences at the front, we were plagued by terrible shortages of arms. The lies were elaborate! Incredible! Staggering! The Stalinist propagandists had rewritten the history of the last few weeks. This was the inspiration for Orwell's 'newspeak' and 'doublethink.' " He banged his mug on the table. "That's what *Nineteen Eighty-four* was: a fictional account of what happened in Barcelona."

Baldwin excused himself to go to the toilet. Once there, he reached inside his shirt and switched off the recorder. This horseshit was a waste of time. He'd need tape when the old bugger finally opened up about Paris.

While Baldwin was away, Dawney fanned the air furiously with his beret, trying to dissipate the stink of pine deodorant, lime cologne and mint mouthwash that swirled around the American.

Baldwin returned and Dawney continued. "After this armistice I stayed in Barcelona. My girlfriend had lost a brother in the fighting. I wanted to comfort her, and guard her. Orwell insisted on returning to the front, where he was wounded in the throat by a sniper. He returned to Barcelona in June. By then the purge had begun."

Dawney's flashlight played across the second picture. There was an idyllic sidewalk café dotted with flower boxes and gaily colored umbrellas. Smiling waiters delivered drinks and squirted soda from enormous siphons. Lovers held hands, little boys shined shoes and students pored over books. All were oblivious to the scene dominating the center of the painting. Here, a man seen only from the rear pointed a delicate white index finger at a young couple. Two uniformed policemen towered over them, nightsticks raised. The young man had thrown up his arms to protect his head. His mouth was contorted with fear. The woman was slumped forward onto the table. Blood seeped from her head and collected in a puddle beneath the table.

Baldwin remembered his instructions: "As many names as possible." "Who are they?" he asked.

"That's me, and that's Anita, my girlfriend." The beam of light lingered on her wounded head.

Baldwin found himself liking this picture, wanting to know more about it. "Is it symbolic, like the first painting?"

"Goddammit, no! That's what happened when they took us. She

swore at them, so they arrested her. She died in prison, but I was even more unlucky, I survived."

"What?"

"Never mind," he said quickly. "The purge started a month after the riots. The riots, of course, were the excuse. They 'proved' that we were fascist sympathizers or, even worse, that dreaded word . . ." Dawney screwed up his face and waved his hands menacingly. "Trotskyites!

"The Republican police arrested a thousand POUM members. Our militia was riddled with Russian agents, NKVD, who gave the police lists of the 'most dangerous fascists.' Police and NKVD agents raided cafés, swarmed onto trolleys and swept through working-class neighborhoods. If they couldn't arrest a POUM militiaman they took his wife and children hostage.

"Overnight Barcelona had become part of the Soviet Union, and 1937, when the Stalinist purges were reaching a climax, was not a good time to be living there.

"The NKVD had set up a state within a state throughout Republican Spain. They had secret dungeons, an intelligence service and paramilitary squads which kidnapped, tortured and liquidated their enemies. Even the Ministry of Justice didn't know the identity of the NKVD agents or the location of their prisons."

"Didn't the Spanish try to control the NKVD? After all, it was their country."

Dawney laughed. "Christ, laddie, get out of your cloister or library or wherever you spend your fucking time. The leaders of the Spanish Republic were bloody terrified of the NKVD. So were the Russian generals and commissars Stalin sent to Spain. Even the man who set up the NKVD network in Spain, Alexander Orlov, was bloody terrified."

"How do you know?" Baldwin had great admiration for the KGB, the present-day descendant of the old NKVD. Momentarily he was finding Dawney fascinating.

"How do I know? Because when Orlov learned that his bosses in Moscow were sending out a twelve-man bodyguard to 'protect' him, he recruited a squad of German Communists to guard him day and night."

"I can't picture those KGB goons running around Spain in their cheap suits. They must have really stuck out."

"They were called NKVD then and everyone in Spain wore cheap suits. Besides, Stalin sent very few Russians to Spain. He was afraid they'd be corrupted. Those who did go were liquidated when they returned to Mother Russia."

"Then who staffed the NKVD, Spanish Communists?"

"No; too unreliable. Most of the NKVD in Spain were from Europe and America, Communist idealists who had emigrated to the Soviet Union—the land of their dreams—during the early 1930s. Some became commissars in the International Brigades; others became NKVD agents.

"They found it easy to infiltrate the other parties and militias. Like many of us, some chose a *nom de guerre* on arrival and then reassumed their real names when they left. You could never be sure who was who. Dawney was my *nom de guerre*."

Baldwin glanced at his watch. "Sir, it's getting late and I still don't see what this has to do with Paris."

"You will, but first try to appreciate the atmosphere in Barcelona that summer, the impossibility of knowing for sure someone's motives or politics, or even their real identities."

"But Orwell trusted you?"

"Completely, though he felt the poisonous climate. Do you know what he said afterwards?" Baldwin shook his head. "He said: 'You had all the while a hateful feeling that someone hitherto your friend might be denouncing you to the secret police.' "

"Was he right?"

"Yes! Even before he recovered enough from his wound to return to Barcelona, the police had searched and staked out Eileen's room as the Hotel Continental."

"Eileen?"

"His wife. She had followed him to Barcelona. Didn't you know that?"

"Yes, of course. Of course."

"When he returned from the front line she met him in the hotel lobby and warned him to hide. For a week the police stalked him. He slept outdoors at night and ate in fancy restaurants by day. Finally, with the help of the British consul, he fled to France. When the train crossed the border he was dressed in jacket and tie, eating in the first-class restaurant. It didn't occur to the police that a wanted Trotskyite would travel first-class. He escaped. I was not as lucky."

He trained the flashlight on the third picture. "That was what happened to me."

A man in a black suit, his back to the viewer, sat behind a desk holding a gold-papered cigarette in a delicate white hand. Smoke from the cigarette spiraled toward the ceiling. The surface of his desk was empty except for a blank piece of paper and a fountain pen. Dawney moved the light around the edges of the painting, picking out a wall calendar—September 1937—a clock and a file cabinet.

"Just an office like any other," he said. "Except for this." He held the light steady on the middle of the picture. A young man was tied to a chair. His face was a patchwork of hollows, black stubble and bloody smears. His eyes were empty, sockets without pupils.

"Every day for four months the same NKVD agent interrogated me. My cell was so small I couldn't lie down. After four months of starvation, exhaustion and brutality, four months of never seeing the sun or talking to anyone but my interrogator, I admitted to being a fascist spy. I filled that blank piece of paper with a detailed confession."

"Which torture was the worst?"

"Christ almighty, lad, do you think I compared them, like some fucking wine connoisseur? I don't remember what they did, only the results."

"Were they responsible for your fingers?"

Dawney wiggled the scarred fingers on his left hand and said, "These were courtesy of the Gestapo. I was trapped in France during the war and fought with the Resistance until the Germans caught me. I was imprisoned in the worst of their torture chambers, the tunnels at Ivry. Quite a life I've had: tortured by Stalin and Hitler."

The lights in the pub suddenly flashed on and off. Only the chandelier over the bar remained lit. Except for the beam of Dawney's flashlight, the corner where they sat was now completely dark.

A barmaid shouted, "Time, gentlemen, please."

"Why not continue the interview at your studio," Baldwin suggested. "Is it nearby?" He reached for his pint, planning to drain it as quickly as possible.

Dawney seized his wrist, gripping it with surprising strength. "They won't toss us out for another ten minutes. Enough time for the last masterpiece." He trained the light on the fourth canvas and said, "After I confessed, they took me to a beach outside Barcelona."

To the right, hundreds of men, some naked, others in suits, uniforms, overalls and rags, stood erect, shook fists, kneeled, prayed, shielded faces with hands and lay dying on the sand. Surf crashed on the shore behind them. The rising sun had turned the horizon blood red.

On the left side of the canvas, a line of soldiers, their faces identical and impassive, fired rifles into the crowd. The commander of the firing squad held a revolver in a delicate white hand. It was pointed into the air like a starter's pistol. The straight lines of executioners and ragged lines of prisoners stretched down the beach until they finally met, like railroad tracks, on the horizon.

"I was only wounded," Dawney said. "I hid under my comrades' bodies. Later, I slipped into the surf and floated down the beach."

Baldwin shook his head and willed his eyes to water in sympathy. "What a horrifying experience. Hard to imagine people can be so cruel." He paused as if in contemplation. "I hope you'll forgive me for saying it, sir, but I still don't understand the connection between that beach and Paris."

Dawney trained his light on the white hands gripping the machine gun in the first picture. "There's your bloody connection!" he shouted.

He jerked the light over to the second painting, where it illumi-

nated the delicate white finger pointed by the policeman in the café.
"And there!"

Then the light was on the elegant hands of the interrogator.
"And there again!"

And on the white hands holding the pistol in the last painting.
"And bloody there!

"The man who provoked the Barcelona riots was the same man
who arrested and interrogated me and commanded the firing squad.
He was an NKVD agent who had infiltrated our militia unit. For
months the bastard posed as our comrade. Then he betrayed us."

He slammed the penlight down on the table, cracking open its
plastic case and spilling the batteries on the floor. The corner where
they sat was now totally dark.

"Eight years later, Blair and I met that bastard again in Paris."

Baldwin slipped his hand underneath his shirt, clicked on the
recorder and said, "Blair?"

"Yes, of course." Dawney waved his hand impatiently. "Eric
Blair."

"I'm sorry, sir, but I must have missed something. Who is Eric
Blair?"

Suddenly the barmaid turned on the overhead chandeliers and
bright light flooded the entire room. The pub was like a theater after
the curtain has fallen. Puddles of beer spotted the linoleum and
clouds of smoke hung in the air. They were the last patrons.

Dawney studied Baldwin's soft boyish face. Clearly, the young
American had no idea who Eric Blair was. Dawney slipped his hand
into his coat pocket, clutched the handle of the knife he used to cut
his canvasses and ran his thumb along its sharp curved blade. With
his other hand he gripped the edge of his chair, restraining himself
from lunging across the table and ripping the knife across Baldwin's
throat.

It was inconceivable that someone who had studied Orwell's life
could forget that his real name was Eric Blair. Dawney had read all
the books and articles about Orwell, and in every one this fact was
prominent and inescapable. Dawney's instincts had been correct; he
had been wise to treat the Baldwin advertisement with caution, wise

in his plan to observe Baldwin on Jura before making himself known. He had never imagined Baldwin would come to London and stake out the Tattered Flag. Thank God he had always kept his *nom de guerre* separate from his current identity. He only visited the Flag two or three times a month and the regulars there knew him as Dawney—"the bloke who did the paintings." None of them knew his real name. He could still undo the damage. But he would have to stop coming to the Flag and he would have to kill Baldwin.

He drained his beer and said softly, "Care to come round to my studio? We can finish the interview there."

"Where is it?" Baldwin asked. If he learned the address he could kill Dawney on the way and disguise it as a street robbery. Again he rubbed his legs together and felt the outline of the pistol: first the handle, then the barrel and silencer.

"Just around the corner. Five minutes' walk at most."

Once they were outside Baldwin said, "You were going to tell me about Eric Blair."

"I'm sorry, I seem to have confused the names."

"Was it this Blair who betrayed you in Spain? Was *he* the man you saw in Paris?"

"No. Blair is . . . well, he's not really important."

Dawney guided them into a deserted mews. They walked past lines of shuttered garages. During the day these were automobile repair shops and warehouses. At the very end the mews kinked left and then ended in a cul-de-sac.

"Then what was the name of the man in Paris?"

"Oh, laddie." Dawney laughed tonelessly. "I think you bloody well know."

Baldwin wished there was more light so he could see Dawney's face. Was he joking? Was this another "symbolic remark"? Did he finally suspect the truth? And why had this fucking Eric Blair made him so wary? It was time he had his gun in his hand. Baldwin bent over as if to retie a shoelace and slipped his hand under the cuff of his trousers.

Dawney plunged the tip of his knife into Baldwin's neck and ripped its curved blade across the man's throat. The flesh was far easier to cut than canvas. Baldwin screamed and fell to his knees. Instinctively he dropped the revolver and clawed at his neck. Blood poured from the wound.

Dawney calmly picked up the revolver, unscrewed the silencer and dropped both into his pocket. "I was just in the nick of time, laddie, wasn't I?" he said in his scratchy smoker's voice.

Baldwin fell backward onto the cobblestones. Dawney bent over him and stared into his open eyes. "All those lovely smells and pretty teeth," he whispered. "All gone, all wasted." He watched the man die, committing the scene to memory so that, if he chose, he could paint a fifth masterpiece. His revenge had already begun, and if it was not according to plan, it was nevertheless hugely satisfying. He pictured those delicate white hands, by now cracked with age and speckled with liver spots. What would their owner do when he learned that his pretty young messenger had been killed?

Baldwin's corpse stopped twitching and the blood slowed to a trickle. Dawney searched him and found the recorder, its cartridge still spinning. It had immortalized the death, almost as well as a picture.

The photograph in the young man's passport looked like Baldwin, but the name was John Birch. Dawney kept it. As he turned Birch/Baldwin's pockets inside out he wondered if this was Baldwin's *nom de guerre*, or was there a genuine Baldwin living at Barnhill? After imagining this revenge for so many years he could not stop now. He would have to stick to his plan and go to Jura, even it if meant walking into Ekman's trap.

CHAPTER 7

"Has it ever occurred to you," Nat Beale asked Adam as he detached three lottery tickets from a string clipped to the shirtfront of an armless vendor, "that Gore runs TropicAmerican like a network of Communist cells?"

Adam shook his head. He had heard Gore called a fascist, but never a Communist.

Beale patted the pockets of his madras jacket to indicate that as usual he had left his wallet behind. *"Un momento, Carlos,"* he said to the vendor. Beale was well known in the town and had learned the names of beggars, bartenders and taxi drivers. He questioned them about conditions at the resort and the refinery and raised their complaints at board meetings. Adam supposed he imagined himself some sort of patrician Democrat. But unlike most patrician Democrats, he had no inherited wealth, so he survived on lecture fees and the honorariums Tropic and other corporations paid him for joining their boards.

Adam stuffed twelve pesos into the vendor's pocket. The man turned to Beale and said, *"Muchas gracias, Señor Fonda."*

"They're convinced I'm Henry Fonda," Beale said. "They had one of his films here last month. It's touching."

"But he's dead."

He lowered his voice. "I don't think they know, or perhaps it doesn't make any difference." He turned back to the vendor. *"Yo soy Nat Beale."*

The man grinned conspiratorially and winked. *"Bueno, si tú quieres. Muchas gracias, Señor Beale."*

"No, no, Señor Nat." Beale folded the lottery tickets and carefully slipped one into his wallet, the others he left on the table as a tip.

The man bowed and disappeared through the curtain of colored plastic strips separating the bar from the plaza. The bar had been popular with members of the island's upper class who drove out from the capital on weekends. Then they had moved on to the TropicResort, leaving behind bottles of exotic liqueurs and photographs of obscure entertainers and politicians embracing the owner. Beale called it the Hemingway Bar because, he said, it reminded him of the Floridita in Havana.

Adam gulped his first daiquiri. Two more and he could imagine that the postal clerks and grocers standing at the bar were gun runners and coup plotters, and the shoeshine boy and whore, informers. He would see himself as a soldier of fortune, but one with a conscience. In keeping with this fantasy, he always came to this bar dressed for the part: reflecting wraparound sunglasses, a khaki aviator's shirt, British "bush trousers" with oversized pockets and a twenty-feature wristwatch ordered from an airline catalogue during a dull flight. He liked to imagine he was starring in a film. The camera would track him through the seedy but picturesque town; then a shot through an overhead fan as he entered the bar. "He drinks daiquiris in an atmospheric Caribbean café with the former Director of the CIA." So much for the fantasy. But what was he really doing here?

"Here's what I mean by 'Communist cells,' " Beale said. "Ever since that appalling fishing trip, Victor's been giving everyone secret assignments. Fiore's rushed back to New York, Hochmeyer's gone to the R-Tube plant in Taiwan and Hacker slipped away yesterday afternoon taking Pine and Ash with him; that's half the forest, and no one has seen Birch or Maple for weeks.

"What I'm wondering"—he paused and stared hard at Adam—"is what's *your* assignment?"

"Nothing, aside from changing the board meeting to Scotland. But he may pile on something else tomorrow night. He and the Duchess have summoned me for dinner in the fishing village."

Beale looked as if he had eaten something rancid. "What a vulgar place that is. For what it cost they could have fixed up this whole town and brought the guests in by bus every evening. Would have done wonders for the local economy."

Adam shrugged. "It's kept the Duchess busy for five years."

"Promise you'll call me afterwards and let me know what Victor wants."

Adam looked puzzled. "Nat, are you actually asking me to spy on Victor for you?"

"We've always exchanged information in the past."

"But in a casual way. You've never pressed me; never pushed. Why now?"

Beale looked wounded. "I thought we shared a certain sensitivity —an instinctive dislike for Hacker, for Victor's absurd expeditions and that hideous village."

"I like the expeditions."

"And you're always poking fun at the Duchess."

"Just because I joke about them doesn't mean . . ."

"But it's a first step." Beale grinned and patted Adam on the back. A teacher encouraging his prize pupil.

"I don't hear you telling me what he's asked you to do."

"That's because he hasn't asked me to do anything. He's frozen me out of the R-Tube launch."

"Frozen out ain't the least of it, old buddy." Adam imitated Hacker's drawl. "You've been wiped off the screen."

"What?"

"Received any calls in your room recently?"

"Yes, of course. What do you mean?"

"When?"

"Yesterday morning, before we went fishing. It was my lecture bureau."

"Any since then?"

Beale looked puzzled. "I suppose not. What are you getting at?"

"That the R-Tube has wiped you off Directory Inquiries. You're not staying here and you never arrived. Reception never keeps paper records anymore; everything's on the R-Tube. So, for the record, you don't exist."

Slowly Beale nodded. "And I flew in on the company plane. And landed on our airstrip. All the flight plans and immigration cards are programmed through the R-Tube." He closed his eyes. "God almighty, I've disappeared."

Adam grinned. "Maybe the R-Tube's angry. It overheard what you said on the boat and it's teaching you a lesson."

"It's possible." He was serious. "I shouldn't have spoken up. Stupid, stupid of me! But I can't bear those junkets. The careless expense: did you see the captain throwing the extra box lunches overboard? The killing for the fun of it, so wasteful and bloodthirsty. Have you noticed that Victor never eats what he kills? And then everyone pretending to enjoy it."

"Most do." Adam pushed up his sunglasses. Beale was still agitated. "Nat, I was joking about the R-Tube hearing you."

"No, in a sense you're right. Victor is upset that I'm opposed to installing the R-Tube in Georgetown. He's programmed it to give me a characteristic Gore warning: 'Support me or disappear.' It's like South Africa, where political dissidents are 'banned.' Suddenly their names can't be published in the newspapers and their friends can only visit them one at a time, if at all. We should sell the R-Tube to South Africa."

"Nat, how the hell did you end up running the CIA?"

"Oh, I thought everyone knew that. The previous Director resigned nine months before the presidential election. They needed someone to pinch-hit. At the time the President and the Agency were feuding. The career men thought he was a weak sister. To teach them a lesson he appointed me. A fox in the chicken coop," he said.

"Or a chicken in a fox's den."

"Say what you will, but I succeeded in blocking some of their more outrageous schemes and made some deserved enemies, Hacker among them. The only problem was that the President lost the election and I found I couldn't go back to my university." He looked fierce and shook his fist in the air. " 'No tenure for CIA mass murderers!' No one else wanted me; I'd become too controversial. So here I am, Victor's cut-rate Kissinger. But he has been generous.

The director's fee is twice what the others pay, and I get three thousand dollars a day as a consultant. In fact, I'll be here off and on until the board meeting, negotiating with the government. Victor wants to construct another TropicResort on the north coast."

"But you hate the one on the south coast."

"Well, *I* certainly wouldn't choose it for a holiday, but some people seem to like it. It's clean."

"That's great, Nat. So while you're hauling in three grand a day of Victor's money you want me to risk my job by spying on him. There are about four things wrong with that."

"I assume you'd be insulted if I offered to pay you. I wouldn't ask unless I thought the R-Tube posed a threat, particularly if it's installed in Washington."

"A threat? To whom? Christ, it's only Victor's toy. There are just five hundred sets in the test markets, only fifty thousand interactive subscribers in the entire country, and they're scattered among more than a dozen systems. That's a threat?"

"How many people had television in 1945? Almost none. Twenty years later ninety percent of all households had it. The same thing's going to happen with interactive, only faster." He finished his drink. "Let's walk."

They stopped on the north side of the plaza, opposite a taxi stand. The drivers shouted greetings and sounded their "La Cucaracha" horns in Beale's honor. Adam saw one man jump from his cab and hurry to a telephone box.

"You're probably thinking I overtip them, aren't you?"

Adam shook his head, though it was exactly what he had thought.

"Look at their taxis. What do you see?" He had become Professor Beale.

"Pimpmobiles."

"Fine. That's just what my son calls them. Now we're getting somewhere. And what makes them pimpmobiles?"

Adam shrugged. "I suppose it's because they have knobs on their steering wheels, little bronze statues on their hoods, pink pussycats with eyes that light up in their rear windows, multicolored mudguards, pennants flying from aerials, furry dice hanging everywhere,

tinted glass, and inside there are bars, tape decks, television sets
. . ."

"Forget those last things, the taxis don't have them. Summarize:
what's the essence of a pimpmobile?"

"Accessories."

"Very good! Now do you see it? The R-Tube is a pimpmobile. It's
nothing new, not a real invention, just the combination of two old
ones—the computer and the television—tarted up with accessories,
or what Victor calls 'enhancements.' " He gave a dry New England
cackle and guided them to a bench in the middle of the plaza.

Adam looked up. They were directly under a coconut palm.
"Mind if we move?" he asked, pointing to one of the cracked coconuts on the pavement. "I'd hate to be hit by one of those."

Beale was bewildered. "I'd never considered that. But the odds of
being hit must be infinitesimal."

Adam stood up. "Why risk it?"

When they were seated on a safer bench, Beale said, "Of course,
the analogy with a pimpmobile only goes so far. Add up a
pimpmobile's accessories and all you have is bad taste; add up the
R-Tube's and what do you get? One machine that does everything.
Instead of needing a telephone company, a television network, a
security service, a computer, a bank, a shopping mall, et cetera, et
cetera, you have the R-Tube. And because it does everything"—he
leaned over and whispered loudly into Adam's ear—"it *knows* everything."

"Nat," he said patiently, talking to a child. "It's a machine."

Beale stared hard and spoke in a monotone. "At TropicResort the
R-Tube head-end computer sweeps individual units every six seconds, recording every R-Tube activity. Homes will be the same:
every six seconds a steady stream of personal information will leave
the unit. It's an automatic, perpetual, never-ending invasion of privacy. Anyone using one of these contraptions at home is writing his
own dossier."

"There's nothing new about dossiers. You know that."

"We called them 'profiles'; 'dossier' sounded too sinister. Assembling a comprehensive one takes weeks, months, and a lot of man-

power. The R-Tube does it in seconds. The information is already there, retained in the head-end computer. It has the subscribers' bank records, financial transactions, polling responses and household purchases, even what drugs they take and size shoes they wear. It knows their taste in music, books, television, pay movies and pornography. Anyone with access to the head-end knows if you've made hotel or plane reservations, where you're going, what kind of car you're renting. They've got the floor plans of your house and your medical history. The security sensors reveal how many people are in the home and where they're standing. You use the 'messaging enhancement' and they know which other subscribers you're contacting and what you're saying."

"So don't use it."

"That's what Victor says, isn't it? But soon there won't be any choice. There'll be one public utility supplying communications, entertainment, security and banking and shopping services all through interactive cable systems like the R-Tube. There may not be one big national monopoly, but there'll be local monopolies, that's for sure."

Christ almighty, Adam thought, no wonder Victor has wiped him off the screen and tied him up on some bullshit consulting assignment. He's a fucking loose cannon. Victor doesn't want him running around lobbying the rest of the board.

"Nat," he said. "Who is this 'anyone' who's got unrestricted access to the sweeps? You know that we have a security system protecting its confidentiality."

"I'm disappointed. You're sounding more like a PR man every minute."

"Good. That's what I'm supposed to be."

"Is this the kind of PR nonsense you're planning for Washington?"

"It's what we've used to gain acceptance in the other test markets."

"It's a damned lie."

"What PR isn't?"

"You know no one can guarantee the security of computer records and transactions. Let's imagine that Victor wants to keep the profiles secure, which I don't believe for a minute. Computer thieves could still steal them. Remember the New York schoolboys who tapped into the Canadian Ministry of Defense? There's no such thing as a foolproof security system. Anyone with access to the Washington profiles will have a number of congressmen, journalists and, yes, even CIA and FBI agents by the balls. And don't forget who'll be in charge of security for the Washington head-end, 'old buddy.' "

"Nat, there are laws against this kind of thing."

"If I want to hear Victor's PR, I can hear it from him, thank you very much. The courts have ruled that individuals have no legal interest in records about themselves owned by others. There's some protection for bank and medical data, but not much. Furthermore, subscriber profiles are not the R-Tube's side dish, they're the god-damned main course! Ask Fiore. Advertisers will buy our customer profiles so they can target their campaigns on particular neighbor-hoods, even on individual families. Without the sale of profiles, interactive cable is a bust."

"That's way down the road," Adam broke in. "Washington is just a test market. Later on there'll be laws and regulations protecting people. The liberal congressmen, journalists and bureaucrats will see to that."

"I disagree. When the time comes, a surprising number of them will do nothing at all."

"That's ridiculous. We're not talking PR now, just common sense."

"A great many will do nothing because Victor will already have their profiles. How many, do you think, will have nothing to hide? Remember, we're talking about Washington, not Des Moines. The R-Tube may not reveal their peccadillos in full splendor, but it *will* point Hacker and his 'trees' in the right direction. It's happened elsewhere." He pulled a crumbling newspaper clipping from his pocket. "I brought you this."

The clipping, dated 1981, described how a politician living in one of the small R-Tube test market areas had managed to obtain the sweeps results. They had revealed that someone in an opponent's family—his opponent was a born-again Christian—had been watching pornographic movies.

"That's out of date," Beale said. "These days the R-Tube is more efficient. Now each family member has a separate access number. If this had happened last month, the sweeps would have shown exactly who in that man's household liked dirty movies. Let me give you another example. An interactive system on the West Coast has a popular program called 'Tell Your Tube.' Subscribers are asked questions such as 'What do you gargle with?' 'How many times have you been given a speeding ticket?' 'What do you think of capital punishment?' 'Should the local mall have drinking fountains for the handicapped?' Last month one of the questions was 'Answer yes or no: I have a friend, relative or acquaintance who is a homosexual.' Forty-three percent of the viewers answered yes."

"I'd say yes too. So what? You can't blackmail someone for knowing a homosexual."

"But you can narrow the field; check the sweeps to see who among the forty-three percent regularly watches gay movies, and who uses credit cards at gay bars. Once you've got a manageable list of suspects you know who to follow, spy on and persecute."

Before Adam could raise another objection Beale jumped off the bench and said, "Let's see what's doing in the market."

The narrow streets were lined with stores selling either scrubbing brushes and detergents or gambling devices—pyramids of dice, decks of cards fanned out and plastic roulette wheels. "It's sad," Beale said, "the men gamble and the women clean. Not very liberated." He greeted everyone as he walked with a phrase of high school Spanish. Adam wondered if they were humoring the *loco norteamericano,* or did they think he really was Henry Fonda? He was tiring of Beale's lectures, of his paranoia and his grinning "friends."

"What are you really suggesting, Nat? That I sabotage my own public relations campaign?"

"I hoped, if you understood the threat . . ."

"If I throw in with you, the major threat I see is to my job. I've done so many damned different things in the last ten years I need a five-page résumé. I don't want to start a sixth."

"It was because of your background that we were so sure you'd help us."

" 'We'? Who is this 'we'?"

Beale squeezed his arm and whispered, "Former colleagues who think the way I do. Let's wait until we're inside the market. Plenty of folks there gabbing in Spanish. You can't imagine how easily they can pick up a conversation with their damned gadgets."

The market was covered and smelled of too ripe fruit baking under a shimmering tin roof. "Have a mango," Beale offered, reaching down to pluck the blackest, most bruised one from a pile. "She looks like she'd appreciate a few customers." A spindly girl had fallen asleep next to the mangoes with her lizardy hand outstretched. Adam filled it with small coins.

"Don't overpay," Beale ordered. "You'll spoil her."

Adam straightened up and caught a glimpse of the armless lottery ticket vendor ducking behind a pile of used tires. So much for Señor Fonda's friends.

Beale had not noticed. "As you can imagine, I was none too popular at the Agency. The Neanderthals kept me in the dark and, to be honest, I still have no idea how the place operates. I was rather lonely, but then I met a fine set of young people, very sensitive and independent-minded; they were all 'analysts,' not operatives like our 'old buddy.' Most had doctorates from good universities, and in the academic world they would certainly have had tenure. They were all in different specialties: communications, energy, the Middle East, everything. They were charming people, from the finest families. Two were sons of my college classmates."

"Kind of a CIA branch of the Mayflower Society."

"Oh, there was also a fine young black woman, and several Jews. They met at each other's homes for wine and cheese, the sort of informal gatherings that are common on campuses. Colleagues meeting colleagues and exchanging ideas informally. No one ever did anything disloyal, although it was understood that if the Neanderthals were doing something dangerous it was perfectly all right, as a matter of principle, to leak some fact to the press or put up some roadblocks."

"Hacker was a Neanderthal of course."

"Low-level."

Amazing. Beale was making him feel sorry for Hacker.

"My friends have been tracking the development of interactive cable. They're convinced it should never be installed in Washington, particularly by a company controlled by a close friend of this President, by a company with Hacker as chief of security."

He handed Adam's mango to a beggar. "You wouldn't have to worry about your job. All you'd have to do is tell me what Gore and Hacker are planning for Washington. My friends can then set up their roadblocks. No one would know you were helping us."

Adam shook his head. "You don't know how this place works. Your friends sabotage the R-Tube and I'm finished. Victor would hold me responsible. As he says, it's my baby."

"Victor won't be around much longer to hold anyone responsible for anything. Sometime next month the Secretary of Defense will be resigning and Victor's friend the President plans to nominate him for the post. It's supposed to be a secret, but my friends know all about it." He smiled proudly. "Victor is very keen to launch the R-Tube in Washington before he's confirmed."

Adam shook his head. "I can't believe he would leave Tropic-American, simply hand the company over to someone else."

"Oh, he's told the President he'd only serve for two years. He's considering it as sort of a high-powered sabbatical. Victor will see to it that the Tropic board appoints a frail elder statesman to replace him, a caretaker who will step aside gracefully whenever he decides to return."

Adam wiped his forehead with the sleeve of his shirt. The heat, combined with the pills and daiquiris, was making him dizzy. Fainting would be embarrassing. He made a show of consulting his watch. "Nat, I have an appointment back at the Resort."

"But you haven't given me an answer."

His legs felt rubbery. He turned and pushed his way toward an exit and fresh air. Beale followed. "That's because I haven't decided."

But in fact he had. It was no contest: Gore versus Beale; Beale's liberal clique versus TropicAmerican and the Pentagon. The news of Victor's becoming Secretary of Defense was affecting him differently than Beale had anticipated. If he pleased Victor with his handling of the R-Tube, maybe Victor would take him to Washington. He was old enough to be an assistant secretary.

Victor, Adam thought, was like a sailfish, sleek and fast-moving. But no one would ever hook and stuff Victor, certainly not Beale and his "fine set of young people." Because they disdained or feared power, they never accomplished anything, never risked doing good because they were afraid of doing evil. Instead they stood aside and criticized men like Victor Gore. Of course Victor was not perfect. He made mistakes, sometimes went too far and pushed too hard. But at least he was a player. Adam pictured himself as Victor's trusted pilot fish, darting ahead to explore a reef, swimming alongside, passing slower, less daring fish and then racing behind Victor as he suddenly dove into the deepest and coldest fathoms of power.

CHAPTER 8

Gina shifted the cheese and tomato sandwich into her left hand and unlatched Brigadier Paget's front gate. In the States a military man of equal rank would have retired to a luxury condominium or a small country farm. The Brigadier lived in a two-story house on a street lined with identical buildings distinguished by their names and the number of roses in their gardens. The Brigadier's was called "Parade Rest," and it had lots of roses.

She lingered to admire the front garden. Once she rang the doorbell she would be playing her last and best card. Paget was the only person who had met her impersonator. On the plane down from Scotland she had convinced herself that Piers was orchestrating everything. The only question was whether he wanted to kill or scare. If she were dead there could be no unpleasant divorce proceedings and the only publicity would be sympathetic to Piers, something along the lines of: "Poor Mike, terrible blow for him. Lost his wife in a ghastly hunting accident. Entirely her fault. She went stalking without knowing the slightest thing about guns. One of those headstrong Americans."

But if Piers wanted to kill her, why bother hiring someone to steal her thesis and impersonate her? Perhaps he wanted to trick the police into searching for a nonexistent academic competitor. No, more likely he was hoping to push her into a nervous breakdown, then shut her away in some hospital. Even better if she ran home to Wisconsin. Then everyone could say: "Poor Mike. Wife ran out on him, just when he needed her. Mental problems."

When she first left Jura she had planned to return to Oxford unexpectedly and confront him with her suspicions. But when the moment came she lost her nerve and simply told him that her thesis had disappeared. He had appeared genuinely surprised, but then again she had never been able to decipher what really went on behind that smooth, featureless face. Later he had said, "That vegetarian restaurant off the High Street has just gone bust. Perhaps you'd like to try running it?" He was offering her another hobby.

Despite his performance, she was convinced he was guilty. She wanted him to be guilty. She pictured waking up on a beautiful spring morning, sun streaming through the windows, and enjoying a leisurely breakfast while leafing through newspapers with headlines such as: MP GUILTY OF WIFE MURDER PLOT . . . MIKE SOBS AT SENTENCING . . . MIKE GETS 20 YEARS. Her mother was fond of saying that revenge is a dish best eaten cold. This revenge would be ice cold, delicious.

She hoped that Paget would lead her to the impostor and the impostor would lead her to her thesis and, she prayed, to Piers. She pushed the Brigadier's buzzer.

An erect elderly gentleman wearing a double-breasted blazer and striped regimental tie jerked open the front door. "Dammit, man!" he boomed. "You're more than an hour late."

"Yes, I'm terribly sorry."

His voice softened. "Excuse my rudeness. Can't see as well as I'd like and I assumed you were your brother, or is he your husband?" She was too surprised to answer. "Last week he was smack on time. Miss Stevens and I have been getting jolly hungry waiting for him to arrive with the lunch. I don't suppose you've brought . . ." He squinted at her sandwich. "Only enough for one and it looks like British Rail catering."

After he had ushered her into a tiny parlor and introduced her to Bella Stevens, she said, "My brother's never been to England. He lives in Chicago."

"Well, you both have the same surname and you're both Americans."

Suddenly she realized what he meant. "You're talking about the Baldwin who interviewed you last week."

"Who else?"

She thrust her passport and a copy of her bill from *The Times* into his hand. "He's an impostor who's been sabotaging my work." While Paget was examining her documents under a magnifying glass and reading them out loud to Bella Stevens, she explained everything.

When she had finished, the Brigadier said, "Well, somehow he must know you're on to him. That's why he hasn't kept his appointment." Another reason for suspecting Piers, she thought. She had mentioned that she was going to Bournemouth.

Bella Stevens shook her head. "How can we be sure, Geoffrey? I think we should notify the police. They can set a trap, catch him red-handed."

"What? And if no one comes, have me look the fool in front of some young constable? Certainly not! He's an hour and a half late already. Obviously he's changed his mind. You two go off to the Moti and gossip about your beloved Orwell. I've heard enough about him recently to last a lifetime." He reached for Gina's sandwich. "I'll eat this, no sense wasting it."

Before they could protest, he had turned on the television full volume. Bella motioned Gina to follow her out of the room. "It's no good arguing with him, dear, not when he's in a mood. Best do what he says."

Once they were seated in the Indian restaurant she said, "I'm afraid the Brigadier is slightly jealous of rivals, even if they've been dead for over thirty years."

Gina felt her pulse quicken. "Should he be jealous?"

"I'll let you be the judge of that." Bella laughed merrily; she was enjoying being with someone so young. "To be precise, and I know you academics love precision, I met Eric—George Orwell to you—for the very first time in September 1934 when he picked me up in the reading room of the British Museum. After that we often picnicked in Russell Square. Neither of us had very much money, so for amusement we'd watch the changing of the guard at the palace. For Eric, it was always good for a laugh: all those huge, stony-faced men strutting about while a military band played 'The March of Time,' which of course sounds like a nursery song. In a way, that's what I remember most about him, his laughter." Well, that's not *really* what I remember most about him, she thought, but under the circumstances it's probably best not to mention *that*. What an extraordinary crush this young woman has on him!

Gina's cheeks flushed and a drop of perspiration trickled down her arm. She knew from her early encounters with Piers's mistresses that, for her, these were the physical symptoms of acute jealousy. She hid her face behind a menu. It was absurd. How could she allow herself to be jealous of a seventy-five-year-old woman who may once have had an affair with someone who died the year that Gina was born?

"It's odd," she said from behind the menu, "but I've never read or heard of anyone describing his laugh as particularly memorable. You must have known him very well indeed."

"We were what was then delicately referred to as"—she smiled sweetly and paused—"very good friends." There it is, young lady, she thought. You forced me to say it. "He also had perfectly marvelous hands, large yet very elegant. I thought they perfectly matched his temperament: masculine yet at the same time kind and gentle. And for such a tall, gangly man he had a distinctively graceful walk. I suppose these days it would be termed 'sexy.' "

A waiter with dirty cuffs brought rice, yogurt, a luridly orange chicken curry and a jar of chutney with Bella's name written across the label.

"You can put down your menu, dear," Bella said. "I never order here. They know what I like." She held the chutney up to the light and examined it closely. "A friend sends this to me from Lahore. It's so tasty that the chef tries to snitch it and I have to mark the label to keep him honest. But you are welcome to taste it, although I shan't give you much because it's quite dear and very, very hot." She spooned a dab onto Gina's plate.

Gina thought she had swallowed hot coals. She inhaled small discreet gasps of air and prayed that she would not start hiccuping. Why did she always go to such lengths to please the English and to imitate them? She had been doing it for ten years. Even as a teenager she had been a fanatical Anglophile. She had spent one snowy Wisconsin winter reading books by and about famous British female explorers. Bella had been her favorite and she had often entertained fantasies about accompanying her to Persia or North Africa.

Bella frowned. "Don't be stupid. If it's too hot for you, just say so. There's no disgrace involved."

"No, no, no! It's delicious. Please go on. What happened between you and Orwell? I mean, didn't you ever consider marriage?"

"Ha! What a laugh," Bella said. "I've never wanted to marry anyone. Against the rules."

"What rules?"

"Mine. Besides, he was the one who got married. In 1935 our picnics in Russell Square suddenly became less frequent. Later I learned he had met Eileen, his future wife. He invited me to the wedding, but I went to Persia and Palestine instead."

"But surely you kept in touch . . ."

"No. Out of sight, out of mind. Another rule."

"Then it was fate that you met again ten years later in Paris."

"Not fate, chance! But it was not all that surprising. Paris in 1945 was the kind of place where everyone who was anyone was meeting everyone else purely by chance. The months between the liberation and the end of the war were particularly stimulating and gay. Everyone had been served a small taste of peace and was hungry for the feast, yet a few hundred miles away the great crusade went on. It was one of those electrifying times when people were certain the future was going to be a huge success. They were exhausted and starving, yet at the same time possessed of tremendous energy.

"On the other hand, those months were a very dreary time indeed for those who were only concerned with their appearances and their stomachs. They were very weary-making people and one did one's best to avoid them because they were always sniveling about what they couldn't do, or wear, or eat.

"They complained because there was no butter from Normandy. It went rancid because there was no salt to preserve it. There was no sugar because the sugar-beet farms had had no rain, which also meant that the imitation coffee—there was no real coffee—tasted even more like dust. There was no water except between noon and two and no soap that foamed properly, so people smelled badly when they jammed into the Métro to keep warm. There was no heat because there was no transport for the coal, and without coal there could be no electricity, which made the streets so dark that everyone slipped on the ice. Their bones couldn't be set properly because there was no plaster of paris, and so on. What a dull bunch of nancys the complainers were.

"I said, 'So what if the streets are dark, makes it more romantic. There may be no heat, but everyone's drinking more brandy, making more love.' It was all such an adventure. There were no proper shoes, but the wooden clogs made a delightful clip-clop on the cobblestones. New clothes were scarce, so the Sorbonne students kitted themselves up in ski clothes. The Resistance was known to have worn them and they were considered *très chic*. No taxicabs, so the wealthy rode about in little painted, curtained boxes drawn by bicycles, sort of a combination rickshaw and sedan chair.

"But these were only the props. The actors made the city, and in 1945 a particularly distinguished cast had gathered there. Some came with the Allied armies as officers, correspondents or camp followers; others had suffered through the Occupation. In the space of four months I interviewed Sartre, Gertrude Stein, Simone de Beauvoir and Picasso. Marlene Dietrich was staying at the Ritz, a few doors down the hall from Hemingway. He insisted I interview him in the bathroom, while he was shaving. That Dietrich woman was there the whole time, perched on the edge of his tub, gulping champagne, swinging her legs and singing. Hemingway was the only correspondent who could afford the Ritz. The rest of us were crammed into the Hotel Scribe."

"Isn't that where Eric stayed?"

"Don't rush me, dear, I'll get to him soon. Before the war the Scribe catered to middle-class foreigners and provincial French. The Wehrmacht made it their headquarters during the Occupation and then afterwards it became the official Allied press center. It was the scene of the military briefings and the official censors and Western Union representatives had offices on the ground floor. Anyone with a story to peddle turned up at the bar. There was no way for a correspondent to avoid the Scribe, which was a shame because it was a perfectly vile place for a woman, even a woman like me. I remember it as a cross between a rowdy public house and a seedy men's club—puddles of booze, cigarette butts and frayed furniture. My room had an aroma of stale Hun: spilled beer and cruelty. The first and only night I slept there I kept imagining some SS officer terrorizing a French whore. I lay on the floor rather than the mattress, and moved my clothes to a friend's flat the next day.

"The Scribe bar was a poorly ventilated, noisy den that was extravagantly stocked with bottles liberated from the Hun. The boys, and I mean 'boys,' were there at all hours drinking, punching, pimping for one another and pumping some sodden colonel for a story. Every few hours some drunk hero sang the 'Marseillaise.'

"A 'honk-honk' was the only thing that drew them out of the bar. The Scribe was wired with the same kind of horns that sounded the alert at air bases. They went off at the Scribe whenever there was to be a briefing or an important communique distributed. Since the army never printed quite enough bulletins to go around these 'honk-honks' touched off a riot. Everyone scooped up their poker winnings, bolted drinks, hid bottles of scotch and rushed onto the narrow staircase. Suddenly scores of British, French, American, Canadian, South African, Chinese, Brazilian and what-have-you journalists were all on the stairs at once, elbowing, cursing in ten languages and fighting their way to the briefing room. It was during one of these 'honk-honks' that, for the first time in ten years, I came face to face with Eric.

"He and an elderly man were calmly walking up the stairs, bucking the traffic. He looked marvelous. Many correspondents dressed in the most ridiculous army uniforms; sometimes the bar resembled a Mad Hatter's tea party. Eric was wearing battle dress too; he had an officer's rank, but he had obviously taken great pains to look like a private. He stood out from the other correspondents, a pearl among swine.

" 'Eric!' I screamed. 'You're going the wrong way.'

" 'Why, hello, Bella,' he said, as if we had parted the day before and he had fully expected to see me. 'We're not going to the briefing. I've only been here two days, but I've already learned that one's never told anything important at briefings.' He pushed his elderly companion forward. 'Here, meet Mr. P. G. Wodehouse.'

"I had always assumed Wodehouse would be bluff and blimpy, like Bertie Wooster. Instead, I found myself shaking hands with a quiet, shy, awkward sort of chap.

"Eric said, 'Mr. Wodehouse and I are just on our way to lunch. Care to join us?'

"I was so startled by our unexpected meeting that I hesitated.

" 'Not to worry, we're not eating here. Five years of English rationing have made these American army meals too rich for my stomach. We're going to the hotel where I used to work in the scullery. The food will be ghastly, but we'll have fun seeing if anyone recognizes me.'

" 'Damn! I promised to lunch with a brigadier chap, an old friend from Palestine.'

" 'Bring him along. More the merrier. But I must warn you that we're going to be discussing revenge. In the last few days Mr. Wodehouse and I have become experts.' "

At "Parade Rest," someone was ringing the buzzer. Brigadier Paget bellowed twice for Perkins before he remembered that Saturday was her day at the pictures and there was no one in the house but himself. He squinted through the letter box at his visitor, but saw only a blur of pink flesh and dark suit, another damned salesman. At her house, Bella scared visitors off with a sign: "Beware— Bad Dog." Well, Paget didn't have a dog and he refused to lie. He opened the door.

A nasal voice said, "I'm terribly sorry to be so late, Brigadier Paget." Paget recognized the kind of exaggerated courtesy sometimes affected by Americans.

"Save the polite chitchat, Mr. Baldwin or whatever your name is. You're a damned fraud." Paget slammed the door. It jarred against the American's foot.

"Too slow." Now the visitor spoke in a soft monotone.

Paget turned and ran to the telephone. He was dialing the third digit of the police emergency number when the American ripped the phone from the wall and pushed him backward into an armchair. "Still too slow. Baldwin is . . . well, he's not feeling a hundred percent, so he sent me instead." He leaned over and stared into Paget's eyes. "But you can't see clearly enough to tell the difference, can you?"

"You Americans all look the same to me: too well fed and too soft in the face."

"O.K., cut the crap. Hand it over."

"Hand what over?"

"The diary. The one you read Baldwin over the phone."

"Bugger off."

"Your age doesn't matter to me. I'll make you."

"I dislike bullies almost as much as liars." Paget bent forward and tried to focus his eyes. He'd look a damned fool if he couldn't describe this man to the police.

But the American had disappeared from his narrow line of vision. He heard him moving about the room, pulling open drawers and dumping their contents—letters, a checkbook, pictures of his sons and a box of medals—on the floor and kicking through them. The sound of smashing china meant he had tipped over some of the miniature porcelain soldiers arrayed across the chess table.

"Stop smashing things!" Paget shouted. "Those were a present from the brigade."

The American flung a handful of the soldiers against the wall. They shattered inches over Paget's head, showering him with shards.

"You can't intimidate me," Paget said. "I never give in to bullies. And you won't find what you're looking for by pulling my house apart."

"Why not?"

Paget had to restrain himself from saying, "Because I'm bloody well sitting on it, you idiot!" He had been reading the diary when the doorbell sounded and had left it in the armchair—the same one the American had just shoved him back into. Perhaps it *was* wiser to hand the diary over before the ladies returned. This man might have already tried to kill Mrs. Baldwin. But to surrender under these circumstances would be craven. He might jump up and grab the penknife or the poker, but what if the American had moved them about? And if he left the chair the diary would be in plain sight. The American's brutality had confirmed his suspicions as to why his Paris diary was so valuable, and to whom. All the more reason to keep it hidden at all costs.

"I haven't got all day, gramps."

"I'm not your grandfather, thank God."

"Tell me where it is . . ." The American pressed the palms of his hands against the sides of the Brigadier's head and, with his index fingers, stroked the old man's eyelids. "Tell me where it is, or the lights go out forever."

Bella borrowed a pencil from Gina and marked a new line on the bottle of chutney. She had consumed a fourth of the bottle. "I'm not sorry you didn't care for it," she said. "All the more for me."

Gina laughed. "Let's forget the tea and have another lager." For the first time in days she felt safe and relaxed. She was beginning to understand why Eric had liked Bella. Replacing her earlier jealousy was the affection that can grow between two women who have loved the same man.

After the waiter had poured the lager, Bella continued: "As we walked from the Scribe to the hotel where Eric had worked he regaled us with stories of how he and the other *plongeurs*, or dish-washers, had been mistreated by the waiters and cooks, who were in turn persecuted by the headwaiters and the *patron*. As we walked up the steps he turned to the Brigadier and said, 'When I worked here there was a secret vein of dirt running through the entire building, like an intestine.'

"Not the sort of talk to stimulate one's appetite. Despite his jolly 'more the merrier' chitchat, I think he resented the Brigadier tagging along and hoped he might change his mind and return to the

Scribe. Perhaps Eric was jealous. The Brigadier had fought in Syria and won a decoration, whereas Eric's health had kept him in England, drilling with the Home Guard.

"Eric had booked a table, so they were ready for us. There was a nervous jug-eared boy wearing a frayed bow tie and a gray-faced old man in tails. We were the only diners and they were the only staff.

" 'It's Claude,' Eric whispered, nodding toward the man. 'A nasty character, used to box our ears if we dropped a saucer.'

"Claude bowed gravely and distributed hand-lettered menus. There was carrot soup to start, then onion *tarte*, and apples for dessert, though, being French, they had given the food grand names like *pommes au façon du chef*. Eric's former tormentor doubled as the cook. He disappeared into the kitchen while the boy scrambled around filling water glasses and pouring red wine from a dusty bottle. The room had once been rather grand, but now the mirrors were cracked and the tablecloths ripped and patched. They had set the plates over the holes, which made for interesting table arrangements. The silverware, however, was glorious; a heavy antique set so beautifully polished it all but illuminated the room.

" 'What happened to the mirrors?' Eric asked the boy.

" 'The Germans.'

" 'And the cherubs?' He pointed to the molding and told us there had been a handsome set of painted sconces in the shape of cherubs.

"The boy shrugged. 'The Germans.'

" 'But you still have the silver.'

" 'The waiter hid it. They tortured him but he refused to surrender it. He is now'—he lowered his voice and tapped his forehead—'a little touched, an imbecile.'

" 'Does he mistreat you?'

The boy shook his head emphatically.

" 'Good. And the rest of the staff?'

" 'The Germans.'

"The meal was delicious. The waiter had decorated the onion *tarte* with an Eiffel Tower of carrot sticks, and crisply fried onion bits floated in the carrot soup. Isn't it extraordinary what one remembers? The room was so gloomy that Eric went out of his way to be jolly. He always loved playing host. When we picnicked he used to unfurl a small tablecloth with great ceremony. During lunch he and I discussed the French attitude toward the Germans. He was obsessed with the subject of postwar policy toward Germany and afraid there was going to be a repetition of the mistakes made after the first war. He thought that a policy of revenge—stiff reparations and deindustrialization—was utterly immoral. I'm sure you've read the articles he sent back from France and Germany. Most mention the immorality of revenge.

"Wodehouse pushed his food around his plate and scarcely said a word. He was going through a bad patch. Our government was making up its mind whether to try him for treason. One used to say that someone had had a 'good war' or a 'bad war.' Well, Wodehouse had had a very stupid war. He began by staying in France too long in 1940. The Germans interned him in Berlin, where he foolishly agreed to make what he thought were amusing broadcasts about life as a German internee. He used the phrase 'whether Britain wins the war or not,' and this did not go down very well at home, where we were then enduring the Blitz. The BBC banned his work from the air and libraries swept him from the shelves. Eric wrote an article defending him.

" 'What do you think, Brigadier Paget?' Eric asked after we'd eaten. 'Should Mr. Wodehouse here be shipped back to London in leg irons? Locked up in the Tower for high treason?' If Eric thought the Brigadier would rise to the bait, he was disappointed.

" 'Of course not. It's an absurd farce. Happened four years ago and should be forgotten. He never gave away any secrets or spied for the enemy, did you, Mr. Wodehouse?'

" 'Certainly not! But I'm accused of weakening national morale, like Lord Haw-Haw.'

" 'Nonsense!' Paget said. 'All the writers who are jealous of you had a marvelous time bashing you about.'

"Wodehouse smiled weakly and tipped an imaginary hat. 'Glad to have been of service.'

"Eric was slightly taken aback. He'd been hoping for a Blimpy foil for his notions about vengeance. He tried another tack with more success. 'What's happened to Mr. Wodehouse is all part of this poisonous atmosphere of revenge. Here in Paris the hunt for traitors and Quislings is practically a national sport. The French have always delighted in humiliating the Germans. Now they hope to turn Germany into a vast rural slum and ship off its workers as slave laborers.'

" 'And why shouldn't they?' the Brigadier demanded. 'The Germans did the same to them.'

" 'Which is precisely why we shouldn't do it to the Germans.' Eric smiled. At last the Brigadier was running to form. Eric rolled one of those awful cigarettes to celebrate.

" 'But think of the damage the Germans did. Surely they should be required to rebuild what they've destroyed,' the Brigadier argued.

" 'Most Germans won't have the strength to rebuild their own homes and factories much less travel a thousand miles to rebuild someone else's. Besides, what can half-starved children and old men build?'

" 'Say what you will, but it strikes me as simple justice.'

" 'Justice means bringing the big rats to account. The Germans who'd be shipped off as lend-lease slaves aren't the guilty ones. Look at France. Who's being punished? Lowly policemen, and whores who slept with German officers. Most of the schemes being advanced for postwar Germany are not just, they're precisely the opposite. What's happening to Wodehouse, the witch hunts for collaborators in France and these ugly schemes for Germany are all expressions of this sordid lust for vengeance.'

" 'Granted it's not a pretty emotion, but isn't it just human nature to want . . .'

"Eric thumped his fist on the table. 'Because it's human nature doesn't mean it should be indulged! Consider this hotel. I freely admit I was attracted here by the prospect of lording it over my former tormentors. I had contemplated a sarcastic essay at the hotel's expense. But look what I found, a sad ruin of a place; and look who I'd be hurting, not the owners, but a boy and an old imbecile who've done their best to please us. Precisely the "spoils of war" one's likely to find in Germany.'

"Finally the Brigadier lost his patience. He imagined that Eric was attacking him personally, but I knew it was nothing of the sort. Eric often developed his essays by staging arguments. 'It's all very well for you to be so magnanimous,' the Brigadier said. 'You haven't had to fight the bloody Nazis and lose comrades in battle.'

"This struck home. Eric was sensitive about missing the war. He straightened up and reddened and I knew he was struggling over his response. At last he said, 'I fought fascism in Spain, at a time when I daresay many in our army considered Hitler and Mussolini nothing more than 'jolly good disciplinarians.' I lost several brave comrades there and I certainly haven't forgiven Franco or Stalin. I would applaud if they were brought to justice. But as for their henchmen, the men who did their bidding and pulled the triggers, should they be punished almost a decade later? I don't think so.'

" 'But, Eric,' I said. 'Doesn't it depend on what they did? What if they shot prisoners or tortured hostages?'

" 'What of it? Shouldn't the intervening years be taken into account?' He looked around the dining room to see if anyone else was listening, then finished his cigarette and gave a handful to the boy with instructions to smoke them in the kitchen with the cook, 'with our compliments.' When the boy left he said, 'Let me give you a hypothetical illustration of what a complicated and tricky business revenge can be. I'd appreciate your not repeating it since I may use it in an essay.'

"We all agreed and he continued. 'Imagine that last week, just after arriving in Paris, I happened to meet a former comrade from Spain in the bar of the Scribe. He had been a brilliant young painter, a man of great fun and sensitivity, of whom I had been extraordinarily fond. He had disappeared during the purges in Barcelona and I had mourned him as dead, a victim of the Stalinists. Now suddenly here he is . . . but *who* is he? An altogether different man—withdrawn, brooding and suspicious—who has aged twenty years in eight. He refuses to discuss the past, except to say that he was arrested during the purges and then escaped to France, where he fought with the Resistance and was later arrested by the Gestapo. I soon discover that he is a melancholy alcoholic who spends hours in the Scribe cadging whiskey from correspondents and recounting the most fantastic, and in all probability fabricated, stories of his experiences.

" 'Two days following our first meeting he bursts into my room, extremely agitated, and pulls me downstairs to the bar. From a distance he points out an American colonel bearing a remarkable resemblance to an American who fought in our Spanish militia unit. My friend tells me that this is the same man, but he has changed his name. This is hardly surprising, given that the Americans consider it treason to have fought fascism in Spain, whereas fighting it in France eight years later is heroic.

" 'My friend hurries me out of the bar and back to my room. He is literally shaking with fright. He swears that in Spain this American colonel was a Soviet agent who betrayed our comrades to the pro-Stalinist Republican police and then helped interrogate and execute them. *Now*, given this hypothetical situation, what do you suggest?'

" 'Why, expose him, of course!' said the Brigadier. 'Have him arrested and interrogated. He may still be a Soviet agent.'

" 'But what if he isn't? What if my friend is mistaken, either about the Colonel's identity or about what happened in Spain? Remember that my friend is now a somewhat bizarre figure. The Colonel's reputation and career could be seriously and unnecessarily damaged. Can you imagine what the American army's reaction would be? Bad enough to have fought in Spain, but to have betrayed one's comrades as well . . . it's a diabolical combination.'

" 'But suppose your friend is right?'

" 'Yes, but perhaps, eight years after the event, the Colonel has repented and changed his name to hide from his former Soviet associates. He is a different man, a heroic and gallant officer.'

" 'But, my God, man, if he was a torturer and murderer, shouldn't he be made to account for his crimes?'

" 'By whom? That pathetic band of Spanish Republican exiles in Mexico? What legal right have they to try anyone? Where would the court be located? The sentence carried out? And besides, the Republic approved of the Barcelona purges. If the Colonel is guilty, he was only carrying out their orders. Everyone committed terrible atrocities in Spain and he was by no means the mastermind. The real villain is in Moscow and now he's an ally. If anyone is to be punished for what happened to my friend, it should be Stalin, not one of his minor lackeys.'

"The Brigadier threw up his hands. The argument had exhausted him and he was eager to escape. 'I concede. You win your point. There's too little evidence, too much risk of an injustice and too much time has passed. But there's one remaining question: Suppose this Colonel is still working for the Soviets?'

" 'Then he would certainly bear watching.'

" 'And whoever watched would have to be jolly careful he didn't cotton on, wouldn't he? If your Colonel is still in the Soviets' pay, he wouldn't take kindly to someone nosing around. He'd have plenty of allies to call on. Just now the French Communists are very influential in Paris.'

" 'Which is precisely why one wouldn't want to confront him directly.' "

A scowling Indian waiter interrupted to hand Gina the check. The restaurant had filled and people were waiting. Bella snatched it out of her hand. "My treat, particularly since you didn't enjoy it."

"But finish the story first; what happened next?" She had never heard any of this before; it would make her thesis a success.

"Oh, nothing very much. Eric changed the subject, the Brigadier beetled off to headquarters and Wodehouse went to meet his wife. What a non-event he had been, though, poor man; one can understand why he was so gloomy. Eric and I walked back to the dreadful Scribe. I said, 'If you think you fooled me with all that "hypothetical" claptrap, you're dead wrong.'

"Eric laughed. 'I didn't want to tell that story, but your Brigadier egged me on so. I fooled him, though, didn't I?'

" 'Don't be so sure. Paget is nobody's fool. But what's going to happen now?'

" 'My friend has made me swear not to approach the Colonel directly. Yet, solely on the basis of his word, he expects me to expose the man as a mass murderer and Soviet spy.'

" 'Then what *are* you planning to do?'

"Eric stopped and faced me. I could see that he was tremendously excited. Remember that he had spent the entire war cooped up in England. Finally he was on the Continent, faced with the kind of moral dilemma and political intrigue he relished. 'I'm going to set a trap for the Colonel,' he said. 'Provoke him. His reaction will reveal whether or not my friend is telling the truth.'

" 'Isn't that dangerous?'

" 'I never thought I'd hear *you* ask that.'

" 'You're right. I'm ashamed of myself.'

" 'It could be less dangerous if you helped. Are you game?'

" 'And you should be ashamed of *that* question. What kind of trap do you have in mind? What's the bait?'

"Eric grinned and pointed at himself."

Bella pocketed the change and rose to leave. "I'd rather continue this at the Brigadier's. It will be new to him and I don't want to tell it twice. Eric *did* swear me to secrecy, but I'm sure he'd forgive me for telling you. And it may have something to do with that unpleasantness in Scotland."

Brigadier Paget heard the American drag the tea chest in which he kept his diaries into the center of the parlor and overturn it. School exercise books, leather-bound notebooks, loose-leaf binders and bundles of hotel stationery tied with ribbons spilled onto the floor. There was an odor of dust and mold perfumed by tea.

"Which is the Paris diary?" the American demanded. "Help me find it and I'm gone."

Paget sat rigid in his chair, refusing to answer. The American's threat to blind him had been a bluff, proof that the best way to handle bullies was to ignore them.

The American flung a notebook across the room at the Brigadier, opening a deep gash over his left eye. Blood splashed onto his shirt.

"Is it that one?" the American shouted. "Or this one?" He hurled another.

"I have such a good memory for everything but names," Bella said. She pursed her lips and stared at the ocean. She was one of the few elderly women on the Bournemouth promenade not bundled into a wheelchair, leaning on a nurse's arm or inching along on a walker. She looked purposefully over the other strollers' heads. "It's terribly inconvenient. I can be introduced to someone, have a delightful time and then find I've forgotten their name. I'm always calling afterwards and saying, 'Now who was that charming man?' "

Gina broke in, "But you remember that lunch so clearly. Surely if you concentrate you'll also remember the Colonel's name."

Bella glanced at her. Gina had crossed her arms and was holding her shoulders. "Are you chilly, dear?"

"Not at all. It's quite mild."

"Then why are you hugging yourself?"

She dropped her arms. "It's a habit."

"It gives the wrong impression; makes one think you're timid. No wonder your husband imagines he can frighten you. But I'm not sure I agree that your husband is behind it. What was his name again?"

"Piers."

"The danger of being caught far outweighs the benefits of frightening you, don't you agree?"

"He wouldn't look at it that way. He never thinks he'll lose, ever. One weekend he took this course in 'self-realization training.' It taught him that if you think you'll succeed, then you will; if you think you'll make piles of money, you will; if you think you'll be elected to Parliament, you will; and so on."

Bella sighed. "Poor old church, what tempting competitors it has." They walked for a minute in silence. Finally Bella shook her head in frustration and said, "It's no good. The name simply won't come, but there's a chance the Brigadier may remember it or have it scribbled in one of his diaries."

"But I thought he left the restaurant in a huff and never saw Eric again."

"That's right. But later I asked him to arrange a meeting between me and the American colonel. This was step one of Eric's plan. I claimed I wanted to interview the Colonel about American plans for administering Germany. Brigadier Paget was very obliging. It was an understandable request since he and the Colonel both worked at Allied headquarters.

Brigadier Paget heard the American crumpling newspapers and breaking kindling wood. There was a puffing of bellows and a crackling and spitting as the fire flared. The room became warmer.

The American said, "So much for 'Jerusalem, 1936,'" and Paget heard the thump of a book landing in the fireplace and smelled a sweet animal odor as flames scorched a leather binding.

"Give it up or I'll burn every one."

Paget shook his head. He was too angry to speak. He heard another thump and then a clanging as the American stirred the fire with a poker. The man was murdering his past.

"Since you can't see, I'll give you a report: I've tossed five of your fucking diaries into the fire."

"You're bluffing. Why destroy what you came to find?"

He jerked Paget out of the armchair, dragged him across the room and thrust his hand toward the fireplace. "There! Feel the heat? Those are your precious books going up in flames."

Paget reached behind with his free hand and swept the rug, searching for the poker. He had stumbled over it when the American pulled him across the room. It was just within reach. He grabbed what he thought was the handle. Pain shot through his hand. He had seized the hot tip. He moaned, but willed himself not to drop it.

"Fire too hot for you, Brigadier?" The American thought he had singed his hand in the fire.

Paget swung the steel rod at the voice. The poker missed its target and crashed into the mantelpiece. Paget whirled around and swung again, hoping to catch the American sneaking up behind him. It crashed into a mirror. Blood from the cut in Paget's forehead seeped into his better eye. He was now totally blind, unable to focus on even a small corner of the room.

The American had slipped across the room and was standing near the armchair. "You sly old coot," he said. "All the time you were sitting on the diary. Well, cheerio, Brigadier." He laughed again. "Now you go easy on the furniture, you hear?"

Paget kicked off his house slippers and, still holding the poker, tiptoed to the parlor door and listened as the American walked down the front hall. When the American stopped, Paget slipped into the hallway and froze, listening. He knew the American was pausing to open the front door.

When he heard the handle move, Paget ran the six paces from the parlor to the front door and swung the poker. It slammed into the American's body and flew out of Paget's grasp.

The American swore, giving away his position. Paget jumped on his back and pulled him down to the carpet, all the time clawing his face, ripping at his ears and poking at his eyes. The American punched him in the side of the head and rolled away. Paget stumbled to his feet and began fumbling with the door, trying to escape. As he turned the handle, a weight crashed into his head and he sensed, but could not see, a flash of brilliant white light.

Bella and Gina turned off the promenade onto a path leading through the public gardens. A band played to lines of gray heads peeking over the tops of canvas deck chairs. "Just look at it," Bella said. "Bournemouth has the warmest winter, the most sunshine and the least rainfall on the south coast, and the dullest collection of old wrecks. How I hate it!"

"Then why stay?"

"I couldn't abandon the Brigadier. Reading to me makes him feel useful."

She loves him, Gina thought.

"What's your next move?" Bella asked. "I trust you're not giving up without a fight."

"Certainly not!" She hoped she sounded determined and

unafraid. "I'm returning to reinterview the islanders who knew Orwell, reconstruct my manuscript and await the arrival of my mysterious Mr. Dawney."

"That's it!" Bella shouted and clapped her hands. "That's the name!"

"The American colonel?"

"No. Dawney was Eric's friend, his comrade from Spain who recognized the American in the Scribe. You *see,*" she said triumphantly. "I knew your troubles began in Paris."

"Just because this Dawney answered my advertisement doesn't mean Piers is innocent. After all, Dawney knew Orwell in Paris; he might be replying in the normal course of events."

When they reached the Brigadier's cottage Bella said proudly, "I'm the only one he trusts with a key, although it took me six months to persuade him to part with it."

At her touch the door swung open. Glancing at Gina, she pushed it open all the way, and saw him. The Brigadier was sprawled on the hallway floor, breathing heavily, his face smeared with blood.

Bella gasped and fell to her knees. It was Gina who recovered from her shock first and dashed into the house to summon an ambulance. Then she saw the parlor. The table was tipped over, the floor littered with glass from the mirror, broken toy soldiers and the Brigadier's diaries. More diaries smoldered in the fireplace. Despite her brave talk she had been considering abandoning everything, never returning to Barnhill. But now she was no longer the only victim, and she had no choice. She would meet this Dawney, confront Piers, do whatever was necessary to punish whoever was responsible for this outrage.

She returned to the hallway to see Bella stroking the Brigadier's head and wiping the blood off his face with a handkerchief. "Geoffrey, tell me what happened," she whispered. "Tell me who did this . . . this unspeakable cruelty." Her voice became harder. "Tell *us*" —she looked at Gina—"so we can avenge you." Then she whispered in his ear, "Squeeze my hand if you understand."

His hands were clenched into tight fists. She gently pulled back his fingers one by one. As she slipped her own hand into his, something fell onto the floor. "What was that?" she said. Her voice was sharp and commanding. "He was holding something in his hand. Find it."

Gina picked it up. She wiped it on her shirt and held it up to the light. "I don't understand," she said. "It's a woman's gold earring."

CHAPTER 9

The Duchess's straw made a raspy, greedy sucking noise as it vacuumed a puddle of piña colada from the bottom of her frosted glass. Victor was late, leaving her and Adam alone in the Lily Pad, a patio restaurant bordering the TropicResort golf course. She pushed aside the empty glass—she had bitten through the straw—and said, "Someone wants to destroy all this beauty." She gestured toward the fairway and the "native village." "They're trying to smear Victor."

"Someone's always trying to smear Victor. Once they stop, I'm out of a job." Adam smiled, a skillful doctor calming a nervous patient. She was notoriously paranoid about attacks on her husband. "When Victor acquires a company he's a 'megalomaniac.' When he shuts one down he's the 'unacceptable face of capitalism.' Too many people have made too many accusations. No one listens anymore."

She fixed her eyes on him. Her face had been expertly creamed, oiled, caressed and smoothed, but her eyes were an older woman's, milky and runny. Now they were scared. "You're wrong," she said. "They'll listen when Victor is accused of being a Communist."

"Now that lie is"—he screwed up his face like a connoisseur tasting an unpleasant wine—"too brash, too absurd, an impudent, green little lie. We'll have to send it back, no one will drink it." He saw she was not laughing. "You're joking?"

"It's true," she said flatly. "Victor was an idealist. He joined the Communist Party for a single semester while he was a student in 1932. All the best and the brightest flirted with Communism then. It was *long* before my time, of course, but I found out when one of his former classmates wrote a weaselly letter demanding a 'loan.'"

"Blackmail?"

"Goddamned right! I happened to open the letter by mistake. Victor handled it and we never heard a squeak from *that* little man again. Now it's starting all over again, except this time whoever's behind it doesn't want money, they want Victor. Doesn't it remind you of that horrid Senator McCarthy?"

To stall for time Adam looked down and fiddled with the miniature Japanese parasol floating in his drink. Christ almighty! This was the last thing he'd expected. He'd screwed himself again! Bet on another loser! Half his friends and prospective employers would think he got what he deserved; the other half wouldn't touch someone who'd climbed into bed with a Commie. Fuck Victor and his sophomoric ideals! But what could he say to the Duchess? What was the best reaction? Sympathy? Disbelief? Or outrage at Victor's predicament? He settled on a safe, neutral response.

"Who do you think is behind it?" he asked.

"It could be anyone! The Soviets hoping to embarrass the President. Think of it—his closest friend a Communist!"

"*Former* Communist. A Communist for . . . How long is a semester? Six months? We'll make it five. A man who was a Communist for five months fifty years ago." Perhaps he *could* protect Victor. If he succeeded he could ask for the earth. Could it be that Nat Beale and his "fine set of young people" were doing this in the hope of sabotaging the R-Tube?

She looked at him approvingly as she signaled for a refill. "That *does* sound better." The drink came in an instant. The piña coladas at the TropicResort, all premixed to her specifications, bubbled and churned in clear plastic containers. The Duchess cultivated a reputation for being creative and had picked the 'themes' for the Resort's restaurants. The Lily Pad's theme was frogs. They leapt across menus, plates and napkins.

She blew into her straw and the surface of her new drink erupted like a volcano. "It's so damned *unfair*. Particularly now when the President is going to offer him a cabinet post."

"Does the President know?" For a conservative anti-Communist President, the revelation would be embarrassing, at the least. Gore and the Duchess would be ostracized by their wealthy friends and excluded from their glittering social events. Adam might come to resemble one of Nixon's faithful aides, following his leader into a golf exile, living in a cottage on the grounds and conducting briefings for a shrinking circle of reporters.

"The President doesn't know, at least not yet," she said. "And he won't—that is, if you help poor Victor. Mr. Hacker has already been recruited for the battle, but he's proven something of a disappointment. Now it's up to you."

Gore pulled alongside their table in a golf cart. It was bright pink and shaded by a lime-green awning, his wife's favorite colors. A man in a red blazer followed at twenty-five yards in a cart marked SECURITY.

"Mind if I borrow Adam for a few minutes, dear?" he asked.

"Of course not." She waved her hand at Adam, dismissing him. "Hop in, Adam. We'll go for a ride."

There were no sidewalks in the TropicResort and walking was discouraged. Every guest was issued a numbered electric golf cart. A card, affixed to every dashboard, said: "For your safety and protection, when not in use plug cart into an electric outlet." Adam had been puzzled at first, not understanding why a plugged-in golf cart was "safer." Then Hacker had explained. Each cart was tagged with its own computer signature. Plugging it into the electrical system connected it with the head-end computer, thereby enabling the R-Tube to locate a guest instantaneously.

Gore's cart was supercharged, twice as fast as the guest vehicles. He shoved the accelerator to the floor and they lurched forward. "We'll have to hurry to catch the sunset," he said.

Adam moved restlessly in his seat. He had to know what Gore was planning. Would he call a press conference and admit everything, hoping to defuse the issue? Or would he stonewall? Was a cabinet post now out of the question? Gore owed him an explanation. It was his future as well. He broke the silence. "Victor, your wife has just told me something incredible . . ."

Gore held up his hand. "No talking. Admire the view."

They sped past caravans of golfers in straw hats and polo shirts.

Whenever he drove around the Resort he was tempted to play bumper cars and ram the other carts; or to attach a "Cucaracha" horn to his cart and shatter the Resort's eerie quiet, disrupt the purring of air conditioners and golf carts, the flip-flop of sandals, plip-plop of tennis balls and the slapping of bodies hitting water, all the reassuring sounds of efficiently managed health, leisure and exercise.

Gore sped along the perimeter road, following the barbed-wire-topped wood fence encircling the Resort. Through the slats, Adam could see glimpses of taxis bouncing along a potholed highway, workers walking to the refinery and a monotonous rolling countryside of scrubby bushes and stunted trees. Gore swerved away from the fence, toward the ocean, and now the view was of golf carts gliding across fairways like gigantic bugs, and the Aunt Jemima maids carrying towels and linen past palms, bougainvillea and the shrubs Beale called "house plants with elephantiasis." He had once described the Resort as "a Connecticut country club dropped into a tropical East Germany."

In the distance was one of the striped wooden barriers which blocked all entrances to the TropicResort. Guardhouses next to the barriers were wired with computer terminals which read employees' identity cards and the "Tropic Fun Passes" issued to guests. At night guards cruised the paths connecting the Resort's facilities. But guests found their presence more reassuring than ominous. Gore was fond of saying that nowadays people would accept anything as long as you prefaced your request with the phrase "For your protection . . ."

Gore parked on a rise overlooking the beach. The sun was fifteen minutes above the horizon. "Do you know what major-league rule number one is?" he asked. Without waiting for an answer he said, " 'Never write it down.' Whatever you commit to paper depletes you, subtracts from your power and thrusts a weapon into your enemies' hands. What you haven't written you can later restate, reinterpret and redesign.

"Which brings us to major-league rule two: 'Never say it.' No direct questions; no clear answers. Instead, you construct an invisible pattern: you pause, stress a word or phrase, tell a joke, then a story, then smile, laugh, touch the hand, squeeze the arm and . . . click!" He snapped his fingers in Adam's face. "The information is passed, the deal done, and it's safer than invisible ink or microdots because later, if some smart-ass lawyer corners you and says, 'Now, isn't it a fact, Mr. Gore, that on such and such a date you and Mr. Jones met at such and such a club and agreed to raise the price, depress the price, manipulate the price, to sell, to buy, to dump, to hoard . . . ?' Well, then you can stare right at him and say, either indignantly or innocently, depending on your mood, 'We said nothing of the sort! We discussed our golf handicaps, our children, the presidential election.' You see how it works? You don't have to lie. The only person who can betray you is you."

"Or whoever you talked with."

"Not at all. They can only testify to what you actually said. How they interpreted it is their problem."

"But why can't . . ."

Gore snapped his fingers again. "Listen, don't interrupt." He paused for almost a minute, staring at the setting sun before he said abruptly, "Weren't you once married?"

Adam hesitated. Was he meant to be answering or listening?

"Weren't you?"

"For two years, yes. The Peace Corps made us think we had a lot in common. But we didn't."

"Well, even in that short time I'm sure you learned how protective wives can be; how fierce they become if someone threatens their mates. It's a failing that's usually excused."

Adam laughed. "That wasn't a problem in my marriage. My wife, Katie . . ."

Gore tensed. "Would it help you concentrate if we went inside, away from the view?"

He shook his head. Of course Gore was not interested in his marriage. He was supposed to be listening, deciphering Gore's "invisible pattern." Yet he couldn't resist pretending this was a genuine conversation. Why couldn't he control himself? This was just like playing the silly games with the R-Tube or making childish remarks about Hacker's earring.

Gore said, "The more I accomplish, the more enemies I make. The more things I build"—he pointed toward the "native fishing village" that anchored one end of the beach—"the more people line up for a chance to destroy them. The more power I have, the more vigilant I have to be, the harder I have to fight to keep it. It's a perpetual battle, a never-ending war, but with an important difference. Often I don't know who I'm fighting or what they want. So before I counterattack, before I send out platoons to guard my flanks, I have to find that out, don't I . . . don't I?"

"Yes, of course." He was beginning to understand what Gore wanted, although the military metaphors were making him uncomfortable.

"Yes. I have to know their strengths . . their objectives . . . and most of all, who's paying." He spoke slowly and deliberately, as if communicating with a child or a foreigner. "So I dispatch a loyal and trusted officer to spy, to raid and probe the enemy. I think of him as my skirmisher."

The TropicResort airstrip was directly below the bluff, bordering the beach. Gore paused as a TropicAir Saberliner circled and landed. "That's your plane," he said. "It'll take you to Miami to connect with a London flight. I want you in Scotland tomorrow. Stan has just telexed that a real estate agent in Glasgow has located a shooting estate. Check it out, see it's not too shabby. You'll have time to do an exposure analysis of the island. Map out zones of protection, zones of movement. The status, location and nature of local threats. Small islands are usually safe because they're easy to control. There's only one ferry to Jura, so it's easy to know who's coming and going. The bad news is that islands like Jura attract eccentrics and anti-establishment types."

"Isn't this more up Stan's alley?"

"You're both paid to protect me. Get to know the islanders. Soften them up. Defuse the minefields."

Gore climbed out of the cart and walked to the edge of the bluff. When Adam joined him he asked, "Do you know Sarah Bailey?"

"The vice-president for office systems?"

"In 1950 she was my stenographer and she's as loyal now as then. Every time we've grown, moved headquarters and diversified, I've taken her with me. Whenever I succeed, so does she. My success is hers. If I have the honor to serve my country, she will too."

A small propeller plane taxied down the runway and took off. "There goes your friend Beale," Gore said. "If I'd known how difficult he'd be over the R-Tube I never would have recommended him for the board. I wonder how much longer he'll be with us? Ever heard of the Luddites?"

"Weren't they English . . ."

"Mechanics and workers who vandalized factory machines in the last century. They were afraid the machines would steal their jobs. They were right, but they were fighting the inevitable. The R-Tube is inevitable too, and Luddites like Beale aren't going to stop us either. The objections he raises are irrelevant. What's important is who's at the head-end. Who's got the sweeps. I think it should be us, don't you?"

"Yes!" He hoped he sounded enthusiastic.

"Good." He started back to the cart. "I'll take you back to my wife now. She'll be in the fishing village, rehearsing her dancers."

As they drove in silence—they had not waited for the sunset—Adam figured out what he'd just been told. Some enemy wanted to destroy Gore by revealing his former membership in the Communist Party. One or more participants in the conspiracy could be found on this Scottish island. Gore planned to counterattack, perhaps during the board meeting, but first he wanted Adam to "skirmish."

Well, he'd do his best. According to the Duchess, Hacker had been a disappointment. He recognized Gore's favorite management style: overlapping assignments. Give two men the same job and see who performs. It was obvious to him now why Gore had entrusted the factual portion of his briefing to the Duchess. Gore did not want to be linked to any attempt to suppress these damaging revelations. If somewhere down the line his past was exposed, then he still had the option of calling a press conference, admitting everything and shrugging it all off as an insignificant and long-forgotten episode. He could say that any attempt to suppress it had been made without his knowledge by a wife who was overprotective and by two overzealous employees acting on her instructions. And if there *was* any fuck-up Adam would not be able to hide behind any written or even verbal orders. He would be exposed; Gore would be protected.

He accepted the risk, for Gore had made clear his reward. Like Sarah Bailey, he would follow him to Washington, to a new adventure. Once he was in the government, who knew what might happen? Perhaps he would resign from the Pentagon to protest a dangerous nuclear weapons policy, a heroic act of sacrifice for the cause of world peace; or, alternatively, he would defend a controversial weapon crucial to national security. His current job—the ridiculous public relations, "skirmishing" for Gore—that was not him. He wanted to do something important, even brave. And his heroism would be authentically his own, not guided by some borrowed ideology, but by his experience. But first he needed Victor.

The TropicResort fishing village was built on a landfill at the end of the airstrip. It had flickering gas lamps, red tile roofs, quaint whitewashed houses reminiscent of Mykonos and a California mission church crammed with Greek icons. (The Duchess, who had chosen everything, had a Greek grandmother.) Old men squatted on stools repairing nets that were never used. A plaza lined with sidewalk cafés faced fishing boats that never left the harbor.

Closed-circuit cameras perched on every roof and lamppost, their lenses pointed downward, white vultures ready to swoop. Some of the buildings were false fronts with doors that never opened; others housed the picturesque workshops of the "international artists" bribed by the Duchess to paint, sculpture and hammer jewelry for the amusement of guests. None of them lived in the village, and at night it was deserted, illuminated by yellow spotlights and the flashlights of patrolling guards. It was obviously bogus but, as in the case of Disneyland, no expense had been spared; a classy fraud, built to last.

"I hate the tropics," Gore said as they walked past the "fishermen." "They're out of date. The towns are nothing but decayed imitations of nineteenth-century provincial Europe. No tourist wants to dodge rabid dogs, cheer at cockfights and brush off cockroaches. You have to avoid everything native and build something newer and safer."

He found the Duchess sitting in one of the cafés, nibbling on creole pizza and shouting directions to her folk dancers: busboys and chambermaids wearing Greek peasant outfits and frozen smiles. Adam noticed that, like Hacker, some of the boys had gold rings dangling from their earlobes. When Gore left he asked the Duchess why.

"I told them to," she said.

"Is Stan Hacker under orders too?"

"No." She laughed. "He volunteered. Didn't Victor tell you that the Vice-President was here last weekend? We had a traditional pirate party in his honor. Every table had a treasure chest, and the waiters and dancers dressed as pirates, earrings and all. Stan and his young men wore them so they could mingle without spoiling the atmosphere."

"But Hacker is still wearing his earring."

"Is he? Well, so are some of the busboys. They must like being pirates."

"Pirates weren't celebrated for their loyalty." He smiled wickedly. "They preyed on all countries equally. You'd better tell Victor to keep an eye on Stan."

"But we don't have to worry about *your* loyalty, do we?" And then she was back onto the threat to her husband's reputation. "When I found out," she explained, "I asked Mr. Hacker to investigate. He doesn't seem to have had much success, though he promises some developments when Victor arrives in Scotland."

"Is that why Victor shifted the meeting?"

"No! Mr. Hacker and I suggested the change of venue to Victor. He agreed without knowing our motives. You must remember that *everything* has been done on my orders." She stopped, gave a discreet wink and then handed him two photographs and said, "Mr.

Hacker took these. It's possible she's innocent, merely a conduit for these poisonous stories. But it's more likely she's not. Her husband is a notorious left-wing politician, even *admits* to being a Marxist. He's always jetting off to conferences in Algeria and those sorts of places. The kind of man who'd enjoy destroying Victor. Mr. Hacker thinks the Russians are behind it. They'd have the records of Victor's membership, wouldn't they?"

Adam studied the first photograph. It showed a woman bending over to feed some hens. Behind her, slightly out of focus, was a large white house. The second photograph was an enlargement, showing her face. She had high cheekbones, long brown hair and freckles. She was handsome, but had dark circles under her eyes and wore the intense expression of a student who had stayed up too late smoking too many cigarettes and drinking too much coffee. A woman living alone on a remote island should look more relaxed. Her appearance was evidence against her.

He handed the pictures back to the Duchess and said, "Attractive, isn't she?"

"She's just young, I'd say."

"I'll do my best." Now it was his turn to wink. "Don't you think it might help if she liked me?"

PART II

PART II

CHAPTER 10

"More desolate, but more beautiful than I'd imagined," Bella Stevens said as she surveyed Jura with her telescope. She and Gina sat on the lawn of the Port Askaig Hotel in Islay, awaiting the departure of the ferry that crossed the straits separating the two islands. "Reminds me of Patagonia or the Falklands; they both have this purplish, boggy barrenness—real commando country." She leaned forward and twirled the eyepiece impatiently. Gina wondered how much she could see and how much was pretense, although her description of the island was accurate. "Islands like this appear even more deserted when it's clear and sunny. In foul weather you always wonder if the mist and fog aren't concealing a village or farm. But today you can see everything; see that there's nothing." She swept her telescope across the far shore. "Just a jetty, a deserted cottage and a road disappearing into those hills. That battered white van is the only thing spoiling the view."

"That's the postman. He's the only outsider who calls at Barnhill." At least let's hope he's the only one, she thought, remembering the Irish stalker.

"And towering over the island are those three volcanic hills. I imagine you can see Northern Ireland from their peaks. Naughty of Eric not to have invited me here. Forty years ago I could have climbed all three in a day."

Gina laughed for the first time since finding the Brigadier. "The Paps are about twenty-five hundred feet high. Most people barely manage one in a day. I've never been up any of them."

"Paps! That's rather sinister—I mean, given there are three of them. Perhaps whoever named them was thinking of cows or cats."

Gina was relieved Bella was talking again. Since leaving Bournemouth yesterday morning she had hardly said a word. Whenever Gina had asked about the Brigadier, or about Bella's meeting with the Colonel in Paris, her eyes had watered and she had shaken her head sadly. Once she said, "I'm much too distraught to launch into that now, dear." They had driven north in Bella's antique Rover, stopping to eat in transport cafés and sleeping in the car wrapped in scratchy Bedouin robes Bella stored in the trunk "for just such an emergency."

But Bella was too much of an old campaigner to be permanently daunted. By the time they crossed into Scotland Gina noticed that her companion's eyes were dry again. She spent the remainder of the drive staring at the horizon and jotting notes on a memo pad. During the trip over from the mainland Gina saw her reread the notes, then crumple them up and toss them overboard.

Bella seemed to have a plan, which was a relief to Gina. Her own instinct, at first, had been to remain in England and rely on the police. But the earring and the ransacked cottage had convinced them that the Brigadier, now in a coma, had been assaulted by a punk bent on robbery. When Gina had attempted to explain the other possibilities, Bella had shot her a look that silenced her. After the police had left she said, "Dear, I doubt the local constabulary have either the inclination or the resources to pursue this matter properly. Don't you think it best to leave the *real* investigation to us, the two people with the most to gain? After all, you want your papers returned and an end to this worrisome harassment. And I want the man, or woman, who assaulted the Brigadier. Mr. Dawney may be of help, but I rather doubt it. If he's as I remember him, he's rather a nervous, peculiar little man. No, I'll have to accompany you to Jura. I can recognize Dawney and he knows that Eric trusted me. I wonder where he's holed up all these years."

Gina protested, but halfheartedly. She wanted Bella's company and dreaded returning alone to Barnhill. Having Bella join her would also prevent her driving to Heathrow and jumping on a plane to New York. It was harder to desert in front of an audience. And although Bella certainly wanted to avenge the Brigadier, Gina suspected that she also wanted one last, grand adventure.

Bella dropped the telescope into her lap and said, "This little port has just the atmosphere one finds at a remote frontier railway junction. First the big ferry brings us over from the mainland and then we wait for the connection to Jura. The single hotel and shop are mostly here for travelers. Is this the only way to get to Jura?"

"Unless you hire a boat or take a helicopter."

"Splendid. Then this is the choke point: the only entrance and exit."

"We could stay here," Gina suggested. "Book into the hotel, meet every boat and wait for Dawney. He said the third week in October and you're so convinced you can recognize him."

"But suppose he's already on Jura waiting for us?" Bella unlaced her square-toed hiking boots, hitched up her tweed skirt and turned her face to the sun. "My appetite's back," she announced. "Let's eat the *cuisine du pays:* Scotch ale and Scotch egg with plenty of mustard."

When Gina returned with the food, Bella said, "I think I've remembered everything about that blasted American colonel except his name."

"The day we met, he doused me with the nastiest scent imaginable. I'd asked him for an interview and he'd suggested we meet at a department store, of all places. I think it was Au Printemps, but it could have been the Galeries something or other. It hardly matters which, because in 1945 they were all much the same. They had these seductive window displays, but when you dashed inside waving a fistful of francs you saw nothing but empty shelves, pyramids of cheap scent in expensive boxes and bins overflowing with hideous souvenir knickknacks that had been manufactured for the Hun. You know—things like cheap lace embroidered with pictures of German tanks.

"The store where I met the Colonel was as grim as its goods. The lifts didn't work, the lights were dim and the Germans had pinched the carpets. Over the telephone the Colonel had insisted on the scent counter at noon. He had that mechanical, efficient voice that SHAEF officers affected. We couldn't have met in his office because that would have made the interview formal, requiring all sorts of clearances.

"What had happened was this: the day before, the Brigadier had nobbled him in the canteen and said"—she cleared her throat and imitated the Brigadier—" 'A well-known lady writer, friend of mine, wants to do an article about the plans you chaps have for your zone. She needs an informal chat, someone to point her in the right direction, give her the true gen. All confidential of course. Consider it a big favor . . .' blah, blah, blah . . .

"The Colonel took the bait, as I knew he would. It was a time when none of my colleagues were vastly interested in his specialty. The Americans had just captured a Rhine bridge and taken Cologne, so the best stories were coming from the front. I think he was chuffed that someone was interested in his sideshow. He described himself in detail over the telephone so I'd be sure to recognize him. I was left with the impression I was meeting Cary Grant.

"I must say the store he chose for our meeting was extraordinary. It was deserted except for the aisles surrounding the scent department, and they were absolutely packed with people. From a distance all one could see was a forest of enormous turbans and green combat helmets belonging to American soldiers. They'd drive all night from the front and arrive in combat fatigues. Then they'd sightsee, drink, do something shameful and, to atone, buy scent for their wives or mothers. Some were so drunk and exhausted they fell asleep on their feet and the salesgirls had to shake them.

"The absurdly high turbans were worn by Frenchwomen who thought the scent counter a first-class spot for trapping an American boyfriend, particularly if they could snare him before he'd spent too much. All in all, I thought it was a peculiar place to discuss the fate of the German people. But it was the Colonel's choice, not mine.

"I found him standing at the edge of the crowd. Not bad-looking, but definitely not as advertised. Isn't it extraordinary how some people see themselves? The words he'd used most were 'thin,' 'lean' and 'sharp.' He had 'a thin nose,' 'a lean build' and 'sharp blue eyes.'

I found myself shaking hands with a bald young man—young for a colonel anyway—with a close-cropped fringe of prematurely gray hair. His nose *was* thin, but out of kilter, broken several times in several places. And his famous blue eyes were slightly out of control, unfocused.

"He immediately grabbed a spray off the counter and squirted scent on my cheek and neck. 'This is the most expensive,' he said. 'Eisenhower buys it. What do you think?' It stung horribly, as if someone had dragged nettles across my face. Before I could answer, he squirted another fragrance on my hand. 'Don't worry about the price,' he said. 'My treat. Have them both if you like.' Before I could jump away, he squirted a third scent on my hair. I gagged on the fumes and coughed. One of the shopgirls giggled.

"First I thought that swaggering around Paris squirting scent had become second nature for Americans, something they did whenever they had a chance with a woman. But then I caught him eyeing me coldly, without passion. His vulgar assault was calculated. He was reminding me that he was rich and powerful, and he was testing me. Would I accept a present offered so offensively? Most of all, and I'm not certain he realized this, he wanted to humiliate me.

"I pulled out a handkerchief, borrowed water from a soldier's canteen and slowly and deliberately dabbed the scent off my hands and face. When I told Eric the story afterwards, he whooped with laughter and said, 'That's just how to handle bullies.'

"I told the Colonel I loathed scent and then turned and walked down an empty aisle. He followed. For half an hour we talked while strolling past heaps of those awful German souvenirs.

"Eric had given me three assignments: probe the Colonel's background, scrutinize his appearance and then offhandedly mention Eric's name and say he was quartered at the Scribe. If I could manage it, I was to insert Dawney's name into the conversation too. Eric suggested I think of myself as a gamekeeper dragging a fox's scent across the path of a nervous, hungry hound. A rather disturbing metaphor.

"But first I had to dispense with the pretext for our meeting. I'd swotted up on the Colonel the night before. He was in G–5 at

SHAEF, responsible for planning the German occupation, and personally in charge of some of the ECAD—I think it stood for European Civil Affairs Division—detachments that were to follow the American First Army into Germany. These troops were trained to become the first civil authority in occupied Germany. I remember the Colonel telling me he was going to Cologne in several days to oversee ECAD operations there.

"Then he said, 'But it's not what happens in the first weeks of the Occupation that matters; it's what we do afterwards, and that, contrary to what you may have heard, is still the subject of secret and intense debate among the Allies, and within each Allied government. There are so many competing schemes that the different factions are presently stalemated. There's a power vacuum and I plan to fill it.'

"I realized then that, like most civil servants who agree to off-the-record chats, he had some pet scheme to push. He probably hoped for an article praising his ideas. He certainly wasn't the first one peddling a master plan for postwar Germany. Around this time I recall reading the most outrageous article in one of your magazines. Some bureaucrat had the splendid idea of making the Germans construct gigantic monuments on their main thoroughfares depicting German crimes throughout history.

"The Colonel presented himself, as people with totalitarian schemes often do, as the sanest alternative to a clutch of even more awful possibilities. 'There are some creepy plans circulating through G–5 these days,' he said. 'Wholesale sterilization of Nazi Party members, fifteen years' forced labor for German males so they can rebuild Europe, compulsory weekly attendance at films of Nazi atrocities, the partition of Germany into twelve states. One of my French colleagues wants to ship SS men back to the scenes of their crimes for execution.

"'I'm pushing for a more humane and effective policy. First, ask yourself: What do the Germans worship?' Before I could answer, 'Hitler,' he said, 'Power.' 'For generations Germans have revered power. Our first task is to persuade them to worship *our* power. And to do that we have to overcome our distaste for dominating the defeated. If we act like conquerors, we'll have no problem bending the Germans to our will.'

"Suddenly the Colonel paused for several seconds and pointed to the huge turbans worn by the women buzzing around the scent counter. 'Aren't these hats fabulous?' he asked.

" 'No, they're perfectly ghastly.'

" 'Oh, I don't mean how they *look.*'

" 'What else *is* there to a hat?'

" 'Its effect. Haven't you wondered why Parisian women wore such ridiculous clothes throughout the Occupation? All these high hats and turbans, the oversized boxy suits and high-soled cork shoes made it possible for even the smallest woman to stand up to the Krauts, even intimidate them. Believe me, those clothes drove the Nazis crazy! This is the sort of detail we'll have to remember in Germany.'

"Well, score one for the Colonel. He was on the mark about the fashions. But his other ideas were more sinister than kitting up our MPs in big hats. Afterwards Eric questioned me closely about his plan. Essentially, it entailed sealing off West Germany from the rest of Europe like a leper colony. Rather than execute the older Nazis, we would let them die of natural causes; this he called 'the humane alternative.' Meanwhile the rest of the German lepers would be raised to detest the elder generation and love the Allies, presumably Allies such as the Colonel. They would also learn a new version of German history which would portray all German military triumphs as defeats. Schools and public gathering places would be wired with microphones to ensure that teachers and politicians followed the Colonel's script; to ensure, in the Colonel's words, 'that a totalitarian state never again flourishes in Germany.'

"I told Eric that he spoke completely without emotion, in the same mechanical voice I remembered from the telephone. He didn't hate the German race and he wasn't a Jew. He hadn't faced Nazi troops in combat, nor was he a left-winger.

"As he paced up and down the aisles of that shop explaining his plan, I began to feel as if I were alone in a darkened theater, watching an actor performing for himself. He paused between sentences, but became irritated if I spoke. I longed to know if these pauses were strategic—was he constantly stopping to decide how best to impress and convince me?—or were they merely devices enabling him to step back and admire his performance?

"Finally I said, 'You really must meet a journalist friend of mine named Eric Blair who's keenly interested in all this. Perhaps you've heard of him? He uses the pen name George Orwell.

"Everything he did and said next convinced me that he knew Eric. Instantly, he stopped pacing and faced me. He had stepped down from his personal stage. 'I suppose he's staying at the Scribe?' he asked. His voice was strained, not mechanical. For the first time he wanted me to answer.

"'I should have said, 'No, he's leaving Paris tonight.' Instead, like a fool, I followed Eric's instructions and said, 'He's in room 329. If he's out, you can probably find him in the bar. He spends his time there reminiscing about the war in Spain with a wizened little man named Dawney.'

"The Colonel suddenly saluted, said, 'Thank you, you've been more helpful than you can imagine,' and turned abruptly on his heel and strode away. Heading, I imagined, straight to the Scribe to murder Eric."

CHAPTER 11

The Jura ferry blasted its horn, interrupting Bella and forcing her to bolt her food. She and Gina shared the ferry with two Land-Rovers belonging to one of the estates on Jura. Leaving the other drivers to sit with their windows rolled up against the spray, Gina climbed the iron stairs leading to the pilot's house, the better to watch the Jura shore draw closer. Even on this calm, sunlit day, the water was gray and speckled with whitecaps; the current so strong that the ferry left Port Askaig with its bow pointing a quarter mile west of the Jura dock. For her this was more than a five-mile ride on an open ferry; it was the crossing of a frontier, one that separated past and present. Behind was the present: Islay and the mainland, Piers, and the Brigadier in a coma. Ahead were Eric and Barnhill, prehistoric standing stones and caves, a landscape which encouraged the imagination to shatter time.

Bella's account of Eric's luncheon with Wodehouse and the Brigadier had forced her to alter her daydreams of revenge on Piers. Since Eric had disapproved so of revenge, she would have to re-evaluate her plan. In any case, the attack on Brigadier Paget made it unlikely that Piers was responsible for the earlier attempt on her life. Why would he care about an elderly brigadier and his diaries?

After pulling off the ferry she parked beyond the stone jetty and motioned for the Land-Rovers to pass her. She wanted the road to herself. As she waited for them to disappear, she rolled down the window and hailed Euen. He had just unloaded a mail bag from the ferry.

"Back for good, are you?" he asked.

"Wish I were. Everything calm at Barnhill?"

"Aye."

"No more poachers or prowlers?" She strained to sound casual.

"None I've seen, though I haven't been poking about with you away."

"You're always welcome to use the kitchen, whether I'm there or not."

"I fed your hens. Greedy beasties!"

"I'll pay you for the feed when you bring the mail."

"I'll take it in tea and cakes. I've been stopping with Malcolm's Mary, and a sad mug she brews. Besides, it's I that's owing you—on account of two of your hens disappearing while I was in charge. Must have scratched under the fence. I know I didn't leave the gate open. Perhaps there's a bad dog loose."

Once Euen had driven off, Gina put the Rover in gear and headed slowly northeast, toward Craighouse and Barnhill. "Please go on with the story," she begged. "You mustn't think I'm bored if I don't comment or look at you from time to time. The roads here are tricky."

"Well, as soon as the Colonel was out of sight I dashed back to the Scribe, hoping to see Eric before he did. Luckily, I found the bar at its best, which is to say the piano was silent, a fan had blown away the cigarette smoke and there were only two drunken Brazilians, dressed like Mussolini, standing at the bar. Eric was sitting alone at a remote table, drinking cheap red wine but stinking of expensive whiskey. Before I could say hello, he proudly announced, 'I've just been at the Ritz, boozing with Ernest Hemingway.'

" 'Good for you,' I said. 'I've been at some ghastly shop. Your Colonel tortured me at the perfume counter.' "

"I hoped this would grab his attention. But instead he continued yapping about Hemingway as if he hadn't heard me. Perhaps he hadn't; I'd never seen him in such a state of high alcoholic excitement. The giveaway was that drink made his high-pitched Eton drawl even more high-pitched. It wasn't the right kind of accent for a socialist, and he struggled to keep it under control and compensated by using proletarian words such as 'boozing.' I could under-

stand why he had drunk so much. He was such a shy man it must
have taken courage for him to barge into Hemingway's room and
introduce himself, which is what he did. I'd palled around with
Ernest before Eric arrived in Paris, but I didn't admit to this now. It
would have spoiled his fun.

" 'I caught him just in time,' Eric said. 'He was tossing everything
into these battered cases. Said he was catching a plane for the States
at dawn day after tomorrow. His room was chaotic: champagne
bottles rolling around underfoot, an arsenal of rifles, pistols and grenades on the bed, and chambermaids and valets dashing in and out,
collecting and delivering bits of his uniform. The tables were clut-
tered with vases stuffed full of red roses and an avalanche of petals
covered the rug. The flowers were a present from Marlene Dietrich,
whom he called "the Kraut." She was billeted down the corridor and
she swept in and out while I was there. Ernest claims she sits on the
edge of his bath and sings while he's shaving. I'd say my friend
Ernest was having a "good war," wouldn't you?

" 'All the time the telephone kept ringing and Ernest shouted at
every caller: "Assemble at my command post tomorrow at eighteen
hundred hours." I told him I hadn't realized journalists had command posts. "You're in it," he said, sweeping his hand around the
room. "There's a farewell party here tomorrow evening. You come
too."

" 'As we talked, he field-stripped and cleaned one of the rifles—
the Ritz will never get the grease off its pink coverlet. Then he
scrambled around on hands and knees collecting what he called his
"trophies," mostly Nazi caps, medals and campaign badges he'd
plucked off dead Germans.'

" 'You two must have got on famously,' I said. 'You want to save
Germans when the war ends; he hopes to slaughter as many as
possible beforehand.'

"Eric ignored me. 'Ernest has read my books,' he said, 'though I
doubt he really waded through Clergyman and Aspidistra. His favorite was Down and Out. He praised it extravagantly, but intelligently.
Claimed he'd once lived a few hundred yards from my old digs on
the Pot de Fer, but hadn't appreciated the neighborhood until he

read *Down and Out.* He also pointed out something that I'd never noticed: in *The Sun Also Rises* his Jake Barnes walks down my rue Pot de Fer. Ernest called it the rue Coq d'Or but it was the same street. He said I should consider the coincidence a tribute to *Down and Out.*'

" 'What do you mean 'tribute?' That book of his was published several years before you even wrote *Down and Out.'*

" 'That's not the point!' he said indignantly. But then he paused, and I knew he was seeing Ernest in a new light. 'Well, there's nothing quite as seductive as informed flattery, is there?'

" 'Obviously not.'

" 'But I told him the truth: that I'd always admired his prose. Simple, clean sentences, and always the words of the common man. No stilted language you have to pronounce in a toffy accent.'

"That was a real howl, dear," Bella told Gina, "because Eric himself was telling the whole story in this undeniably Eton drawl.

" 'On the other hand,' he continued, 'in conversation Ernest uses all these mock-heroic clichés. Told me that his plane would be taking off "at first light." You'd think he was going over the top, not climbing onto an army transport plane for a quick journey back to America. And while he was sweeping up his trophies he kept muttering that he'd "hired out to be tough." Now what do you think *that* means?'

"Well, dear, I really didn't care. I wanted to report on the Colonel before I forgot something important. And I wanted to get out of that tight little corner of the bar. Eric kept leaning toward me, and the truth was, he smelled quite bad."

"Of whiskey?" asked Gina.

"Yes, that. But Eric also had a characteristic bad smell. I imagine it came from the disease that plagued his lungs. Whenever I smelled it—which wasn't all the time, by any means—I felt a mixture of attraction and repulsion: repelled by the rotten, decaying odor, but attracted by how stoical Eric was about his health—never whining, always driving himself as if he were fit. He was in no condition to be charging around Europe during the war, and I was not surprised to learn that later he came apart in Cologne.

"Anyway, there was no escaping him that afternoon. He went on and on about Hemingway, and both of their adventures in Spain. I knew they had a lot in common, of course. Both of them had lived in Paris in the twenties and fought for the Republic in Spain; they were brave and fearless in battle, almost foolhardy; they'd written books about that war which were condemned by Communist sympathizers, and both were terribly frustrated over missing most of the Second World War. They were also great exaggerators, not above embellishing purportedly factual accounts. The liberties Eric took in *Wigan Pier*—I can't tell you.

"But I was amazed, frankly, that the two of them had been able to spend more than ten minutes together. Hemingway was so naïve compared to Eric. He went to Spain looking for a great crusade, or some such, whereas Eric went there fully understanding the moral issues. Even worse, after he left Spain, Ernest became precisely the sort of fact-bending propagandist Eric loathed, although, to his credit, that period didn't last long. In the end he was just as disillusioned with the Communists as Eric.

"At bottom, though, they were just very opposite personalities. Ernest needed his gaggle of admirers, whereas Eric could be painfully shy. If Eric hadn't been stuffed so full of Ernest's whiskey and compliments, he might have seen more clearly how very different they were. After all, he claimed to detest bullies—even though he could be one himself—and Ernest was certainly that. If they'd met again under less convivial circumstances, they could easily have come to blows. That was another thing they had in common: neither shied away from a punch-up.

"Anyway, they managed to part that afternoon without any brawling. 'As I headed for the door,' Eric told me, 'Ernest grabbed a bunch of Dietrich's roses and shoved them into my hand, saying, "Here, take some of the Kraut's weeds."

" 'Next he grabbed a revolver off the bed and thrust it into my other hand, suggesting that it might "come in handy" in Germany. He called it his "veteran Kraut killer." He was oblivious to the irony of offering these gifts simultaneously.'

" 'Did you keep the revolver?' I asked. After my meeting with the Colonel I rather hoped he had.

"But Eric looked horrified. 'Just because I've enjoyed several comradely hours with Ernest doesn't mean I've adopted his worst traits. I'm not going to Germany to "kill Krauts." I tossed the gun back on the bed and he muttered something derogatory about "Limey manhood" and said I could "go pound salt"—whatever that means—before he'd offer it to me again. We parted on this sour note. But I kept the roses.'

"Eric suddenly bent backwards and fished out half a dozen roses from their hiding place behind his chair. With a great flourish he plopped them in my lap.

" 'These are for bearding the Colonel for me,' he said. I thought he'd forgotten all about the American, but this apparently was my chance. I repeated everything, including my fear that he was bent on killing him, but he remained calm. I think an hour of Hemingway had made him keen to have his own little heroic sideshow.

" 'He doesn't exactly resemble the American chap Dawney and I knew in Spain,' he commented after I'd described the Colonel. 'I don't recall a squiffy eye, nor that he was bald, just thinning. But there's nothing like a war to change one's appearance.'

"The Colonel's plan to quarantine Germany appalled him. 'Just think of it,' he muttered. 'Set up one totalitarian regime to prevent the re-emergence of another. Just place a new pair of hands—his, presumably—on the old Nazi gears. You can be sure that's Stalin's plan for his slice of Germany.'

"He paused for a sip of wine and said, 'I have a theory—that war encourages heroism, comradeship and compassion in your average man in the ranks. But take the fledgling stockbroker or civil servant who joins up. Merely because he went to some fifth-rate public school, he suddenly finds himself ordering about several hundred men: next thing you know he's having all sorts of totalitarian fantasies. Our Colonel sounds like a splendid specimen of the type, *Officiarius Totalitarianus Americanus*. What if he isn't poor old Dawney's bogeyman? It'd still be instructive to put him under a

microscope, don't you think? In the process I might have to pin
back his wings. I'd enjoy that.'

" 'Well, I'm convinced he *is* Dawney's bogeyman. He couldn't
hide his interest in your whereabouts. You'd better be jolly careful.'

" 'Even better if he is our long-lost comrade,' he said. 'Let's celebrate!' He hailed a waiter and ordered another carafe of cheap
claret.

" 'Honestly, Eric,' I said, 'why go to all this trouble? Why the
intrigue? Why not march into his office and say, "See here, I used to
know you in Spain. What's all this I hear about you changing your
name and becoming a torturer and traitor?" '

"He slapped his leg and roared with laughter. 'That's just what
you'd do, isn't it?'

" 'And I may yet do it. Unless you come to your senses.'

" 'You won't, and neither will I,' he said quickly. 'At least for the
time being. What's needed here is a rather tricky balancing act.' He
set down his glass and moved his graceful hands up and down as
though they were scales weighing something precious. 'On the one
hand, I want to stop Dawney from murdering the Colonel, which
he's quite capable of doing. On the other hand—he raised one hand
above the other—'I don't want the Colonel to murder Dawney.'

" 'Or you.'

"He sighed. 'Yes, or *me*, if you must be melodramatic.'

" 'I'm being realistic. Even if he's no longer in Stalin's pay he
might kill you to protect his new identity. People have been killed
for a lot less recently.'

" 'Don't think for a second I'm running back to London! I have a
responsibility to see this through. If the Colonel is still with the
NKVD, he could do great harm, particularly in his current position.
And his scheme for Germany *does* sound suspiciously Stalinist.

" 'But I have an equal duty'—he moved his hands up and down
again—'not to become the instrument of Dawney's revenge. It
would make a mockery of everything I believe about not punishing
the Germans. I must be sure of the Colonel before I act. I also have
to stall Dawney, persuade him that I believe him but I'm moving at

my own pace. Meanwhile, I can discover the truth. Now do you see why I asked you to drag the fox across the Colonel's path?'

" 'I see someone in poor health drinking too damned much and being bloody foolhardy.'

" 'I'll ignore that. Let's consider what your interview has set in motion. Suppose comrade Dawney is mistaken. Then our Colonel, as he leaves the scent counter, shrugs his shoulders and thinks: Who is this Orwell? Later I persuade him to describe his totalitarian daydreams. I write a splendid article identifying him as *Officiarius Totalitarianus Americanus.*

" 'But suppose he *is* Dawney's bogeyman. Then he won't be thrilled to learn that Dawney and I are sitting in the Scribe bar comparing notes, having a kind of Civil War Old Boys' Day. First off, he might bolt, take himself far away from us and Paris. Then he's out of Dawney's sights; we're out of his. But I'll still have to follow him to make certain he's not an agent. I hope he doesn't flee to America.

" 'Or he may seek me out, admit his wickedness in Spain and convince me he's a reformed character. Then *I* have to convince Dawney.'

" 'Or he may break into your room and, as Ernest might say, "rub you out." Don't forget you made me give him your room number.'

"He grinned and said, 'Then we'd be sure he's a bad hat, wouldn't we?'

"Blast him! He knew I cared for him. I suspect he took a perverse pleasure in seeing me fret. Sometimes his playfulness was almost sadistic. 'You seem to have plotted everything except how to protect yourself,' I said. 'You might remember that officers carry sidearms.'

"He suddenly became serious. 'If he attacks me, I'll be expecting it. Don't you think I can manage some power-mad American?'

"No, I thought. As usual, he looked gray and sickly. Still, I believe he relished a punch-up with the Colonel. Did you know he was once arrested in Glasgow for drunken brawling? And that he beat up a flat-mate in London? He struggled to keep these violent impulses under control. They didn't fit comfortably with his moral outlook."

Gina jammed on the brakes and barely avoided a cow that had wandered into the road. Bella shot forward and was caught by her seat belt with her head only inches from the windshield. "Sorry," Gina said. "I warned you about the tricky road."

"Are we almost there?" Although Bella never would have admitted it, the rough drive was making her queasy.

"No, miles to go."

"Oh," she said in a tired voice. "Well, I hope all this is worth it. What do you think, dear? Does it strike you that Eric's little intrigue in Paris is connected with our difficulties?"

"Not sure. But isn't that what *you* think?" There was a note of exasperation.

"Well, yes, I suppose so. But it's interesting in any case, isn't it? I mean, isn't the whole complicated scheme typical Eric?"

Gina shrugged and resumed driving.

"Well, I think you'd agree if you knew him as well as I did. It was so typical of him—because it was so brave *and* so foolhardy. As you know, he was *very* reckless in Spain, always walking along the tops of trenches and exposing himself to fire, which is how he got that nasty wound in the throat. When a comrade was arrested in Barcelona, Eric marched into prison to visit him even though the police were looking for him to arrest too.

"And it was so typically Eric, his plan, because it offered hope of saving both men from themselves and from each other. Eric loathed unnecessary bloodshed. Remember in Spain when he was sent up as a sniper and saw one of the enemy, a man running back from the latrine? He held his fire and later said, 'A man who is holding up his trousers isn't a fascist, he is visibly a fellow creature.'

"He believed revenge was the most unnecessary bloodshed of all. That condemned man he saw in Burma sidestepping a puddle as he walked to the gallows made a huge impression on him. 'I saw the mystery, the unspeakable wrongness of cutting a life short when it is in full tide,' he wrote afterwards. 'This man was not dying, he was alive just as we were alive.'

"Of course, Eric was no saint. I suspect his 'tricky balancing act' also appealed to him because he so adored secrets, and manipulating people. *He* would decide who was being truthful and *he* would orchestrate their salvation or punishment. His secretiveness was well known, of course. It's been documented by his biographers. And I imagine it's why none of them learned anything about those weeks in Paris. Your revelations of it all should create quite a sensation— although you'll need more proof than the ramblings of a blind old eccentric."

"Yes, Bella, I can't thank you enough," Gina said impatiently. "But what happened next? Who *was* the Colonel?"

Bella sighed and stared out the window. "That's all I know."

Gina was incredulous. "You must mean you can't *remember* any more! But that's impossible. Except for the Colonel's name, your memory has been extraordinary!"

"It has, hasn't it? I pieced it together on the drive up and wrote it down. But I'm afraid that's all there is. Later that evening I returned to the flat where I was staying—the one I'd moved to from the Scribe. As I was climbing the stairs the concierge stopped me and, with a smirk, handed over three beautifully wrapped boxes. Inside were huge bottles of the three foul scents the Colonel had offered me that morning. I recognized the smells when I poured them down the drain. How had he discovered where I was living, and so quickly? Officially I was still quartered at the Scribe with the rest of the correspondents.

"The concierge gave me an envelope too, from the SHAEF press officer. I had suddenly been assigned to a press tour of the Rhine crossings leaving early the following morning. It was a trip I'd been begging to be included on for weeks. I wrote Eric a note and left Paris the next day, without seeing him or the Colonel again. After the war I discovered that soon afterwards Eric had pushed on to Cologne. Several days after arriving there something happened and he was admitted to a military hospital. Then he suffered a more serious tragedy.

"Back in England his wife, Eileen, died during a routine operation. Eric left the hospital, still unwell, and dragged himself home for her funeral, then dashed back to the Continent. His friends, myself included, thought it odd that he returned to the war so quickly. He was very fond of Eileen. And even stranger that he chased after the American armies. He had never been to America and didn't care much for things American. Since he was writing for British newspapers, you'd think he'd have spent more time with our forces. I've always assumed he was chasing the Colonel, *Officiarius Totalitarianus Americanus.*"

Gina could not mask her irritation. "Surely you wrote to him? Saw him after the war? Didn't you want to know the end of the story?"

"Dear, I know this all seems fascinating to you, but for me it's one story of a great many. I was not as famous as Eric, but I've had every bit as eventful a life, perhaps more so because it's been longer. Naturally I wrote to him at Barnhill asking about our Colonel. He replied with chatty letters that never answered my question. I didn't press him. He'd obviously survived whatever happened in Cologne. But I needn't tell *you* that. You're the expert."

Damn right I am, Gina thought. And I'm fed up with being told "If you knew him as well as I did."

"You're being very silent, dear. Is anything wrong?"

Gina glanced at her: an exhausted, distraught old woman. Had it been a mistake to bring her? What protection could she be? Someone younger would have been more useful—would not always be trying to usurp Eric and Barnhill.

"If it's any comfort to you, dear," Bella said sweetly, "Mr. Dawney may know what happened next. He shuffled into the bar as I was leaving. At first, because he wore that filthy red beret, I thought he was French. We only exchanged the usual pleasantries, but I'm sure I'd recognize him again. Eric had told me quite a lot about him, and besides, he had memorably filthy hands and teeth."

Gina hoped Dawney would keep his promise and appear on Jura soon. Then she could send Bella back to Bournemouth and her vigil at the Brigadier's bedside. She could be alone again with Barnhill and Eric. She accelerated and drove on to Craighouse in silence.

Craighouse was not a cozy village. There was too much space and not enough people. The hotel, distillery, store, petrol pump, community house and semi-detached stone cottages were strung out for half a mile along the road, mostly on the side facing the harbor and the abandoned pier. The village was dominated by the pale, muted colors typical of the island's landscape. Only the telephone box, red as an angry boil, stood out against the gray stone cottages and the islanders' camouflage-green Land-Rovers, Wellingtons and anoraks.

"Is this all there is?" Bella asked as they parked in front of the Jura Hotel.

"It's actually rather crowded today," Gina said. A boy bicycled from the shop with a newspaper rolled under his arm, and the young fish-farmer pushed a baby's stroller along a small stretch of sidewalk. Two stout women tramped past the car, their string bags bulging with tinned food and cornflakes. The village smelled of manure, sea and baking scones.

"Good!" Bella said, with exaggerated enthusiasm. "Just the type of settlement I like."

"Barnhill's another two-hour drive. We won't be staying here, just stopping for a quick tea. You must be thirsty after all that talking."

The hotel parlor was stuffy and overheated, and after they ordered, Bella muttered about fresh air and fumbled with the window catch. Gina took pity and helped her raise the window. When she turned around a slim, boyish-looking man stood awkwardly next to the tea trolley, pretending to inspect the display.

"I saw you arrive from my window," he said in an American accent. "Since we're the only guests, I thought I'd introduce myself." He thrust out a hand and said, "Adam Frost."

His handshake was firm, but Gina thought he seemed nervous. Probably lonely, she thought, and embarrassed to be forcing himself on strangers.

Bella frowned. "Young man, stop rocking back and forth on your heels. Either go away or sit down and join us."

He gave a relieved smile and pulled over a chair. "I was hoping you'd say that."

CHAPTER 12

"Have lobster," Adam said. "I'm on expenses."

Gina looked up from the menu. "They trap it here but rarely serve it. It fetches too much in London."

"I'm buying everything they catch and I've persuaded them to set more traps."

"Whatever for?" Until that moment she had assumed he was an American academic forced into an overdue sabbatical and had therefore been suspicious. A young American had impersonated her and here was one suddenly turning up on Jura. She had not eliminated an unknown academic competitor from her list of suspects and this man certainly looked the part of the young professor. He had intelligent pale eyes, a baggy tweed jacket and a boyish shock of brown hair he was constantly sweeping back from his forehead. His playful, almost childish sense of humor reminded her of Piers's colleagues, men who became less mature and more boyish the longer they stayed at university. And he was hopeless with machinery. When the Rover refused to start, he had bumbled under the hood, becoming filthy and exasperated as Bella shouted directions. Finally she accepted his suggestion that they stay at the hotel and summon a mechanic from Islay in the morning. Beforehand, during tea, they had talked about Jura's weather, the easiest route up the Paps and the best fishing lochs. He said nothing to challenge her assumption that he was a lonely academic on holiday.

"You're not one of those clever entrepreneurs who pop up here every few months with a plan to build a holiday village or air-freight Jura lobsters to Paris?" she asked. "Most quit when they discover it's almost cheaper to fly the Frenchmen here and tie bibs around their necks."

Adam laughed and shook his head. "No, my company has rented one of the estates for a week starting Wednesday for a meeting of our board of directors. They're deciding the fate of cable television, so logically they've decided to gather in a place where there's hardly any television at all."

"We get several channels here. In my opinion the islanders watch too damn much."

"Comparing two or three channels to our cable system is like comparing a roller skate to a Rolls-Royce. No, big decisions like this call for big brains, and our directors insist on nourishing theirs with top-quality grub—lobster, salmon and venison. None of your bangers and mash. So you see, I need enough lobsters to feed eighteen big brains, their wives, husbands, girlfriends, boyfriends and camp followers. In case you're wondering, I'm a sort of advance camp follower."

She laughed. "Just like a swarm of locusts. By the time you leave there won't be an unbutchered stag, uncaught salmon or unboiled lobster for miles." She was relieved that Bella, after gorging herself at tea, had begged off dinner and turned in; and she was relieved that he came from a world of board meetings and technology, a world so foreign to hers that it was impossible to believe he was the "Baldwin" who was so interested in her literary research. It was relaxing having a silly conversation with someone her age.

"How does someone who resembles a college professor become a corporate camp follower?" she asked.

For twenty minutes he described in detail how he'd backed in and out of professions, causes, political attitudes and sets of friends. By comparison she had not done badly. She had made only one big mistake. Each of his errors, though, must have taught him something, and he seemed to have been everywhere, done everything. Life as a corporate camp follower had its advantages.

As he pressed on relentlessly, she became restless. Had she misread him? He hadn't seemed the type to thrust his biography on strangers. She wanted to stop him before he gave her reason not to like him. He would be a good antidote to Bella. She might invite him to lunch at Barnhill.

"So, after all that," she interrupted, "you're now feeding delicacies to the overfed, catering to your spoiled bosses. Shame!" She had tried to keep her tone light, but she had hit a nerve.

"Aha!" he said. " 'Spoiled bosses,' you sound like a socialist." Again he was watching her intently.

"Tell my former husband that and he'd have a heart attack." Immediately she regretted mentioning Piers. She was falling into his trap, trading intimacies. And why had she lied? Legally, they were still married.

"Oh, why is that? Who is"—he paused—"I mean, who *was* your husband?"

She sighed. He had spelled out so much of himself that she had to answer or appear rude. It was the danger with listening to someone's life history: they wanted yours in return.

"His name's Piers Baldwin," she said, praying for a blank stare.

"The name's familiar. Is he an author?"

"You're thinking of the man who wrote about the cannibalized plane passengers. Mine's a politician. He's known as Mike Baldwin."

He clicked his fingers. "I just read about him. Isn't he very leftwing? You must be appalled to find capitalist bloodsuckers camped on your doorstep."

His manner was beginning to irritate. Did he take anything seriously? "I couldn't care less if you camp here," she said sharply. "The islanders could use your money. Make sure you let them suck a lot of your blood."

He stared at his plate, making her feel, in spite of herself, that now she had to explain. "I'm sorry," she began, "but everyone assumes that because I married him I share his politics. I don't."

"Then what *are* your politics?" He was back on the offensive.

"I don't have any." Where are those lobsters? Did he order them because he knew they would take forever?

"Everyone has some political beliefs. For example, I think that . . ."

"O.K., O.K." She couldn't bear any more. "Let's say I think—no, it's more a feeling than a thinking—that, despite their shortcomings, there's something basically good about the democracies. And despite the theoretically good intentions of Communism, there's something basically evil about the Soviet Union. My husband, though he would never put it so simply, believes that the opposite is true. Does that satisfy you?"

"Political disagreements usually don't ruin a marriage."

"Oh, I knew about his politics when I married him. It was when his political career replaced his academic one that our disagreement became so important."

"Well, if what you say is true . . ."

"Of course it's true. Why should I lie to you?"

". . . then we're the good guys!" He seemed surprised, and pleased. "The newspaper article said your husband's current wife is also American. He must have a weakness for capitalist women."

"Look, I sort of lied, O.K.? We're not legally divorced, but we've been living apart for a year. I don't think of him as my husband. In fact, I try to think *and* talk about him as little as possible."

He flushed and bolted his beer. Now she was angry with herself for being so blunt. When had she started treating every man as though he were Piers? The lobsters arrived as she was formulating another apology.

The waitress bustled around the table, pouring water and rearranging the silverware, while the cook, who had carried the platter of lobsters out from the kitchen himself, hovered while Adam took the first bite. "They're slightly undercooked and light on the butter, Mr. Frost," he said. "Just the way you like them."

"That's a first," she said when he had left. "The food here is perfectly good, but I've never seen them fuss so."

There was a silence while he pretended to concentrate on his food. At last he said shyly, "Well, I think it's because we've rented the entire hotel as an annex. Perhaps we're paying too much."

"I'd say so."

"Our president insists on tight security. By leasing the hotel we can prevent strangers staying on the island."

"You're the strangers."

"Well, yes, but you see the point, don't you? Wherever we meet we rent all the rooms in the hotel, whether we need them or not. It's a security policy."

"A pretty damned wasteful one."

"Enjoying the lobster?" He was ignoring her barbs, doing his best to remain friendly.

"I insist on paying my share."

"You can't." He rocked back in his chair, grinning mischievously. "Our lease on the hotel began at noon. I'm the manager and you're my guest." He smiled. "And I won't let you pay for your room either. And if you protest too much, I'll buy you breakfast as well."

Why is he being so nice to me? she wondered. When I'm difficult, he smiles; when I'm impossible, he jokes and changes the subject. Perhaps he *is* terribly lonely?

After the waitress removed their plates, he said, "You haven't told me anything about yourself." She tensed for more questions about Piers or her personal life, but instead he said, "You mentioned earlier writing a thesis about George Orwell. Tell me more. I studied twentieth-century literature but I'm shamefully ignorant about him."

She was so relieved that for the next half hour she described Barnhill and her theories about the factual sources for *Nineteen Eighty-four*. He asked perceptive questions and was curious about her research techniques. Although no one had ever been so interested and appreciative, she did not trust him enough, yet, to recount her recent adventures, and she described Bella as an old family friend. When she finished, he said, "Care to go dancing?"

"Where do you think you are, Las Vegas? During the summer they have dances, known as ceilidhs, in the community center, but on Jura in October, believe me, there's no action."

"Bet you a steak dinner there's a dance tonight."

"It's venison here."

"Forget it then. I'd be up all night thinking of Bambi. I can see the point in hunting deer on an island like this that's overrun, but I still don't think I could bear shooting or even eating one myself, could you?"

Before she could answer, he said, "I know there's a dance tonight, because I'm paying for it. It's a present from the company, to thank everyone for putting up with the inconvenience." He leaned across the table conspiratorially and said, "If you thank someone ahead of time for being understanding, it makes it awkward for them to protest later, don't you think?"

"I think you're a clever advance camp follower. But what inconvenience? All the gillies, fishermen and drivers are going to earn nice Christmas nest eggs."

"There may be some inconvenience associated with our security requirements."

"Now you *are* sounding like a corporate mouthpiece. Why are you all so paranoid about your security?"

"We've had bomb threats, even a bombing. Several executives have been kidnapped." He paused. "And there's always blackmail."

She shook her head in disbelief. "Your biggest worry on Jura will be keeping your cars out of ditches. The islanders will haul you out, but not for love."

"Are you *sure* that's all we should worry about?" He looked at her intensely.

"Of course! But what *are* those 'security requirements'? Sounds too ominous. You should call them something else."

"Why are you so interested?"

"If I'm going to be locked up in my house all week, I want some warning."

"Nothing like that. We may ask the islanders to let us suspend the ferry for several days."

"You're going to seal us off?" She pictured herself cooped up with Bella in Barnhill, with Dawney unable to reach them. He might give up and return to London.

"Does that upset you? I wouldn't think you'd care. We'll also ask everyone to use the road between here and the estate only during certain hours. But that's not the only reason for the dance," he added quickly. "We might sponsor another one while the directors are here. Our president's wife is a maniac for local culture and folk dancing."

As they rose to leave he said, "You haven't asked me the name of the company. You don't by any chance know it already?"

"How could I?"

He stammered, "Well, I thought one of the islanders might have told you."

She shrugged. "I don't know anything about American business. Unless it's IBM or Coca-Cola I won't recognize it."

He stopped in the hotel doorway and, facing her, said, "It's TropicAmerican."

She shrugged again. "It sounds vaguely familiar, like the rest of those conglomerate names . . ."

"How do you know we're a conglomerate?"

"It's that kind of name. Isn't there a TransAmerica too, and a RapidAmerica, and a . . ."

"You really haven't heard of us, have you?"

"You have this offensive habit of being surprised that I'm telling the truth." Why, she wondered, had he sounded more relieved than hurt? "Are you all that bad? What do you do? Exploit South African workers? Sell tainted baby formula?"

"Nothing like that," he said quickly. "We're mostly a family entertainment company. I guess we're not such a household word over here."

As they strolled onto the hotel lawn she said, "And you never told me which estate you've leased. Or is keeping that secret another 'security requirement'?"

"We've rented Ardlussa."

"My God, I lease Barnhill from them, it's on their property."

He laughed nervously and gave her shoulder a playful squeeze. "I know. I guess you could say that for the next two weeks we own you."

As they crossed the lawn he stopped to finger the fronds of one of the palm trees that grew in front of the hotel.

"How strange to find these here in Scotland," he said.

"They're not uncommon," Gina explained. "It's damp here on the west coast but it rarely freezes. There used to be tropical plants on the south coast of Jura. Atlantic currents brought the seeds from the West Indies."

"It's almost a West Indian night," Adam agreed. "Cloudless, a full moon reflecting on the water, a balmy breeze and a palm tree. Now that it's dark you can almost imagine the hills covered with lush vegetation. If the weather holds, our guys will feel at home. We might even have the pub serve rum punches."

She ignored this and slipped her arm through his. It was a gesture she liked: casual enough to mean nothing, yet under some circumstances it could mean everything.

She had never seen the village so bustling. On most evenings the street was deserted and windows glowed with the arctic-blue light of the islanders' televisions. A few cars, at most, would be parked near the hotel, with a lone teenager standing in the red call box. But tonight, cars lined both sides of the road and whenever the pub door swung open there was a blast of shouts and laughter. A cluster of children stood outside the only store, surrounded by a litter of empty boxes and torn cellophane. Lights blazed in the windows of the community hall. It reminded her of one of the Sunday newspaper puzzles—"How many things are wrong with this picture?"

"Funny," she said. "Usually the store is never open this late."

"I paid them to," he said, guiding her inside. "TropicAmerican is sponsoring an hour of drinks at the pub and I thought it only fair to give the children a treat. They're getting free candy and cakes, up to a reasonable limit."

Simply walking into the store usually made Gina's teeth ache. There was hardly a thing for sale, aside from detergent and toilet paper, that wasn't heavily dosed with sugar. Everywhere you bumped into trays of caramels, jellies and licorice. The shelves were stacked with chocolates, Danish butter cookies, hard candies and cans of baked beans and fruit in syrup.

Adam selected a fudge caramel from an open box and handed it to Gina with a flourish. "I always give my dates candy before the big dance."

Before she could decline it, he had detached one of the cellophane bags of marshmallows that hung from a rack like a bag of plasma. He shoved the marshmallows under her arm and was reaching for a box of Smarties when she dropped everything on the floor. Then she picked up the marshmallows, slowly and deliberately putting them back.

"Aha," he said lightly, "so you don't like sweets either. Good, neither do I. In fact, I have an ulterior motive."

"So you said. You're bribing them to be nice to your bosses, and you're wasting your money because the people on this island are friendly enough anyway."

"Aha! There it is again: 'the bosses'! Now you're sounding more like Mike Baldwin's wife."

"Not funny."

"There's only one boss," he said quickly, "and he and his wife are obsessed with security. That's one of the many things I'm supposed to be doing here, you know, 'skirmishing,' making sure there's nothing and no one on Jura to threaten them. I'm hoping the kids and their parents will be so grateful to TropicAmerican for all this free drink and candy that they won't stone our motorcades, and the Duchess—that's what we call the president's wife—can sleep without fearing an attack of armed locals. Don't you think I'm brilliant?"

She looked at him in bewilderment. "I can't decide if you're serious."

"Good. Neither can I."

His dance was a flop. As she came in, Gina saw women and girls on wooden folding chairs along the wall, whispering and giggling. Children raced through the room as if at a birthday party, and young men stood in huddles talking loudly and commuting to bottles of beer and whiskey hidden outside. As was usual at local dances, one of the distillery workers had dressed in tartans and was playing reels on the bagpipes. These alternated with pop tunes coming from a battered victrola. All this was the same, yet the atmosphere was different. Perhaps, she thought, it was because only half the usual number had come. Or was it that the women had not baked scones and cakes for the intermission tea?

"Not much of a turnout," he said. "Why isn't anyone dancing?" He looked round sheepishly.

"The men are drunk on your whiskey and the kids bilious on your candy. Are you surprised they're not enthusiastic about reels?"

"I suppose you're right. Well, *we* might as well dance."

He was a smooth and practiced dancer. She became dizzy and clutched his hand tightly, and when he at last danced closer she pressed her cheek lightly against his. After nine years of Piers, she knew she was too easily excited. But she liked this man, his mixture of playfulness and seriousness. He had tolerated her and kept his good humor. He reminded her, but only a little, of Eric.

"How long are you staying at the hotel?" she asked.

"Until Wednesday. Then we move up to Ardlussa."

"Have you seen Barnhill yet?"

He stopped dancing and faced her. "No, but I'd like to."

"It's a big house, four bedrooms. You could stay until Wednesday, unless you need to be here in Craighouse."

He scanned the hall. Most people had drifted away. The victrola stopped and the piper began again. "I think I've done more than enough here, don't you?"

She liked him for that. "Well?"

He pushed back his shock of hair. "I'd love to come. There's not much for me to do in town; that's probably why I engineered all this nonsense." He broke into a wide grin and held out his hand. "I accept with pleasure. I'll drive up tomorrow afternoon."

"Be warned, there's even less to do at Barnhill, unless you're self-sufficient."

"But you'll be there and so will Miss Stevens, our chaperone. And I can read your thesis."

Before she could decide how to answer, a booming American voice behind her said, "Mind if I cut in, old buddy?" Adam's face froze. She spun around and faced an American who reminded her of the beefy Texan oilmen she had often seen boarding planes for Aberdeen, former high school athletes gone to seed. The American had his arm around old Malcolm, who was grinning stupidly, drunk on Adam's beer.

"When did you get here?" Adam asked.

"An hour ago."

"How? It's too late for the ferry."

The beefy American made a circular motion with his index finger, indicating a helicopter. "No shortage of landing fields here, old buddy. Parked the whirlybird next to the school and stumbled onto your party. My old buddy Malcolm here"—he squeezed the old man's shoulders hard enough to make him wince—"has been giving me a swell briefing." He looked around the room. "This the disco?"

"I'm afraid I'm too tired to dance anymore," Gina said.

"That's all right, sweetie. My old buddy here is probably a better dancer, real light on his feet." As he turned to leave, his arm still wrapped around Malcolm's shoulders, she saw that his left earlobe was red and swollen.

CHAPTER 13

"Don't you find it curious," Bella asked, "that yesterday your young man was hopeless under the bonnet, yet this morning he pushes this, tweaks that, and now my old Rover is running a treat?"

"He's not 'my young man.'"

"Well, I do. I find it very curious."

Gina slammed on the brakes and the car stopped inches from one of the gates that prevented sheep wandering between fields. Bella pitched forward, smashing her knee against the glove compartment.

"Another gate, I'm afraid," Gina said. "Do you mind?"

The old woman limped from the car and ran her hand up the post, feeling for the hook. As Gina drove through the open gate and rattled over the cattle grid, she had a sudden urge to accelerate, leaving Bella behind. Instead, she waited until the older woman struggled back.

"That's the last gate before Barnhill," she said. "The house is over there." She pointed to where the dirt track vanished into the mist. The visibility today was poor, the weather more typical of October. Low-flying clouds shuttled across the sky from west to east, squirting rain. Gina had been turning the wipers on and off ever since leaving Craighouse.

Bella unfolded her spyglass and trained it on the rock-capped hills to their left, the same hills where Gina had stalked and been stalked by the soft-voiced Irish boy. Would he return, now that she had?

"Aren't you ever lonely here?" Bella asked. "Deserts like this are splendid for short stays, but I could never stand them for more than a few months, particularly if I was alone. I don't imagine you have many curious natives stopping by?"

"Only old Malcolm and his wife from up the road." Speaking of Malcolm reminded her of the revolver. It was still in her shoulder bag. How had he come by it? In Britain handguns were strictly regulated. And why give it to her? Did he really expect the poachers to return? She would question him when he was sober.

Bella lay down her telescope and sighed. "Eric must have been going through a very pessimistic patch to shut himself away here."

"A hundred and eighty people live 'shut away' here, most very happily."

"I'm sure you're right, dear, but they're not George Orwell, are they? For him, coming here had to be a negative vote. Think of it: his wife had just died, there'd been such a terrible slaughter everywhere during the war and now it seemed that the main result was that left-wing dictatorships were going to replace right-wing ones. So he closeted himself here, away from any reminders of what a mess we'd all made of things. Pessimism must have brought him to this island, and prompted him to write that pessimistic book. Don't forget how it ended: 'He had won the victory over himself. He loved Big Brother.' There's your proof of Eric's pessimism." She turned to Gina. "You weren't drawn here by similar feelings, were you?"

"Point your telescope into that valley," Gina said, "and you'll see Barnhill." The house appeared peaceful and undisturbed, except for marks left in the meadow by Piers's helicopter. First thing tomorrow she would set Adam to work mowing the field, obliterating them.

When they were a hundred yards from the Barnhill gate, a stray ewe darted in front of the Rover. It raced down the middle of the track, feinting left and right, too terrified to choose an escape. Gina sounded the horn and it ran even faster until finally slamming into the closed gate. Gina bounded out and grabbed its horns. Straddling it, her legs locked around its head, she steered it into a field.

"I think I'll walk from here," Bella said. "The drive has left me a trifle queasy and I'd enjoy the fresh air."

Gina drove on alone and parked behind the house. Before going inside she stopped to count her chickens. Euen was wrong: there were four missing, not two. Was Malcolm snitching them?

From outside, the house appeared undisturbed. Nevertheless, she paused briefly after opening the front door, sniffing and listening as she had last week. There were no strange noises, and no odors because a moist cross draft was sweeping through the front hall. She cursed herself. She had left a window open in the kitchen.

The kitchen floor was slippery with blood. The first thing she saw was two of her chickens lying in the sink: plucked, bled and decapitated. Then she noticed the unconscious teenage boy, strapped to a kitchen chair. His naked body was as pale, bony and death-white as the chickens. It was a body that had never seen the sun, never been properly fed or exercised.

Gina shook his shoulders violently, shouting, "Alive? Are you alive?" He moaned through swollen lips, vomited and then slumped forward again. As she wiped him clean with a wet dish towel she noticed his legs. Then, for the first time, she screamed.

A line of six evenly spaced red welts crowned with blisters started at each knee and marched up his thighs, converging on his groin, halting an inch from his line of red pubic hair.

A scratchy voice behind her said, "Pitiful bloody specimen, isn't he? Another inch, though, and he'll tell the truth."

She whirled around and faced a shrunken man wearing a filthy red beret. He gripped a revolver in one hand and, in the other, the metal poker she used for stirring coals in the Aga. "You wouldn't know from looking at him," he said. "But he's a tough lad." He laid the poker on the table and it sizzled a burn into the surface.

"Rise and shine, Charlie lad, visiting hours," he said. The boy groaned, but kept his eyes tightly shut. The old man drew a glass of water, dashed it in the boy's face and then circled his chair, inspecting him with a critical eye, like a physician preparing to explain a case to a bedside circle of medical students. He rubbed his hands together. "Like to know what he's said?"

She nodded, too horrified to speak.

Keeping his revolver trained on her, he grabbed the long-handled feather duster from over the sink and brushed the tips of its feathers

across the boy's blistered skin. "I tied him down while he was unconscious from the blow." He tickled the blister just above the boy's
left knee. "Before this first one he said, 'Bugger you, old man.' So I
gave him a quick tap of the poker, and he told me his name was
Charlie O'Paddy, or some such name. Said he was a fisherman
who'd had a squabble with his mates. They dumped him here.
Teach him not to be Bolshie."

He moved the feathers to the next blister. "Here we made prog-
ress. He admitted being an IRA lad who'd been dropped on the
island for a training course. Said they use the deserted west coast all
the time. That was such an outrageous lie that I gave him two quick
ones." He made a hissing, sizzling sound through yellowed teeth and
dragged the duster up the boy's leg. "At last, some real results. As I
marched north, coming closer to his fortress here"—he tickled the
boy's scrotum—"he became more sociable.

"Now it seemed he came here with a mate to kill someone. His
first, an IRA graduation exercise, and a favor to an American who
briefed him in Belfast.

"But here the pain wore off and he lied again. Instead of the
truth, that he'd been ordered to murder me, he insisted that he was
sent to kill the woman living here." He pointed the duster at her.
"Then his story became ridiculous. Shocking what the young think
you'll believe if you're past sixty. He claimed to have liked you so
much—and without knowing you—that he missed on purpose and
did a bunk on his mates. 'I saved her fuckin' life,' he said. 'And now
she'll fuckin' well save mine.' Ha!

"I told him there'd be nothing to save if he didn't stop lying." He
tickled him again with the duster. "Now you're just in time for the
moment of truth."

"He's not lying!" She noticed the boy's head moving in a slow
circle as he regained consciousness. He *was* only a boy. A red-headed
Irish runt who had refused to murder. "Someone *did* shoot at me!
And they *did* miss. Afterwards a young Irish voice called my name."

"A proper little Irish saint, is he?" He poked the boy's balls.
"Such a saint, he won't need these." He stood in front of the boy,

facing Gina. "I'm old, but not senile," he snapped. "You're both working for Ekman."

"Who's Ekman?"

"You know bloody well! First you smoke me out with your cunning query. Then I stupidly trust you with the name of the pub. Next your friend Ekman sends his Yank to kill me. Save me the trip here. Very considerate.

"But old Dawney is too quick for Ekman's pretty young Yank. He tips the tables; tips them right bloody over. Now Ekman knows he's got to catch me here. Sends Charlie lad to wait until I put my head on the block, so he can chop it like those chickens. He ate the first two, by the way; the ones in the sink are mine."

"Wrong. Mine." She wanted to needle him and postpone Charlie's "moment of truth." She was more terrified of seeing the boy burned than of what might happen to her.

"But again Dawney tips the table bloody over," he said. "And this time it lands on Charlie lad. Everyone's expecting Dawney to arrive on the ferry. Instead he pays a fisherman twenty quid to bring him over and catches your friend asleep."

"Where's his weapon?" Gina asked. "If he'd come to kill you he'd be armed."

"Good idea! Let's find out where he's hid it." He jabbed the boy's chest. "C'mon, lad, time!" He picked up the poker and thrust it into the fiery heart of the coal box. "Then again, pet, perhaps he thought he'd find his weapon here. Look around. Your kitchen's a regular chamber of horrors. What with those lovely knives and cleavers, the roomy sink and this handy fire."

Gina jumped in front of the boy. "He can't tell you anything more. He's innocent!"

"Innocent? Then why did he attack me?"

"Perhaps you scared him."

Dawney aimed the revolver at her stomach. "And why was he here all cozy, warmed by a fire, feasting on your birds?" He yanked out the poker. Its tip was glowing. "Now he'll tell me about Blair's notebooks. You must want them, too, or you've found them. Why else are you on his island, in his house?"

"You wrote me about them," Gina said quickly, "but I don't know what they are or where they are. That boy probably doesn't even know who Orwell was."

"If he can't tell me about Blair's notebooks he can still sign a confession accusing Ekman. That'd be worth something." He had placed a pen and a dated blank sheet of notepaper on the kitchen table, facing the boy. "CONFESSION" was written across the top in block letters.

"All right, pet," he said, gesturing with the revolver. "Step back. Not your turn, yet."

She remembered Malcolm's revolver: still in her shoulder bag and still loaded. She had dropped the bag when she saw the chickens. She glanced down. Three steps away. She edged around the table and bent down. Suddenly Dawney kicked the bag out of reach.

"You shouldn't look down, pet," he said. "I always watch the eyes, they tell the story." With his wet eyes fixed on hers, he rummaged inside and found Malcolm's pistol. "Was there a bullet in here for old Dawney?" He flipped open the chamber and six shells clattered onto the linoleum. "I'll have two confessions now," he said, "first his, then yours."

"Dawney!" Bella's voice echoed through the room. She was standing in the door, far enough for her failing eyes to see him. Gina blocked her view of the naked boy.

"Very convenient, you being here already," she said, squinting up and down, making doubly sure he was the genuine article. "Remarkable! You haven't aged at all. You looked seventy when we met in Paris, and you still do, except that by now you must *be* seventy, mustn't you?" Her eyes lingered on his head and she wrinkled her nose. "That's not the same nasty beret, is it?"

"No . . . no . . . of course not . . ." he stammered. "Buy a new one every few years." He was visibly bewildered, not prepared for Bella, not sure who she was or how she knew his name and so much about him.

"You probably don't recognize me since, unlike you, I've aged considerably." She thrust out her hand and approached him. "Bella Stevens."

"Yes! Yes! The lady explorer. You were there! In the Scribe bar with Blair. We spoke only briefly, but one remembers meeting someone famous."

"I'm not famous any longer. My audience is dead."

"What are you doing *here?*" He looked from her to Gina to the boy in the chair. He sounded perplexed, unsure what to do or whom to trust.

Bella was confident and commanding. "Why, I've come to see *you!* Discover why you've suddenly popped up. Why you've been so infernally mysterious. Imagine saying you'll arrive *sometime* this month and then 'make yourself known.' I'm relying on you to tell us who's been persecuting this poor girl and stealing her thesis, shooting at her and then impersonating her." She stopped when she noticed the naked boy. "Who's that?"

"One of the enemy."

She saw the revolver in his hand. "Good! You've come armed. We may need that before we're finished. A kind and brave man, a dear friend of mine, was brutally assaulted. That can't go unpunished. I think—no, I'm sure!—everything involves those schoolboy games you and Eric played in Paris."

Dawney stood immobile, his face a mask, as Bella and Gina told him everything. When they finished, he laid his revolver on the table and fell into a chair, his back to the boy. Gina held a cold towel to Charlie's forehead, reviving him gently.

She covered his groin with a dishcloth and dabbed ointment on the blisters. They were not deep; mild second-degree burns. By mistake or design Dawney had only touched him lightly with the fire iron. The boy would heal without hospital attention.

"We've told you a great deal, Dawney," Bella said. "Now it's your turn. You might start with what happened after I left the Scribe."

"What happened," he said, regaining some of his confidence, "is that after you ran off to Germany for your front-line thrills, Blair came to his bloody senses and finally agreed that Colonel Ekman had to pay for his Spanish crimes. That's what bloody happened!"

"Ekman . . . Ekman . . . Colonel Ekman . . ." Bella shook her head. "Doesn't ring a bell."

"Colonel Peter Ekman. A bloody Kraut who'd emigrated to America as a boy."

"Less of the 'bloody,' Dawney. And you'll have to elaborate if we're to trust one another." She turned to Gina. "What would you think, dear, of a little informal alliance?"

The idea repelled her, but she nodded.

He told them about meeting "Baldwin" in the pub, and that he had given him the details of Ekman's betrayal. "There's one little secret I kept from my sweet-smelling Yank," he concluded. "But since we're allies I'll tell you."

He leaned across the table and, blowing his cheesy breath onto Gina's face, said in a stage whisper, "I loathed that fucking Eric Blair."

CHAPTER 14

"What did she say, old buddy?" Hacker had cornered Adam in the front door of the Jura Hotel.

"Who?"

"That bitch."

"Fuck off, Stan."

"Be cool, old buddy. Stan knows what you're doing. We both want to protect Victor."

"So?"

"So, we cooperate."

"Victor didn't tell me to cooperate; not with you or anyone."

"If I know Victor, he didn't *tell* you anything."

He tried stepping around Hacker, but the big man put up his arms and blocked the doorway. "You driving up there to fuck it out of her?"

"What makes you think I'm going up there?"

"My buddy Malcolm. She tells him, he tells me. Pays to have buddies. Hope you do fuck it out of her. If you don't, I'll beat it out of her."

"You beat anything out of her and the only people cheering will be journalists. They have a lively press here. Victor can't buy them. He'd be happy too, he likes that kind of publicity."

"Fuck Victor."

"Yes, that's what you'd be doing." He paused. Had he heard Hacker correctly—had he actually said "Fuck Victor"?

"You quit or something?" Adam asked.

"No, I'm just not a suck-butt. To protect Victor, sometimes you got to say 'Fuck Victor.' "

Adam tried pushing Hacker out of the way.

"Move it, Stan, I'm late."

"And I know what you're late for. Last chance: we allies or not?"

"Not."

"Too bad. You don't get laid."

"What does that mean?"

"This." He dangled an oily metal object. When Adam grabbed for it, he yanked it away. "Your car won't start without it. Don't look so surprised. Malcolm saw you under the hood of her car. Under her hood? That's where you'd like to be, isn't it?"

"I'll pay someone to . . ."

"Do what? Drive you up there? Two hours up, then two hours back alone in the dark? It's too late." He dropped his arms so Adam could pass. "I'll be in the bar. You come when you want to talk about the bitch."

Dawney said, "Blair was an upper-class Eton twit who holidayed as a worker for thrills and to grub material."

"His family was impoverished middle class," Gina snapped. "He went to Eton on a scholarship." He had been ranting for some time now, venting years of rage, and Gina had let him talk. But this was a twisted fact, a lie. It could not go unchallenged.

"There's no such thing as a truly impoverished gentleman. The poor starve because they're poor; that doesn't happen to the Blairs of this world. Someone always rescues them and they always escape, leaving someone like me behind.

"Barcelona shows what happened to the Dawneys and the Blairs. Dawney risked everything he possessed: his health and his talent, and Ekman stole them both. Dawney and his wife—his *Spanish* wife, the daughter of a tram conductor—were tortured. But Blair and his fine English wife could afford the Continental Hotel, and during the day they avoided capture by dining in expensive restaurants. They escaped using exit visas provided by the British Consul, probably an Old Etonian. Would he have done the same for Dawney and his beautiful, Spanish wife? Not bloody likely!"

Bella interrupted. "Dawney, you're welcome to your opinions, wrongheaded as they are. But I fail to see what they have to do with our problem."

"They have every goddamned thing to do with it! The less you interrupt, the sooner you'll understand. In Spain I never told Blair how I felt, because I hoped he might use his fancy education and friends to help me."

"Perhaps he tried," Gina said defiantly. "He tried rescuing other comrades from prison."

"What's important is that he failed. In Paris I chummed up again because I needed his connections and reputation. I gave him a chance to atone for Spain. I had no proof Ekman had become an American colonel. Who would believe me? But if Blair pointed one of his ugly, bony fingers at Ekman, everyone would listen. Others who knew the truth might come forward. He'd be exposed, ruined, perhaps imprisoned if he was still working for the Soviets.

"I know what you're asking." He paused and scanned the kitchen. Bella was sitting at the table watching as he paced around the room. Gina was ministering to Charlie's burns. "Blair would have loved that," he said. "Charlie lad set out to kill you, but now you're more interested in his wounds than in your friends.

"What you're asking yourselves," he continued, "is why didn't Dawney just kill Ekman and be done with it? The answer is that I was terrified of being caught. First Stalin's lads in Spain had had a go at me, then the Gestapo in Paris. I didn't fancy ending my life in some capitalist nick. That would have been a grand victory for Ekman. No, I had a different dream: I was free, painting and waking up every morning in an elegant suburb to the cheery thought of Ekman locked in some miserable prison. For that to come true, I needed Blair. And that was why, after you left the Scribe, you old pussy, I indulged him, smiling and laughing while he bored me with that crap about Hemingway. When Blair finally got to Ekman, he was bloody useless. From the way he interrogated me, you'd think that *I'd* tortured Ekman. I had to repeat every detail of Ekman's crimes. If I scrambled a date or confused a name, he pounced. His obsession with details was obscene. 'What's more important,' I said, 'people or history?' 'Inseparable,' he said. What rot! You could tell by his answer that he had never suffered, had never ached for justice.

" 'I must be convinced,' he said, 'before I write anything; before I accuse him publicly and ruin his career. Justice seven years after a crime is a trickier business than justice seven hours or even seven weeks later.' "

"Dawney," Bella said, "please spare us your imitation of his accent."

Dawney continued in his own voice. "As soon as he described his plan I knew he'd be no more use to me then than he'd been in Spain, probably less. First he puts you up to telling Ekman our addresses—"

"Only Eric's," Bella interrupted indignantly. "Not yours."

"And then he expects me to hang about, and for what? For Ekman to kill me so Blair could be certain I was telling the truth? Bloody marvelous, wasn't it?

" 'Give me a few days, Dawney,' he said." Dawney fell back to mimicking his accent.

" 'In a few days, mate, we'll be dead, thanks to you,' I said. 'Besides, I have a friend in SHAEF who says Ekman's leaving for Cologne.'

" 'Then I'll follow him.'

" 'You won't be alive.'

" 'Less of the melodrama. He's an American colonel, not an American gangster. You'll have to trust me for a few days.'

" 'I trust you to do fuck bloody all!'

" 'You haven't any choice,' he said. You'd think he was the laird and I was the crofter begging for another acre.

"Oh, but, ladies and Charlie boy, old Dawney *did* have a choice. Though I wasn't letting Blair know. That same morning my SHAEF friend had slipped me a memorandum. At oh-nine-hundred hours the next morning Ekman would accompany a delegation of

American politicians on a tour of what was delicately described as 'the former German facility at Ivry.' It was a 'facility' I knew well.

"So I pretended that Blair had convinced me. I slid off my chair, bowed, salaamed and tipped my hat." At this, Dawney yanked off his red beret. Gina gasped. His bald crown was deformed by a circle of pink scar tissue.

"Like that, do you, pet?" Dawney shouted triumphantly. "That's the Gestapo. Ekman did the same thing to what's inside."

He replaced the beret and said, "I left Blair puffing grandly on a cigarette, humming a ditty and drumming his fingers on the zinc tabletop. He thought he'd won, thought he had all the time in the bloody world to handle Ekman in his gentlemanly way. But the clock was ticking, and after Ivry, it was ticking as bloody fast for him as for Ekman.

"At oh-eight hundred hours I was at Ivry cutting my way through the barbed wire blocking the entrance to Ekman's tourist attraction. Christ, what a dreary pesthole that Ivry was! A squalid little river port outside Paris with a single attraction: some ancient fortifications that had once protected the city. And underneath those walls . . ." Dawney stopped and wiggled his stubby fingers at Gina, imitating, she imagined, lines of worms crawling underground.

"Underneath the walls," he continued, "was a labyrinth of underground galleries and passages connecting with similar ones elsewhere in Paris. During the war the Nazis converted these tunnels into torture chambers and prisons, and for several weeks I was their 'guest.' When the city was liberated hundreds of Germans fled into them and hid underground, eating rats and refusing to believe the battle was over. Months later they were still being flushed out at gunpoint, which explains why the entrances were blocked with barbed wire: to keep the curious from being attacked by the vermin nesting inside.

"Once I had hacked through the wire I hurried into the central Ivry passage and trained my electric torch on its walls. Everything was just as I'd remembered: stone walls seeping mud and water, high ceilings lost in darkness, pools of fetid water, splashing rats and fluttering bats. Some of the small corridors were dead ends; others fed into even smaller corridors leading to walled-off rooms with grated windows the size of bloody envelopes. The Germans threw us into these rooms and then bricked up the doors. There was no food, no light, and nothing to drink except water licked off walls. Some of us betrayed our comrades in hope of being led outside and executed. That was the reward."

Dawney stopped pacing and stood over Gina. "What do you think, pet? If Blair and I had shared quarters at Ivry, would he have ached more for truth or justice?"

Before she could answer he went on. "I heard Ekman's voice echoing down the corridor before I saw the yellow eyes of the congressmen's torches and heard them cursing the cold and splashing into puddles. I'd bundled up, because I knew the climate. Within ten minutes you shivered. Thirty minutes later your clothes were damp. Imagine how you felt after thirty days.

"Ekman was saying, 'The Germans locked prisoners in these rooms until they died. Think of it! Men, women, even children, imprisoned without food, blankets, light or hope. Living as long as their bodies could endure the hunger and cold, and their souls the horror that their tormentors were other human beings. Or were they? Was there *really* anyone human here besides these wretched prisoners?'

"I realized then that Ekman's tour was more than a macabre titillation for the congressmen. It had a serious purpose: to persuade them to support a strict and vengeful occupation of Germany. My former torturer was now my avenging angel.

"Following him deeper into the main tunnel were about thirty people: the half dozen congressmen and their aides, a military contingent from SHAEF, members of the French Resistance who, like me, had survived Ivry, an interpreter and a squad of MPs, presumably to protect everyone from the crazed Germans who devoured the unwary.

"When they passed my hiding place I fell into step and flicked on my torch. I was one more light, another dark silhouette among many. I quickly flashed my torch across the group. For an instant, caught in my spotlight, was that familiar face, frozen, expressionless. How could Blair doubt that he was the same man we knew in Spain?

"I edged my way through the group, homing on the familiar voice now indignantly describing familiar tortures. 'As we entered the tunnel,' he said, 'I pointed out a small brick building on the left. It was once a French army bakery, but during the war the German army used it to bake people. The German "bakers" crammed a prisoner into a metal-lined wooden box, then hung it from iron hooks over a hot oven. As the box became hotter, the prisoner twisted and turned, desperate to escape. If he tried standing, he burned flesh off the soles of his feet. He grabbed for the overhead hooks and incinerated his fingers. He arched his back and his hair burst into flames and his scalp melted. But the Germans were humane. They kept the fires low enough so they could hoist a prisoner from a box for questioning. The walls of the bakery echoed with the screams of human beings begging other human beings to release them from this agonizing slow death. What kind of people could stand there, listening impassively, even taking pleasure from such agony?'

"Here Ekman paused dramatically, and said, 'Now do you see the danger of Germany?' He then pleaded for a long, strict and vigilant German occupation. 'We quarantine sick people until they are well,' he thundered. 'We must be willing to do the same to the Germans.'

"When Ekman stopped, there was applause from the French. They are always very realistic about Germans. For the moment I had an urge to join the applause and scream, 'Good for you, Ekman!' "

Dawney stopped and wiggled the scarred, yellowed fingers on his right hand. "My mates at the pub think I got these from careless smoking. Ha! Truth is, I grabbed for the hooks." He pointed to his beret. "This is another souvenir of the bakery. They hauled me out for a quizzing just before the old gray stuff spewed out! Next morning, before they could fire the ovens, Ivry was liberated. What a bloody charmed life I lead!

"Anyway, by this time the politicians were shivering and muttering about double pneumonia. Suddenly they cut short the tour.

Thirty electric torches about-faced and pointed home, everyone stampeding toward sunlight and clean air, splashing through puddles and tripping over suspicious piles of rubbish, the remains of French patriots. Everyone, that is, except Ekman.

"I had jammed my pistol into his neck and whispered, 'Shut off your torch or die.' Blair would have criticized this as 'melodramatic,' but it was bloody effective. For several minutes we stood in the dark, silently watching the other lights grow dimmer, hearing the echoes grow fainter. Finally I flicked on my torch and marched him deeper into the labyrinth of narrowing corridors and perspiring walls.

"I shoved him into a small cell and ordered him to squat on the dirt floor, hands over his head. My torch was trained on him, blinding him. Over his head were names and prayers scrawled in charcoal by dying prisoners. The dripping water had made them illegible. In front was a heap of ashes from one of the small fires that we prisoners, like prehistoric cavemen, built to warm ourselves.

"I let him enjoy the atmosphere before shining the torch on my face and asking him why I shouldn't kill him. I preferred he spend his last minutes believing he might live, begging for his life.

"He swore I was mistaken. He didn't know me; his name wasn't Ekman. I cocked the pistol and he admitted everything. He screamed that the MPs would return when he was discovered missing. If I freed him now I might escape.

"I pointed the pistol at his nose. Now he ordered me not to shoot. He was trying to dominate me, re-create the atmosphere of that Spanish jail.

"I took a step closer and at last he begged for his life. Now everything was perfect, precisely as imagined." Dawney made a little kissing noise, like a chef pleased by a tasty sauce. "He was suffering, terrified, and would die knowing who killed him and why. Most important, I could escape. His murder would be blamed on renegade Germans.

"Yet, at the moment of triumph, I felt flat, depressed." Dawney circled the kitchen table as he spoke, pacing faster and faster as if depicting the accelerating revolutions of his brain as he faced Ekman. Gina found herself swiveling her head to track him, like a spectator at a tennis match, not wanting to lose sight of him, or show him her back.

"My eyes went to those dissolving charcoal names on the wall," he said. "And it came to me that my justice would be similar: fast-fading and soon forgotten. Ekman's death would be an instant; his suffering brief. Mine would be endless. Again I wanted what I'd always wanted: for him to live as long as I did, but humiliated, stripped of everything. Blair *was* right. I had no choice. I needed him.

"Thinking of Blair gave me a brilliant idea. As I closed in, I told Ekman I was acting with the approval of several of the comrades he had betrayed in Barcelona, among them Eric Blair. We had drawn lots for the honor of confronting him. Then I moved closer. I wanted his wound to be superficial, but momentarily crippling. After firing I would feign panic and flee, leaving Ekman to chase down Blair. Soon enough he would have had his proof that Ekman was dangerous."

"But suppose he killed Eric!" Bella exclaimed.

"Would have served him right. Taught him to believe old Dawney. Even better, his murder would have prompted a thorough investigation. Ekman would have been arrested."

"How could you be sure?"

Dawney giggled. "Some anonymous letters would have assisted the police in their inquiries. I wouldn't have let Blair die unavenged. Luckily, none of this was necessary, because Ekman himself unexpectedly rewrote the script, improving it!

"While I was maneuvering, deciding where to wing him, juggling the revolver in one hand and the torch in the other, he leapt up and slammed me against a wall. The torch flew from my hand, crashing into the far wall. Now the room was dark. He wrestled me down, covering my body with his, pinning my arms, grabbing for the revolver. He found it, still clutched in my right hand. I held on and we rolled through the ashes and dried excrement. His knees were pumping like pistons, pounding into my stomach, then my thighs, searching for my groin. I could have fired, but I was afraid of hitting myself or missing him. Then the bullet might ricochet off the stone walls, perhaps killing me.

"But he'd feasted on American butter and chocolate while I'd been fed by the Nazis. My strength was ebbing and my grip on the revolver slipping with every second. I had to risk a ricochet. I jerked the revolver from his grasp and squeezed the trigger. The bullet ripped into my upper thigh. I screamed and rolled away.

"The sound was deafening, as if a shell had exploded in the tiny cell. Ekman was stunned. Was I dead? Wounded? Did I still have the revolver? Would I fire again? He could not be sure, so he ran. I froze, listening as he stumbled out of the cell, then kicked and slapped the walls as he searched for the main tunnel. When the noise ceased, I swept the ground until I found the torch. I turned it on and inspected my wound. It was perfect: the flesh wound for which every line soldier prays. I could retire from the front with honor. And with the comforting knowledge that now Ekman would go for Blair's jugular and Blair, once he saw my wound and heard my explanation, would take the offensive against Ekman.

"An hour later, caked with dirt and dripping blood, I burst into Blair's room at the Scribe. 'How's this for melodrama?' I said. 'Now do you believe that Ekman is dangerous?' "

"I limped into his bathroom. He followed and dressed my wound. I wanted my blood to be smeared all over him.

"He reacted as I'd hoped: horrified and outraged, and guilty he hadn't taken my warning seriously. I told him I was fleeing Paris, leaving Ekman to him. He repeated his promise to follow him to Cologne. He had no choice. He had too huge a conscience, and too much of my blood on his hands."

"Your blood, hell!" Gina shouted. "You slunk back to England, leaving them to kill one another."

"Yes! But each knew the other was dangerous and felt justified in killing the other in self-defense. Fair fight, I say."

Bella spoke up. "No! Eric was unarmed. Hemingway tried to force a revolver on him, but he refused it."

Gina glared at Dawney. "You bastard! You set them up to fight a duel."

CHAPTER 15

Hacker was drunk and smiling like a beauty queen. "Glad you came, old buddy," he shouted. "Have a beer, beer and shot, whatever you want." He leaned across the table and slapped a chair with his palm, indicating where Adam should sit.

Instead, Adam slid in right beside him, so he was facing the bar and other customers rather than Hacker. The pub was a small, smoky room attached to the hotel, but with its own entrance. The atmosphere was vaguely Scandinavian: blond wood tables, a scrubbed floor and homey curtains that were usually closed. Someone placed two pints and two drams of whiskey in front of them and said, "Cheers."

"Once they hear you're from TropicAmerican," Hacker said, "you can't stop them buying. Must be the only place on earth we're popular. I've made lots of buddies real quick."

"We've already been somewhat generous with them."

"Oh, is that it?" He looked disappointed.

"Stan, I need my car. I have to be mobile. Victor'd have a fit if he knew . . ."

Hacker tossed an oily handkerchief onto the table. Inside was the missing part. "Car won't run without it, right?"

"Right."

"Thought so. Here." He pushed it over to Adam.

"Stan, I can't promise to . . ."

He waved his hand as if batting a fly. "Shit, you don't have to *promise* anything, just have a drink with your old buddy." He gargled the whiskey, then swallowed it with a loud gulp.

Adam examined the part. "What is it?"

"Damned if I know. Reached in and unscrewed the first thing I touched. That what you did to her car?"

"Yes."

"You don't know diddly-shit about cars either, right?" Adam nodded. "Nor me. Hate the fuckers, nothing but problems. I like copters." He made the rotor motion with his index finger. "See, we got a lot in common; both hate cars and both love action—which is the big reason we both love Victor."

"Action?"

"Sure. You know, excitement . . . movement . . . change . . ." He gave up searching for the perfect word. "You know what I mean. Only difference is, I've had the real thing, but you still want it. Real bad, too. I figure that's why you don't like me: pure envy. That what you figure?" He drained another pint.

"No."

"We'll pretend you said yes, seeing as how we both know I'm right. And seeing as I'm right, I'm going to give you a piece of advice." Someone put another round in front of them and Adam found himself drinking just as steadily as Hacker. "I know you, old buddy. You want to go to Washington with Victor because you think it'll be exciting. Well, it won't."

"What makes you think . . ."

"Don't bullshit your old buddy. Just listen. When you work for the Washington agencies—even *the* Agency—you're still working for the biggest, dumbest organization in the world. You think it's the big time. Bullshit! Truth is, every time you really want to *do* something, some guy behind a desk is telling you no. You make a stink and you get sent to another guy sitting behind a bigger desk. He's the guy that told your first guy no. So what do you do?" He finished the rest of his pint. So did Adam.

"Let's say, old buddy, that you decide to do what you think is right, but without asking. When they find out, are they happy? Hell no, they slap you down. Do it again and they slap you down again *and* toss you out. You've been fired by the only company in town, you think you're fucked, but then you find out there's plenty of people willing to pay for skills like yours."

"You mean Victor?"

"Sure, who else? See what I mean about us having stuff in common? He's been good to us both. Not many would've offered a good job to someone like you, someone who's always getting bored, changing his mind about everything."

"I think Victor enjoys having people in his debt."

The beauty queen smile vanished. "Victor's not doing *me* any favors. I work for him because it suits me. No matter who pays, I'm always working for myself. Victor pays me the regular freelance wage. I like that. Like that word too, 'freelance.' It's got 'free' in it. You ever been freelance? No. Not enough guts!"

Adam stood up and shoved the automobile part in his pocket. Time to leave. Hacker's drunk was turning ugly.

"Whoa, old buddy!" Hacker said, grabbing Adam's forearm. "Too early to be leaving."

Adam shook off his grasp. "I've heard enough."

"No. Still too many things you don't know."

"Like what?"

"Like . . . like, for example, my earring." The forced smile returned.

Adam slowly sat down. Hacker had played his trump. Now he was too curious to go. "What happened to it?" he asked.

Hacker fingered his swollen lobe. "Some drunk ripped it off. I killed him. Damn! I loved that thing. Never could have worn *that* working for the government. Now you see why I wore it? Reminded everyone I was on my own: a free man."

Adam sat down. Someone brought another round. Soon he found himself disliking Hacker less. Was he becoming drunk as well or was he just grateful for the return of his car? Or was it that they shared Victor's secret? Finally, to his surprise, he heard himself say, "I'm positive she's never even heard of TropicAmerican."

"Who, that bitch? Impossible. Everyone's heard . . ."

"No. She's a bookworm. Been living cooped up in some university. Hates newspapers."

"She's lying."

"Then she's a fabulous actress.

"No, you've got it wrong. I've figured that Nat Beale must be behind it. He hates the R-Tube and he told me about a clique of liberals within the CIA . . ."

"*Everyone* knows about those faggots. Scared of their shadows. They'd never challenge Victor."

"But they might have access to records of Victor's membership in the Party, and Nat said they were determined to block the R-Tube."

"What else did Nat say?" Hacker asked quickly.

Adam paused. Was he betraying Beale? But his views on the R-Tube were hardly secret and Hacker had already known about his group of "fine young people." Better to point Hacker toward Beale, and away from Gina.

After Adam had summarized his conversation with Beale, Hacker rocked back in his chair and said, "Interesting, but no sale. It's the Soviets who are after Victor and they're using that bitch and her husband as conduits. Now listen to your buddy Stan."

In credible and well-documented detail Hacker described Piers Baldwin's contacts in London with foreign socialists and Communists. He had no proof, but Adam believed him. Hacker was a man who knew secrets.

"They only *pretend* to hate each other's guts," Hacker said. "It's a game, a cover. It'll make whatever she says and writes about Victor more credible. If she really hated her husband so much, wouldn't they get divorced?"

"At first she told me they were."

"I thought she didn't lie to you, old buddy." Hacker grinned broadly. He knew he'd won. "We allies now?"

Adam nodded slowly. "I can't see why not."

"O.K. Here's what you do . . ."

We're like a family, Gina thought as she carried a pot of chicken stew into the parlor: a bizarre, eccentric, J. D. Salinger family, but a family.

Charlie is the weak, sensitive younger brother. Upon regaining consciousness he had screamed and then burst into tears at the sight of the woman he'd saved and the man who'd tortured him standing together. When she touched his shoulder, he shivered and wept even louder. He thought she was allied with Dawney; that his burns were God's reward for his Good Deed. He was a religious boy, and this shook his faith. She convinced him Dawney had made a mistake. She had stopped him and now they were equal: she had saved his life. Then she led him into the bathroom, bathed him with a sponge and gave him a pain-killer. She paid attention to his hands. As she dug dirt from his stubby, cracked fingers she imagined them rigid, refusing to squeeze the trigger. When she finished, he said, "I'm trapped here on account of you. Can't go home; can't leave the island. They'll be waiting on the dock." She promised to save him. Could she persuade Adam to smuggle him off the island?

Bella was the once domineering matriarch, reluctant to admit that her faculties were failing, her mind less acute. The long drive had weakened her. She squinted and used the telescope more often and she did not question Dawney or defend Eric as aggressively as Gina. Perhaps she had overestimated the old lady's attachment to him or perhaps for her it really had been all "just one of many adventures." She had come to avenge the Brigadier, but now seemed willing to let Dawney punish Ekman for both of them. While Gina was bathing Charlie and stewing the chickens, Bella had collapsed on a bed. She had to be coaxed downstairs for supper.

Gina plunked the pot of stew onto the table they had pulled out from the parlor wall. Bella and Dawney sat together along one side: aging parents who had formed an alliance against their rebellious children. Where would Adam sit when he came? Was he the nervous suitor seeking parental approval? He would never get it from Bella. He had said to expect him late afternoon, but now it was evening. Perhaps he had changed his mind. If he did come, how could she explain her peculiar "family"?

She slammed a plate in front of Dawney and covered it with shreds of pale chicken, floury gravy and canned carrots. She had cooked a disgusting meal on purpose. She was the rebellious older daughter, fed up at being ordered about by a domineering, cranky old man. She was only tolerating him because she believed he knew what had happened to Eric in Paris and Cologne and why this had brought them all together.

"Not still angry, are we, pet?" he asked. She had slapped the food on his plate so carelessly it had splattered his shirt. "After all, your beloved Blair survived Cologne, though he did spend time in hospital there. I wonder if that was Ekman's doing." He smacked his lips. "Delicious stew, pet."

Had his taste buds also been fried in that box? "What happened next?"

He laughed merrily. "I've no idea what happened in Cologne during what you call 'their duel.' But I know that afterwards Blair was even more convinced I was right." He stopped to eat a watery chicken leg as if it were corn on the cob, rotating it slowly in his mouth and methodically tearing at it with stubby teeth. "Don't you think it's disgusting?" he asked suddenly, dropping his food to his plate. "My teeth, my fingers, the way I have to eat?"

"If you don't know what happened in Cologne, how do you know Eric agreed with you? I think you're making it all up."

She wanted to provoke him into saying more, but he answered her evenly. "I wrote to Blair after the war. He answered from this island. Said that what had happened in Cologne had convinced him I was right. He had followed Ekman around Europe afterwards, taking notes, collecting evidence and building a dossier. As soon as he finished his current work he'd start on a factual account of Ekman's treachery. He said he had already written an outline.

"Another year passed and I became impatient and wrote again. I was afraid he'd lost his nerve and I considered sneaking up here and pinching his notebooks. Finally he replied, promising to begin the Ekman book when he regained his health. In the meantime he was leaving the notes and outline 'in a safe place.' " He looked up from his plate. "I sent you a copy of that letter with my reply to your query.

"Then he died. For years I waited for the penny to drop, for that outline or his notebooks to surface. When his collected essays and letters were finally published I remember snatching them off the librarian's desk even before they were catalogued. The old heart raced as I ran my fingers down the index. I wondered if Ekman was doing the same thing, not with the delicious anticipation I felt, but with terror and dread. What would he do when some clever biographer uncovered the truth? Kill himself? That was almost enough to console me after each disappointment.

"But since there was no mention of Ekman or myself in his collected letters, I decided that his outline and notebooks were irretrievably lost."

"Did it occur to you," Gina asked gently, "that they never existed?"

"No! Blair was not a liar. There was also a third possibility: that when he left this island for the last time he hid the notebooks or gave them to someone for safekeeping. That would explain why they weren't included with his other papers."

Gina surveyed the table. Charlie was drowsy from the pain-killers, and Bella was accepting Dawney's version of events uncritically. She was the only one willing to challenge him and to ask the questions Eric would have posed.

"If you thought your precious outline was on Jura, why wait so long before coming here? Why answer my query? Why risk sending a copy of Eric's letter to someone you'd never met?"

Dawney calmly licked gravy off his scarred fingers and then examined each one, as if noticing them for the first time. "Pet, you may know something about literature, and about Blair, but you know fuck-all about justice. For example, can you imagine how unpredictable the hunger for justice can be?"

"Revenge, not justice."

"Same thing. Ever had malaria? I have. It's like that. Soon after being stung by the mosquito you have a nasty bout of fever. You survive, and for months, sometimes years, the fever lies dormant. You almost forget about it. Then boom! Suddenly you have an attack as bad as the first.

"During the war I was too busy hating Nazis to give Ekman much thought. His atrocities were, for a while, replaced in my mind by the

Gestapo's. They handled me with an impersonal efficiency I came to appreciate. I was a cow on a slaughterhouse assembly line with many anonymous hands performing the little cuts and chops that would transform me into a string of sausages. Rooms were changed, and interrogators rotated. Shift work, and bloody hard shift work too! Because, poor fellows, they were operating on an empty shell. Ekman had already stuck in his pin and sucked out the rich yolk." He scratched his beret, adding another greasy stain. At last Gina understood how it had become so filthy. He liked rubbing the scar tissue underneath. Did it itch or was he reminding himself what was there?

"Ekman was different: the personal touch. We were weeks together, just the two of us, in the same room. Imagine how it would be if Judas, after betraying Christ, had tortured and interrogated him, then driven in the nails himself. Would Christ have been so bloody forgiving then?

"Which was why, when I saw Ekman again in Paris seven years later, my malaria struck. He was vigorous and healthy, an American officer who had flourished, pushing papers around the War Office. I also discovered he was married. Who would marry me? Was that justice?"

"Is justice all there is? Suppose he'd reformed? Suppose he was horrified by what he'd done?"

"Yes, yes, very good, pet," he patted her hands. "That was precisely Blair's line of chat." She jerked her arm away and wiped it on her skirt.

"After Paris my malaria subsided. I lived alone, drank in pubs and sold my masterpieces."

"You see how destructive revenge is? Once you ignored Ekman your career flourished."

"Oh, pet." He shook his head and laughed tonelessly. "All I can paint is smiling clowns, girls with tearful eyes, beefeaters and the bloody Tower of London. Sell them off the fence at Hyde Park to Arabs. No, I never *forgot* Ekman, I just hadn't worked out the 'where and how': where he was and how to punish him.

"Last year I found him in, of all bloody places, *Time* magazine.

Some tourist left a copy on the underground. There was an article about the American President and alongside it, in a little box, a picture of one of his friends: Victor Gore."

"That's it!" Bella shrieked. "*That* was the Colonel's name. Victor Gore! I knew if I only heard it . . ."

"Of course it's his name, his *new* name. I call him Ekman because that's his *real* name, his Spanish name." He watched Gina. "Does the name mean something to you, pet?" he asked.

"Nothing at all," she said truthfully.

"Well, it meant a lot to old Dawney. My pulse pounded, my stomach heaved. The old malaria returned. He was described as 'innovative,' 'dynamic,' 'a forceful leader' and a 'hands-on manager,' whatever that means, although he'd had his hands on me all right. Ha-ha. The only unflattering comment was about his 'passion for secrecy and intrigue.' Bloody straight! He had a lot to keep secret!

"I started buying *Time*, *Newsweek* and the *International Herald Tribune*—cost a bloody fortune! He was often mentioned, a real celebrity. Christ, they even published a letter from some Nip nominating him to be 'Man of the Year.' Suddenly I wanted justice as badly as when I crawled off that beach outside Barcelona, or looked across the Scribe restaurant and saw Ekman in his fancy uniform. No! I didn't want justice *that* badly, I wanted it much more!"

"You didn't want justice," Gina said. "You wanted to destroy a man because he'd become successful."

Dawney forked a chicken breast onto Charlie's plate and slapped him on the back to wake him. "Eat hearty, Charlie boy," he said. "We may need your skills soon." He turned back to Gina. "Call it revenge if you like. But don't scold me. Does anyone scold those elderly Jews for chasing *their* torturers? For decades many of them tried to forget, then they find they're over seventy, close to death, and BANG!" He slapped his hands together. "One day they're staring at a picture of some ex-Nazi. He has a lovely house and an adoring family. He's healthy, unrepentant, perhaps living in luxury. Like me, they suddenly realize that *now* is their last chance for justice. Now do you understand how I felt when I saw Ekman's picture?"

"But why contact *me?*" Gina asked.

"Because you seemed to be on the trail—living on Jura, asking for information about Paris in 1945, a period that had never interested any of Blair's biographers or critics. If you had found Blair's Paris notebooks, my testimony might have made your case stronger, persuaded you to publish. I had already approached several journalists. They all muttered about 'libel' and dismissed me as a crank when I couldn't produce what they called 'proof.' I had the note from Blair, but it only referred to the 'Ekman outline,' it said nothing about Victor Gore. I sent you a copy so you'd take me seriously and wait for my arrival.

"But I failed to anticipate what *did* happen. Which is that Ekman must also have seen your query. You've said your papers were shuffled about a week before they were stolen. The first time Ekman's men must have photographed everything. Then he reads the copies back in America and what does he find? A note from me! Oh, pet, I wish I could have seen his face. Now he panics! Orders your notes stolen—perhaps you'd stumbled on another bit of the puzzle without knowing it—and both of us killed. Everyone else who answered your query is interviewed by the impostor to make sure they're ignorant."

"But the Brigadier!" Bella exclaimed. "Why ransack his house and attack *him?*"

"You've already answered that. His diaries reported your lunch with Blair and that he arranged an interview with Ekman."

"But surely *that* wouldn't be enough to warrant . . ."

Dawney shrugged. "Perhaps there was more, something Paget didn't tell you about."

Gina jabbed her finger at Dawney. "This is all speculation. Where's your proof? Something we can take to the police." Eric had resisted being manipulated by this man, becoming the instrument of his revenge; she was determined to do the same. "Why should a successful American businessman, even if he is your Ekman, order people killed on the off chance they *might* reveal something about his past? He's taking a greater risk being charged with murder."

Dawney looked at her appreciatively. "I had the same thought. But suppose he's still working for the Soviets. Now, just when he can be extraordinarily useful to them, you pop up, threatening to expose him. Don't you think that then he'd be uncommonly thorough? Even hire Charlie here? And what's one retired brigadier to people who're willing to murder the Pope?"

"More theories, not a single fact, not a shred of proof."

Dawney snapped his stubby fingers in her face and mimicked her. "Facts, facts, facts. I'll give you some bloody facts!" He jumped up and swept her library of Orwell books off a shelf and onto the floor.

"Fact bloody number one! After seeing the wound on my thigh, Blair was so terrified of Ekman he dashed over to the Ritz and borrowed a revolver from Ernest Hemingway."

"Now, I don't think that's *quite* true," Bella said gently. "Ernest offered him a pistol, but he refused it."

"Balls! Read that Hemingway biography by someone named Baker. Hemingway said that Blair barged into his room and begged for a pistol to protect himself from Communist assassins."

Gina gestured toward the jumble of books. "But surely *one* of the Orwell biographies and essays would mention such a sensational claim, if only in a footnote, in order to challenge it."

"But you missed it too, pet, didn't you? Even with all your fancy research. So did the rest of them. Guess Blair's fans don't much care for Hemingway.

"You want proof that he borrowed that revolver?" He grabbed one of the books. "Here, this is the definitive Orwell biography, by Bernard Crick." He found the page he wanted and read, " 'Susan Watson remembered that when a lorry came to Barnhill to fetch a bull . . . Orwell locked Richard and Susan in a bedroom while he stood at the door of the house with a loaded service revolver in his hand.'

"Where did he get that 'loaded service revolver'? The army didn't give it to him. Hemingway did, just as Baker says." He turned to Bella. "So you see, it *was* going to be a fair fight in Cologne after all. Both men were armed."

Before either woman could reply he shouted, "Fact bloody two: Blair was hospitalized in Cologne several days after arriving."

"His lungs were always troubling him and . . ."

He snapped his fingers to silence her but then hesitated several seconds before resuming. Gina was reminded of Bella's description of the Colonel: an actor alone on a stage, pausing to criticize and appreciate his own performance.

"Next fact . . ." He scuttled over to the pile and snatched up Gina's copy of *Nineteen Eighty-four.* "Next fact is that Blair couldn't wait to use the Ekman material." He quickly found the passage he wanted and read in a thundering voice:

> "Here we reach the central secret. As we have seen, the mystique of the party, and above all of the Inner Party, depends upon *doublethink.* But deeper than this lies the original motive, the never-questioned instinct that first led to the seizure of power and brought *doublethink,* the Thought Police, continuous warfare, and all the other necessary paraphernalia into existence afterwards. This motive really consists . . .

"Blair left that sentence unfinished. He never identified that 'original motive,' that 'instinct.' But you know what it is, don't you, pet?"

"It's the lust for power, the craving after power for its own sake."

"Bravo! And that evil, that lust for power, domination and control, who does that drive?"

"Big Brother."

"And Peter Ekman!"

"Oh, Jesus. You *are* mad."

Bella wasn't really listening; her mind was running in a different direction. "But what I don't understand is how this Ekman character could disappear from Spain and then pop up in America as Gore."

"His Russian friends could have easily handled that. When an American volunteer arrived in Spain, political commissars confiscated his passport and turned it over to the NKVD. If he died the passport was sent to Moscow to be used again. Passports belonging to orphans, recent immigrants and men estranged from their families—which was the case with many volunteers—were prized. These passports were 'adapted' for American or European NKVD agents who were then infiltrated back to the United States. I'll bet Ekman was one of them. And *voilà*—Victor Gore, the hands-on manager of the TropicAmerican Corporation."

"TropicAmerican?" Gina cried. "Is that the company he's head of? Then Victor Gore is coming *here!*"

"How do you know? I thought you'd never heard of him?"

"I hadn't," she said, too shocked to tell him anything but the truth. "But I met one of his advance men in the village. I invited him here, in fact. I had no idea . . ."

"Splendid!" Dawney was beaming. "More the merrier! And the great man himself will be here in several days. Obviously he's coming to get me. He missed me in London, so he plans to catch me here. Satisfied, pet? Believe me now?"

She nodded. Of all Dawney's theories, facts and pseudo-facts, this was the most persuasive.

"When's he arriving?"

"He's late. He promised to be here this afternoon."

Dawney drew a stubby carved knife from his pocket, caressing its stained blade with his thumb. He lay it beside his plate as if it were an eating utensil. "Charlie lad!" He shook the boy. "Good news! Someone's coming to take your place."

CHAPTER 16

"Why not rip it out?" Charlie asked reasonably as Gina dug carefully around the roots of Eric's overgrown azalea.

"Because I'll want to replant it afterwards." Nearby, Dawney had already gouged a deep hole underneath where Eric's rhubarb had grown. He had woken before the rest of them and laid waste to Eric's garden before breakfast. He had hacked up the plant, tossing its leaves onto the compost heap, and given the giant stalks to Bella. She was boiling them to make fool.

Charlie tried to bend down and help but had to stop midway and gasp in pain. If he stood still his burns only throbbed dully, but when he attempted to sit, squat, run or in any way stretch the muscles underneath them, the wounds became suddenly more painful. After slowly straightening up he asked, "What are we looking for?"

"Dawney thinks a man who once lived here buried something valuable. He put in the rhubarb and azalea. Other tenants replanted the rest of the garden."

"You think it's a waste of time, don't you?"

She nodded. "I know this man rather well. He wasn't the sort to bury things in gardens. If he left anything behind, it's not here."

"Good. Let's leave, then. I can hide in the boot. They'll be watching the dock for sure."

"I'm afraid we'd both have to hide in the boot."

His narrow shoulders slumped. "Someone else is after you—besides me, I mean?"

"You're not the only gun for hire."

"Then I'll protect you."

Dawney peered into their hole, shook his head and muttered. "We'll have a go at the house next. Floorboards, ceiling, behind the cabinets . . ."

Gina stood up. "This is insane. We should be summoning the police, planning to escape before TropicAmerican seals the island."

"There's no telephone here," Charlie said. "But we could ask the postman . . ."

Gina shook her head. "Euen only comes twice a week and he's just been . . . but we could drive to Ardlussa and call from there." She did not tell him that Malcolm, who lived only a mile away at Kinauchdrach, owned a fishing boat and shortwave radio. She was keeping those in reserve.

Dawney pointed at the road. "I tell you, Ekman's lads are parked over the next rise, waiting."

"We can't just sit here."

"Why not? We know the house. You know the land. We can set up an ambush. And we have two guns, they won't be expecting that, and Charlie, our trained killer who won't kill. No scruples this time, right, Charlie lad?" He cuffed the boy roughly on the back of the neck. "You help us and we help you escape."

Gina threw down her shovel. "You're planning to murder Ekman and make us your accomplices."

"Execute, not murder. But I'd prefer he live in disgrace. Find Blair's notebooks and save Ekman's life . . . 'Blair's notebooks' bloody hell! They're *mine*. Don't you think I've earned them? Find his notes, and I'll swim to the mainland holding them in one hand."

"You can't be expecting him to walk through the door alone and unguarded."

"No. I have a plan that's somewhat like Blair's, except that you'll be the bait instead of him, and this time I won't miss."

Charlie nudged her, and she heard the faint hum of an automobile. Sounds traveled great distances on Jura. The car was still a mile away. She refilled the hole. "There's nothing out here, you might as well start on the house." Anything to get rid of him now.

As Dawney disappeared inside, a black automobile appeared on the crest of the hill. He was driving slowly, very cautiously. Dawney had not noticed.

"Do you think that's my replacement?" Charlie asked.

"I'm afraid so."

"Wouldn't want to be him. Should I protect him too?"

"I'm not sure." She wiped her filthy hands on the boy's shirttail and ran them through her hair. Dawney's "facts" were impressive, but they warred against all her instincts. She only had Dawney's word that Eric had finally believed him about Ekman's identity. The proof would be in his notebooks, and these were probably lost forever. Why was she still so skeptical of Dawney? Because of Eric, or Adam, or both of them?

"Who's he?" Adam asked, staring at Charlie. She had intercepted him as he climbed out of the car.

"He comes with the house," she said quickly. "He tends the garden."

Adam glanced at the uprooted flowers skeptically.

"I thought you said you were alone here."

"I am, except for him—and Miss Stevens, whom you've met, and her houseguest."

"Another guest. If you're expecting any more you should tell me."

"Why? Because you're suddenly my landlord?"

"No. Because the ferry is going to be disrupted. We could make special arrangements for them." He picked up his overnight bag and started toward the house.

Charlie cut him off. "We're all going for a walk," he said sullenly.

"That's right," Gina added quickly, and then improvised on Charlie's lie. "Up to Kinauchdrach to visit Malcolm. There's a standing stone along the way; you'll like it. One of the island's attractions." Adam's arrival had forced her hand. Once he and Dawney met there'd be bloodshed. While there was still time she would summon the police on Malcolm's wireless. She might even call Piers.

Adam stepped around Charlie. "I'll leave this bag inside, then."

"Miss Stevens is resting," Gina said. "You'll disturb her. Leave it in the car; no one will steal it here."

He locked it in the boot and joined her. Charlie lagged behind, walking slowly and glancing over his shoulder at the house.

"We expected you yesterday."

"I'm sorry. There was more to do than I'd thought. Must have everything perfect for our leader. Just three days to go and counting."

"Your president reminds me of one of those rock musicians who throw tantrums if their fridges aren't stocked with tequila and brownies."

"I'll tell him you said that. He has a great sense of humor. Would you like to meet him? I could arrange an excursion up here."

"You can do what you want. You've let the estate and we're part of it."

"Good. Then you'll show us around?"

"If you give me some warning." Dawney would have been proud of her.

A standing stone shaped like a miniature Matterhorn sat on the slope of a hillock midway between Barnhill and Kinauchdrach. It was five feet high and covered with moss and lichens, like an ancient tombstone. It attracted animals. Spiders had spun webs between it and surrounding ferns, and rabbits hopped out of nearby underbrush. Gina had once seen an adder coiled around its base.

She had brought him here on purpose. "What do you think?"

"Seeing it from the road, it appears to be an ordinary rock. Then you climb up here and there's no mistaking that it's special, and a bit spooky. I suppose it's like this island. See it from the mainland and it's one more barren island. You have to come here to understand how wrong you were."

Good for you, she thought; he had seen what many visitors to Jura did not. She pointed out similar rocks on surrounding ridges and said, "They're part of a primitive Druid calendar. This standing stone is at the center. You line it up with one of those on the ridges and depending on how far to the left or right the sun rises or sets you can tell the time of year. When the sun sets directly in line with both stones, it's the summer solstice, time to plant. The Druids dragged these stones into place before the pyramids were built."

"Things have a way of surviving on this island, don't they?"

"Yes. You saw us digging up the garden. Those plants date from Orwell's tenancy. Some of his possessions may still be lying around Barnhill."

He turned away before she could study his reactions. As they climbed back down to the track, he said, "Didn't you say you were estranged from your husband?"

"That's right."

"Then that guy in the pub was wrong. He said your husband flew in here last week."

"Island gossip."

"It's not true?"

This can't go on, she thought. Enough fencing. No more balancing act. She had to know whom to trust: him, Dawney or no one. "It wasn't a social visit. He and his mistress came to grab some publicity." She scarcely recognized her own voice. It was hard and her sentences short. She needed to shock him. "Last week someone tried to murder me. Took a shot at me while I was stalking with Malcolm. They missed. We hid overnight in a cave. Malcolm's wife reported us missing and Piers came to lead a search party. Malcolm convinced the police it was a poaching vendetta, but now I know the truth: someone wanted me dead. I also know who it was. We're walking to Kinauchdrach so I can call the police on Malcolm's wireless."

Adam stopped and stared at her in disbelief. But was he shocked because of what she'd said, or because she was summoning the police? Now was her moment of greatest danger. She thrust her hand into her shoulder bag and clutched the handle of Malcolm's pistol.

"Who do you think . . ."

"Wants me dead?" She started toward Kinauchdrach. "Come along and find out. The police will take whatever I say very seriously. Don't forget, I'm still Mike Baldwin's wife."

Malcolm's farmhouse was at the end of a string of barns, garages and workshops which lined one side of the dirt road from Barnhill. A small courtyard, crisscrossed with drying laundry, separated the road from the rear of the house. Gina ducked under the flapping sheets and overalls and pounded on the kitchen door. Malcolm opened it a crack and peered out with bloodshot eyes. He was unshaven and stank of whiskey. "Wife's on the mainland," he said, explaining his binge.

"I didn't come to see Mary." She pushed on the door but his foot was jammed hard against it. Over his shoulder she could see into the kitchen. Two enamel mugs flanked an open bottle of liquor; smoke curled from two cigarettes lying in a saucer. He was not alone.

The door flew open. The large American from the dance stood behind Malcolm, grinning. "Join us for a drink, little lady," he said. "Malcolm here sure knows a lot about this Eric Blair. You might want to include it in that book of yours, if you ever finish it."

He grabbed Adam's elbow and pulled him into the kitchen. "Real nice timing, old buddy," he whispered loudly. "We gonna sort everything out right now."

"How did you get here so quickly? There's only one road and you didn't pass me."

Hacker made the rotor motion with his finger. "Flew up the west coast and parked behind the barn."

Charlie had lagged behind the others. He limped into the kitchen, but then jerked to a halt when he saw Hacker. His mouth dropped open, as if he was witnessing a miracle. "Jesus Christ, Gina," he said. "It's him, the Yank who hired us in Belfast!"

Hacker swore and lunged for him, but the boy was too quick. He kicked over the table, shattering the bottle and spattering everyone with whiskey. He dashed for the door, bent almost double to reduce the target, and willing himself to ignore his painful burns. Hacker hurled a chair. Charlie ducked and was gone, heading toward Barnhill and Dawney's pistol. He started with a fifty-yard lead. But his sneakers were old, their treads as bald as a dangerous tire. He slipped and fell in the muddy lane and Hacker gained ten yards.

He slipped again in wet manure. Another ten yards lost, but Charlie kept going. He knew that Hacker wasn't armed; if he were, he would have fired. Of course, if the American killed him the police would just award him a medal. One less IRA lad. Why hadn't he grabbed a knife in the kitchen?

He glanced back. Another five yards lost. The American was fast for a big man, but his pain was easing and once they were outside the farm he might widen his lead, and beat him to Barnhill. He was the hare, leading the fox into a trap.

The gate was closed. Gina had slammed it shut and rehitched it. He grabbed the top rung and tried to vault it like a gymnast, but the gate was too high, his arms too weak. His sneakers slipped against the wire and he fell backward. He jumped up and fumbled with the clasp. He could hear the American swearing as he gained. Less than ten yards.

The clasp sprung open and he shoved the gate. Wrong way. He had to pull it. As he yanked it with one arm, his other was jerked backward. The American slammed him onto the ground, then grabbed a handful of his hair and ground his face into a pile of manure.

"Only three kinds of Irish," the American said. "There's lace-curtain, shanty, and wheelbarrow-pig-shit. You're the last kind, so you must like this, right?" He whipped the boy's head back. "We're going back now. You tell her anything and you'll die with shit on your tongue." He plunged the boy's face into the manure again.

When they got back the others were standing in a line in front of the garage. Hacker marched the boy past them in an armlock, his prisoner of war.

"Caught me an IRA boy," he shouted.

"How do you know?" asked Adam.

"My job to know. Malcolm, you bring some rope. We'll tie him into one of your chairs. Gag him too if he makes any noise."

Gina waited until they were inside the cramped kitchen before drawing Malcolm's pistol. If she had to shoot she didn't want to miss.

"Let him go," she said, pointing the gun at Hacker.

"Fuck you, little lady." To prove he was not intimidated, he twisted Charlie's arm so violently that the boy screamed and his body convulsed with pain.

"Stop hurting him!" She tightened her grip on the handle.

"Or what? You'll shoot?" He laughed and sprayed her with saliva.

She took aim and he jerked the boy in front of him. "Go ahead, shoot," he said, backing away. "Kill him and you'll hit the jackpot. Got to be a bounty for this one."

Without releasing Hacker from her stare, she jerked up the revolver and fired over his head. The bullet shattered a china platter standing on an open shelf, showering him with shards. He swore and, for an instant, released his grip on the boy. Seizing his chance, Charlie twisted free and scrambled across the room to Gina.

She transferred the revolver into his grip, all the time keeping it aimed at Hacker. "You were right," she said. "I couldn't have shot you in cold blood, but I wouldn't chance him if I were you."

"Now?" Charlie asked. He'd have no trouble killing *this* time. And the sooner, the better. He could see Hacker's eyes darting around the room, looking for weapons.

"No! Wait!" She dashed from the room.

There was a moment of silence. At last Adam spoke up. "Stan, what's all this about Belfast?"

"No talking!" Charlie shouted. "Stand next to your friend."

Then Gina was back, carrying a rifle and two revolvers she had found in Hacker's helicopter. "Now go," she ordered Hacker. "Tell Gore, or Ekman, or whatever he calls himself, that nobody bullies me. I know the truth about him, and I plan to use it."

"How?"

"Let him sweat over that."

"It's you should be sweating, little lady."

Charlie was disappointed. "I say keep him as a hostage."

She shook her head. "No, he'd only cause trouble." Once he left she would radio the police, then flee to the mainland in Malcolm's boat.

Hacker started backing out the door. "See you soon, little lady." Adam had not moved. "C'mon, old buddy. Time to retreat."

Adam took two steps backward, still watching Gina, his eyes never leaving hers. He stopped. She was armed, and had just admitted wanting to ruin Victor. Perhaps she also planned to assassinate him? But if she was the enemy and Hacker his friend, why was he hesitating?

He stumbled on the overturned table, picked himself up and, still staring at her, detoured around it. If he left with Hacker, he would never find out what she knew and who was behind her. If he stayed, she might trust him.

He stopped again. If he abandoned her now, what would Hacker do? Kill her? Was that what Victor wanted? Were those really his orders, or was Hacker out of control, acting on his own in some private adventure? And what was there between him and Gina's "gardener"? How did Hacker *know* Charlie was a terrorist? And why was the boy so afraid of him?

He heard himself say, "I'm staying, Stan."

"No, you're not!" Charlie shouted. "We don't want you." He looked at Gina. "Do we?"

"I don't know." She had not expected this. "I suppose he could stay . . ."

"No more jokes, old buddy. Time to go."

Adam was silent. He wanted it both ways: to win Gina's trust without losing Gore's.

"You're making one big fucking mistake."

"I'm staying." He remained facing Gina, his back to Hacker.

"O.K. But you haven't won this one."

Suddenly something heavy landed with a crash on the floor. Adam spun around. Hacker had swept Malcolm's wireless off the shelf. Tubes sparked and flashed and the room was filled with acrid smoke. The set was smashed beyond repair, and Hacker had vanished.

CHAPTER 17

Gina and Adam left Kinauchdrach walking side by side, close enough so their arms brushed and they could speak without the wind stealing their words. She seized his hand to stop him from nervously snapping his fingers, and after that holding hands seemed appropriate. She pictured them as relay runners, brushing fingertips as they passed a baton back and forth after completing laps. Except they were exchanging information—everything they knew about Ekman, Dawney and Éric. And, like runners, they had to accomplish their transfer rapidly. This was why she insisted on leaving the kitchen. Malcolm and Charlie might interrupt the delicate exchange.

"How long do we have?" she asked.

"Three or four hours. Hacker was alone this morning, but two of his assistants—Pine and Ash—are arriving midafternoon. He'll wait for them."

"We could hide in the caves or walk overland to Craighouse . . ."

"Why Craighouse? There must be a closer telephone."

"Yes, Ardlussa."

"Let's drive there?"

"Hacker might cut us off."

"Not if we hurry." He stopped and was about to turn back. "It's an hour at most to Ardlussa."

"There's another problem," she said. "We'd have to go back through Barnhill and there's someone there who wants you dead."

Dawney stood inside the open doorway of Malcolm's garage, surrounded by clouds of midges and oily Land-Rover parts, watching Gina and Adam walk into the hills. They were even holding hands! He had run to Kinauchdrach after the helicopter swooped low over Barnhill. He was worried Ekman had kidnapped Gina or mounted a surprise attack. Instead, he arrived to see her and this young man—who had to be one of Ekman's—leaving the farmhouse together. Long after they disappeared from sight, he remained standing in the garage, immobilized by rage. The midges stung his face and flew under his beret and bit his wounded scalp. A rat leapt from a broken refrigerator, and Malcolm's chickens pecked around his feet. But nothing distracted him from his fury.

She had betrayed him. She worked for Ekman; was part of the plot to lure him here, discover what he knew and then kill him. Now he was trapped, alone, without a means of escape. When his eyes adjusted to the dark he surveyed the garage. He smiled when he saw a pile of rags and a can of kerosene.

Malcolm's rheumy-eyed retriever panted alongside Gina and Adam; his two mongrel sheep dogs darted along their flanks, flushing rabbits and cutting furrows in the meadow. Hinds with erect ears watched from the ridges. Gina was glad of their protection. As they talked she checked them frequently, guarding against a repetition of last week's ambush.

"So Dawney isn't crazy," she concluded. "I mean, of course he's crazy—but not entirely. If parts of his story weren't true, why would the other 'Baldwin' have tried to kill him? And why did someone attack the Brigadier?" Almost as an afterthought she added, "We found Paget clutching an earring. The police believe he ripped it off his assailant."

Now Adam was certain. Here was irrefutable proof that Hacker wanted this woman dead. But did Gore? That was the crucial question. Was it possible that Hacker's briefing had been as vague as his own, leaving him free to plot his own strategy and enjoy his new "freelance" freedom? But even if Gore had not guided Hacker's hand, did he nevertheless approve of Hacker's methods and tacitly encourage him? The stakes were high enough: his reputation, a cabinet post and the R-Tube.

He struggled to sort out his own position. He was Gore's willing aide, yes, and he was not entirely naïve. He had imagined that Gore's "skirmishes" might involve lying, stealing, even sophisticated blackmail. But one thing was clear: he could not murder for Victor Gore, particularly after meeting the intended victim. Others might consider this a rather cold, northern point on anyone's moral compass, but for him it was a start. From here he might move south.

Of course, Gore had not ordered him to murder. But he *had* put Adam in a position where, if Hacker killed Gina, he could be considered an accessory. And even if the police never discovered the truth, *he* would know it, and so would Gore. He moved another few degrees south: he would not be an accessory to murder.

It was also possible that Gore, through the Duchess, had lied and Dawney's allegations about Spain were true. Gore's involvement with Communism may have been more than a schoolboy flirtation fifty years ago. If he still worked for the Soviets, then things were even more serious. Nat Beale's fears about placing the R-Tube in the capital suddenly seemed less paranoid. The R-Tube would give the Russians detailed dossiers on most of official Washington. And they would have Gore, their agent, in the Pentagon and on intimate terms with the President. He began to understand what he had to do. But did he have the courage?

"So our best chance for escape, then, is Malcolm's boat."

"No!" she said. "That would mean abandoning Dawney *and* Bella to Hacker. I'd be responsible for whatever happened to them. When I leave I'm taking everyone with me."

"But we could notify the police once we reached the mainland."

"I'm not leaving them behind. Most of this has happened because of me and I'm going to sort it out. And don't worry about me accusing Gore of being a mass murderer and Russian agent. For that I'll need more than Dawney's flimsy evidence."

Adam restrained himself from telling her about Hacker's lost earring.

"First off I'm going back to Barnhill by myself to persuade Dawney you're not a threat. Then we'll all escape together, either by car to Ardlussa or in Malcolm's boat, although I'm not sure it could take all of us, especially in this rough sea."

From the hill where they had stopped they had an unobstructed view that included the mainland, the Sound of Jura and, to the north, the neighboring island of Scarba and the Straits of Corryvreckan. There were swells and whitecaps in the sound, lighter swells and foamier whitecaps in the straits. "We'd better go back," Gina said. "If it gets any rougher, we'll have trouble persuading Malcolm to make the crossing."

Malcolm was on the floor of the kitchen attempting to piece together the wireless. "I'm afraid it's a write-off, Malcolm," Gina said from the doorway. "We'll buy you a new one on the mainland. Is there enough fuel to get us to Tayvallaich?"

"Aye, tanks are full." He turned back to the tangle of wires and shattered tubes. "Bloody Yank promised me a thousand quid, then offs and leaves me with a smashed wireless."

"A thousand pounds!" Then she remembered what Hacker had said. "And what did you tell him about Mr. Blair that he found so interesting?"

He turned away from her and muttered, "I had too much to drink."

Gina kicked the wireless out of his hands. "You've seen me fire that gun. You know I'll pull the trigger." She leaned down and looked him in the face. "What did you tell him!"

"Christ, lassie, what's with you! I'm the one that *gave* you that gun. It was Mr. Blair's, if you must know. That's what I told the Yank."

She held up the revolver and examined it, as if seeing it for the first time. "And I think I know where he got it," she said softly, "and from whom."

She knelt on the floor facing Malcolm. "Why did he leave it with *you?*" Her voice was sharp.

"He was sick, afraid he wouldn't return. He said, 'If I'm not back, toss it in the sound and good riddance!' "

"But why *you*, Malcolm? You didn't even live up here then."

"That's right, lived in the village. But I did errands for Mr. Blair. He called me 'my auxiliary postman.' He was sent these food parcels from America. They'd hang about the post office for days till it was time for a mail drop at Barnhill. Someone was opening the parcels and nicking the best bits. So he asked me to bring them up as soon as they arrived. Paid me too, and when he opened them he always gave me the canned fruit and coffee. Said he didn't mind the islanders having his food, but he wanted to decide who ate what. *I* never pinched anything from those boxes, that's why he trusted me with his revolver. He didn't want to take it with him from hospital to hospital, or to leave it lying around the house . . ."

She interrupted. The old man was rambling, still concealing something. "Was that all you told Hacker? I don't believe it. He promised you a thousand pounds. For what?" She grabbed his shoulders and shook him hard. "He hired the men who stalked us. He's tried to kill me once, and he's coming back to try again. We're going to escape, but first you have to tell me everything; otherwise I'll leave you behind."

The old man looked to see if Adam or Charlie would intervene. Both stared at him without sympathy. "Blair left something else with me," he said slowly. "That's what I told Mr. Hacker."

"What was it?"

"Tin box."

"No one pays a thousand quid for a tin box!" She shook him harder. "There's no *time* for this."

Malcolm slumped in his seat. "Mary'll have at me if she finds out. She was always loyal to Mr. Blair. Made me promise to destroy those papers if he died. That was his wish."

"What kind of papers? What did they say?"

"Never read them. Sin to read other people's diaries, isn't it? He gave them to me with his gun. Told me to hold them until he returned from hospital. If he died I was to burn them."

"Why didn't you?"

"He died famous. I knew they were valuable, being in his handwriting and all. But Mary said we'd given our word; we had to burn them. She's not very canny, my Mary. So I hid them, outside the house so she wouldn't find them. Been waiting to sell them, but I never figured out how to do it without being accused of stealing them."

"Why did you tell Hacker?"

Malcolm shrugged sheepishly. "He got me drunk and talking about Blair. Asked if he'd left anything on the island. As I said, I'd been wanting to sell them and this seemed as good a time as any."

"Get them!" Gina ordered. "Get them and let's go!"

"Can't do it, lassie. Not as easy as that. I hid them so Mary wouldn't find them."

"Where are they?"

"Will you pay a thousand quid?"

"More."

"How much?"

She picked a figure. "Two thousand, if we get them today."

"Cash?"

"Yes."

He pulled a jumble of keys from a drawer. "We'll need the boat. Come on, then. Take you to the mainland afterwards."

She was so excited by Malcolm's story that it was not until Charlie shouted "Fire!" that she smelled the smoke and saw it curling under the kitchen door. She rushed to the window. Flames were shooting through the roof of the nearby garage.

Adam was first out of the kitchen door. There were two loud cracks and he fell back inside.

"Gunshots!" Charlie shouted. "He's burning the garage to draw us out."

Malcolm peered cautiously out the door. "Winds are strong and from the southwest. If we don't put it out the wind could carry it here."

"Christ, he almost hit me," Adam said. He slumped into a chair, his face white.

"Was it Hacker?" Gina demanded.

"Who?" He was dazed; his mouth was open and his eyes unfocused.

She leaned over and shouted, "Hacker, your 'old buddy.'"

"No. A small man, much older."

Charlie shook his head in disgust. "It's that fucking Dawney."

She spoke to Adam again. "He must have seen us together and decided I've betrayed him."

"Where was he?" Malcolm asked.

"That small rise just above the house."

"Bloody hell! From there he can watch both doors, front and back."

"How long can we hold out?" Gina asked.

"If the fire doesn't spread, there's nothing preventing him firing the house too. He must have found my kerosene. Plenty there."

"Stay here and burn, or go outside and . . ." Adam was talking to himself.

"Oh, I expect most of us'll survive," Malcolm said pleasantly. "If we all run at once, out both doors, he can't hit us all."

"It's Adam and me he wants most," Gina said evenly. "You because you work for Ekman. Me because he thinks I've double-crossed him."

"Ekman?"

"Gore, then. I've just explained that," she snapped. "Ekman is Gore. Look up, listen. It's *us* he wants. You run out the front and distract him. I'll slip out the rear with the revolver and . . ."

"No one's ever tried to kill me," Adam said softly.

"Will you do it?" Gina demanded.

"Yes, but when?"

"Right now!"

"Which way should I run?"

"Away from Dawney, of course!"

"How will I know . . ."

Charlie jumped up. "Fuck this. I'll go. Even with my bad legs I must be faster than him."

And more likely to succeed, Gina thought. But she admired

Adam for being willing to try, though he hadn't the slightest idea of what to do.

More black smoke drifted under the door and clouded the windows. Charlie ran into the parlor. She heard the front door slam, then Charlie screaming obscenities at Dawney.

There was a shot, then two more.

She slipped out the back door. Dawney stood on the rise, holding his revolver in both hands, tracking Charlie across the meadow. He fired again, but the boy was dodging, jumping and zigzagging like a rabbit.

While he was distracted Gina crept up the other side of the rise. When she was a few feet away she leveled Eric's revolver at his back and shouted his name. He whirled around, still pointing his gun. It was a standoff.

She took a deep breath and said, "We've found Eric's notebooks."

"Ha! Another lie!"

"Malcolm knows where they are."

His eyes darted to the smoldering remains of the garage. The fire had burned quickly, but had not spread. "Not in there, were they?"

"No. At least I don't think so."

He tensed. "I thought you knew."

"Malcolm won't say, but he'll take us to them."

"And your friend?" He waved the barrel of his revolver toward the house.

"He's defected."

"Another lie!"

"He stayed when he could have escaped in Ekman's helicopter."

He lowered the gun. "Can we trust him?"

"We haven't time for this. Ekman's men are coming back. Then, when it's too late, you'll find out who your friends are."

He shoved the revolver into his waistband. She had gambled and won. She lowered Eric's revolver too.

As they walked toward the house he grabbed her hand. "So you like holding hands, do you, pet? Let's hope this time you're telling me the truth, or it'll be the last time." He squeezed her hand until she cried out in pain.

CHAPTER 18

Dawney stood in the prow of Malcolm's boat as it chugged up Jura's east coast. He was laughing, crooning sea chanteys, literally hugging himself, delirious with anticipation. He interrupted his premature celebration to seek reassurance that only minutes and a mile of open water now separated him from Blair's notebooks.

"Do you promise they're safe?" he shouted over the rattle of the antique engine.

"Aye, haven't I said so?"

"But someone could have tampered . . ."

"I was there myself six months back."

"Splendid, splendid." He hummed "Blow the Man Down."

Gina was amazed at how quickly he had put Kinauchdrach behind them. Once more they were allies. He had agreed Malcolm should have his two thousand pounds and had apologized to Adam. His good will and rationality were a relief, particularly since she was unarmed. The weapons she had seized from Hacker were useless because she had left their ammunition in the helicopter. And she had insisted that Charlie take Eric's revolver. Since Malcolm had refused to cross the straits with all of them, she had persuaded the boy to return to Barnhill and stay with Bella. They might need the revolver if Hacker returned, although she hoped they would take her advice and flee into the hills behind the house at the first sound of an approaching car or helicopter.

"Why across the straits, Malcolm?" she asked. "Why hide them on a remote tiny island instead of Jura?"

"Couldn't leave them in the house; the old woman might have

found them. Couldn't bury them; might have rotted. And we've moved so much—down to Craighouse, then to Inverlussa, then up to Kinauchdrach only six months ago—I'd always have been digging them up. A cave was more practical. Things last in caves."

"Only if they're well hidden," Dawney interrupted.

"No worry about that."

"Why not a Jura cave?" Gina persisted.

"Had them in a Jura cave for years. But after McLaine's skull disappeared I worried they weren't safe there. Too many strangers visiting our west coast. So I moved them to Scarba. Except for one farm on the other side, it's deserted. Corryvreckan keeps the Scouts from camping on the south coast."

"I've never seen anyone land there."

"Aye, much too dangerous."

"How dangerous?" Adam asked.

"Plenty of boats lost in these straits. Blair himself had his problems here. The motor fell off his boat and he started slipping towards the whirlpool. He had to swim a distance, holding his young son. Both could have drowned; could have starved too if a lobster boat hadn't happened by."

They rounded the northern tip of Jura and steamed into the three-quarter-mile-wide straits. A necklace of small whirlpools strung together by racing currents circled the Jura coast. Immediately the wind was stronger, damper and louder. The contrast reminded Gina of leaving a warm house and walking into a blizzard. In the middle, whitecaps exploded against whitecaps and whirlpools boiled like pools of molten lava.

Malcolm hugged the Jura shore and scanned the water. "Not bad today," he said. "We're within half an hour of the ebb and the wind's too southerly to stir up the hog."

"The hog?" Adam asked.

"The big one, the Corryvreckan. The hungry hog that eats boats. What we're seeing now are the wee piglets."

"Why can't we see the big one?"

"Wrong conditions. Need a flood tide battling a strong westerly blowing in from the Atlantic. The tide slams against a pyramid of submerged rocks, and whoom! A whirlpool high as a ship's mast. Boat went in a few years back and they never found a plank."

Dawney pointed to a black mountain rising like a wall across the straits. "Scarba?"

"Aye, Scarba." Malcolm grinned stupidly and pointed to the open sea. "And that's Labrador that way, Mr. Dawney, which is where we'll go if the engine fails again. There or the Corryvreckan. Which do you fancy?"

"I fancy Blair's notebooks."

Malcolm chuckled. "Aye, that you do, that you surely do . . ." He jerked sharply on the tiller and the boat shuddered, pitching Dawney forward onto his face. Malcolm giggled. The others gripped the sides as the small boat lurched into a small whirlpool, quivered and then spun completely around. Now they faced the Atlantic.

Gina was horrified. The old man had still not recovered completely from his early-morning binge.

As Malcolm pulled the boat back on course, the engine spluttered and died. He laughed and watched each of the passengers, savoring their fear. Gina said nothing. They had lost power once before, just after leaving Kinauchdrach, but Malcolm had immediately pulled up the boards and tinkered with the engine. She was certain this time he had purposely cut the engine because he didn't like Dawney's orders, or the revolver jammed in his belt. He wanted to scare him, remind him that, out there, he was the boss.

Finally Malcolm said, "She's an old boat." He jerked the starter several times and the engine turned over.

They dropped anchor twenty yards off Scarba, in a protected cove northwest of the Corryvreckan, and rowed ashore in a rubber dinghy. Then Malcolm led them back along the coast toward the Corryvreckan. They leapt between rocks, clambered along ledges like the wild goats and waded through shallow pools. They stopped at a small beach of round stones that ground and squeaked under their rubber boots. They saw the cave, but Malcolm made them sit facing the other way, across to Jura, so he could retrieve the papers unobserved.

"Wait out here," he ordered. "It's a good hidey-hole. Might use it again."

He returned carrying a rusted tin box marked *Biscuits for Cheese* and laid it ceremoniously at Dawney's feet.

Dawney pulled hard, but the lid was stuck. He hurriedly pried around the rim with a penknife, cutting himself. Blood gushed from a wound in his palm. He ignored it until at last the lid flew off and caught the wind, clattering over the rocks until it finally disappeared in the Corryvreckan.

Gina seized Dawney's hand as he reached inside. "No! You'll get blood on everything." She handed him a handkerchief to wrap around the wound and then pulled two brown leather notebooks from the tin.

"Open them!" Dawney ordered. "We'll read them now."

Gina looked at Malcolm. "Do we have time?"

He checked the straits. "Some, but not much. Tide's beginning to flood and the wind's getting up from the west now."

"Half an hour," Dawney said. "You already told us these straits weren't that dangerous today."

"They weren't, but they're changing." He glanced at the revolver in Dawney's belt. "But I suppose we've got some time."

"Good. Open them, pet. Let's see what Blair thought of Ekman. You can have all the credit. Better, in fact, that you never mention me. They'll be your find, you'll publish them, they'll make you famous. All I want is justice." He pulled himself close to her so their thighs and arms touched. Even in this wind she could smell his cheesy breath.

As she opened the first notebook Adam moved behind them so he could read over their shoulders. Malcolm, however, stood at water's edge, watching the whitecaps grow and multiply. "Aren't you interested, Malcolm?" she asked. "Or have you already read them?"

"Don't care to. Not my business. Blair trusted me and I betrayed him because I'm a greedy old coot."

Dawney reached across her with his good hand and impatiently flipped through the first twenty pages. Gina saw they described what they already knew: Eric's arrival in Paris, his lunch with Bella, Paget and Wodehouse, Bella's report on Colonel Gore and Eric's encounter with Hemingway and Dawney.

"Nothing new," Dawney said as he flipped pages. "Nothing new, nothing new . . ." He stopped at a page headed: *EH—Second Visit,* and they all began reading Orwell's words:

Late afternoon. I return to H's room at the Ritz. H opens the door, naked except for a towel wrapped around his waist. He is grasping a drink. His room is tidier, presumably in preparation for the "command post" party. No empty champagne bottles in evidence, ditto fading flowers and hand grenades. New pink coverlet on bed and the desk is covered with dishes of food under moist towels. H's revolver is visible in an open trunk, nesting on top of his rolled socks.

Brief pause while H squints and then remembers me.

"Beat it!"

"I've reconsidered your offer . . ."

"Too late."

I point to the trunk. "It's there on top . . ."

"I've torn up my tickets on you . . ."

"What does *that* mean?"

"Means pull the rag out of your ass and move."

"I need it. The Communists want to kill me."

"They're too busy killing Krauts to worry about skinny Brits. Anyway, that Colt doesn't kill Reds, only Krauts. It's a Kraut killer. Told you that."

I make a stab at stepping around H and grabbing the revolver. Ekman may be waiting downstairs, or at the Scribe. After D's experience, not keen on walking about Paris unarmed.

H tosses his drink on the floor, shattering the glass, and stations himself between me and the trunk.

"Listen, you fairy, I don't like having my presents thrown back in my face."

"I'm taking it." (And I'm starting to lose my temper.)

"Apologize. Then I may give it to you."

"Never."

"You lousy son of a bitch." H rocks on the balls of his feet like a boxer, arms dangling at his side and chin shoved forward. "I'll take you quick, you c—sucker. You'll leave with your ass drumming the tiles; with your egg-shaped glands, if you have any, stuffed in your mouth."

Another brief pause while I consider the reasons for H's behaviour. By rejecting his revolver I have spurned his friendship and shown contempt for his courage. If I had understood this I might have taken the revolver and later tossed it in a dustbin. No one appreciates having a gift refused, particularly someone like H. I bear some responsibility for this unpleasantness. While I'm having these thoughts H trips me up. His towel falls away and suddenly he is on top of me, naked, pinning my arms to the floor. Our faces almost touch and I smell whiskey on his breath. He grins.

"I thought so. Not enough guts to box a rabbit." I struggle but he's too heavy. "Since it's a Colt, we'll fight for it Western style: Indian rassling. Beat me and it's yours. I win and you suck snot."

"What's Indian rassling?"

"Arm wrestling. Got an arm, don't you?"

I nod, though I don't like the sound of what happens if I lose.

"That means yes, c—sucker?"

"Yes." At this point I would have agreed to anything to get him off me. On the other hand, what fun if his "Kraut" walks into the room and sees him straddling me.

He slides off but does not fetch his towel. This is my chance to retreat, but I decide against it because: (i) I still need his revolver; (ii) when fighting bullies the term "fighting fair" loses all meaning and therefore I am confident I can beat H and (not a noble thought) humiliate him.

H outlines the rules. They are ancient American Indian rules and not to be questioned. We lie on the floor facing one another and clasp hands. He is still grinning, presumably in anticipation of a quick victory. (Provided, of course, I obey "Indian rules.") He is in no hurry to win and exerts enough pressure to keep our hands locked in a calculated stalemate. Meanwhile we have the following exchange.

H: "That Colt is worth ten of you. It's a noble gun and it killed plenty of Nazis. On the road to Paris I killed one snotty SS Kraut with it. He was a lot like you. He said, 'You won't kill me because it violates the Geneva Convention and because you are a race of mongrel degenerates.' I said, 'Triple ha-ha, you c---sucker,' and shot him in the guts fast, three times. When he fell forward I hit him topside and his brains flew out of his mouth."

He stares at me, hoping to have shocked, which he has, although I hope that this story is some sort of fable. "And how do you like it now, gentlemen?" he asks.

"What does *that* mean?"

"Ask the Krauts who refused to come out when I asked them to surrender. We rolled a grenade into their cellar. 'And how do you like it now, gentlemen?' "

"Do you enjoy killing?"

"My kills are clean."

"They don't strike *me* that way."

He squeezes my hand but does not slam it onto the floor, not ready yet, I guess, for this "clean kill." I provoke him so I can position my free hand unobserved. "I killed fascists in Spain, but I didn't enjoy it. If I were in the army I'd kill them again, but I still wouldn't revel in it."

"I'm sick of all this moral superiority shit, and who are you to tell *me* about Spain? All the British volunteers were scum. I saw them at Jarama, panicked by the tanks and running like rabbits. They were all cowards and fairies."

I lose my temper completely. "What a disgusting pack of lies. I was in the trenches fighting fascists while you were boozing and hoarding marmalade in Madrid." The rumor that H had hoarded marmalade is just the sort of lie I loathe, mean-spirited and impossible to verify. Under normal circumstances I would never repeat it. But H has goaded me into answering his lies with one of his own.

"You lousy son of a bitch! I was bombed, strafed, shot at . . ."

"Precisely. Shot *at*. Ever wounded? No. I was, through the throat.

You were an observer, a tourist, and not a very perceptive one at that. Took you ages to fasten onto the fact that the Stalinists had turned the Republic into a carnival of treachery and rottenness."

"Balls! After this I'm going to beat the shit out of you." He slams my hand onto the floor and says, "Triple ha-ha, c—-sucker. You played it wrong."

I slam my left fist into his face, shattering his glasses and bloodying his nose. So much for Indian rules. He releases my other hand and I jump up, ripping the coverlet off the bed and flinging it over him. He becomes entangled in it, sweeps his canapés onto the floor and slips on them. He stumbles up, still trying to sort his way out of the bedspread. I am facing an oversized pink punching bag. I hit him twice more, hard, and he falls back onto the bed.

I seize the revolver and am down the hall before he lurches to the door, bellowing obscenities. "You stink of death, you shit!" Et cetera.

Realize as I exit the Ritz that this is not the sort of story he is likely to repeat, at least not as it really happened. Same here. Not proud of losing my temper and groveling on the floor with him. But I can say this in my defence: (i) He provoked me shamelessly; (ii) I needed his revolver and he *had* once offered it to me; (iii) to beat bullies you must sometimes bend the rules; (iv) it was good training for Ekman.

Dawney cackled with pleasure. "Christ, pet, it really worked, didn't it? After seeing my wound he really *was* bloody petrified of Ekman."

"I'd say Eric was more prudent than petrified." In truth, she was shaken. Here was an Eric she had never met: someone who could be cruel and, by his own admission, not always in control.

Dawney stroked her hand. "Say what you will, but my strategy worked. They both went to Cologne with their trigger fingers itching."

"Don't like it," Malcolm said.

"What?" Gina looked up from the notebook for the first time.

"The hog."

"I don't see anything different," Dawney said.

But Gina did. Both clouds and currents were racing faster. The wind was colder and wetter. She zipped up her jacket and blew on her fingers.

"I don't see your whirlpool," Dawney insisted.

"You will," Malcolm said. "Wind is changing, tides are strong and there's a squall coming in for sure."

"There *are* more whitecaps," Adam said. "Let's read the rest on the mainland."

Dawney lay his hand on the butt of his revolver. "Ten more minutes."

Malcolm looked to Gina for support, but she was silent. The straits *were* rougher, but not truly dangerous, not yet.

At last Malcolm said, "If you must, then, another ten minutes."

Gina opened the second notebook.

CHAPTER 19

25 March—Morning

The gargoyles are headless and the stone saints have lost noses, lips and eyes. Three direct hits on the nave of Cologne Cathedral have chocked it with rubble, but the spires have survived. And so have the remains of the Three Wise Men buried, it is rumored, in the crypt. Another church is said to hold the bones of eleven thousand English virgins slain by Huns while making a pilgrimage to Rome.

I am sitting on the top steps of the Cathedral. Above my head is a sign: "You Are Now in Cologne Compliments 1st Bn 36th Armd. Inf. Reg. Texas Spearhead." Next to me three members of the "Spearhead" swill bottles of a fizzy pink Moselle they have mistaken for champagne. These steps are the best vantage point in Cologne. I can see the Hohenzollern Bridge, acres of rubble and the Dom Hotel, headquarters for Colonel Ekman-Gore, whom I have awarded a hyphenated name. I have also delivered a note to the Dom inviting him to meet me on these steps before a sunset. I hope he comes today because my lungs are playing up again and I have a slight fever. By tomorrow he may have me at a distinct disadvantage.

First the bridge. It has two turreted stone towers on each bank of the Rhine, which are more or less intact, but the span itself lies in the river, its metal arches poking from the water like the humps of a sea serpent.

Cologne: Ninety percent is a jumble of jagged walls, buildings without ceilings, overturned trams and scorched trees. Girders thrust from heaps of masonry like giant rhubarb stalks and electrical cables hang like tropical vines. The sun is shining, the sky harsh blue, but the ruins appear grey, virtually colorless except for the red lettering on posters plastered everywhere by the authorities. What has survived are chimneys, church spires, monuments in the middle of roundabouts and forty thousand old men, women and children from a prewar population of three quarters of a million.

These survivors are, in the words of an American officer I met, "Strictly the three D's—Docile, Disciplined and Deferential." In fact, despite the fact that by and large they do all their washing, cooking, working and eating outdoors, one hardly notices them at all, as people anyway. They have the same dusty dull-colored appearance as the rubble. Perhaps that is why one sees them moving blocks of stone and thinks: "Rubble is being carted away." Or sees them threading through the ruins on bicycles and thinks: "There goes another bicycle." Or dragging a cart heaped with bundles of belongings and thinks: "Bundles are passing." It is only when a flight of planes roars overhead and they stop and stare upwards that you see their terrified faces and realize they are human.

I expect that a good many people at home envy me. During the worst of the Blitz this is probably just the scene many must have hoped to see one day. I suspect many could also picture themselves giving one of the passing SS prisoners a sharp kick and thinking that it would be immensely satisfying. But I also suspect that most people, if they were here, would quickly discover the curious fact that when revenge is finally possible it quickly loses its appeal, or is at the very least a great disappointment. So instead of enjoying this scene of unrelieved German humiliation and suffering, one feels mainly sickened by the frightful destructiveness of modern war.

Yet, to follow the lead of the pacifists and condemn the indiscriminate bombing that leveled Cologne strikes me as a very shallow notion. The truth is that the bombs which fell on Cologne killed a random cross section of the population and are vastly more fair than the trench battles of the First War which took mainly young men between the ages of eighteen and thirty. The truly inhumane thing is not bombing, but war itself.

25 March—Noon

Much coming and going of jeeps, lorries, officers and MPs from the American headquarters across the square, but no one resembling E-G has come into view. Have I chosen the wrong strategy?

I decided on this approach because: (i) The Cathedral Square is the busiest spot in Cologne and I don't want to give E-G an opportunity to repeat his attack on D. Although I have H's loaded revolver in my kit bag just in case. (ii) I want to hear E-G's version of what happened in Spain and how Dawney came to be wounded in Paris. Even Nazi war criminals will be allowed trials during which they will undoubtedly attempt to justify and explain their crimes. (iii) I have not fully decided what to *do* about E-G. If his explanations are unsatisfactory, or if he brazenly admits everything, then blackmail seems the best answer. I will bluff and claim to have already documented his crimes and change of identity and left this damaging testimony with a third party with instructions to make it public if there are any attacks on Dawney or myself. As part of the bargain E-G must also transfer to a less sensitive post, perhaps a combat unit, where he will have less influence on postwar Europe.

25 March—Late Afternoon (but written on March 27 from my bed in an American military hospital)

A rat-faced German boy in an oversized army greatcoat flings up his arm and shouts, "Heil Eisenhower!" (Obviously sent by E-G.) He flashes open his coat to reveal a mobile black market department store. Dangling from clips sewn into the lining are silk scarves, nylons, watches, packets of cigarettes and an envelope. He slips this to me while putting on a great show of promoting his wares. An unsigned note inside says simply, "Follow him."

I obey, but not before slinging over my shoulder the kit bag containing H's "Kraut killer." I am too curious and have come too far to refuse E-G's invitation. Besides, saying no would be cowardice. Has he counted on this?

I follow the boy along the military highway connecting Cologne to the front. The Business of War is flourishing. Lorries with supplies and fresh troops roar past lorries crammed with German prisoners, stirring up clouds of dust turned red-gold by the setting sun. The boy accelerates to overtake a column of captured SS. Some officers have sensitive scholars' faces and carry valises plastered with prewar hotel stickers: Hotel Angleterre, Nice; The Ritz, Lisboa; and Shepheards. Their guards shunt them down a side street as if they were a goods train. Next we weave through a mob of Polish workers, each kitted up with an identical knapsack from which dangles the same pink sausage. Supplied by the Red Cross or looted from a sausage factory?

My guide darts down a path snaking through mounds of rubble and I follow, tripping over the rubbish of war—empty field ration tins and ammunition boxes—and wheezing and coughing from the exertion. I am definitely feverish.

Suddenly there are fewer people and soldiers. A lone jeep blaring orders in bad German bumps in and out of craters and a woman pops up from the ruins of her house like a jack-in-the-box. A leprous old man dragging a cart overloaded with turnips and a stinky red weed blocks my way and casts a shadow that reaches my feet. The sun is only minutes from setting. The old man refuses to move until I tell him when I think the war will end. And do I think, now that the Americans are here, that Hitler will bomb Cologne?

Crocuses and daffodils grow in bomb craters and tacked-up notices asking the whereabouts of lost relations flap fitfully in the wind. We trip through gutted houses. Discolored patches of wall where pictures of the Führer once hung identify which belonged to Nazis.

The boy is doubling back. To disorient me or kill time? My only signposts are the Cathedral spire and a ring of blackened chimneys standing out against the darkening sky like Stonehenge. We climb an alp of smashed concrete dusted with plaster, then pick through a gutted shed stinking of hops, a former brewery. Through its shattered roof, stars are starting to glitter in the moonless sky. We could be in a Venetian palace. The boy reappears and tugs on my arm. "Follow! Follow!"

The darkness is pierced by shafts of yellow light, and the cemetery stillness broken by muffled music and murmuring voices, all coming from shelters hidden underneath the rubble. The boy pushes on a steel door and we stumble into an underground, candle-lit room holding fifty people. Blank-faced men and women lie in rows of iron cots. A gaunt man pumps a squeeze-box and a foursome play cards. Just the sort of place into which H might toss a grenade if the "Krauts" did not scamper out fast enough. Everyone falls silent as we walk through. The women, seeing my uniform, turn away.

The boy snatches a lantern from a shelf and lights its candle. We set off through a labyrinth of underground corridors connecting more cellars and shelters. Similar scenes in each. During the bombing people hammered doors through adjoining cellar walls so they could visit, shop and sleep without venturing above ground. We pass through the basement of a looted department store, go down another airless passage and then halt before the type of heavy iron door that in England protects a bank vault. The boy pushes it open, thrusts the lantern into my hand and scurries off. I slip my hand into my kit bag and, holding the butt of H's Colt, go inside.

The room is cavernous, its ceiling high. Impossible, even with the lantern, to see it all at once. Heaped on trestle tables is what, at first glance, appears to be a menagerie of dead animals. My eyes adjust to the light and I see they are foxtail capes, mink stoles, sealskin coats and the like. I step backwards and trip over a stool. As I stumble, my light flashes upwards, illuminating the ceiling. Half a dozen nooses dangle from an overhead beam.

A sharp click sounds across the room, and a powerful electric torch floods the room with light. As I right myself, a flat American voice says, "Quite a combination, isn't it? Fur coats and executions." Holding the torch and leaning against a mound of mink is Col. E-G.

"We bombed the Gestapo out of their upstairs headquarters, so they had to consolidate. This basement was cool enough to protect their furs as well as large and secret enough to accommodate hangings. They dropped nooses over that bar, kicked out the stools and then brought in six more. This is one of countless storerooms. We're still finding others crammed with Nazi plunder. Some are sealed by collapsed buildings."

He sweeps his hand across the table. "Like a fur? Here's a nice one." He throws a white pelt across the room, landing it at my feet. It's big enough to have clothed a polar bear. "Have another." He tosses a coat of jiggling tails. "I prefer stamps myself; I've been collecting them since I was a boy. I just traded a carton of cigarettes for one stamp that's worth a fortune in New York. And easy to ship there too, much easier than these coats. But you might manage to smuggle a few back to England. I could help you." He takes my silence for a refusal, which it is. "Oh, all right. The stamps, then. I've found one that should sell for several thousand of your pounds. You can stick it on a letter and . . ."

"No, thanks."

"We'll return to this later. Meanwhile, let me bring you up to date on what's happened since Spain."

While he talks I observe that: (i) His sidearm is holstered, so there is no need to draw H's revolver. (ii) He is older and balder, but definitely, as he has just himself admitted, the same intense American who served briefly with our militia. I am reminded of a recently dead fish: the eye unfocused, but not yet cloudy, and the skin moist, but not quite alive. (iii) I am becoming iller and weaker by the moment.

For the time being he is more interested in Germany than Spain. He describes the same plan he outlined to Bella Stevens in Paris. As she said, his pill is sugarcoated. He advocates strict security and a strict quarantine, while at the same time keeping the German people so drugged with pleasure they will be oblivious to his manipulations. Germany will be transformed into a gigantic and faintly sinister Riviera hotel, a plan smacking of Huxley's *Brave New World.*

When I think I've heard enough I say, "Well, totalitarianism is visibly on the upgrade these days, isn't it? And, oddly enough, just when it's supposed to be defeated."

He stops talking and looks perplexed, uncertain whether I am endorsing or ridiculing his bizarre scheme. He can take it either way. Time for the main course.

"Which do you prefer?" I ask. "Gore or Ekman?"

"The first. Why don't you just call me Victor? I've put Ekman behind me."

"And Ekman's crimes too?" I ask pleasantly.

"Have you come to Cologne for Dawney's revenge?"

"No, for the truth. And I believe in forgiveness that doesn't interfere with justice."

" 'Justice' sounds suspiciously like Dawney. Is this you speaking, or him?" He is equally pleasant, but he drops his hand so it rests on his sidearm. His revolver is still holstered, but he has surreptitiously unbuttoned the flap. He is now at a decided advantage. I cannot dig into my bag without alerting him, but he can draw his revolver in an instant. If there is going to be any duel, I have already lost. Clearly, Americans know more about "shoot-outs" than we do.

"For the present," I say, "they are Dawney's accusations, not mine." To discourage him from shooting me I add, "But I arranged before coming here that they will be made public if anything happens to me."

"But *you* won't publicize them, will you?" he says. "They would ruin me. Your country is more understanding about Spain than mine. The FBI has lists of volunteers. Ekman could never have received a commission, but Gore can. Ironic, isn't it, that if you fought fascism in 1936 they won't let you fight it in 1945?"

"That's an appealing explanation for your change of identities."

"It's the truth." He shrugs.

"Dawney claims you had other motives."

"He says I tortured him, doesn't he?" He said this in an almost amused voice. "What a f---ing liar that man is, what a f---king, monstrous, monumental liar!"

"He also accuses you of spying for the Soviets and betraying him and others and then supervising their execution."

"Does he have any proof?"

"No."

"Of course not! Is there anything else?"

"You tried to murder him in Paris last week. I saw his wound."

His voice hardens and he moves towards me. "Another lie. Like all his accusations, the reverse is true. He tried to murder *me!* And in a place very much like this one. He said he had your blessing. But now I can see that he didn't. If you were convinced I was such a villain, you never would have followed that boy down here, alone and unarmed."

"And his wound?"

"We struggled for his revolver and he shot himself. By the way, where *was* his wound?"

"In the thigh."

"Did you notice any powder burns on his trousers?" I had. "Do you think if I was that close, and wanted to kill him, I would have aimed there?"

This *had* crossed my mind, a mind rapidly becoming muddled by fever. My vision is blurring and my legs feel hollow. The combination of chasing the boy and then standing in this frigid room has given me chills. Every sentence is an effort and my lungs tighten with each wheezy breath. I long to lie down and cover myself with some of E-G's furs.

"Do you mean to say Dawney is mad? Deluded?" I ask. "That he attempted to murder you because he *imagines* you tortured him in Spain?"

"To the contrary, he has *every* reason to want me dead."

I can no longer stand and have to suffer the humiliation of slumping onto one of the stools.

"You see, it was not *I* who betrayed Dawney," E-G thunders. "Or *I* who interrogated him or supervised that execution. The truth is that *I* was the one who was arrested by the Reds. *I* was the one who was interrogated, tortured and marked for execution. But everything, *everything* Dawney has told you about these episodes is correct down to the finest, most exquisite detail. Except for one fact . . ."

He pauses until I look up from the stool.

"And that is that *Dawney* was the Stalinist spy, the traitor, interrogator, executioner. And I was his victim."

Dawney leapt up, knocking Gina backward onto the rocky beach. "Lies!" he screamed. "More of his bloody lies. The fucking Blair! How could he even write such filth!"

He tore the revolver from his belt and gestured with it wildly. Adam and Malcolm threw themselves onto the beach. "You're not to believe a word of it, not a word!"

"There's another entry," Gina said quietly, trying to soothe him. "Let's read it. I'm sure Eric didn't believe him, or why would he tell you otherwise after the war?"

Dawney jumped back next to her and peered at the notebook. "All right, then, let's have the rest."

"No!" Malcolm pointed to the straits. "We leave now or we'll be marooned overnight. The whirlpool's kicking up. Wind blows any harder and I'm not taking you across."

Dawney flipped through the notebook. "There's only a few pages more. We'll read these and then you'll take us back." He rested the revolver in his lap, gripping the handle with his uninjured hand.

28 March—Cologne

According to a nurse, I have been delirious and feverish for the best part of two days. Both of which have been passed in this comfortable private room in the American army hospital. Presumably E-G brought me here after I collapsed in his vault. Does this in itself prove that he is Dawney's victim rather than his villain? I wonder. It is equally likely that he swallowed my bluff and feared if he left me to die of pneumonia or whatever that someone would release notes in my handwriting revealing his past.

Why is it that atrocity stories are so tricky? One reason may be that they are so often believed or disbelieved according to one's political predilections. Hence the fact that during this century the Right has fervently believed in Sinn Fein atrocities in Ireland and Red atrocities in Spain, whereas the Left has believed equally fervently in Black and Tan atrocities in Ireland and fascist atrocities in

Spain. These are just two examples but of course there are plenty more: the Soviets in the Ukraine, the American Marines in Nicaragua, etc.

Another reason the truth behind atrocity stories is so slippery may be that both the guilty and their victims can become so irretrievably scarred and twisted by their experiences that the world of facts becomes irrelevant. In time their memories come to resemble the Cologne cellars: labyrinths with so many confusing dark passages, gloomy vestibules and noose-filled rooms. Victim and torturer alike wander through these labyrinths until, without suspecting it, they sometimes retrace one another's steps and become transformed, and those who started their unhappy travels as victims end up becoming the opposite and vice versa.

Has this happened to Dawney? Is he tormented by what was done to him or by what he did? Has he subconsciously switched roles in order to soothe a wounded conscience? Has the butcher become the lamb? It is conceivable that the horrors practiced upon him by the Gestapo have made it impossible for him to believe himself capable of having inflicted similar pain on others in Spain. His account of E-G's crimes is then a lie, but a lie so fiercely held that he has come to believe it fervently. Only this could explain him begging me to expose E-G and accuse him of committing crimes that are in truth his.

Or E-G is lying. If so, he is as clever and convincing a liar as I have met. Like Dawney, he has no proof for his accusations except his own convincing passion. A stalemate.

Pause while a nurse looks in and asks if I am up to receiving visitors. I say yes. It is unlikely E-G would pull me from the cellar in order to finish me off in a hospital.

It appears my tricky balancing act will have to continue. At least until either D or E-G admits guilt or supplies credible evidence. I can continue stalling D with promises of sometime in the future writing an exposé of E-G. I can prevent E-G from attacking D, or me, by continuing the bluff that a third party is poised to release diaries I have written detailing D's accusations. Meanwhile I will

have to keep an eye on E-G—*Officiarius Totalitarianus Americanus*
—for the duration of the war.

E-G is here, smiling and cradling in his arms a too large bunch of
daffodils and crocuses, presumably plucked from bomb craters by an
orderly. He tosses them on my bed and some of the stalks fly up and
whip my cheeks. After the customary chat about illnesses and hospitals, I blackmail him.

The deal is this: He can remain Colonel Victor Gore and my
charges will remain secret, providing he agrees to secure an immediate transfer. He must not have any responsibility for executing or
formulating occupation policy. He pleads, argues and makes vague
threats before agreeing. As we both know, he has no choice. I have
what H would call his "egg-shaped glands" in my grip.

"Not a very generous reward for saving your life yesterday, and
fixing you up in this room," he says.

"It's to your advantage to keep me healthy."

"Why must I transfer? My position here has no connection with
Dawney or Spain."

"I have my reasons." If Dawney is right, what he advocates for
Germany may have everything to do with Spain.

He becomes excited and circles my bed. "So you *do* believe
Dawney. You think I'm still in with the Soviets." I stare at him
blankly. "Is that it, dammit?"

"That may be one reason. But to be honest, I can't decide who to
believe. Perhaps you're both lying."

I have said the wrong thing. He slams his fist against my bedstead
and swears, then bats my hand aside when I reach for the buzzer to
summon the nurse.

He points to his squiffy eye. "Did I have this when you knew me
in Spain?"

"I hardly knew you in Spain."

"But did I have it?"

"No." I begin to wonder if he isn't as mad as Dawney, perhaps
more so.

He grabs his nose and shakes it violently. "Do you remember my
nose looking like this?"

"No."

"They're both Dawney's work. And so are these!" Abruptly he unbuckles his belt and drops his trousers. A line of small red circular scars, evenly spaced, climbs up each of his legs from knee to crotch.

CHAPTER 20

Dawney tore the notebook from Gina's hands and thrust it under his shirt. "It's a forgery! This couldn't be Blair's diary."

Gina looked at Adam. "Does Gore have scars on his legs?"

"I've never noticed any . . . but I've never seen him wear shorts or a bathing suit. Which is strange, now that I think about it, at a place like TropicResort." Adam's mind was racing. "This means he's innocent, doesn't it? He fought in Spain, yes, but he never committed any crimes or spied for the Russians. Instead, even better, he was an idealistic young man who was tortured by Soviet agents. He was a martyr, and these diaries will prove it."

"What do they matter, *his* scars?" Dawney shouted. "What about *mine?* They exist. You've seen them!" He moved away from them, still waving, but not pointing the revolver.

"But the Nazis were responsible for your wounds," Gina said. "You said that yourself. And you said Gore was responsible for what had happened in here." She pointed to her head. "Perhaps in a way he was."

Dawney examined the rocky beach and straits as if seeing them for the first time. Then he shook his head and murmured, "No, no, not true."

"Those scars are just like Charlie's. Do you expect us to believe that is a coincidence?"

He looked at her imploringly. "It's a lie, pet. Blair made it up. But why would he betray me . . ."

"Nonsense! You betrayed yourself by torturing Charlie that way." Her eyes jumped to Dawney's revolver. Adam was closest. If he moved fast, he could disarm him. She tried to alert him with her eyes.

"Everything I've told you is true. Ekman *did* torture me, I swear it."

"Then why did you burn Charlie?"

"Because I thought he worked for Ekman."

"No, dammit! Why did you burn him that *way?* Where did you learn that technique?"

"In Spain . . ." he said slowly.

Adam pounced. "So you admit it! You admit torturing Victor Gore in Spain. Everything he told Orwell about you is true."

"Let him finish," Gina said. She wanted to hear Dawney's own explanation. He had recounted his experiences in Barcelona with too much passion and conviction for them to be a complete fabrication.

"You were saying. 'In Spain . . .'" she prompted. "Where in Spain?" But she was too late. Adam's outburst had put Dawney back on the defensive. Now he was making decisions.

"There's no justice for old Dawney here, is there, pet?" He moved further away from them and leveled the revolver at Malcolm. "We're leaving." Adam stood up. "Not you, and not her. Your friend Ekman can rescue you. And while you're waiting . . ." He laughed and kicked the empty biscuit tin toward them. "You can eat these."

From the beach they could see the rubber dinghy. Malcolm was rowing and Dawney sat in the bow, clutching his revolver in one hand and Eric's diaries in the other. A gust of wind swept away his beret and it disappeared into a whirlpool.

"They've only taken two life vests," Gina said as the two men climbed aboard Malcolm's boat. "Good for Malcolm! He's left two behind in the cove."

"I suppose we can use them as pillows, or to stay warm until we're rescued."

"Rescued? We won't see another boat in these straits until this storm quits, and that could be several days at this time of year. Meanwhile we've no food or warm clothing, and no shelter except those caves. And if Dawney kills Malcolm, who'll ever know we're here at all? No, one of us has to swim for it, and I'm afraid it has to be you—I don't know how."

Adam studied the straits again. "Christ, they're at least a mile wide."

"A little less. But swimming them is no big deal. Several summers back a legless veteran did a round trip. And you heard what Malcolm said about Eric Blair: even with his bad lungs he swam to an island holding his son. And you'll have a life vest. Once you reach Jura, get the car from Barnhill and drive down to Craighouse to telephone for help."

"Why not?" Adam smiled and shrugged his shoulders. "I don't think anyone would really give a good goddamn if I drowned. The funeral would be poorly attended, not a wet eye in the house."

"I hope you're joking. I loathe self-pity." But Gina knew how he felt. Who would really mourn her if she perished on Scarba? Certainly not Piers, nor her "friends," who were mostly his. And she had seen her own friends and family only twice in ten years.

The wind carried ashore the stink of diesel and the uneven, sputtering chug of Malcolm's boat. "He's heading the wrong way!" Adam shouted. "Out to sea!"

"No, once he's clear of the Corryvreckan he'll steer south and double back through the straits, hugging the Jura coast. The most treacherous waters are over here, near Scarba. Look there!" She pointed to turbulent waters a hundred yards offshore. "Malcolm was right. The winds have hit the flood tide and set off the Corryvreckan. It's starting to boil; can you hear it? It's the sound of currents slamming into those underwater rocks." As she spoke, a funnel of water shot upward and the spray blew toward Scarba, dampening their clothes.

Malcolm was navigating so close to Jura that she wondered if he would wreck his boat and scramble ashore, leaving Dawney to fend for himself. But at other times he swerved erratically toward the center of the straits and the strengthening whirlpool.

"He's trying to scare Dawney," she said. "Throw him off balance so he'll drop the gun." Suddenly the hoarse chugging stopped and they heard only the wind. "He's cut the engines on purpose—just like he did on the way over."

The currents spun the boat around, pulling it toward the middle of the boiling straits. It slammed against whitecaps and twisted through swells like a gondola on a fun-fair ride. A wave swept over the bow and the boat disappeared into a deep trough. When it reappeared, the two men were struggling, each trying to push the other overboard. There was a sharp crack, like a rifle firing, as the boat crashed into a submerged rock near Scarba before disappearing again. Then it rose once more. Two waves, like hands offering it heavenward as a sacrifice, carried it aloft on their crests. Only Malcolm was visible now, standing in the stern, bent over the engine and furiously pulling at the starter. The engine coughed once, then twice. Puffs of dark smoke shot from the exhaust, but as he turned back toward Jura the engine sputtered and died. The old man jumped forward and slammed his fist against the control panel. The boat was speeding in a straight line toward the big whirlpool, as if a hand beneath the Corryvreckan were pulling it on an invisible string. It pitched forward into the raging waters and the engine at last turned over, a final death rattle, before the boat vanished into the whirlpool.

Gina ran to the shoreline, but there was no sign of any swimmers. Malcolm and Dawney had disappeared, and with them, Eric's diaries. She was silent for a minute and then said, "Right. We'd better see if Malcolm really left those vests." She strode toward the cove where they had beached the dinghy. Adam ran after her.

Hacker had to shout. He had one of those overseas connections combining static with echo. He peered out of the red telephone box in Craighouse, checking that no one was within earshot. Then he shouted the report he had been rehearsing since returning to Kinauchdrach and finding it deserted.

"Yes, just what we feared. That's right, written evidence. . . .

No, I'm not sure if she's found it, but she's threatening to reveal what she knows. . . . No, that's not an assumption, I *heard* her."

He paused and took a deep breath. Now came the part he dreaded. "She's escaped. . . . No, she's just not on the island. If she was, there wouldn't be any problem. . . . I thought we had them trapped. But there was a boat. . . . I've only been here two days. I can't know every boat and . . . Yes, entirely my fault.

"He's defected, gone with her. . . . Don't know why, perhaps he's got the hots for her. I warned you about him, said we should have taken him out. I'm not taking responsibility for him too. . . .

"Will you relax. Haven't I said that I'd taken care of Paget? . . . No, he didn't have anything written down, no letters, no diaries, nothing. But he knew. That's why I killed the old son of a bitch. . . . All right, then, I *thought* I'd killed him but it doesn't matter, he's as good as dead. . . .

"I agree . . . no choice but to hold it at the Resort now. . . . My guess is she'll return home. . . . Because there's nowhere else for her. . . . Are you certain Baldwin will cooperate?" There was a long pause. Hacker looked around nervously, checking the street and his watch. "Fine, fine, you handle Baldwin. . . . I'm flying back tomorrow, just as soon as I get off this fucking island."

As soon as the call ended Hacker redialed the operator and said, "I want to make a credit card call, person to person to a Mr. Victor Gore . . ." After giving the number he noticed one of the island boys waiting to use the telephone. He did not chase him away nor, when Gore at last came on the line, did he bother to lower his voice.

Gina could not see Adam, it was too dark, but she could feel him. Her thighs were pressed against his and his arms were wrapped tightly around her shoulders. And as he slept, she listened to the slow beating of his heart. They had found a dry corner of the cave and stretched out on the life preservers. They would have to sleep in each other's arms, they had agreed, in order to stay warm.

While he slept fitfully she admitted to herself that she needed him: both to swim the straits and to take her to E-G. But did she want him to? She wanted someone and it was hard to imagine someone less ideological, less like Piers. Did she dare wake him with a kiss and then make love, wordlessly, in the dark or should she first persuade him to agree to one of the schemes she had been turning over in her mind? Only one offered the possibility of protecting them from E-G as well as finishing what Eric had started.

She nudged Adam gently and he woke. "Still raining?" he asked.

"Yes."

"Can't you sleep?"

"I've been thinking about what we should do."

"I thought you'd decided to feed me to the whirlpool."

"I mean after that. I don't fancy spending my life hiding from Gore and Hacker."

"Isn't the solution obvious? I tell Gore the diaries were destroyed, Dawney is dead and you and I know the truth: that he was the victim of the Soviets, not their agent. We agree to keep his past secret, he returns your manuscript and we all live happily ever after."

"But don't you see? Everything's much trickier than that. Assuming we avoid Hacker on Jura, he'll still tell Gore that I've threatened to ruin him and that you've thrown in with me. You think Hacker is freelancing this one or at least exceeding Gore's instructions—but are you willing to risk our lives on it?"

Adam had a coughing fit. "God," he complained, "soon I'll be as sick as your friend Orwell. Well, what do *you* suggest?"

"That you be less eager to forgive Victor Gore. That instead of crawling back and asking him to congratulate you for a job well done, you *demand* that Hacker be punished, Brigadier Paget compensated and my manuscript returned. And even if Victor Gore is ignorant of everything Hacker's done in his name, we're still in danger since Hacker will be keen to prevent us from talking to Gore. And if you're wrong, if Gore *did* order me killed, they may shoot us on sight."

"I'm not stupid. All that had crossed my mind, but aside from changing our names and disappearing, I don't see any choice, except to reassure Victor that his secret is safe and hope for the best, unless you're planning to involve the police."

"What evidence could we give them? Dawney's dead, the diaries are gone and I'm sure Charlie would be afraid to cooperate. And if we did call in the police it would have to come out that Victor Gore was once a Communist named Peter Ekman. Eric was reluctant to reveal Gore's past without conclusive proof that he was also a Soviet agent and guilty of war crimes in Spain. So am I, particularly since it appears likely that Dawney rather than Gore was guilty of those crimes."

"What do you mean 'likely'? I'd say Gore's burns were conclusive proof of his innocence."

"Yes, I suppose so," she said slowly. But she was still not completely convinced. She had heard Dawney's indictment of Gore, Adam had not. It was hard to believe such convincing passion could be based on a falsehood. Damn Dawney for snatching away the diary before she could read Eric's reaction to Gore's scars. Eric was right about atrocity stories and the truth behind this one was as "slippery" now as it had been more than forty years ago. Could she really hope to finish what he had started? Discover who was the "butcher" and who the "lamb"?

Adam coughed again, interrupting her thoughts. "I'm still waiting," he said. "What's your suggestion for handling Gore?"

She spoke quickly. "First off, we don't admit that the diaries were lost. We approach him through an intermediary and threaten to publish them if anything happens to us. Then we meet him and describe what they said. This will convince him we have them. How else could we know what happened in Cologne? Next we allay any fears he may have that Eric accepted Dawney's version of events or that we plan to publish the diaries."

"But eventually I'd have to tell him the truth: that the diaries are at the bottom of the Corryvreckan."

"That's just what we *don't* tell him. He's lived most of his life fearing those diaries would surface. We play on those fears." Now came the delicate part. She did not want him to suspect that she planned to pick up Eric's "tricky balancing act" and bring it to a conclusion.

"What you're suggesting usually goes by the name of blackmail."

"And what if it is? We're trading our silence for our lives. What's so immoral about that?" He tensed and pulled away. She was coming on too strong. She pulled him back and rubbed his hands. "Put yourself in his place. He *believes* those diaries exist. Eric told him that in Cologne. Then forty years later Hacker or someone else showed him the letter stolen from my files—the letter Eric wrote Dawney in which he promised to use them as the basis for a book. Then Malcolm told Hacker about them during their binge. Once we admit we don't have those diaries we've lost our advantage. Instead, we bluff." Just as Eric did, she thought.

"You haven't met Gore. He's not a fool. He'll realize that if we *really* had the diaries we'd simply publish them. Afterwards he wouldn't dare touch us."

"Trust me. I'll persuade him we're not publishing for the same reason Eric didn't: it wouldn't be fair. I'll explain what Dawney did to Charlie and how it confirms everything he told Eric in Cologne." There was more silence. She almost had him. "Think on the bright side. He won't dare fire you and if you choose to stay on you can demand almost anything."

"He won't come to Jura after what's happened," Adam said. "Hacker will warn him off. On such short notice they'll have to hold the board meeting at the TropicResort."

"Then you'll take me there."

"Suppose I refuse?"

"I'll go alone."

He sighed. "I'll take you."

They went to sleep but later she awoke and found his hand in the dark, and remembering how marvelous and strong-looking they were, caressed his long bony fingers. She traced his lips and cheeks with her fingertips, brushed back his shock of brown hair and then lightly kissed his forehead, his hollow cheeks and finally his lips. Now he was awake as well. He slid his hands underneath her jacket but when he tried to speak, she whispered, "Shhh . . ." and laid a hand over his mouth. They made love in the dark with their clothes on, never exchanging a word. She fell asleep wondering if she had done it because she wanted him, or because she wanted him to have another reason to swim the Corryvreckan and take her to E-G. Or had she done it because, in the darkness, she could imagine he was someone else?

Early the following afternoon there was a break in the line of storms. Gina and Adam scrambled east along the Scarba coast so he could cross the straits at the narrowest point. As she tied him into the life jacket, he smiled and said, "I look as though I'm about to leap from the *Titanic*."

"I just had the same thought."

"Wasn't it women and children first on the *Titanic?*"

She tied his shoes to the life belt. "You'll be cold and wet on the other side. Better to carry shoes and run to Barnhill than hobble there barefoot."

"Just enough extra weight to drag me under."

"Last night you said you were a strong swimmer. That's the truth, isn't it?"

"I won medals in freestyle. Of course, that was in a university swimming pool, not in a Scottish whirlpool."

She stepped back and checked him a last time. "Remember, once you've called the authorities, the main thing is to see Bella safely off Jura and back to her house in Bournemouth. Charlie can hole up there for a while too. I imagine I'll be taken to the lifeboat station on Islay. If we miss one another, don't hang around waiting for me. Hacker may still be on the island."

"But isn't that just why we *should* wait for you?"

"Don't worry. I'll stick close to the boys from the lifeboat station, and the police are bound to be involved in any rescue." He frowned and stared at the straits. "Go on, then," she urged. "There's a late-afternoon ferry from Jura to Islay; from there you can catch another boat to the mainland. If you hurry you'll be in Bournemouth to-morrow morning. Wait for me at Bella's."

"And you're still determined to confront Gore?"

"Determined." She kissed him and gripped his hands. "If it's too cold, or the currents too strong, turn back. There's no disgrace in it."

He slid off a rock. The cold water stabbed his groin like a knife and he set off swimming a breaststroke. He timed the swells, shutting his mouth and dipping his head when they hit, then gasping for a breath and checking that he was headed toward the Jura cove he had picked for a landfall. Like tides and currents in the Corryvreckan, the waves were unpredictable. He judged one wrong and choked on cold salty water. Another wave slapped his face, then another and he swallowed more sea water. Was this how you drowned, he wondered—slowly, a little at a time, until the lungs filled and you blacked out forever?

He turned onto his back and paddled sideways through a trough, coughing water from his lungs and checking the two islands. Gina was standing on a rock, waving and shouting encouragement. He was midway. The currents here were even stronger, more confusing. A string of smaller whirlpools had created their own world of tides and races. He escaped from one pool only to be dragged toward another eye of churning water. The small pools were hands passing him backward toward the Corryvreckan and the Atlantic.

A wave buried him and he fought the tug of another current. His legs were numb and his head light. The life jacket had forced him to choose between a breaststroke and a slow, clumsy crawl. He had been glad of the jacket at first—he thought it would allow him to float if he tired—but the sea was too cold and the currents too powerful for that. He swiveled his head. Gina was still there, shouting him on. He unhitched his belt and his shoes vanished into a wave. Next he jerked at the straps of the life jacket with numb fingers. At last they ripped open and he squirmed free. He waved the jacket high over his head and then tossed it into the waves. He struck out toward Jura with a powerful and confident stroke.

When he climbed ashore, he lay on a rock for several minutes catching his breath. Across the straits Gina waved her life vest in the air. Was she applauding him? He decided she was. He scrambled up a cliff and ran barefoot toward Barnhill.

CHAPTER 21

Gina heard the powerful engines of the Islay lifeboat and darted from the cave. Its strong searchlight was sweeping the Scarba coastline. The light picked her out, stopped, and a too familiar voice shouted her name over a bullhorn.

As soon as she was on board Piers wrapped her in a blanket, thrust a mug of tea into her hand and led her to a seat away from the crew. The sky was lightening as they sped back along the west coast of Jura. It was almost morning, more than twelve hours since Adam had left. "What took so long?" she asked. "Did you bribe them to wait for you?"

"It's not strange that the authorities contacted me. I *am* next of kin. About the delay, I don't really know. The weather's been ghastly, and I believe there was a mechanical problem with the boat. I was fortunate to arrive in time."

It was just possible that he was telling the truth. Adam had swum the Corryvrecken during a brief lull in the bad weather. Shortly afterward the storm had worsened and was followed by a thick fog that could have delayed the rescue. But it was just as possible that Piers was lying. She preferred to believe that. "You bastard," she said. "You pulled a string or paid someone. I sat here freezing for a few more hours so you could harvest some publicity. Where's the press? Back at the pier with Dorothy? Or has she run off with that pilot?"

His face reddened and he glared at her. Bull's-eye, she thought, she had hit him in his most sensitive spot, his vanity. The more she provoked him at moments like these, the more she learned. In particular, she wanted to know why he had come again. Would he really go to such trouble for some favorable publicity? She decided to wave another red flag and see if the bull charged. "You lied to me, didn't you?" she accused.

"What do you mean 'lied'?" He looked fierce. He had adopted "I'll Never Lie to You" as one of his slogans.

"Last time you swore you wouldn't rescue me again. Obviously that was a lie."

"Christ almighty, you're impossible!" he shouted. But then, worried the crew might overhear him, he lowered his voice and said, "I flew up here at great inconvenience simply to be on hand to comfort you after the rescue. By chance I arrived in time to join the search party and now, as thanks, you accuse me of telling a lie, something I never do, something—"

"That's right," she broke in. "And you've just told another. You haven't come to comfort me. You know damned well the best way for you to do that would be to stay as far away as possible. No, Piers, as usual you're out for yourself."

He leaned toward her, his face twisted with fury. "All right, so there happens to be a reporter waiting on the dock. But he heard about this from the police, not me. In fact, I wish he wasn't here."

She laughed merrily. "That makes three lies."

"No, goddammit! I'm not here for cheap publicity. I don't need it. I'm popular because of my convictions, not because of the capitalist press." He was shouting again. "But you're right about not caring about you. If they'd asked me I'd have said leave her there for a few more days or, even better, a few more weeks."

"Then why are you here?" she asked softly. She noticed that his hands were gripping the wooden seat so tightly that their knuckles had turned white.

"It's not for me," he spluttered. "I'm doing a favor . . . a favor for friends."

"Some favor. You're just excess weight, slowing down the boat." She did a double take. "What 'friends'?"

"I'm taking you home," he said quickly. "Keep you out of trouble."

She leaned across and shook his shoulders. "What 'trouble'? What 'friends' are you talking about?"

His eyes darted to the horizon. She could sense him composing another lie. Finally he said, "*Our* friends, of course. They've all been terribly worried. First you and that old man lose your way, then you're shipwrecked on that island. Christ, isn't that trouble enough?" He turned back and faced her, suddenly more confident. "They've all been concerned that you were much too isolated here; that you were lonely, depressed, not yourself. For months they've been after me to bring you home. Everyone misses you."

"What crap! 'We' don't have any friends; they're all *your* friends and none of them gives a good goddamn what happens to me. They'd just as soon see my bones picked clean by wild goats. Come on, dammit, who are you talking about?"

"For God's sake keep your voice down. You're all keyed up, almost delirious. I've brought some pills to calm your nerves, help you sleep. You must have suffered terribly, stuck on that island in the storm without any provisions. I hired the helicopter again, and there's a plane waiting in Glasgow for us. I'll do my best to keep the press away. We can be in London in a few hours. Then you can sleep."

Dorothy, a reporter and two police constables were waiting on the Port Askaig pier. Gina ignored the reporter and strode over to Dorothy. "Do you have any cash?" she demanded. Dorothy usually carried Piers's funds.

"Yes, but how much do you need?" She was wary.

"A hundred pounds."

"What for?"

"For Chrissakes, it's my money. Give it to me. If you must know, I want to make a contribution to their lifeboat fund. Good politics."

Dorothy counted out the money like a teller. Gina shoved it in her pocket and said, "Thanks. Should be enough to see me to London."

"But we've already arranged transport."

"That's the point." She walked over and joined the men. The reporter was taking statements from Piers and the lifeboat captain.

She interrupted. "I'd like to say something." Piers grabbed her arm. She shook him off and the reporter flipped to a clean sheet of notepaper.

"First off, I want to express my gratitude to the men of the Islay lifeboat station who rescued me. I want also to thank my husband for joining them. For him in particular it was above and beyond the call of duty, since we have both known for some time that I will soon be petitioning for a divorce. I shall charge adultery and mental cruelty. This also explains why we will now be returning to London separately. End of statement." She turned to one of the constables. "I trust you won't mind driving me to the airport?" As she drove away, the reporter was feeding coins into the paybox.

"He's conscious," Perkins said the moment she opened the door and saw Bella. Adam and Charlie stood several paces behind her.

Bella hugged the middle-aged housekeeper and said, "Quick, then, grab your wrap and let's go to the hospital."

"Oh, he's not there. Kicked up such a fuss they finally got rid of him. The doctors were opposed but the nurses insisted, and no wonder too. I've had him ever since and he's been a terror, raving on about that diary of his, and about you running off and leaving him—"

Bella pushed past her and hurried down the hall. "Better not go upstairs now," Perkins said. "I just put him down for his nap."

"Then I'll wake him."

"Suit yourself. I'll be back when I've recovered."

Adam stopped her at the front gate and asked if anyone had telephoned since the Brigadier's return.

"Yes, two calls, but . . ." She eyed him suspiciously. "Who are you to be asking?"

"Adam Frost."

"Suppose it's all right, then. Early this morning a young lady phoned asking for you. At first I thought she had the wrong number. Said she'd be arriving tonight but the pips interrupted before she left her name."

Charlie gave a cheer and Adam slapped him on the back. During the drive from Scotland both had worried about Gina. Several times Charlie had insisted they stop and telephone, but Adam had persuaded him that it was too early. She would still be en route and the Brigadier's cottage was sure to be unoccupied.

"And the second call?" Adam asked Perkins. "You said there were two."

"That wasn't for you. One of your countrymen asking after the Brigadier."

"What did you tell him?"

"That he was dead and buried; popped off just after coming home from hospital. He ordered me to say that to anyone who called. Now if you don't mind, I've had two straight days of the old dear."

"But why . . ."

"Did he want to be known as dead? Guess he thinks he's still in danger. At least the police have more sense. The inspector took a look at the shambles and said it had to be a robbery that turned nasty when the stubborn old thing wouldn't cooperate."

She pushed through the gate before Adam could question her further. Charlie turned toward the house but Adam quickly grabbed his arm. "Let's leave them alone for a while," he said. "You come with me. I'm going to hunt down a travel agent."

"Leaving, are-you?" Charlie asked eagerly. He considered Adam to be his rival.

"Mrs. Baldwin and I are going to the Caribbean." The boy looked at the ground and Adam took pity on him. "But we'll only be away several days and I happen to know she hopes you'll stay on here until she returns. She wants to help you find a job, or go home if you prefer. In the meantime, you could protect the Brigadier in case Hacker decides to finish the job."

The boy threw back his shoulders. "Like a professional bodyguard?"

"Yes, that's right."

"All right, then, but only for a short while. And if I want a job, I'll find my own. Reckon I can look out for myself now."

Bella had to shake Paget several times to wake him. When he opened his eyes he said, "Ha! Ran off and left me for dead."

"Don't talk such rot. You were unconscious and I had a duty to protect that poor girl."

After she had finished summarizing what had happened on Jura, he said, "If that blasted Yank hadn't bashed me over the head I might have saved you the trip, told you all about Colonel Victor Gore."

Bella stepped back and squinted. His face was flushed and his head wrapped in a turban of bandages. "Are you quite sure you've recovered?" she asked.

"Never felt better," he said in a weak voice.

"But last Saturday, before Mrs. Baldwin and I went to the Moti, you never said a thing about Colonel Gore."

"That's because once you left me in peace I finally had time to dig out my Paris diary and reread it to see what the fuss was all about. First thing I discovered was I'd been dead right about having drinks alone with Blair at the Scribe. Happened in April, a month after we lunched together with Wodehouse, and a month after you dashed off without a goodbye."

"But I had to leave suddenly, Geoffrey. It was my job and—"

"All right, all right. Never mind. All forgiven."

"But why did Eric want to see *you?* The two of you hit it off so poorly the first time that I was afraid you'd come to blows."

"Good thing for him we didn't. Anyway, he didn't want to see me, it was I who insisted on our meeting. Threatened to expose what was going on if he refused."

"And what *was* going on?"

"What was going on," he snapped, "was that whenever someone like Blair sees an officer's uniform he jumps to the conclusion that inside it is some silly, easily fooled Blimp. Ha! Wrong! Just like that Yank who bashed me. He sees a pink-cheeked old thing wearing thick glasses, with a carnation in the buttonhole, carrying a cane, and thinks: This old dodderer will be a pushover. I set him straight.

Too bad I couldn't see his face when I went after him with the iron. Few more inches on target and he'd have been in the hospital, or worse, and not me." He raised his head from the pile of pillows and said in a quivering voice, "And in some ways you were just as bad as the Yank, and Blair. First off, during that lunch, Blair goes on about some hypothetical American colonel who may have been a Soviet agent. And then the very next day you ask me to arrange an interview for you with a Colonel Gore. You must have thought I was very dim. It's clear from my diary that from the start I was almost positive that you and Blair were in league and that Gore was Blair's hypothetical colonel."

"Then why didn't you *say* something."

"I was going to. Couldn't have Soviet spies poking their noses into everything. I'd planned to alert American intelligence as soon as I'd warned you to stay clear of the Colonel. I didn't want you caught up in the investigation."

"Is that *really* the only reason you hesitated?"

"All right, dammit! I said I was *almost* positive that Gore was Blair's hypothetical colonel. But I couldn't accuse the man unless I was *completely* positive, could I? And the best way to accomplish that seemed to be to force one or the other of you to admit the truth. But before I could act all of you—Blair, the Colonel and you —suddenly beetled off, leaving me alone with my suspicions."

"Until Eric came through Paris again in April."

"That's right. And once I'd cornered him in the Scribe I didn't waste any time. Told him straight out that I knew about Gore and considered it my duty to inform the Americans.

"It took Blair several moments to think of a reply. I'd obviously caught him off balance. Finally he said, 'I apologize for underestimating you.'

" 'Nonsense,' I shot back. 'Any child could have figured out that—'

"He held up his hand and said, 'Wait, hear me out,' and then related that fantastic story of his confrontation with Colonel Gore in Cologne and Gore's claim that rather than working for the Soviets, he had been their victim.

" 'But how can you be sure he's telling the truth?' I demanded. 'Last month you seemed almost convinced that the opposite was true. Time to let intelligence sort this out.'

"He thumped the table and said, 'No! I gave my word I wouldn't do that as long as he transferred to a front-line command, which he's done. There's still too much uncertainty; not enough proof to warrant besmirching a man's reputation, perhaps ruining his career.'

"I protested some more until at last he said, 'Give me a month before you act. A month to observe him and investigate, to see if I can uncover any conclusive proof one way or the other.'

" 'And in the meantime he could be passing information on to the Russians.'

" 'I'll grant we're taking some risks, but they're small ones. Given his present duties, it's doubtful he has access to anything important.'

"I replied with words to the effect that this entire approach struck me as maddeningly indecisive and weak. This really set him off. He thumped that table again and said, 'Better to be momentarily indecisive, but fair, than the opposite. After all, doesn't that distinguish us from those thugs in Berlin and Moscow? If the situation were reversed they'd simply shoot Dawney *and* Gore, just to be sure they'd eliminated the right man. It's only natural that people who'd favor that approach should also mistakenly confuse our concern for fairness and justice with weakness. Which is precisely why, once we're certain we're in the right, we must act as decisively and ruthlessly as they would. And that's what I promise to do once I've uncovered the truth about Gore.' "

The Brigadier fell back onto the pillows and said, "Satisfied? Now you know everything."

"But did you give Eric the month he wanted?"

Paget looked annoyed. "Yes, though it scarcely mattered since the war ended before his month expired and soon Blair, you, me, Gore and everyone were scattered all over the globe. Blair was right, of course. In fact, I'd been plagued by the same doubts; otherwise I never would have agreed, would have gone to intelligence immediately. Too bad I didn't. Then I wouldn't be lying here wrapped in these damn bandages."

"But, Geoffrey, I don't see why—"

He bolted upright again. "All of this was in my Paris diary. Isn't it obvious that this Colonel Gore, or someone who wants very badly to hurt him, sent someone here to steal it?" He fell back onto the bed and was silent for several moments before taking her hand and stroking it. "Sorry to be so short," he said weakly. "But I've been lying here turning everything over, becoming angry at myself for allowing that Yank to get the best of me. Means a great deal to have you back."

"All understood," she whispered. "No apologies necessary." She wanted to let him sleep but decided that for Gina's sake she had to pose one more question. Gina might be able to use this information if, as Adam claimed, she planned to have it out with Colonel Gore. "And you're certain you wrote down what Eric said about the Colonel?" she asked. "Everything about him being a Communist and then changing his identity?" Paget nodded. "Good! Then there *is* still some written evidence."

"You mean *was*. My assailant made off with the diary. By now it's probably at the bottom of some pond."

"But just suppose it's not," she said quietly, almost to herself. "Then whoever had it could destroy Victor Gore." She looked down at the Brigadier, but he had fallen asleep, clutching her hand. He was right: Blair *had* underestimated him, and so had she. She always had. Stupid. In some ways he was twice the man Eric had been; every bit as sensitive but even more generous, and less the bully and manipulator. While she sat stiffly by his bedside the afternoon sun flooded through the windows, slanting across his face and coloring it a youthful reddish brown. Perhaps it won't hurt, she thought, to break just one of my "rules"—the one about marriage.

PART III

PART III

CHAPTER 22

Nat Beale rocked back in his chair and whistled. "Those diaries are worth a fortune, and imagine the fees you could earn lecturing on how you've discovered them!" The waiter, thinking "Señor Fonda" had whistled for service, hurried over, and to avoid disappointing him Beale ordered another round of daiquiris. He was huddled with Adam and Gina in a dark corner of the "Hemingway Bar," surrounded by out-of-date calendars. This was his first interruption of their story of what had happened on Jura.

"Hard to believe you won't be tempted to publish them no matter what Victor promises," he continued. "Victor may have the same thought."

"He'll have to take our word for it," Adam said. "He hasn't any choice."

"So it seems." Beale grinned. "You've really harpooned him, haven't you? I'd be less than candid if I didn't admit to enjoying this. Where are the diaries now?"

Gina glanced at Adam. During the day they had spent at Bella's and their long air flight from London he had agreed to the plan she had outlined on Scarba. Now she could sense him becoming nervous. If he was uncomfortable lying to Beale, she would do it. "I've given them to a solicitor in London," she said, "with instructions to publish them if anything happens to us."

"Then how can Victor, or I for that matter, be sure they exist?"

"*You* don't need to be sure," she said. "And he'll know we have them once we tell him what they say."

"You want me to run interference with Hacker and arrange a

meeting with Victor, yet you're not willing to trust me . . ." He paused and waved his hand in the air. "It doesn't matter. Diaries or no diaries, Victor is finished."

"That's what I'll have to decide."

"No, young lady, I'm afraid that's for me and our board of directors to decide. Once they learn that he concealed his membership in the Communist Party, changed his identity and ordered a Tropic employee to terrorize people to preserve his secrets, they'll force him to quit."

"How will they find out?" Adam asked.

"Why, I'll tell them of course, unless he agrees to resign. I might even take the helm for a while, but purely as a caretaker."

Gina looked fierce. She had not flown this distance to further Beale's career. "We won't help you, and without our evidence or testimony . . ."

"Too late. I already know enough to convince Victor to bow out. I'll give him the choice between a dignified resignation and having the whole story presented to the board. Which do you think he'll choose? I'll also require that he refuse any position he's offered in Washington."

"You plan to blackmail him."

"No! I plan to act in the best interests of the country. He could still be a Soviet agent." He turned to Adam. "You know my reservations about placing the R-Tube in Washington. Imagine the consequences if Victor is passing the sweep results on to the KGB."

"But what about his scars?" Adam asked. "The same scars Dawney inflicted on the boy."

"I don't find them persuasive. And the other evidence points to a Russian connection." He looked at Gina. "What about those 'friends' of your husband's? Where is someone like Mike Baldwin more likely to have friends—Washington or Moscow?"

"My husband loathes the Soviets. Claims they're as bad as . . ."

"The Americans? That's what he says, but does he believe it? I imagine his 'friends' are more likely to be Vietnamese or Cuban, but they're controlled by Moscow, so what's the difference? Hacker took some incredible risks. He ordered you killed, beat up an old man and

Lord only knows what else. He's brutal but not stupid. I just don't believe that he acted without express orders or that Victor would have given them, unless he was worried about concealing more than a forty-year-old secret."

He drained his drink and rose to leave. "You're staying in that little hotel behind the cathedral?"

Adam nodded.

"Good. Go there now and wait. I'll fetch you after I've explained everything to him."

"You mean you can see him tonight?" Adam asked.

"Why not?"

"Last week he'd wiped you off the R-Tube because of your opposition to Washington."

"Oh, he can't afford to play those games now. I'm still a member in good standing of his board. At least for the next few days he'll have to be civil. And besides, if I know Victor he'll see me right away because he'll assume I've come to apologize and pledge my support."

"How about Hacker?" Adam asked. He had planned to warn Beale that while on Jura he had told Hacker about Beale's group of "fine young people." But now he was so angry with Beale for planning to use his discoveries to promote his own career that he decided to let him take his chances with Hacker.

"Hacker returned last night," Beale said. "And ever since he's been staying close to the Resort, and close to Victor. But don't worry. Once Victor hears you have the diaries he won't let Hacker touch you."

Adam grabbed Beale by the wrist before he could walk away and said, "Your turn to pay for the drinks." Beale sighed, but then unbuckled his belt and pulled a wad of small notes from a secret compartment hidden in the lining.

"Telling him was a mistake," Gina said, back in their room. "We should have telephoned Gore or gone directly to the Resort and caught him unawares."

"You wouldn't say that if you knew how the TropicResort works. Calls are screened by the R-Tube, and Hacker's security force checks every visitor in and out. We need someone to take us to Gore. Think of Nat as our white flag, protecting us while we discuss a truce."

"Gore doesn't strike me as someone who respects white flags."

"He will if he believes we have the diaries."

"I'm taking the revolver anyway." She had reclaimed it from Charlie and brought it along in her luggage.

"If he searches us . . ."

"I don't give a damn. I don't trust your friend Beale and I'm not meeting Victor Gore unarmed."

Adam turned on the overhead fan and pulled down the bamboo window shade. It was late afternoon and the tropical sun filtered through moist hazy clouds. The drinks combined with jet lag and humidity had made him dizzy. He stripped to his undershorts and fell into the groove in the middle of the double bed. They had rented the room as a sanctuary in which to hide until Gore summoned them. Neither expected to sleep there. Within seconds the thin sheets were soaked with his perspiration. Gina slumped into a chair. "What will you do afterwards?" she asked.

"Look for another job, I suppose, and keep out of Hacker's way."

"You've changed your mind about forcing Gore to promote you?"

"How can I if Nat forces him to resign?"

"And if Beale fails?"

"Then I'll make him resign and I'll quit myself. I've had enough." He looked up at her and smiled. "See what a bad influence you've been?" When he closed his eyes she undressed. He woke to find her stroking him and licking his perspiration. When he reached for her, she whispered, "No, don't move, it's too hot. Let me do everything."

When he woke again the room was dark and she was gone. He could recall making love in rhythm to the slow clicking of the fan, and the bed becoming a swimming pool of sweat. But he did not remember her leaving. He jumped up and opened the blinds rather than hunt for the light switch. The streetlights were glowing but the sky was still pink. Her note was on a chair. "Darling. Too hot to sleep. Don't leave without me. Promise?"

When someone opened the door he assumed it was she. "Get dressed," Beale said. "He's willing to see you, but only you. Later he may speak with the woman."

"That wasn't the deal."

"It's the best I could do." He drummed his fingers nervously on the table while Adam dressed.

"I'll have to wait for her to explain . . ."

"No time for that. He insists you come now. Leave her a note telling her to come to my villa. It's Casita 19. I'll tell the guards to admit her."

"Why the hurry?"

"The board is arriving tonight and Victor's throwing a welcoming party. He probably wants time after you talk to plan what he's going to tell them."

"He sounds calm."

"He is, which disturbs me. He was very, *very* understanding about what you'd been through. And he admitted straight out having fought in Spain and changing his identity."

"He's not angry?"

"Only with Hacker."

"Did you pressure him about resigning?"

"He volunteered that it would be best if he left with his reputation intact. For some reason he's tremendously pleased with you. Went on and on about what a splendid job you'd done. If this were the army he'd be awarding you a medal."

A sign at the entrance to the Lily Pad said "Private Party." There were hurricane lamps on the tables and a semicircle of flickering kerosene torches separating the patio from the darkening golf course. Slabs of meat smoked over a barbecue tended by a chef in a gaucho outfit. Gore and the Duchess were the only guests. They sat at a remote table holding hands and sipping through straws stuck into hollowed-out coconuts. Adam was embarrassed to interrupt, but as he stood there hesitating, Gore looked up and switched on a welcoming smile.

"Well, here's our hero," he said, patting Adam on the back as he sat down. "Nat has told me everything and we want to thank you for performing so brilliantly, and honorably." He glanced over Adam's shoulder. "Where is Nat? I thought he was bringing you here."

"He went back to his villa to change for dinner."

"That's fine, just fine." He smiled again. "Better for us to be alone."

The Duchess squeezed his arm and said, "I hope you're joining us too. We're having a late barbecue to welcome the board." She drained her coconut and stood up to leave. "I'll never forget what you've done for Victor."

The guard punched Gina's name into the R-Tube console. The message: AUTHORIZED VISITOR BEALE GC 19 flashed onto the screen. He murmured instructions to her taxi driver, raised the barrier and gave a clumsy salute. She noticed that the driver, who had rocketed along the potholed highway connecting the town to the Resort, now was slowing to a crawl, probably confused by the network of similar roads or intimidated by the guards driving motor scooters and golf carts marked SECURITY. After he had made several wrong turns she was completely disoriented. Each curving drive led to an identical cluster of one-story white stucco villas with red tile roofs and gas lamps. There were no streetlights, and most of the buildings were dark. The golf course surrounding the islands of villas reminded her of the ocean on a moonless night: black, featureless and cold.

"Where are the guests?" she asked the driver.

"No one comes this month. Afraid of the storms."

A small crowd of maids and guards was clustered in front of Beale's villa. Several red SECURITY carts and an ambulance, its rear door open, were parked helter-skelter on the front lawn. She asked a guard what had happened. "Someone must be sick," he said. "The ambulance just arrived."

The door of Beale's villa was ajar, and in the vestibule she could see a huddle of men in white coats and uniforms. The huddle broke and two attendants wheeled out a stretcher. A sheet covered the face, but she was certain it was Beale. Hacker was last to leave. He methodically locked the door, extinguishing the porch light, and then slammed shut the back door of the ambulance.

Gina slipped across the street and crouched in a sand trap, watching as the ambulance drove away. For several minutes its slowly winking red light was visible across the golf course. Hacker and a blond young man wearing a red blazer climbed into separate golf carts and left. The crowd melted into the darkness and she was alone. But not for long, she knew. As soon as Hacker checked the computer he would learn she was here.

"First let me explain everything," Gore said as soon as the Duchess had left. "Then you can ask questions." He smiled and shook his head. "Heaven knows, you have the right to, after what you've been through. And let's have two of those coconut punches, my wife's recipe." To signal the waiter he banged an empty shell against the glass tabletop.

"My wife knows everything. She caught that Baldwin woman's notice in the paper and alerted me. The old alarm bells sounded when I saw she was living on Blair's island. You're probably wondering: Why the alarm bells? Nowadays it's no big deal to have belonged to the Communist Party, or to have fought for the Spanish Republic. Most of those veterans are now drooling old shells who wheel themselves out for peace parades. Nobody pays attention to them, not even the FBI. But that wasn't always the case. During the war it was a great handicap to have fought in Spain. And in the early fifties there was McCarthy. In those days a former Communist never could have put together this company, gained the confidence of bankers and shareholders. Now the climate is better, but it's much too late to come clean. Combine my past with my friendship with the President and you've got the makings of a first-class scandal."

"Then who was Victor Gore?"

"Another American volunteer. He was killed fighting for the Jaca road. That was several months before I was arrested."

"But how did you assume his identity? That's the part that . . ."

Gore's smile vanished. "I asked you not to interrupt. That's an insignificant detail. The important thing to understand is that Peter Ekman was a fool. He went to Spain because he thought it would be an adventure. He didn't give a hoot for politics or Communism. He joined the Party because it would pay his way to Madrid. See what a fool he was? In that war politics was *everything*. He fought with the Lincoln Brigade, but was soon weeded out by the political commissars as "politically unreliable," in need of more education. He didn't like the sound of that, so he deserted and fled north. He had planned to slip across the border to France, but when he arrived in Barcelona he learned that too many foreign deserters had attempted the same thing, and been caught and shot. So he joined the first militia outfit that would have him, the POUM, where he met Dawney and Blair. He figured they couldn't shoot you for deserting the cause if you were still fighting for it. Now do you understand how foolish Peter Ekman was? He never bothered to learn that the Trotskyite POUM was distrusted by the Republic and detested by the Soviets. Because of this gross naïveté he was arrested, starved, beaten, immersed in tubs of water, pulled out moments before drowning and thrown naked into a windowless cell. And while he was lying there, licking his wounds like a helpless animal, he decided he'd never again let himself become so powerless that he could be subjected to such humiliation, never permit anyone to abuse him, never become so helpless." As Gore described the horrors he had suffered, the muscles in his neck tensed and a snakelike vein on the side of his forehead pulsed and strained against the surface of the skin. There could be no doubt that Peter Ekman *had* suffered these indignities, and had been transformed by them.

"And then there were those famous burns," he said. "Since many of the interrogation rooms were warmed by coal fires, that became the prison's winter specialty. On the beach I noticed that many had similar scars. Would you like to see mine?"

"That's not necessary, Victor. I believe you."

"But I *want* you to see them." He pulled up one leg of his red linen trousers to reveal discolored patches of skin. "Everything I told Blair in Cologne was true; everything Dawney told you was a lie.

"When I glimpsed Dawney at the Hotel Scribe my first impulse was to strangle him. But doing that, or accusing him in public, would have meant admitting I had been Peter Ekman, Communist fool. I also assumed that he would be afraid enough of me to flee Paris. Instead he came after me! And when that failed, he enlisted Blair in his bizarre crusade to accuse me of his crimes. To his credit, Blair was skeptical and when we met in Cologne we cleared up our misunderstandings. It is my opinion that Dawney went mad because of what he'd done. But Nat tells me this is all in Blair's diaries, isn't it?" He paused and stared hard at Adam. "Isn't it?"

"Yes, except Blair couldn't decide which of you was telling the truth."

"And you've read the diaries and met Dawney?"

"Yes."

"And who do *you* believe?"

"Why, you, of course. Otherwise I wouldn't be here."

"And why do you believe me."

"Because Dawney tortured you and the Irish boy in the same way. But there is one thing. You must speak some Spanish, so why did you insist I translate during that fishing expedition?"

"Peter Ekman learned Spanish, not Victor Gore. Are you convinced Ekman is innocent?"

Adam nodded vigorously. "Haven't I said that?"

"Yes. But I want to hear it again, and again. It's an important first step."

Thick clouds obscured the stars and sliver of moon, making it so dark that Gina had to wrench the flag from the hole and hold it in front of her nose to see the numeral. It said "6." She was on the green of the sixth hole. Several hundred yards down the seventh fairway the headlights of two security carts blinked on and off like dim yellow eyes as the carts nosed in and out of sand traps and scooted around lagoons.

At first she had followed the curving driveways, hoping they might lead to a main road or to the reception area, and perhaps Adam and Gore. But when she found herself retracing her steps, she adopted a new strategy and left the twinkling lanterns of one island of villas to sprint across dark fairways to another island, then another. But the distances between them were so great, and the night so dark, that each appeared identical. She went in a circle, and returned to Beale's villa. Hacker and his forces had reconvened on it too, like ants drawn to a sugar cube. She pulled out Eric's Colt as she listened to the crackling of their radios, and to someone repeating her name. When they were convinced that the house was empty, they paired off into twos and drove off in different directions. She decided to stick to the golf course, working backward from hole to hole until she reached the first, gambling that it would be near the heart of the Resort. She started at the tenth hole, but somewhere between there and the sixth two security carts had picked up her scent and begun following her.

She felt a sudden gust of wet wind, and a drop of rain, large and hard enough to be hail, hit her forehead. Seconds later rain fell in sheets, obscuring her view. It stopped just as abruptly. There was a brief pause before the insects resumed their chirping and the two security carts started down the seventh fairway. Searchlights mounted on their awnings swept the ground ahead in fifty-yard arcs.

The sixth hole was a dogleg. She ran too far down the first leg and into a strange fairway. By the time she realized her mistake and doubled back, her pursuers were parked near the sixth green, playing their spotlights onto the fairway. She had forgotten to replace the flag. Now they knew her system. The beam of one searchlight slashed through the darkness, passing several feet from where she stood. The other sliced toward her from the opposite direction. She zigzagged across the middle of the sixth fairway and flattened herself against the trunk of a palm tree as the light probed around her. It moved on and she set out running for a clump of marsh grass. One light flashed across her back and for a split second she saw her shadow in its long yellow shaft. The light braked and backtracked as she dived into the tall grass. It bordered a long lagoon, a water obstacle separating parallel fairways. As the carts hummed toward her, she slipped into the water and, holding the revolver over her head and praying it would be shallow, began wading.

Her feet sank several inches into the muddy bottom. The water rose to her waist, her armpits and then her chin. She tried tiptoeing but only sank deeper. Finally she willed herself to kick her legs and pull at the stagnant water with her free arm. The line of storm clouds passed and the sliver of moon illuminated the way ahead. There was another green, a flag waving from its hole. She prayed it would say "1." She needed time to find Adam and warn him.

Beale had blackmailed Gore and now he was dead, killed before he could share the secret of Gore's past. Unlike them, he had no diaries to protect him. But in fact, neither did they. If Adam let Gore suspect they were lying, they would be as vulnerable as Beale.

"I'm going to fire Stan Hacker," Gore said. "That must please you."

"It's pretty light punishment for what he's done."

"You've always disliked him, so I don't expect you to be objective. What pains me is that if he's guilty of anything, it's trying too hard to protect me. After my wife clipped that Baldwin woman's notice, I took Stan into my confidence. At first I didn't say anything about Dawney or Paris. I told him I'd once belonged to the Communist Party, and now feared that the Baldwin woman was collecting information for a damaging exposé. I debated telling him even that much, but then I couldn't go racing around Scotland myself.

"His reaction should have warned me. He became visibly upset and asked several times what effect these revelations could have on the R-Tube. I told him the truth: they might mean the end of it. Did you know that Stan was not happy at the Agency?"

"He told me."

"The Washington project was very important to him. He was counting on being in charge of security for the head-on computer, and having access to the sweep results. I suspect he planned to use them to settle some old scores."

"And you were going to let him?"

"Why not? As long as he was discreet. I believe in rewarding people with what they want most. What's the fun of receiving a bonus you don't need?

"I only took Stan into my confidence because I thought he had a healthy interest in preserving my reputation. His first move was to break into Mrs. Baldwin's house and photograph her papers. He brought the results to me because he didn't know what was important. When I saw the note to her from Dawney I knew I had trouble. I told Stan about what had happened in Spain and ordered him to stop Dawney."

"For Chrissakes, Victor, what does 'stop Dawney' mean? It means kill him, doesn't it? So Stan *was* acting on your orders?" It was the first time he had raised his voice.

Gore looked at him thoughtfully. "It could have meant any number of things: blackmail him, frighten him or, yes, even kill him. That would have been simple justice."

"Or it could have meant 'If you can't stop *him*, kill the woman.' "

Gore shook his head sadly. "Yes, that does seem to be how Stan interpreted it. I won't dispute that he was excessive."

"And wrong."

"Oh yes, that too. He tried to drop an atomic bomb on the whole problem. Blast away everyone who might harm me."

"He could have been charged with murder and you named as an accessory. That would have been more damaging than Dawney's revelations. Why do you think Stan went off the rails?"

"Why, I imagine he thought he was doing his job. What other explanation is there? When his methods failed, he had to tell me that Dawney was on his way to Jura to poison the Baldwin woman with his lies. I decided to shift our meeting there because I was the only one who could identify Dawney, and Jura was the next place we expected him to surface."

"That can't be the only reason. Dawney is not exactly nondescript. Jura is so small Hacker could easily have found him."

"You're right, of course." Gore flashed another smile. "I did have other motives. That island seemed an ideal place to trap him. But because it was so damned small, we needed an excuse to flood it with our people without making the locals suspicious. And if Dawney slipped through our net and reached Mrs. Baldwin, I wanted to be able to persuade her that he was insane and his story a lie. That's why I sent you ahead to skirmish. I wanted to know the best way of handling her."

"Then why didn't you say just that?"

"Because information is power. Hasn't this fiasco taught you anything? I don't tell anyone more than necessary. The fewer people who knew about Spain and Dawney, the better. But my faith in you was justified, wasn't it? You had the light touch, the finesse Stan lacked."

He leaned across the table and punched Adam's arm. "You saved my ass. You not only found those damned diaries but also persuaded her not to publish them. And, best of all, you've disposed of Dawney."

"No! I didn't kill Dawney. Didn't Nat tell you he drowned?"

"Yes, but the main thing is, he's dead, and you get credit, not Stan. I want you to stay on board. Choose between a promotion here or coming with me to Washington. It's being announced next week. Don't look so shocked. Didn't I tell you I believe in rewarding people with what they want?"

Adam's face showed his surprise. "After all that's happened you really want me to . . ."

"What's happened? Someone who destroyed my youth has tried to destroy my reputation. He failed, and now he's dead. That's what happened. What should I do now, retire to Palm Springs?"

"No, I suppose not." Victor had a point. Why should he be victimized again by Dawney? And why should Beale use what Adam had uncovered in order to blackmail him into retiring? He felt ashamed for having employed Nat as an intermediary.

"What about Nat?" he asked. "He said that . . ."

"He'd force me to resign? What crap!" He waved his hand in the air. "Nat is a weak, unprincipled man who pretends to be precisely the opposite. He's already retreated from what he called his 'demands.' Believe me, he's in no position to cause any trouble."

The flag said "1." Gina felt like kissing it. By crossing the lagoon she had widened her lead. Her pursuers were probably still backtracking from hole to hole, hoping to overtake her before she reached the clubhouse. The first fairway was a straight three-hundred-yard run.

When she reached the first tee she saw that her plan had been sound; by following the course she had reached the heart of the TropicResort. She hurried past a shuttered pro shop and lines of idle golf carts, through a maze of deserted tennis courts and onto a paved roadway. The violent rainstorms had driven guests inside. To her right, down a gentle hill, were the lights of the main gate and next to them a sprawling one-story hacienda with swimming pools and open plazas. Up a hill to her left she saw a row of flickering torches. There was a smell of barbecuing meat. The torches were closer, she would check them first.

She approached the restaurant cautiously, keeping outside the circles of light. A chef turned an animal on a spit and a lone waiter leaned against a well-stocked bar. A wiry man with close-cropped gray hair sat with Adam on the outer edge of the patio, smiling and patting him on the back. She pulled Eric's revolver from her bag. She could leap from the shadows and surprise him.

"After what you and the Baldwin woman suffered, I don't blame you for taking Nat into your confidence," Gore said. "I would have done the same thing."

Adam took another sip from his coconut. Could he have everything? A Tropic promotion *or* a powerful position in Washington, and satisfy Gina as well? Perhaps it was time to mend fences. "I think you're being very understanding," he said.

"Not at all. It's *you* who's being understanding. I should have put you in the picture. I blame myself." He reached underneath the table, pulled two bulging manila envelopes from a duffel and slapped them on the table with such force that Adam expected the glass to shatter.

"Stan stole these from Mrs. Baldwin. As soon as she joins us, I plan to return them and apologize."

"I'm sure she'll be pleased."

"As pleased as I shall be to have the diaries that are in her possession."

"But they're not in her possession. They're with a lawyer; didn't Nat tell you?"

"Yes, that's a problem. Suppose she choked to death on a piece of our barbecue, or her taxi crashed? Then what? Her lawyer would release Blair's diaries and I'd be ruined."

"But that's hardly likely . . ."

"Do you think I should live with those diaries hanging over me, knowing at any moment I could be subjected to a nasty scandal? And it goes without saying that if I'm destroyed, you would also suffer."

"I'm sure I can persuade her to destroy them." Adam was becoming uncomfortable; sooner or later he would have to admit the truth. Victor had been generous and understanding. He had promised to fire Hacker; he had produced Gina's manuscript; and his explanations were logical and convincing. Why test his patience? Hadn't he suffered enough from Dawney's brutality and insanity?

Adam took a deep breath and said, "Victor, don't worry about the diaries. Dawney had them when he drowned. We never recovered them."

Gore shot back his chair and clapped his hands together. "Goddammit, I knew it! I thought you'd never risk coming here otherwise. Much safer to sell them to some newspaper. Damn, you'd have made a fortune too." The smile left his face. "I thought you didn't have them, but I had to be sure."

CHAPTER 23

Gina rushed Gore from his blind side. By the time he turned his head in surprise, she was a body length away. She held Eric's revolver in both hands, pointing its barrel at his temple.

"Get up," she ordered. "You're coming with us."

His eyes moved up and down her body and then locked onto hers. Her hand began trembling. "Are you taking me hostage?" he asked pleasantly.

"Until we're safely away." She gripped the revolver tighter, willing herself to hold it on target.

"Safely away?" He smiled. "Impossible. You can't hustle me through the airport at gunpoint. The authorities won't be gentle with anyone threatening their most prominent foreign resident."

"Stop it, Gina!" Adam shouted. "There's no *need* for this. Everything's been settled."

"It's been settled for your friend Beale all right. He's dead."

"I saw him an hour ago."

"I saw the body. Hacker helped it into the ambulance."

Adam looked at Gore. "Is that true?"

"Heart attack, I'm afraid."

Adam jumped up, knocking back his chair. "How do you know that? We've been sitting here ever since . . ."

"Well, that may not be *exactly* how he died, but it's what his death certificate will say."

"You had him killed because he threatened to expose you," Gina said.

"Wrong, on both counts. First, he was trying to blackmail me, not expose me, and second, I didn't order Hacker to kill him. I merely said I hoped he wouldn't be communicating his slanderous allegations to the board."

"You wanted him dead," said Adam, as if talking to himself. "If it wasn't Spain, it must have been the R-Tube. Nat always suspected you were going to feed the sweeps to the KGB."

Gore raised the coconut high over his head and slammed it down on the table. The glass shattered with a bang. Adam threw up his hands to protect his eyes from the shards. Gore had sliced a cut in his forearm. Blood dripped onto his red linen trousers.

He ignored the wound. In a voice boiling with rage, he said, "Nat was a fool! Victor Gore works for himself, not for the goddamned Soviets, not for anyone. I haven't touched the Russians since Spain." He looked at Adam. "I *was* tortured in Barcelona. I escaped and used Gore's passport to come home. Since then I've stayed clear of the Soviets. They'd have killed me, if they'd found me, or forced me to spy for them. But Nat was right about the R-Tube: those Washington sweeps *will* be priceless. Not immediately; it'll take several years to construct useful customer profiles. But when they're assembled, they'll belong to *me*, not to some pack of Moscow bureaucrats. I'll use them as *I* please: to leverage my power in the Cabinet, protect TropicAmerican's profits or influence the President. The possibilities are endless, aren't they? Those I can't use I'll give to whomever I choose: Democrats, Republicans, the CIA— even, if it pleases me, to the KGB."

"You're lying," Gina said. "You're working for them already. When you thought we'd escaped from Jura, you or Hacker must have contacted my husband. He let slip that 'friends' of his had asked him to 'keep me out of trouble.' I think he planned to sedate me and wait for instructions. My husband is a Marxist; he doesn't do favors for 'friends' who run companies like yours, unless they're Communists."

"Why didn't you tell me about this before?" Adam asked quickly. "Why keep these suspicions to yourself?"

"Because until Hacker murdered Beale—and I'm convinced that's what happened—that's all they were: suspicions. And I was afraid if I shared them you'd refuse to bring me along. You only agreed in the first place because you believed Gore was innocent."

Gore looked perplexed. "I know all about your husband," he said slowly. "Stan said he was orchestrating everything for the Russians, helping them embarrass me and the President. That made sense. This doesn't."

"It's no use lying anymore," she said. "You may have destroyed Brigadier Paget's diaries but . . ."

"Paget's diaries? Now you're the one who's lying. Stan never said anything . . ."

There was a loud crash behind them. Gina quickly looked around. The chef and waiter had fled, one of them knocking over a table in his haste. They would alert the guards. "There's no time for this. We're going. Move!" He turned his back to her. "Get up or I shoot."

He stood and faced her. "You won't shoot. First . . ." He paused and checked her eyes. "First . . . kill me and you'll never leave here alive. Second . . ." He stopped and snapped his fingers in her face. She was reminded of Dawney. Both men had identical mannerisms, the snapping fingers and long pauses while they fixed you with their eyes. Had the torturer seared these habits into his victim's subconscious?

"Second . . . you won't fire because I'm unarmed. It's one thing to kill in self-defense. An execution is different; I know that from experience. Even Dawney, when he had the chance in those Ivry tunnels, couldn't do it. He stalled, wasted time arguing with himself until I could jump him. If he couldn't do it, neither can you.

"And third . . ."

"Stop it!" She lowered the revolver. "We'll leave without you. Tell your men to let us through the gates."

"I'm in control here, not you."

"We have the diaries."

"Oh yes, I've been told all about that."

"Then you understand that if anything happens . . ."

"You'll what, publish them? Won't that be rather difficult?"

"What do you mean?"

"It's no use," Adam said softly. "He knows."

She shook her head in disbelief. "You really *are* a fool, aren't you?"

"He's nothing of the kind," Gore said. "Simply more like me than he realizes, or cares to admit." He turned to Adam. "Why do you think I hired you—Hacker too, for that matter? Because I know how you think. You both want what I want: power and action. We all want to be players. You could never surprise me. If I want to know how you'll react, or what will tempt you, I look to myself."

"But Hacker *has* surprised you," Gina said. "It showed in your face when I told you that my husband had become involved."

Suddenly, as if a gigantic flash bulb had exploded, the restaurant was flooded with light. Gina shielded her eyes and a voice shouted, "Surprise, old buddy!"

There were two searchlights, each mounted on a golf cart. She aimed at the nearest. There was the bang of Eric's revolver, then a split second later a louder crash as the gigantic bulb shattered. As she and Adam ran from the restaurant she heard Gore yelling, "Don't kill the woman."

They stopped in the shadows of the tennis pavilion to catch their breath. The main gate was a hundred yards down the road, the hacienda containing shops and restaurants across the way.

"Let me explain," Adam begged. "I didn't betray you."

"Save it. Even if you did, it hasn't done you any good. I didn't hear him order Hacker to take *you* alive."

The Resort was quiet. The threat of more rain was keeping guests inside. "No one appears to be following us," she said.

"They don't have to." He pointed to the main gate. "Look." The guards had lowered the barrier and were rolling striped barrels into the road. A taxi arriving from town was waved away. "They've sealed us off."

"If we could slip through we might flag down a car."

"And the guards?"

"I've got four bullets. If we disarm them I won't need to fire."

"Too late." One guard was handing another a Sten gun.

"At least we've lost Hacker. We have time to think, to figure out the best way . . ."

"You don't understand how it works." He slumped into one of the director's chairs overlooking the tennis courts. "By now he and Gore are sitting in the blockhouse with the head-end computer. They can monitor the entire Resort. They're still after us but they're waiting until we're cornered."

"How about the fence? It must stop somewhere."

"It encircles the whole compound."

"Could we climb it? Cut through it?"

"Electrified. By now they've switched on the power. The plowed ground on each side is dotted with pressure pads. Step on them and you alert the R-Tube."

"We'll wait them out. Hide and then contact one of your board members. There are hundreds of empty rooms and villas. They can't search them all."

"They don't need to. They're also equipped with pressure pads, as well as heat sensors and other anti-theft devices. We'd be detected the moment we broke into a vacant room."

"There must be public telephones. We could call the police."

"That's the same thing as calling Victor."

"There's an American embassy in the capital."

"Calls go through the switchboard and the R-Tube before a connection is made."

"Isn't there a beach? Doesn't the fence stop at the water's edge?"

"It runs several yards into the ocean. Even at low tide the Resort is protected."

"We can swim round it."

"I thought you couldn't."

"We'll wade, then, or you'll carry me on your back, or . . ."

He jumped out of the chair. "There are boats in that damned fishing village."

Suddenly all the clusters of spotlights attached to poles around the tennis courts clicked on together. Across the golf course they could see lights blaze in one island of villas after another. Yellow sodium lamps mounted along the top of the electrified fence glowed, illuminating the plowed no-man's-land.

The brightly lit, eerie silence was shattered by the soft purring of a machine. At first Gina thought it was a cart approaching the tennis courts. Then she looked up. One of the boxy white closed-circuit cameras mounted below the roof of the pavilion was swiveling back and forth, scanning the tennis courts. There was another whirring and a second camera panned the pavilion's interior. Its lens passed them by, then stopped and backtracked until it pointed over their heads. Slowly it moved downward, jerked to a stop and fixed them in its gaze. A small red light in its base winked.

Gina stared into the camera's eye, frozen by loathing and fascination, imagining for a moment that she could see Hacker and Gore. She moved to the left and the camera found her again. She raised Eric's revolver and fired a bullet into the lens. The white box exploded.

Adam pulled her away. "Are you crazy? We only have four bullets."

"Three now, but it was worth it. How far to that boat?"

"Two miles."

"I know how we can get there fast."

Before he could question her she was running toward the golf shop. As he raced after her he could hear motor scooters and see headlights converging on the tennis courts.

The shed housing the idle golf carts was lit by harsh phosphorescent bulbs. Thick cables attached to the rear of the carts allowed them to feed from a trough of electrical outlets. Before Adam could shout a warning, she unplugged one and switched it on. "Camouflage," she explained. "At a distance we'll resemble the others."

"Gore already knows we're here," he said.

"How? We just arrived, and those cameras haven't moved," she said, pointing to three white boxes suspended from the ceiling. "The red lights aren't even on."

He snapped the electrical cable she had disconnected from the outlet and it disappeared into the cart. "Each cart has a computer signature and all the electrical outlets are monitored by the head-end. Right now he knows that a cable in this shed has been unplugged. It's too late and dark for a guest to be playing golf." As he spoke the camera began to move, searching for the gap in the line of carts.

"O.K. He knows we're here. But unless we plug in when we stop he won't know where we've gone." She jumped into the driver's seat. "Come on. I'll drive. You direct. We'll stay off the paths and cut across the golf course."

Heavy rain resumed as they left. Adam looked back. The cameras had finally picked them up. Victor was watching.

The fishing village was brightly lit and deserted. She halted in the plaza and asked which way to turn. He looked left and right. The cameras perched on roofs and underneath streetlamps were stationary. Streets and alleyways branched off from the plaza in all directions. He knew that some turned back on themselves, led onto the airstrip or narrowed into culs-de-sac. The Duchess had ordered her architects to construct mazes of quaint streets.

"Which way, dammit?" Gina implored.

He guessed and pointed to the widest road.

They bounced over cobblestones, swerved around benches and fountains and past the shuttered windows of artists' studios, gift shops and galleries. Each street looked the same—lines of white stucco buildings, gas lamps, stone fountains and tubs of flowers. On his instructions she turned left, left again, then rounded a corner and unexpectedly sped out of the village and onto the airstrip. As they retraced their route to the plaza a loud droning echoed through the village.

They shot back into the plaza, almost colliding with Gore and Hacker, who were sitting in Gore's golf cart, with the supercharged motor humming loudly as they waited. Hacker cupped his hands over his mouth and yelled, "Give up, old buddy?"

Gina reversed, wheeled the cart around and sped down the nearest alley. Gore's cart lunged forward in pursuit with Hacker whooping like a cowboy.

Gina veered onto a wider street. It snaked left, took a sharp right turn and suddenly there was nowhere to turn, only a solid line of buildings on both sides. There was a final ninety-degree corner before the road narrowed and ended in a dark cul-de-sac. Ahead she saw a stone archway, a courtyard and then a building proclaiming itself to be a *taberna*.

She slammed on the brakes and spun the wheel as Gore rounded the last turn and swung his cart into the middle of the street. He and Hacker climbed out slowly. They were less than fifty yards away. They had cornered their prey.

"Split up!" Adam whispered. "When you get to the beach wade around to the left until you're clear of the fence."

When she hesitated, he pushed her out of the cart. "You go through the *taberna*." It was the only building he knew led somewhere. The rest might be false fronts or empty shells.

She dashed under the archway, through the *taberna*, and emerged in a weed-filled lot. In front was a high stone wall and a door. She pushed through it and found herself in another street. She rounded a corner and saw the water.

Back in the cul-de-sac, Adam yanked at a doorknob. The door was only painted on, so his hand scraped against rough stucco. He turned to see Hacker stalking him. Gore followed several paces behind. He was carrying a hunting rifle.

Adam ran next door and tried to pull open a window. It was another of the Duchess's special effects. He zigzagged across the street and threw himself against another door. It swung open and he stumbled into a windowless room hung with paintings. The only exit was back through the same door. He ran outside and into Hacker's arms.

Hacker slammed him against a wall and kicked his legs apart. While patting him down for weapons he said, "Never should have unplugged that cart, old buddy. Your girlfriend do that? When we saw you leave the golf shed Victor guessed right off where you were headed. You're real lucky. He wants to talk first. You get to live a few more minutes."

"Turn him around," Gore ordered. "Then raise your hands and press yourself against that wall." Gore stood across the street, aiming his rifle at Hacker's chest. "What the hell are you doing?" Hacker shouted.

"Hard to decide who to shoot first. What do you boys think?" He paused briefly but both men were too stunned to speak. "No opinions? Then I'll have to choose."

"Are you fucking crazy?" Hacker screamed.

"You've both disappointed me," Gore said. "But, Stan, I think you win the prize. When did you contact Mrs. Baldwin's husband and ask for his help? He was your ally, wasn't he?"

"No, Victor. I told you I suspected him of being behind it, doing a favor for his Marxist buddies, putting his wife up to everything. Christ, don't you remember . . ."

"Yes, that's what you *said.*"

Hacker lowered his hands slightly and began edging away from the wall. "Then what the fuck is all this about?"

"It's also about Brigadier Paget's diary."

"What diary?"

"I knew you'd say that." Gore looked pleased. "The diary you stole from him; the one you were planning to use to blackmail both me and your Russian friends."

"I can explain."

"Too late." Gore whipped down the rifle and fired. Hacker pitched onto the cobblestones, writhing in pain and clutching his left knee. Gore looked at Adam. "Try anything and you'll join him."

He closed in on Hacker and said, "You sold me to the Russians, didn't you?"

Hacker moaned and shook his head.

"Hurting too much to talk? Good. Then I'll tell you what you've done. You can grunt yes or no. Lie to me again and the next bullet goes in your head.

"Fact number one: As soon as I trusted you with the information that I'd belonged to the Party, you shopped it to the KGB, right?"

Hacker nodded.

"They must have been delighted. Suddenly they had themselves a first-class mole. They could wait until I was confirmed and the R-Tube installed and then threaten to reveal everything unless I played ball. A real triple play for them. They'd get a close friend of the President, the Secretary of Defense and the R-Tube sweeps. They'd have most of Washington by the balls. For that package they'd have paid anything, given you whatever you wanted. And all the time you'd have the satisfaction of knowing you'd given your former employers a first-class screwing."

"I was going to tell you," Hacker whispered. "We could have double-crossed them. Got paid by both sides. I had a plan."

"You know I'm not interested in money anymore." Gore stopped and glanced back and forth between Adam and Hacker. "How does the rest go? Let me guess. You and the Russians must have been terrified that Dawney or Mrs. Baldwin would expose me. You can't blackmail someone once their secret is out. That's why you ordered the woman killed; why you sent Birch after Dawney; why you took so many risks. And of course stumbling on Brigadier Paget's diary must have been a splendid bonus. Now you could also double-cross the Soviets; threaten to expose me unless they paid. And they would have paid too, almost anything to protect my reputation; so would I. You could have collected from both sides and, even better, controlled both sides. The only thing I can't understand is why you didn't kill Brigadier Paget."

Hacker groaned and rolled over, still clutching his bloody knee. The longer he kept talking, the more time he would have to figure out a way of disarming Gore. "Wish I had killed the old bastard," he said. "But when I met him I didn't know exactly what was in his diary, only that it mentioned your name. Birch had told me that much before Dawney killed him, but he didn't understand the importance of the rest. I hadn't trusted him with the whole story, so all he knew was that . . ."

"But you knew the whole story," Gore interrupted, "because I was stupid, and trusting enough, to tell you. I first became suspicious when I learned how much you'd done behind my back. At first I thought my instructions had been too vague, even for me, and that you were using your initiative, trying to please me and protect your stake in the R-Tube. Then, when the Baldwin woman mentioned

her husband's involvement and Paget's diary, everything fell into
place."

Hacker rolled over again. Suddenly he sprang forward, lunging for
Gore's feet. Gore jumped out of range, whipped down the rifle and
shot him. Hacker screamed and flipped backward, pumping and
twitching his legs, his body quivering with spasms. Gore leaned over
and, like a hunter putting down a wounded animal, pumped a final
bullet into his brain. Adam was reminded of the captain clubbing
the sailfish, except Hacker was not as handsome a kill.

Gore stepped back to admire his trophy. "Can you believe it?" he
asked. "I spend my life hiding from the Russians, and that son of a
bitch, the first man I trust with my secret, he sells me out to them.
Serve them right if you and that Baldwin woman run around telling
everyone the truth."

Adam slowly lowered his hands and asked, "What is the truth?"

Gina crouched in a fishing boat, hoping to see Adam emerge from
the maze of streets. She would not leave without him. When she
heard the first shot she ran back along the pier. She had three
bullets left; enough, she hoped, to cover his retreat. Then she heard
a second shot and then a third echo from deep within the village.
He was trapped, perhaps wounded. She would have to retrace her
steps to the cul-de-sac.

"The truth," Gore said, contemplating Hacker's corpse, "is not
my most pressing problem."

"Then what is?" Adam wanted to keep him talking, postpone
whatever he was planning. Since killing Hacker, Gore seemed relaxed. Had that been satisfaction enough? Or did he prefer to space
his kills? He had said Hacker had disappointed him most. Did that
mean Adam would receive a lesser punishment? He inched tenta-
tively away from the wall. To his relief, Gore's gaze was still fixed on
the dead man.

"Isn't my problem obvious?" he asked.

"You mean Stan?"

"Hell no!" He prodded the corpse with his foot, as if checking a dead dog for signs of life. "He's easily explained, at least to the police here. No, I'm worried about the Russians. They won't fold their tents merely because Stan's out of the picture." He looked up at Adam. "How would you handle them?"

Adam replied immediately. If he hesitated, or challenged Gore, he might lose him. "You've got two options: stonewall, or damage control." He moved a step further. "Stonewall means deny everything and take the offensive. Charge that you're the victim of a KGB disinformation campaign designed to smear you and embarrass the President. You could get away with it. After all, what do the Soviets really have? Only what they've learned from Stan. Orwell's diaries have been destroyed."

"I see problems there, one or two things you don't know yet, but go on . . ."

"Damage control means admitting you belonged to the Communist Party, perhaps even that you fought in Spain. But while there you realized that Communism is the Great Satan. You changed your name to escape a youthful mistake. Beg everyone's understanding and prayers, et cetera."

"Under the circumstances I prefer that option." Gore paused to check that his rifle was loaded.

"What circumstances?" Adam asked quickly. "If I'm going to help, I'll have to know everything."

"You already do . . . well, almost everything." He stopped, and Adam imagined he was deciding how much to reveal. Finally he said, "Several years ago my wife had her face lifted. The doctor did a marvelous job. A tiny cut, a little tuck, and she woke up considerably more attractive. I did the same thing with Spain, at least with the account of my activities there that I gave Orwell in Cologne, and to you a few minutes ago."

"But those scars on your legs, they must be genuine."

"Oh, I was tortured by the Communists all right; that's why Blair believed my story. It's hard to lie about experiences as horrifying as those, and convince someone as quick as Blair."

"But then Dawney must have lied, and he convinced Blair as well."

"I think Blair was unable to decide between us because he believed us both, which is not surprising, since we were *both* telling the truth. You see, the Communists had tortured Dawney *and* me."

Gina flattened herself against the back of the *taberna*'s archway. Adam and Gore were twenty yards away, their voices echoing down the enclosed street. Gore covered Adam with a rifle and Hacker lay at his feet in a puddle of blood. If she fired from here, she would hit Gore in the back; if she missed, he could kill Adam and turn the rifle on her.

Gina hesitated. Perhaps Adam's life was not in immediate danger. And why was Hacker dead? But she knew one thing for certain: if she challenged Gore again with Eric's revolver, she had to be prepared to kill him. This time there could be no hesitation or doubts.

Gore checked the street. None of the Resort's guests had wandered into the village. "Dawney was interrogated and tortured first," he said, "by me." He flashed a quick smile. "A month later I was thrown into the same cell and tortured in the same rooms until I confessed to Trotskyite 'crimes.' You see, the Spanish purges mirrored those in the Soviet Union. In both, torturers soon became the tortured and those who ordered the first wave of executions found themselves in the second."

"But why did Dawney inflict those scars on the boy if he hadn't inflicted them on you and others before?"

"I told you about the coal fires. It may have been summer when I questioned Dawney and I didn't want to overheat the room. In any case, he escaped being burned, but he certainly knew about others who weren't so lucky.

"Understand what I mean by doing a little plastic surgery on the truth? Everything I told Blair, and you, was so near the truth that it was believable. For example, Peter Ekman was the son of one of the many American Communists who emigrated to Russia during the 1920s. Ten years later I was sent to Spain to spy on British and American volunteers. While I was there my father, like most foreign Communists living then in the land of their dreams, was executed. Several weeks later I was arrested.

"Most everything I told you about Peter Ekman was really true of Victor Gore. *He* was the silly young American who went to Spain on a lark. After he was killed, I checked his background for the NKVD to see if his papers might prove useful. As it turned out, he was a natural: an unmarried loner with no family except a father who'd disowned him because of his politics. By this time reports of the Stalinist purges had spread to Spain, so I took the precaution of stealing Gore's papers and taking them with me when I was sent to Barcelona to infiltrate the POUM. I entrusted them to the owner of a small bar for safekeeping. After escaping from that beach I recovered them, fled to the States and assumed Gore's identity. Until that bastard Hacker sold me to the KGB I'm sure the Soviets had never connected Peter Ekman to Victor Gore."

"But Dawney swore that you supervised the execution on that beach."

"Perhaps he caught a glimpse of me there and thought I was acting in my former capacity—an understandable mistake for someone in his condition.

"He and I weren't the only ones to escape by running into the water. The Spanish Communists who did the dirty work weren't very accurate. As I treaded water, dived to escape bullets and then finally swam down the beach, away from Peter Ekman and toward Victor Gore, my mind clicked and snapped for the first time in weeks. During that swim I concluded that fascism, Communism, capitalism and all ideologies only *pretend* to be the means for achieving glorious ends. But they're really all just useful instruments: tools to be picked up or laid down according to circumstances; tools for seizing control and constructing walls to prevent people seeing the truth."

"And the truth is . . ."

"That power is everything."

Gina checked Eric's revolver. Two bullets in the cylinder, another in the chamber. Would Eric have fired it in Cologne if he had known what she did now? Perhaps. But he would not have shot Gore in the back. That was an execution.

"O.K.," Adam said. "I can see why it'd be difficult to stonewall. The Soviets might still have some evidence or pictures of Peter Ekman."

Gore lowered the rifle so its barrel pointed at the cobblestones. "Now you see why I prefer damage control. We admit some of the truth so the Soviets can't make a big splash, then perform some skillful surgery on the rest. You could be my surgeon."

Gore was now pacing and snapping his fingers as he spoke. If he came closer Adam could risk jumping him. Or should he say yes to his offer? Once he was safe he could double-cross Gore.

But why did Gore want to avoid killing him tonight? Perhaps two bodies at once were simply too much to explain, even for the president of TropicAmerican. But what if Gore too had considered the possibility of a double cross? Was he unafraid of Adam because he held some secret trump card? Or was he just confident that he still knew what Adam wanted and could easily control him; that he was unprincipled and easily bought?

Adam heard a voice, his voice, saying, "No."

Gore jerked up the rifle. "You crazy? I've offered you a chance. You want to join Stan?"

Adam smiled, shrugged and moved a step closer. No choice now, he had to tackle Gore. "It's my usual problem," he said. "I can't seem to control my instincts."

Gore leveled the rifle at his stomach. "Maybe it's all for the best. Sooner or later I'd have had to do this. You'd always have been a loose cannon."

"Drop the rifle!" Gina shouted. He spun his head around and smiled in relief when he saw her. "You still won't shoot," he said.

Adam edged forward. He was balanced on the balls of his feet, ready to spring. Then Gore suddenly turned back and saw him.

A split second separated Gore's shot and Gina's. Adam jumped and Gore's bullet went wide. Gina's was deadly accurate. She stood for a moment frozen to the spot, staring at Gore's body. When she was certain he was dead she started running toward Adam. Halfway, she suddenly stopped, looked at Eric's revolver and flung it over the wall. Then she ran into Adam's arms.

EPILOGUE

"Will you be at the funeral?" Jim Fiore asked as Gore's casket was forklifted into the hold of a TropicAir jet. Adam and Gina were taking the same plane, but only as far as Miami.

Adam shook his head. "I'm accompanying Mrs. Baldwin to England . . ."

Gina broke in. "After what's happened, do you really expect him to attend?"

"What happened," Fiore said carefully, "is that Victor caught Stan Hacker selling corporate secrets to the Soviet Union. He confronted him, and Hacker tried to kill him. Both men died in the ensuing gun battle."

"But you know that's a lie!"

He ignored her and turned to Adam. "Victor Gore was a great patriot: a decorated war veteran and a visionary capitalist. That's what the President will say when he delivers the eulogy at his funeral. Are you going to contradict him?"

"We've already said we have no interest in destroying a dead man's reputation." Adam took Gina's arm and walked toward the plane.

Fiore followed them. "And I appreciate that. But are you sure I can't persuade you to remain on board? These next months are bound to be difficult and I could use your experience, particularly for the R-Tube launch in Washington."

Adam stopped and faced him. "You must be joking."

"Not at all. The board has voted to proceed with the R-Tube as a tribute to Victor. I've told the President that installing the R-Tube in Washington was Victor's dream, and he's promised to make it possible for us. Stan's plan of promoting the R-Tube as a security system was a good one. The campaign lifts off next month and I was hoping you'd manage it."

"Stan was a Soviet agent. His plan was the KGB's."

"I've talked to the FBI," Fiore said quickly. "They've agreed to oversee the security of the Washington head-end to ensure the sweeps don't fall into the wrong hands."

Gina shook her head in amazement. "Then they'll have access to the data."

"Yes," Adam said. "And what's to prevent them from using the sweeps to . . ."

"We're going to be very strict about that. We'll only let them access the head-end if a threat to national security is involved." Before Adam could protest, Fiore held up his hand. "I guess you're not the right man for Washington after all. It shouldn't be hard to find someone who loves the R-Tube as much as Victor."

Adam and Gina climbed aboard in silence. As the plane banked over the TropicResort, Gina said in a flat voice, "It was a bright cold day in April, and the clocks were striking thirteen."

Adam frowned. "What does that mean?"

"Never mind," she said. "Eric knew. And we'll all find out soon enough."